TRANSFORMERS
RESCUE BOTS

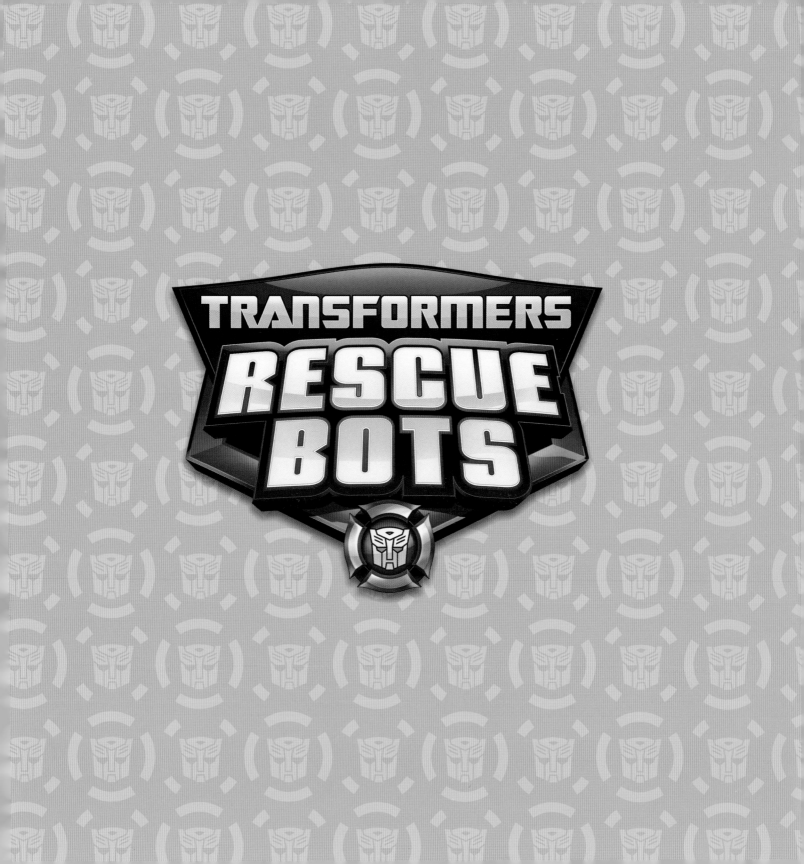

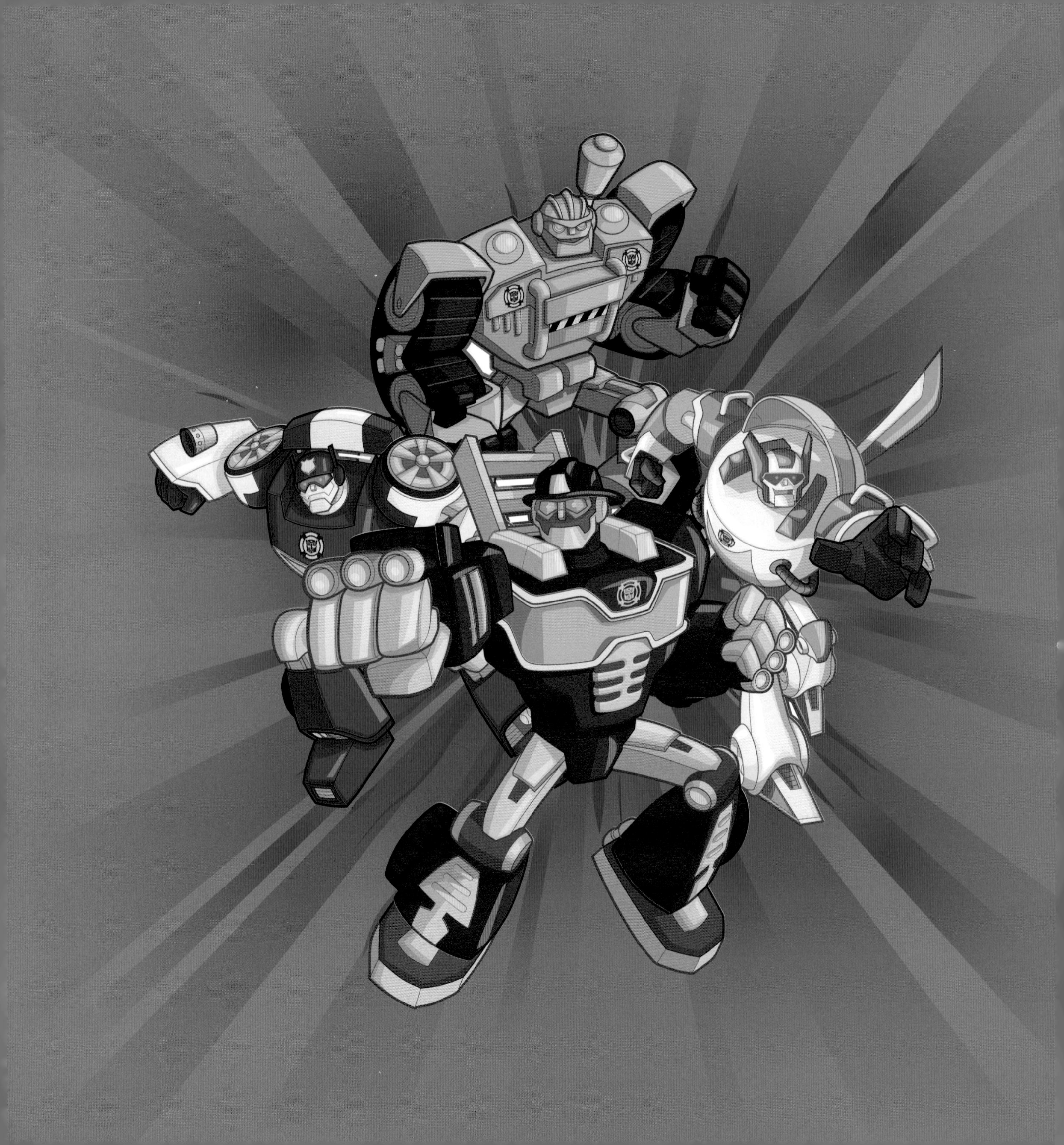

TRANSFORMERS

RESCUE BOTS

Storybook Collection

Little, Brown and Company

Hachette Book Group
1290 Avenue of the Americas, New York, NY 10104
Visit us at lb-kids.com

LB kids is an imprint of Little, Brown and Company.
The LB kids name and logo are trademarks of Hachette Book Group, Inc.

The publisher is not responsible for websites (or their content) that are not owned by the publisher.

First Edition: October 2016

Transformers Rescue Bots: The Mystery of the Pirate Bell originally published in September 2013
by Little, Brown and Company

Transformers Rescue Bots: Return of the Dino Bot originally published in June 2014
by Little, Brown and Company

Transformers Rescue Bots: The Ghosts of Griffin Rock originally published in September 2014
by Little, Brown and Company

Transformers Rescue Bots: Land Before Prime originally published in January 2015
by Little, Brown and Company

Transformers Rescue Bots: Blast Off! originally published in June 2015
by Little, Brown and Company

Transformers Rescue Bots: Attack of the Movie Monsters! originally published in October 2015
by Little, Brown and Company

Transformers Rescue Bots: Dangerous Rescue originally published in January 2016
by Little, Brown and Company

Library of Congress Control Number: 2016932933

ISBN 978-0-316-41091-5

10 9 8 7 6 5 4 3 2

1010

Printed in China

Licensed By:

Hasbro

TRANSFORMERS RESCUE BOTS

Storybook Collection

LITTLE, BROWN & COMPANY

LB kids

TRANSFORMERS
RESCUE BOTS

The Mystery of the Pirate Bell
9

Return of the Dino Bot
35

The Ghosts of Griffin Rock
61

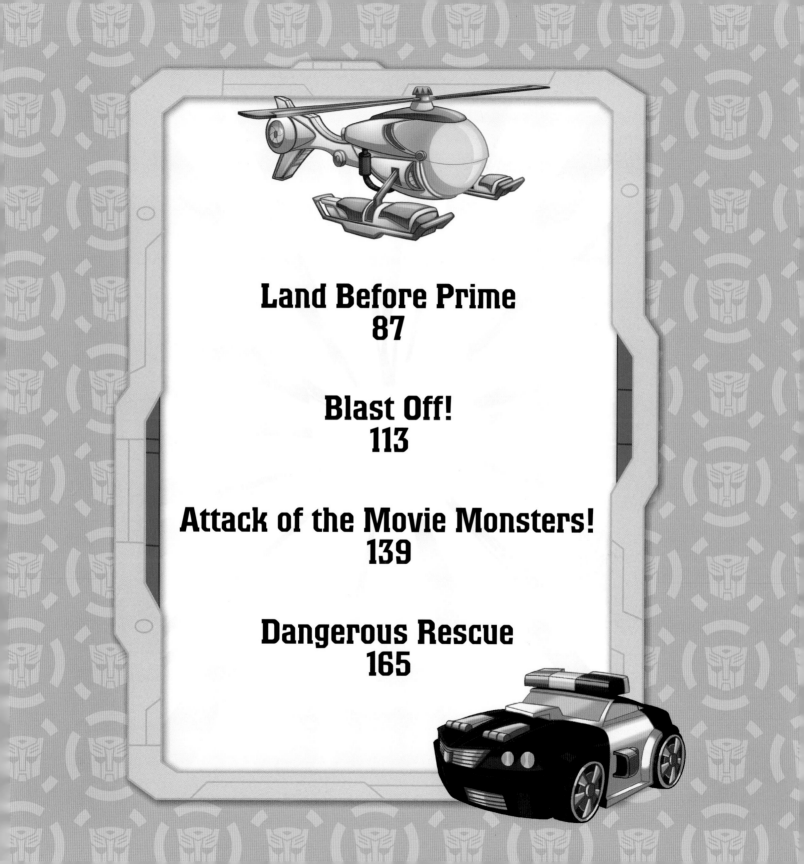

Land Before Prime
87

Blast Off!
113

Attack of the Movie Monsters!
139

Dangerous Rescue
165

The Mystery of the Pirate Bell

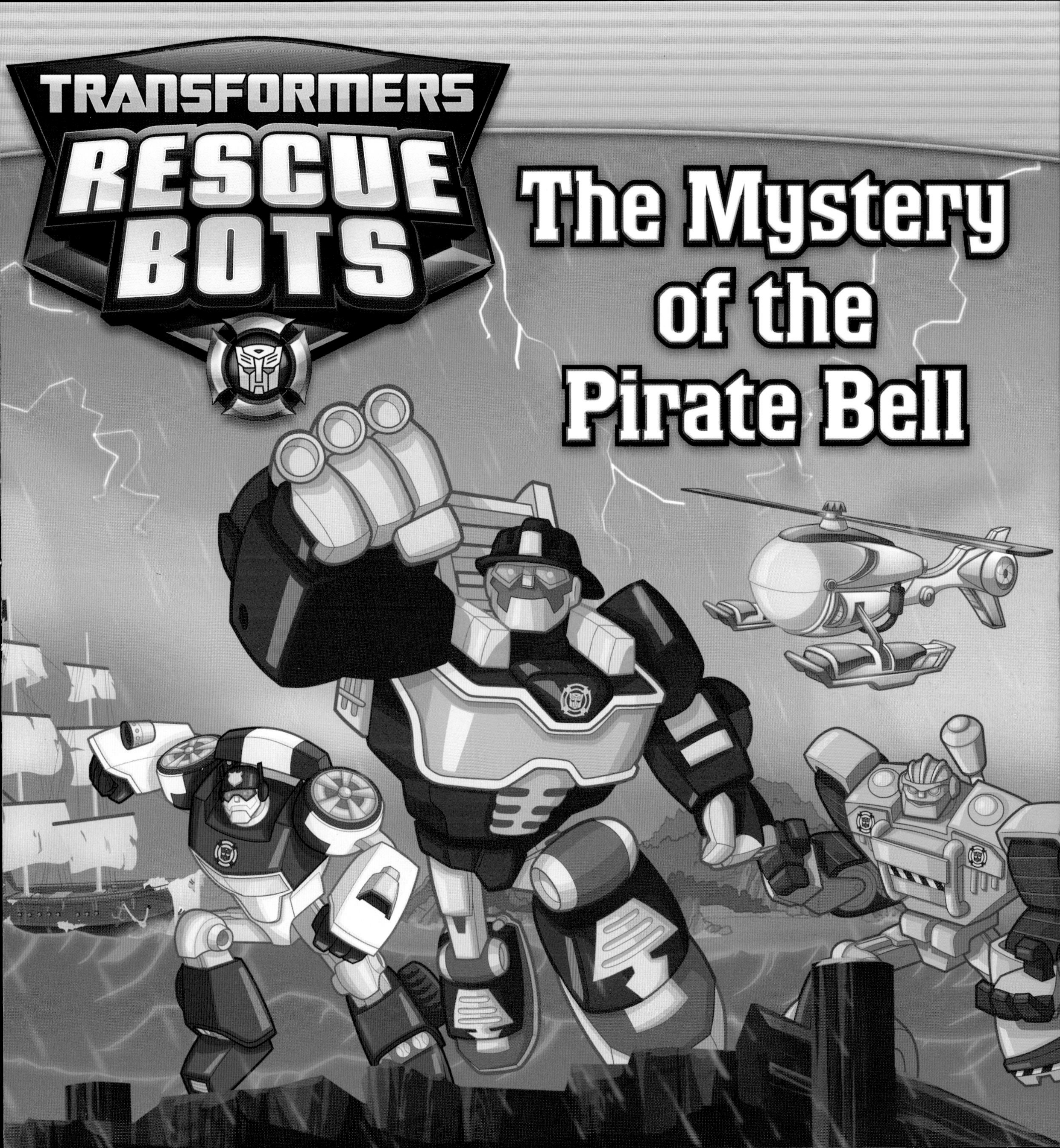
TRANSFORMERS
RESCUE BOTS

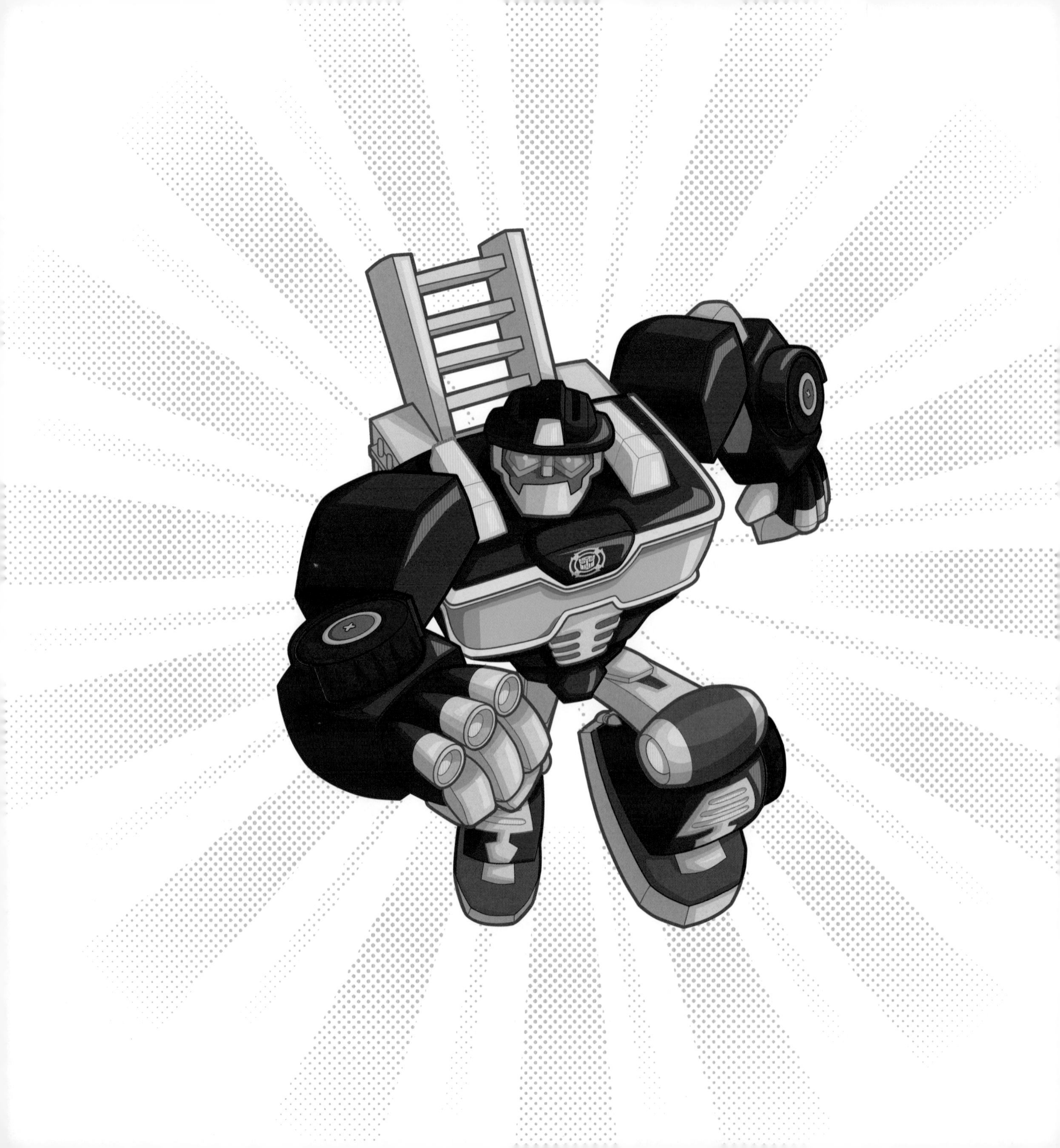

TRANSFORMERS
RESCUE BOTS

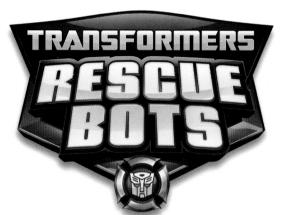

The Mystery of the Pirate Bell

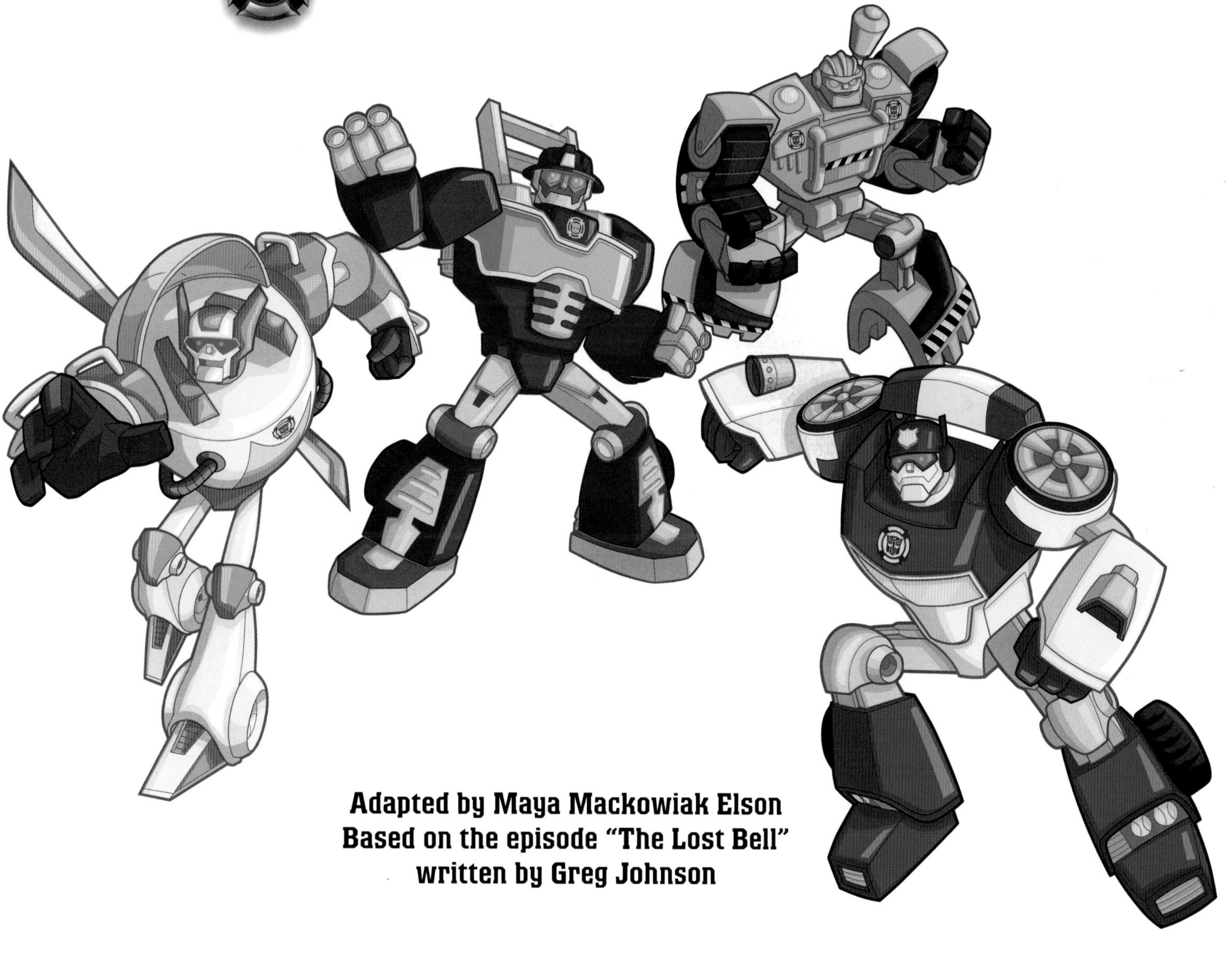

Adapted by Maya Mackowiak Elson
Based on the episode "The Lost Bell"
written by Greg Johnson

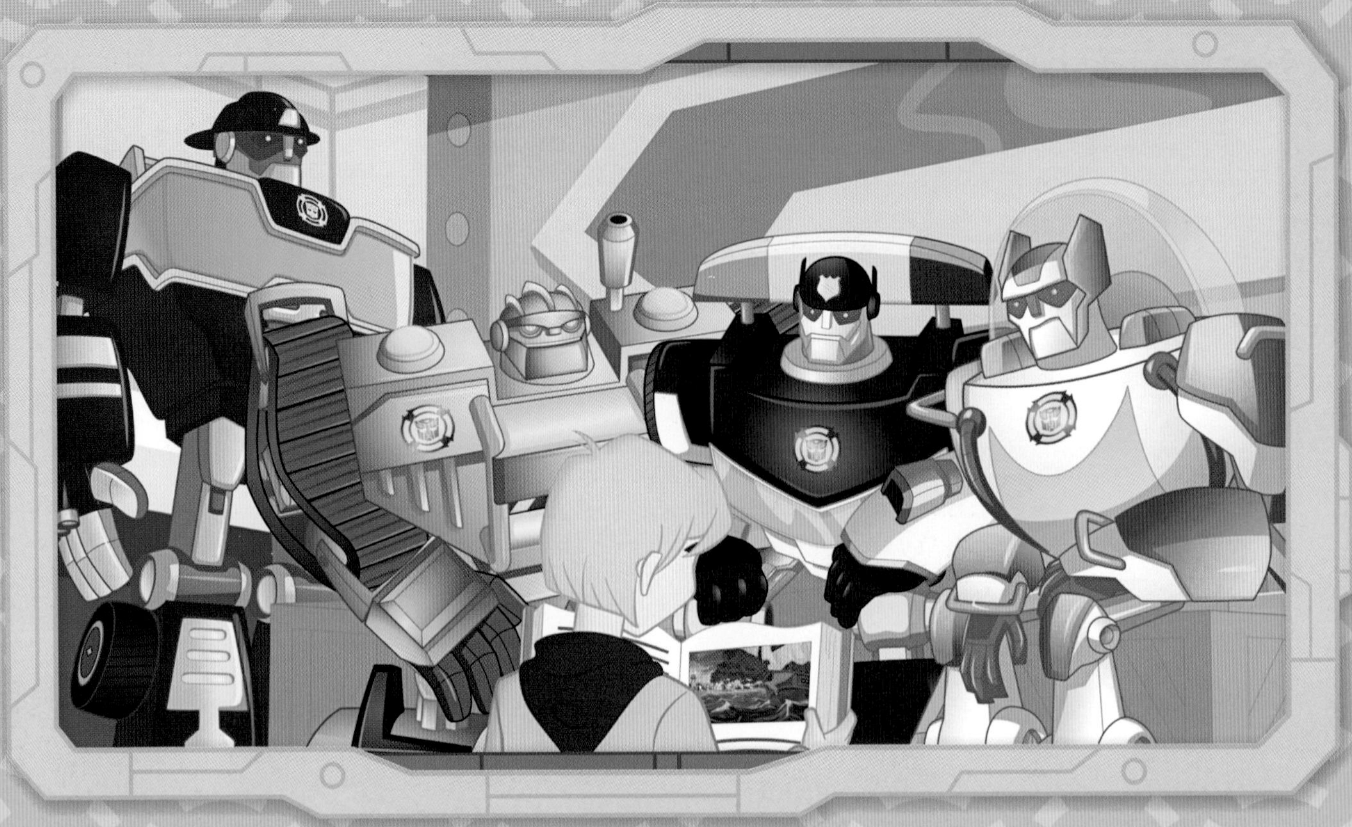

One dreary morning, Cody is reading about an important event in Griffin Rock history. "'Pirates sailed in on a ship called the *Oaken Crow*, and looted!'" he reads. "'Before they escaped, the swashbucklers set fire to the entire island!'"

Heatwave interrupts, "Humans spend too much time thinking about the past."

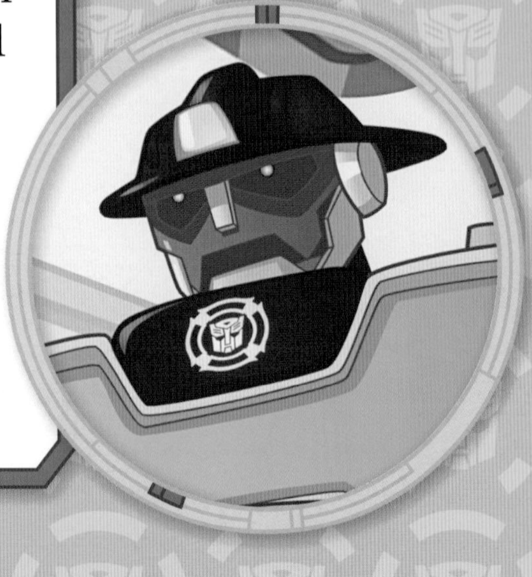

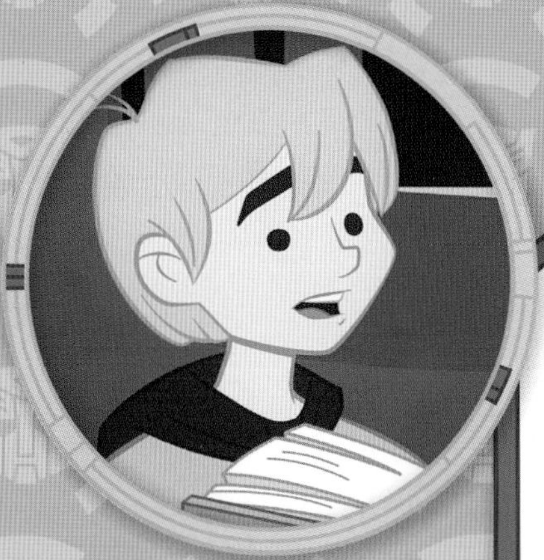

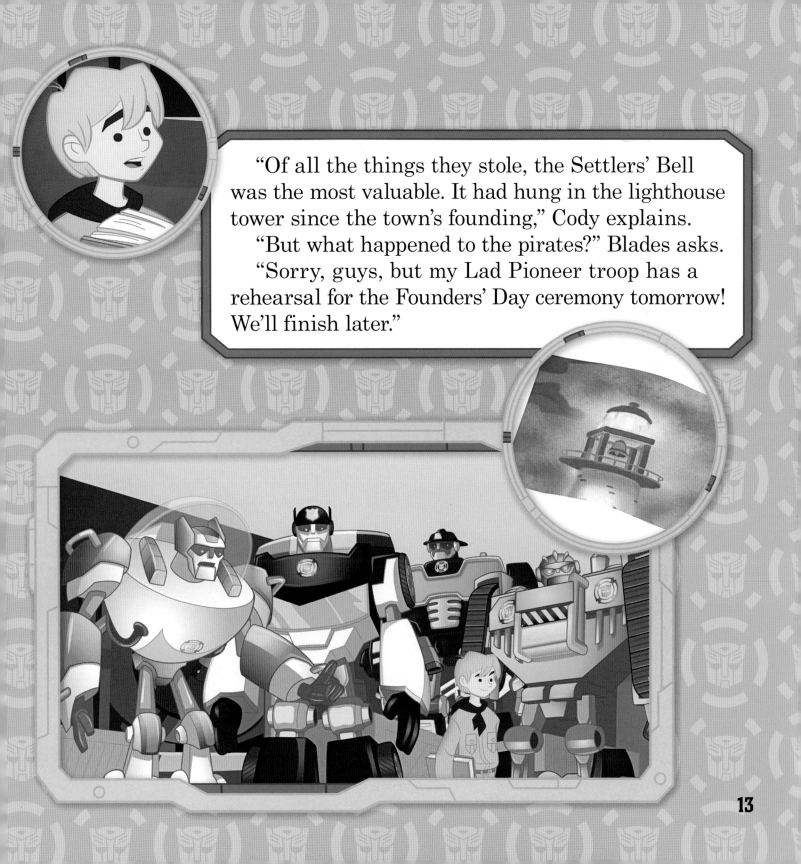

“Of all the things they stole, the Settlers’ Bell was the most valuable. It had hung in the lighthouse tower since the town’s founding,” Cody explains.

“But what happened to the pirates?” Blades asks.

“Sorry, guys, but my Lad Pioneer troop has a rehearsal for the Founders’ Day ceremony tomorrow! We’ll finish later.”

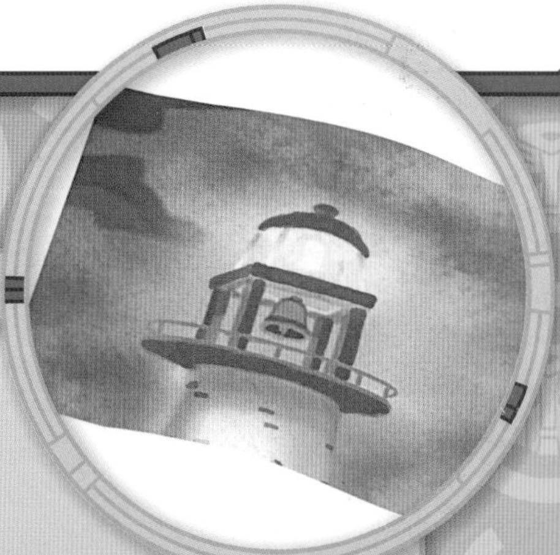

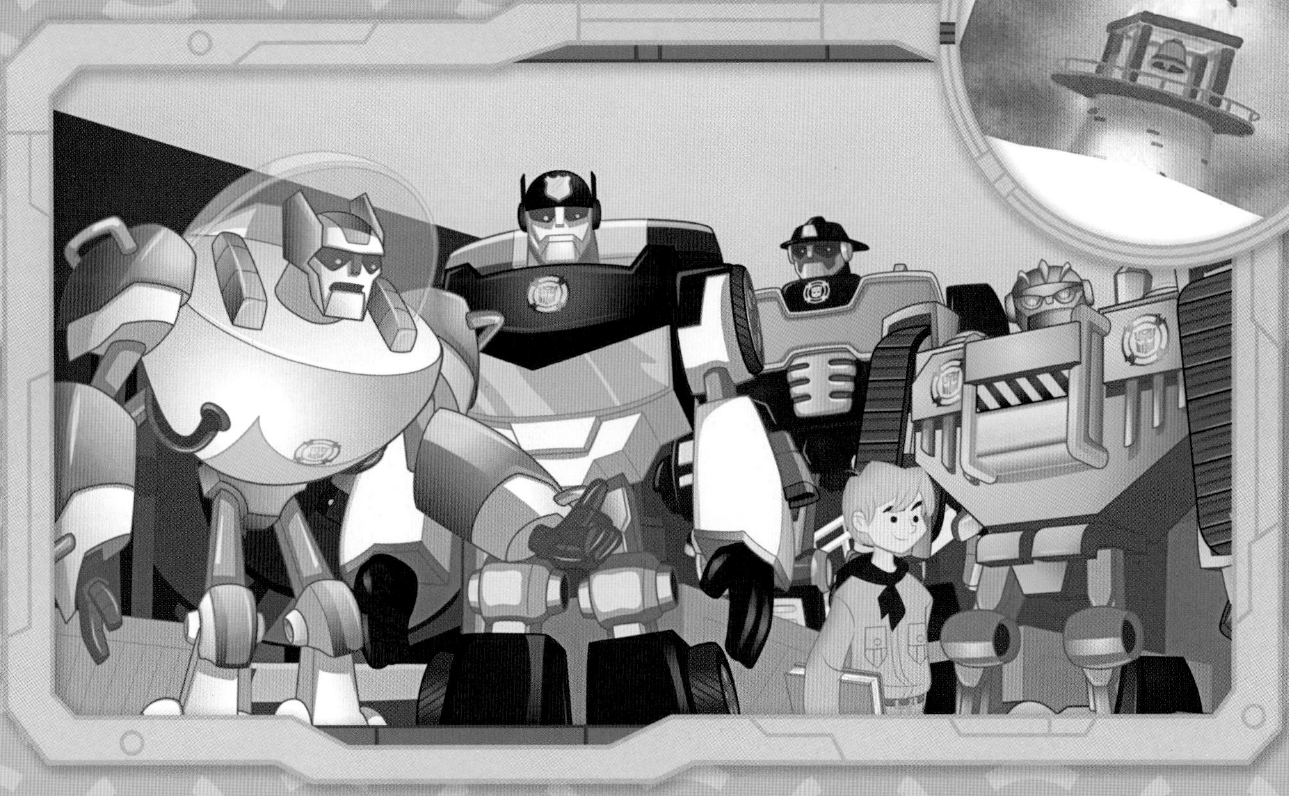

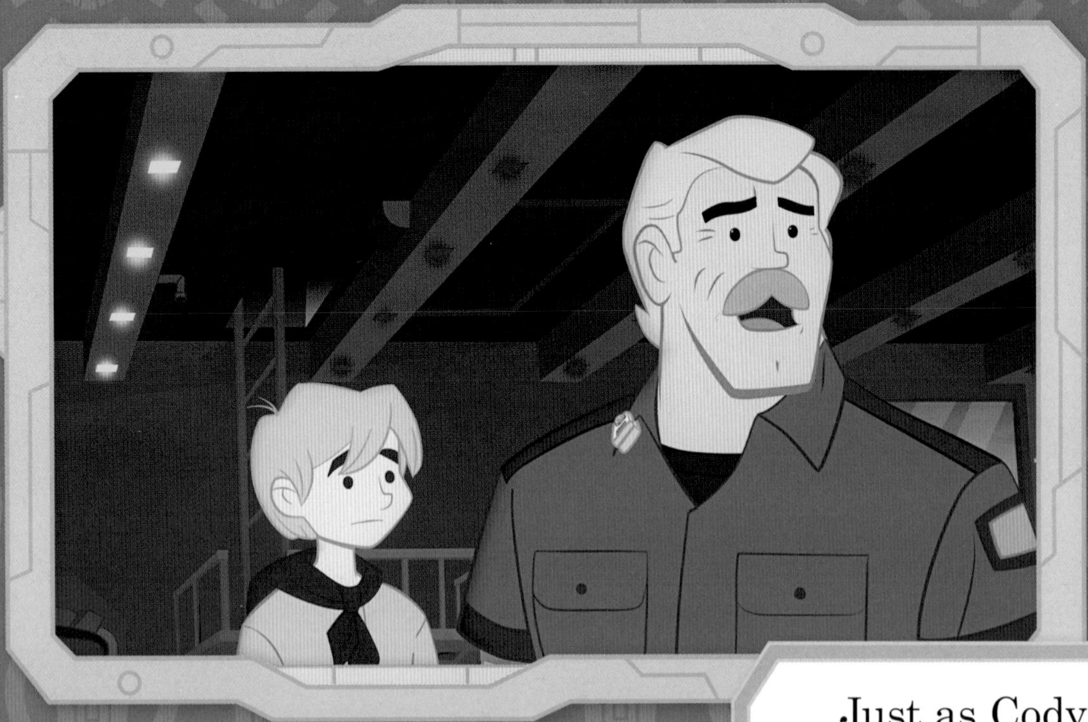

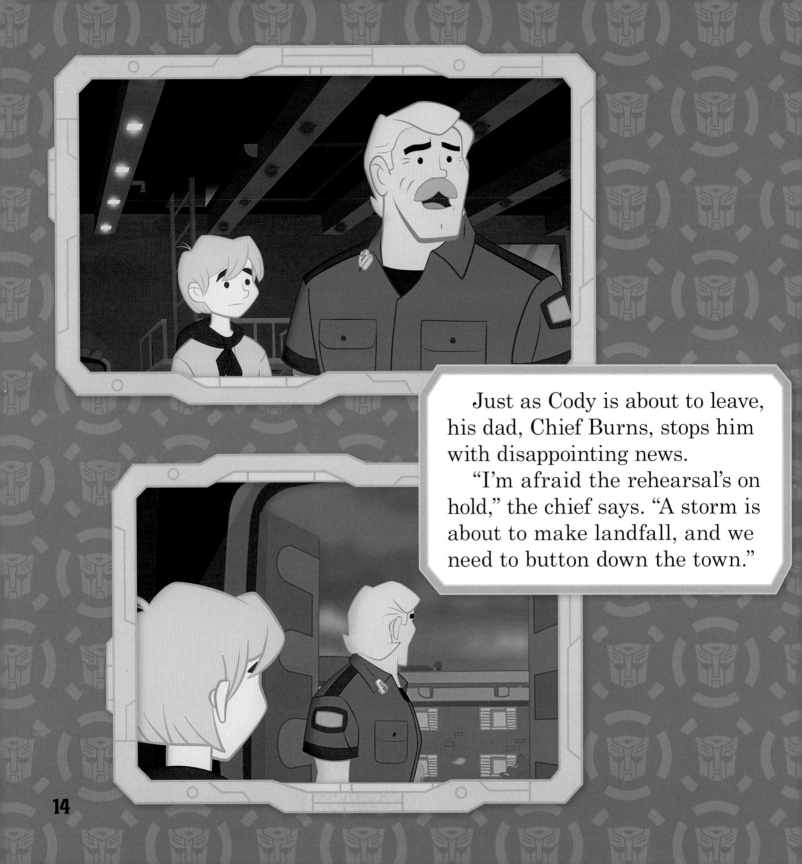

Just as Cody is about to leave, his dad, Chief Burns, stops him with disappointing news.

"I'm afraid the rehearsal's on hold," the chief says. "A storm is about to make landfall, and we need to button down the town."

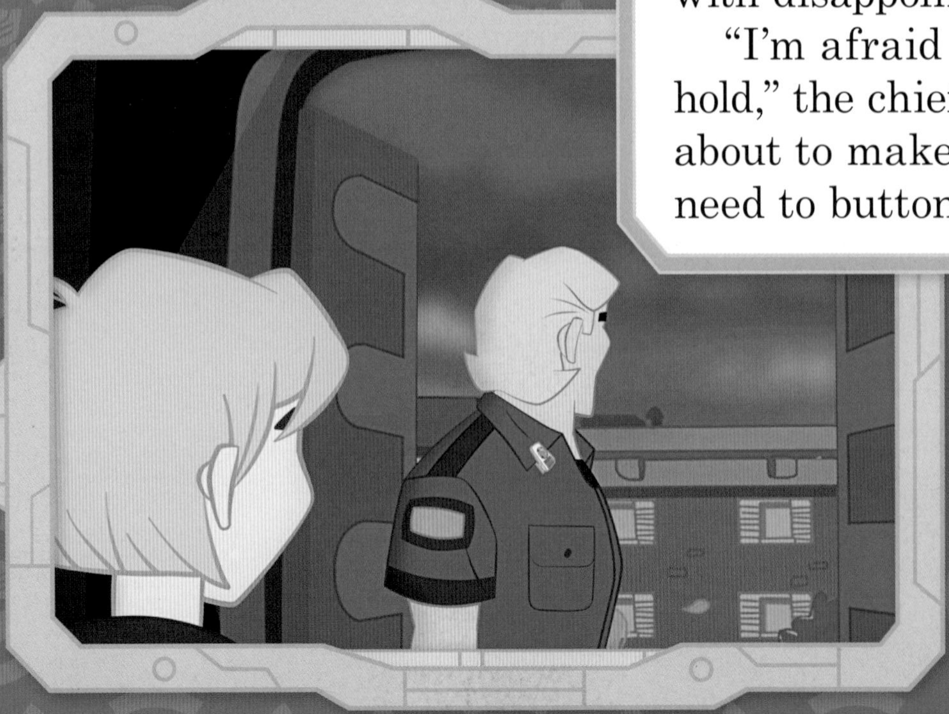

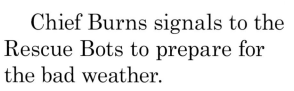

Chief Burns signals to the Rescue Bots to prepare for the bad weather.

Rolling to the rescue, the Bots pick up branches from the street, board up windows, and secure traffic-bots.

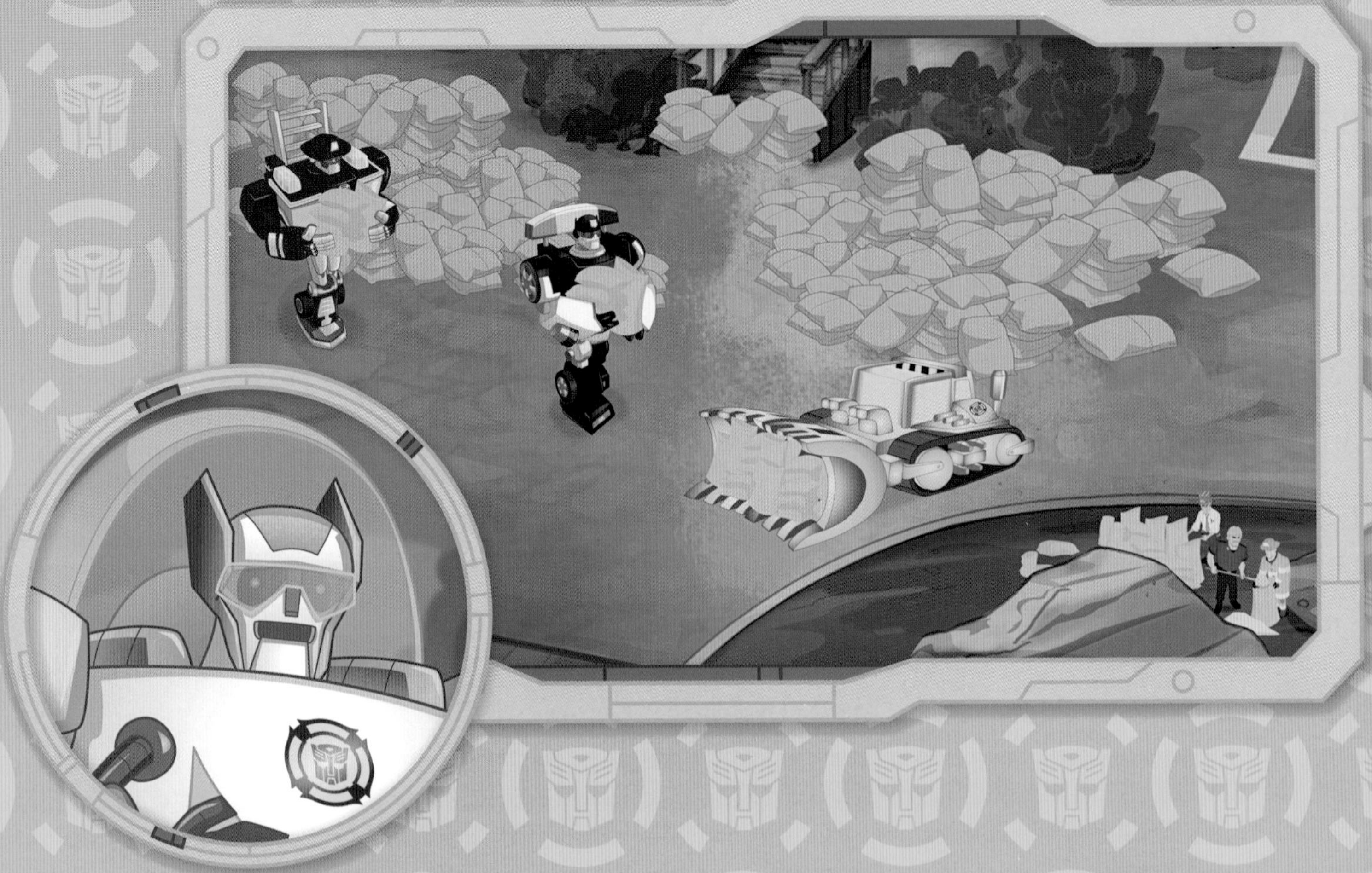

While the team is building a sandbag wall, Blades brings up the pirates again.

"So, what did happen to them?" the Copter-Bot asks.

"They sailed into a storm like this one," Cody says. "The *Oaken Crow* disappeared, and nobody ever heard from them again!"

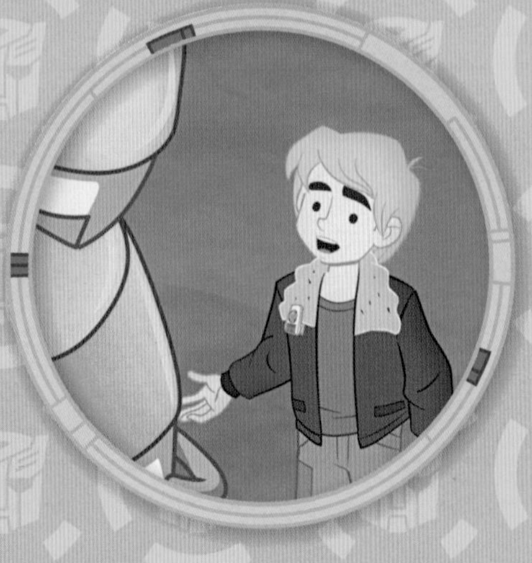

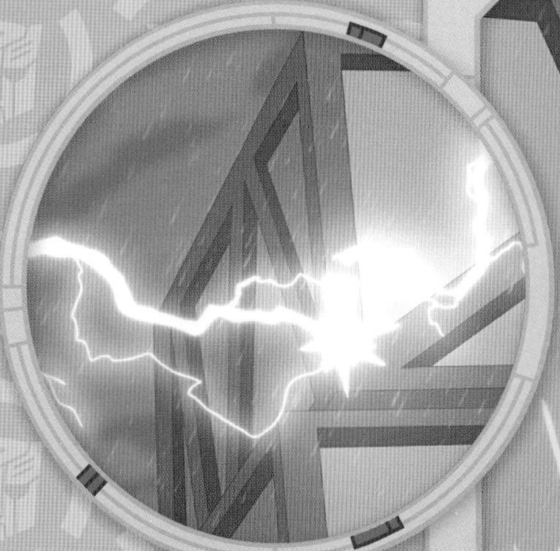

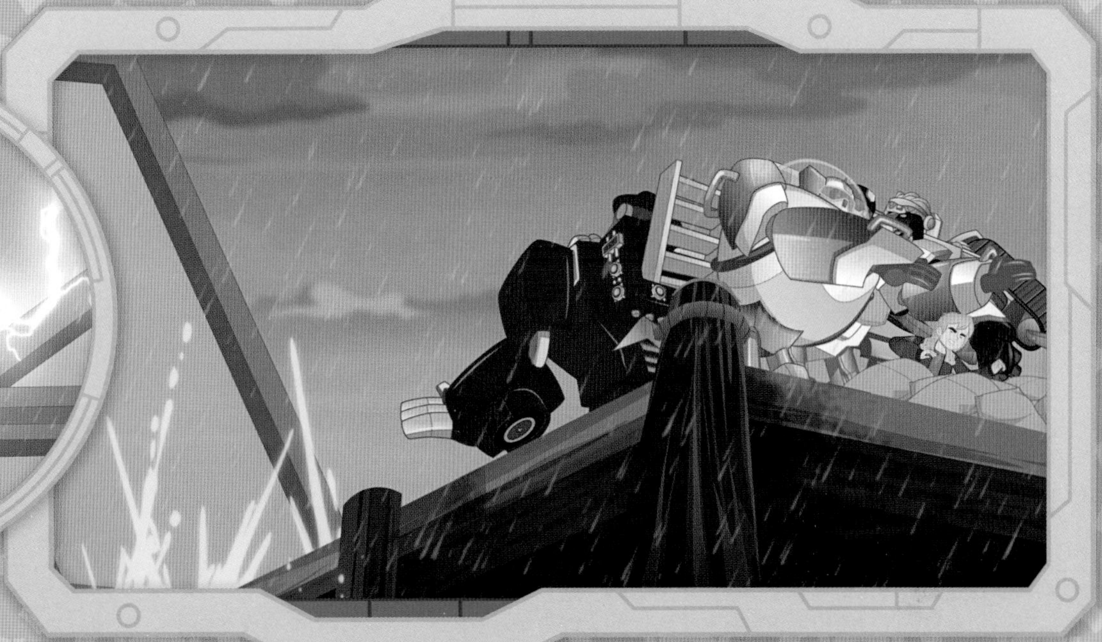

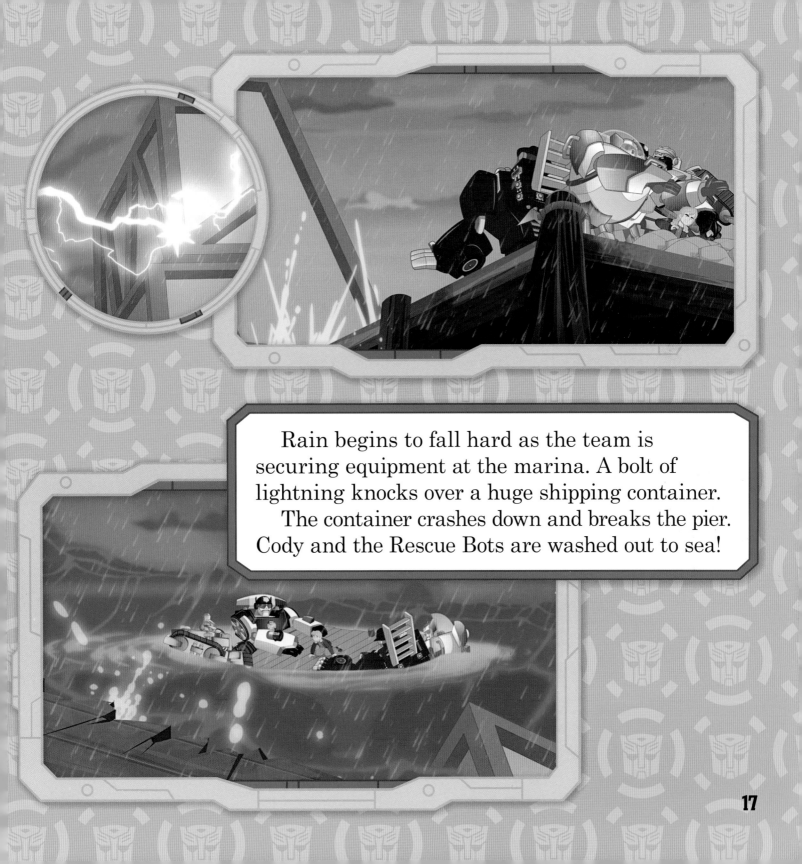

Rain begins to fall hard as the team is securing equipment at the marina. A bolt of lightning knocks over a huge shipping container.

The container crashes down and breaks the pier. Cody and the Rescue Bots are washed out to sea!

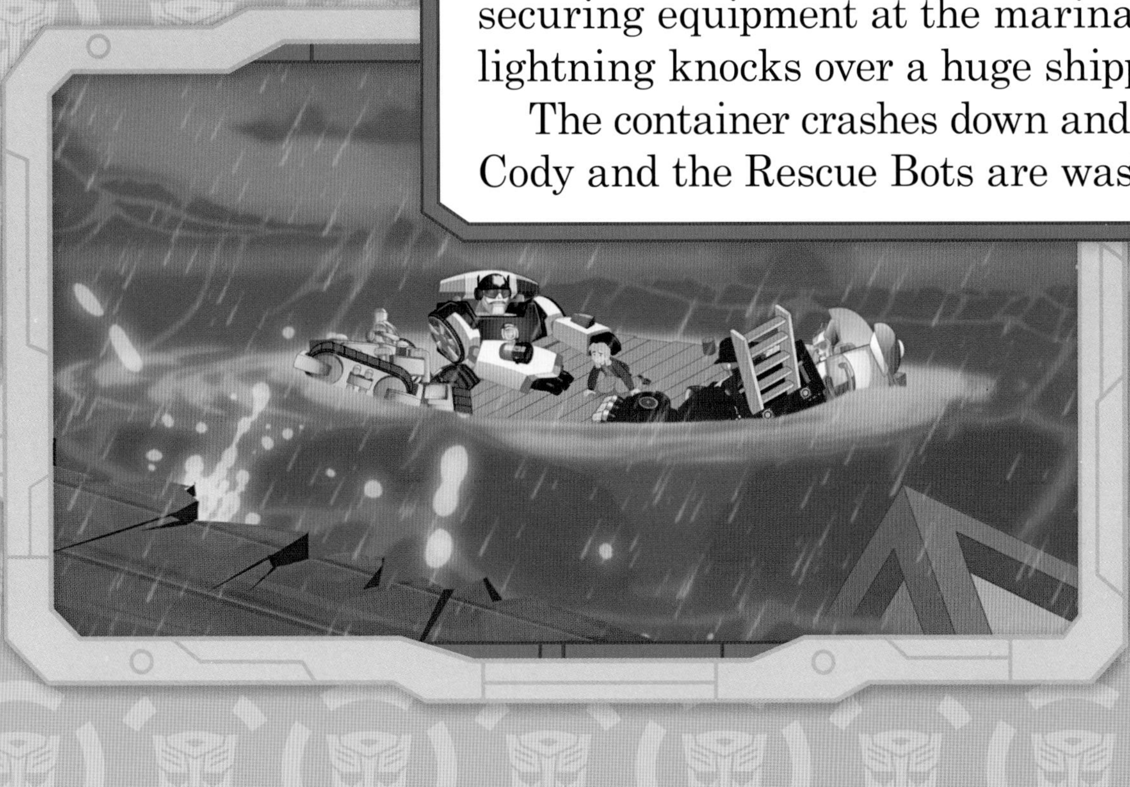

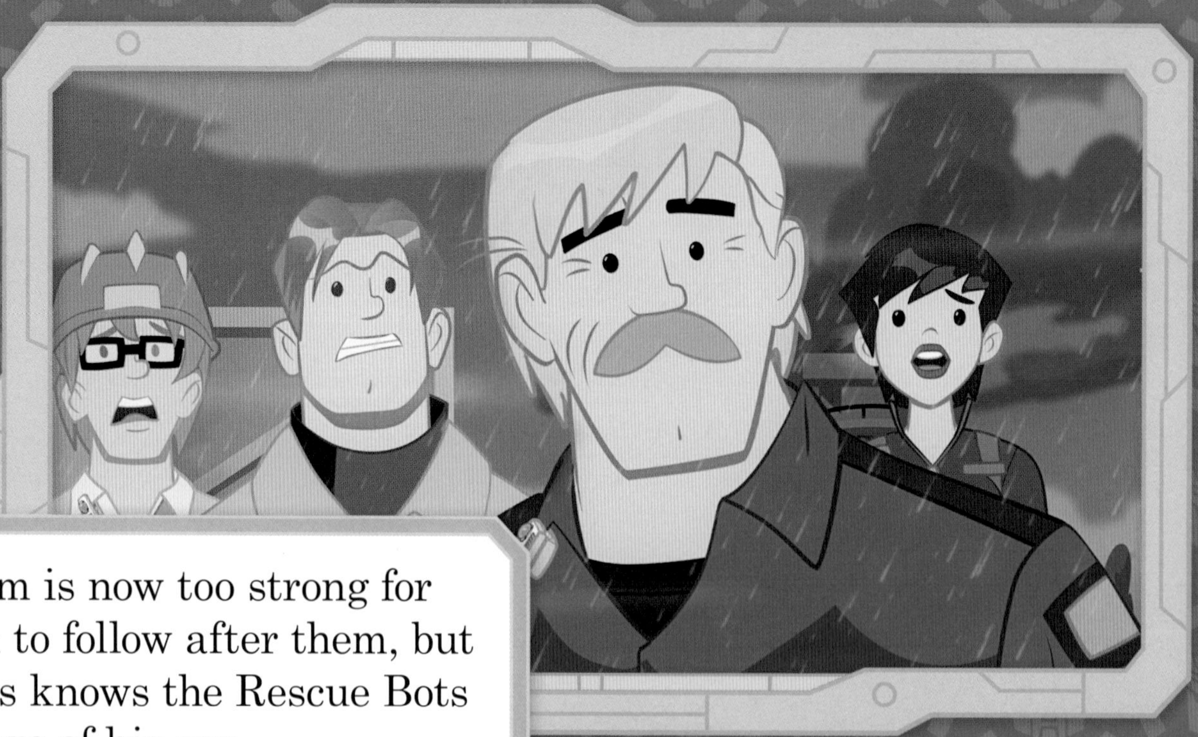

The storm is now too strong for any human to follow after them, but Chief Burns knows the Rescue Bots will take care of his son.

Soon, Cody and the Bots find themselves in calmer waters, and they go ashore on a deserted beach.

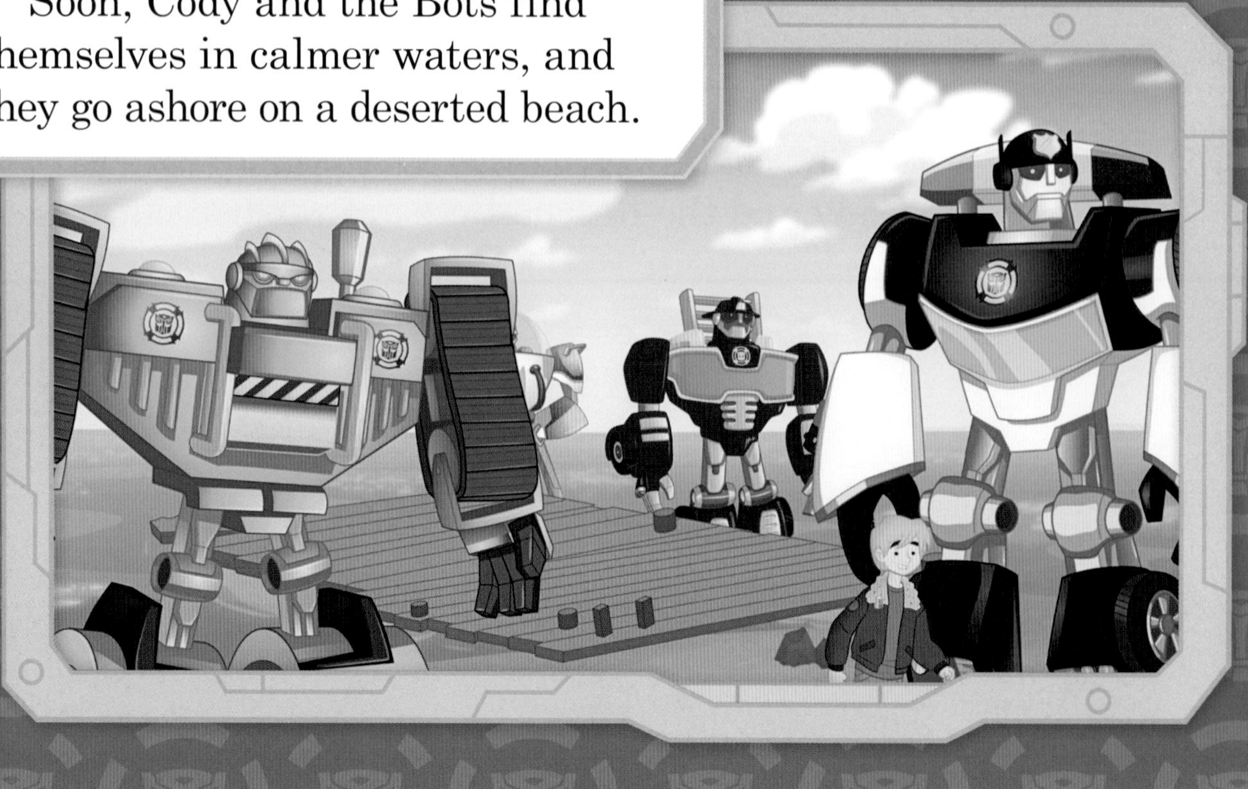

“We’re castaways!” Cody exclaims. “Isn’t that cool?”

“You know what would be cooler?” Blades sighs. “If my rotor wasn’t bent. Then I could fly for help!”

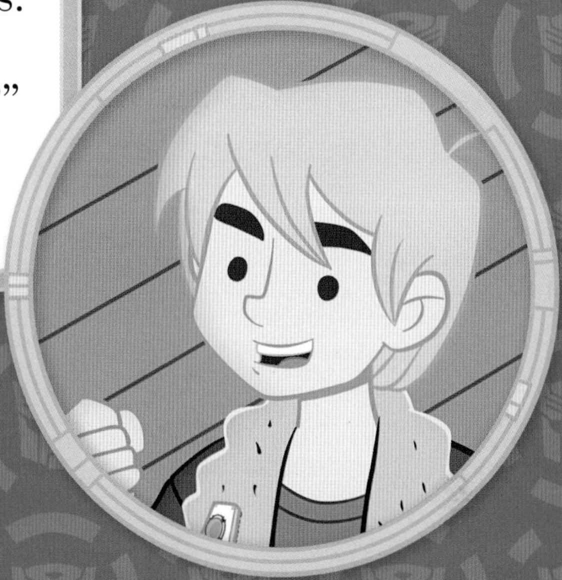

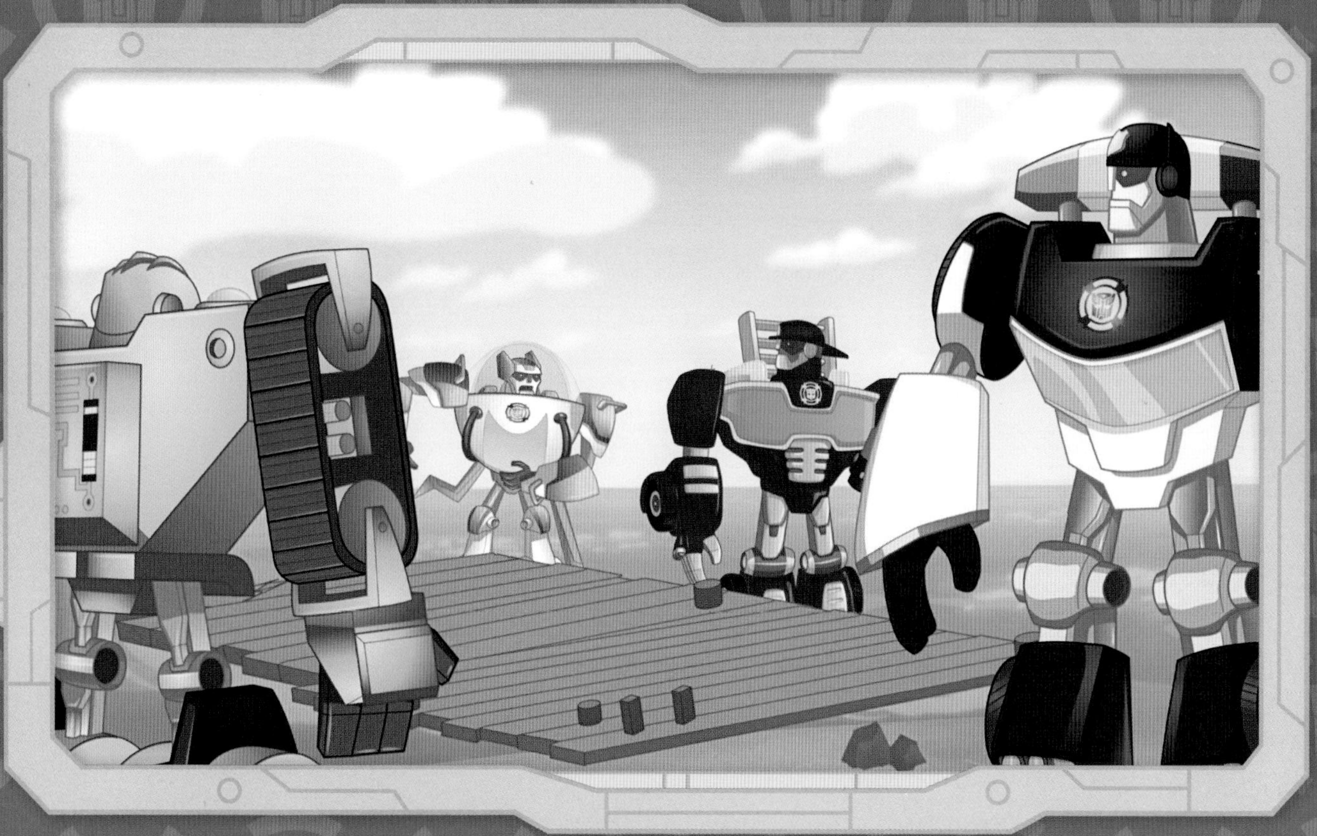

Exploring the island, Cody and the Bots discover a small clearing with a waterfall and a stream. "This is a good place for shelter," Cody says.

"One shelter, coming up!" Heatwave exclaims.

"I can help!" Cody insists.

"I'm afraid this is a job for heavy machinery," says Boulder.

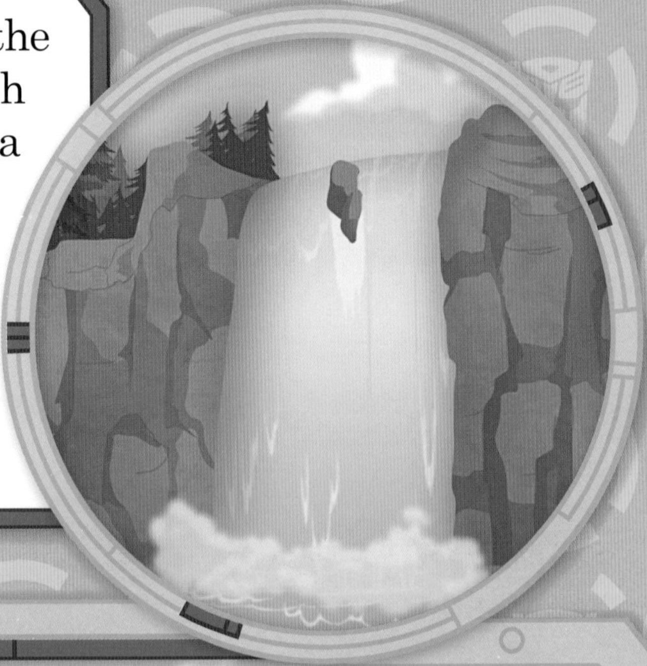

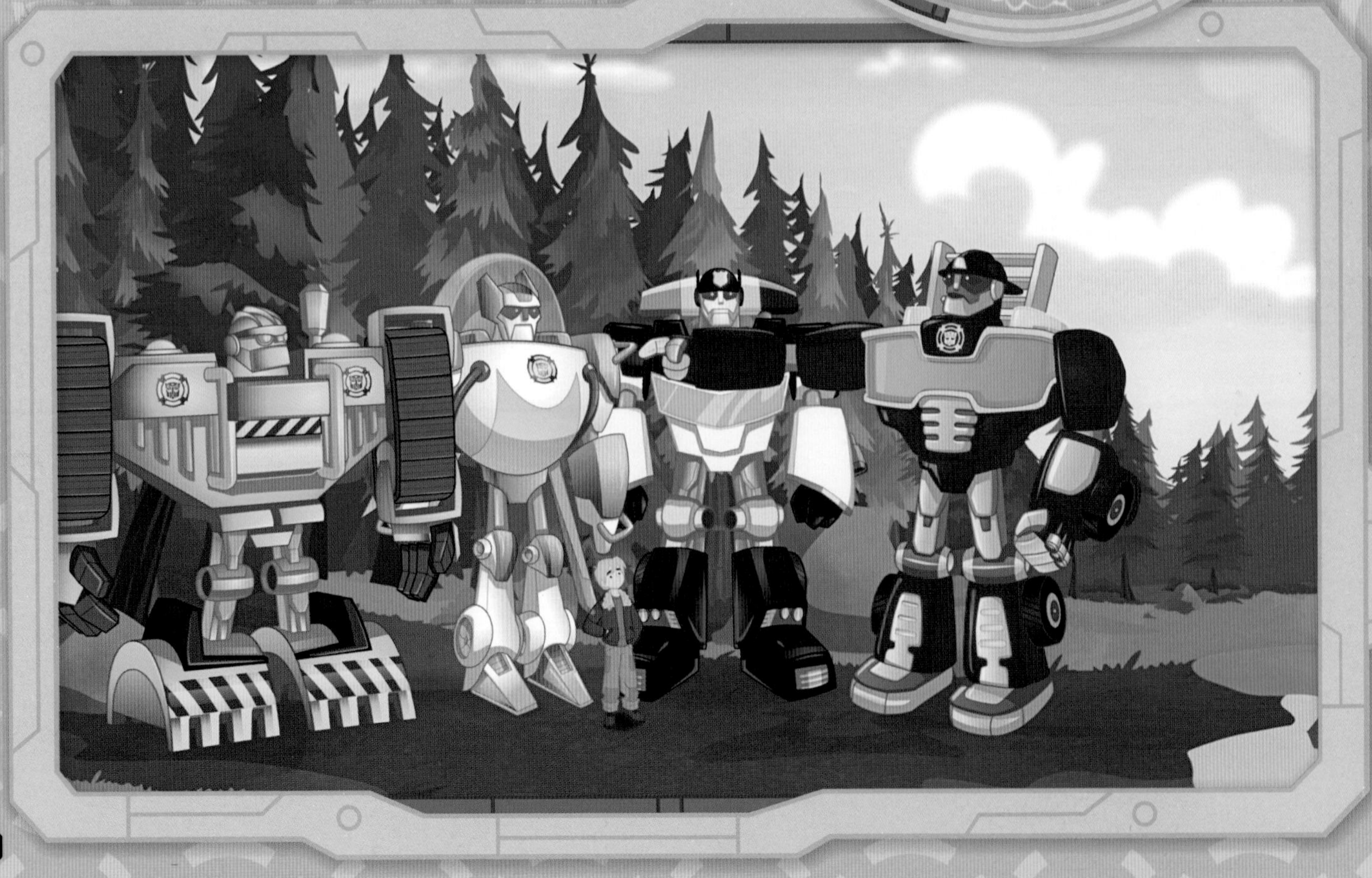

The Bots gather supplies and start building an unsteady structure of rocks, mud, and logs. As Boulder opens the door, the shelter collapses into a pile.

"It's okay, guys," Cody says when he sees the ruins. "I built my own."

Cody's shelter is small, simple, and just right.

"How did you learn to build that?" Heatwave asks.

"Lad Pioneers," Cody says. "See? It pays to learn about history and how things were done in the past."

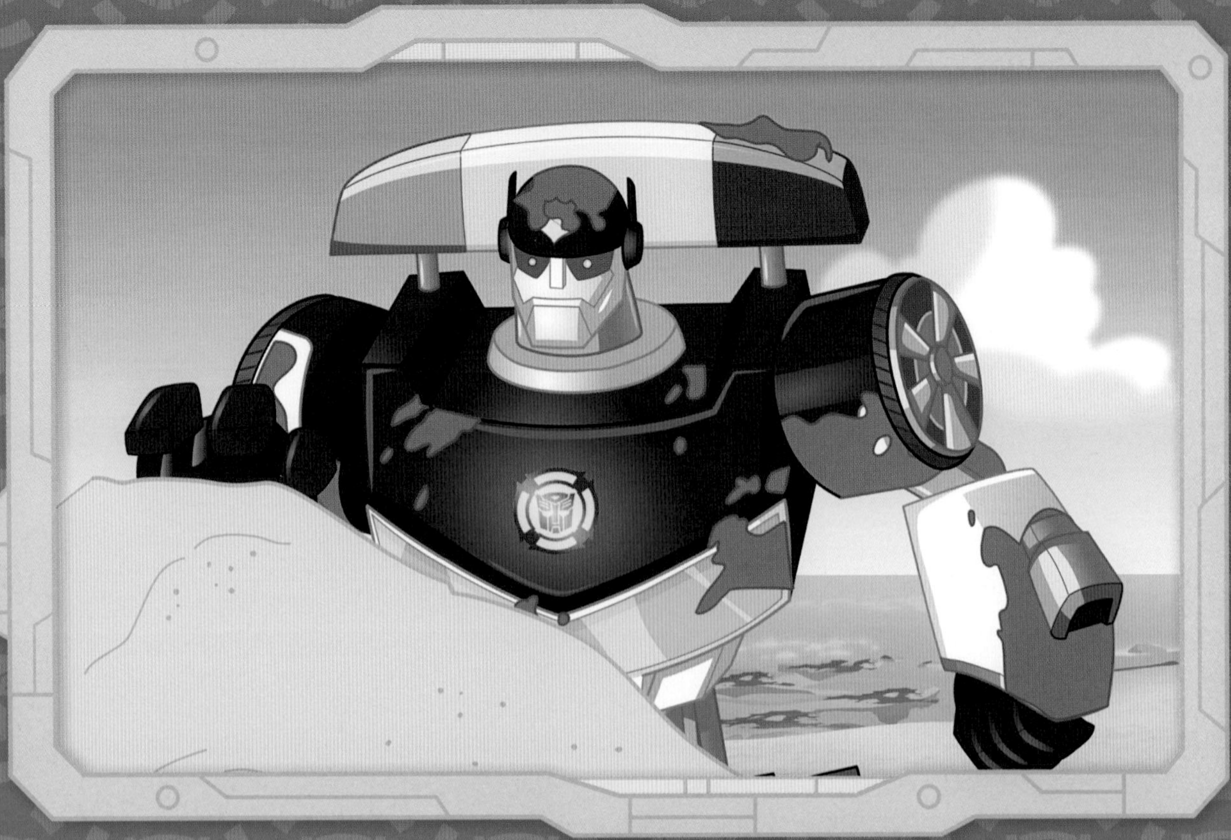

With a shelter built, Cody realizes he's very hungry. The Bots are determined to find their friend some food. They search the beach and tide pool but find very little.

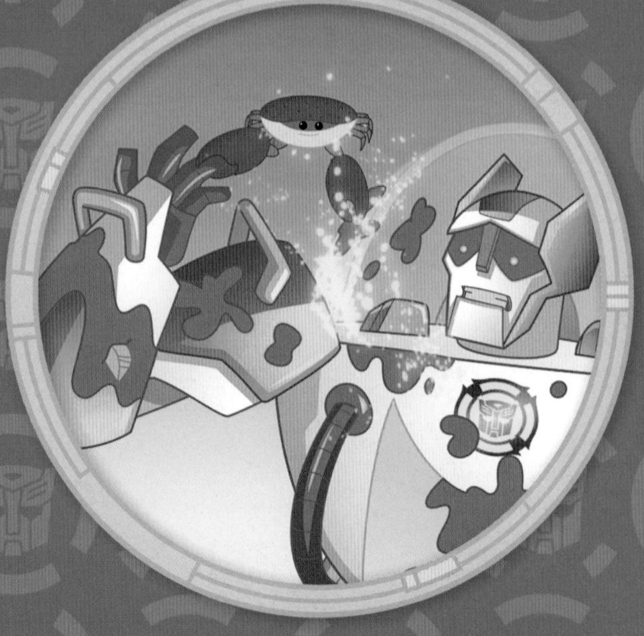

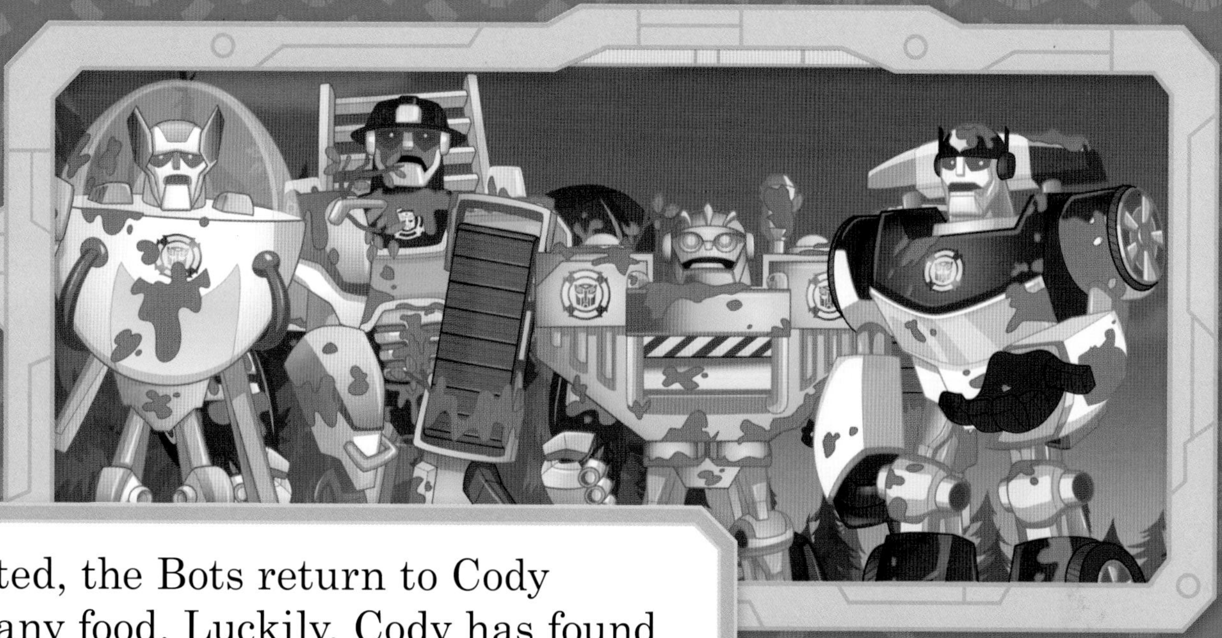

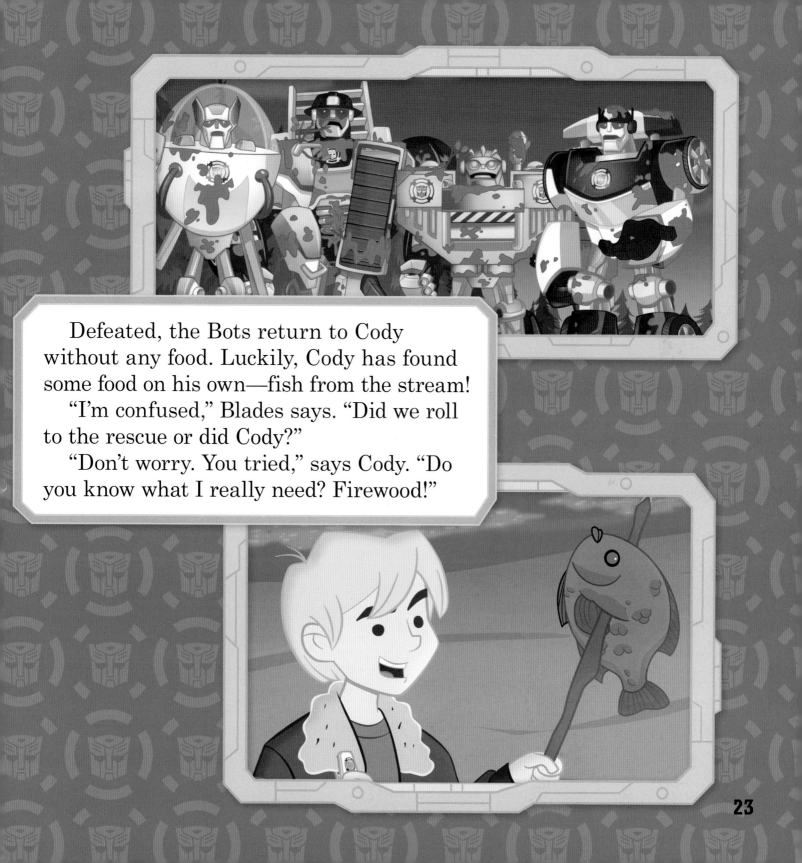

Defeated, the Bots return to Cody without any food. Luckily, Cody has found some food on his own—fish from the stream!

"I'm confused," Blades says. "Did we roll to the rescue or did Cody?"

"Don't worry. You tried," says Cody. "Do you know what I really need? Firewood!"

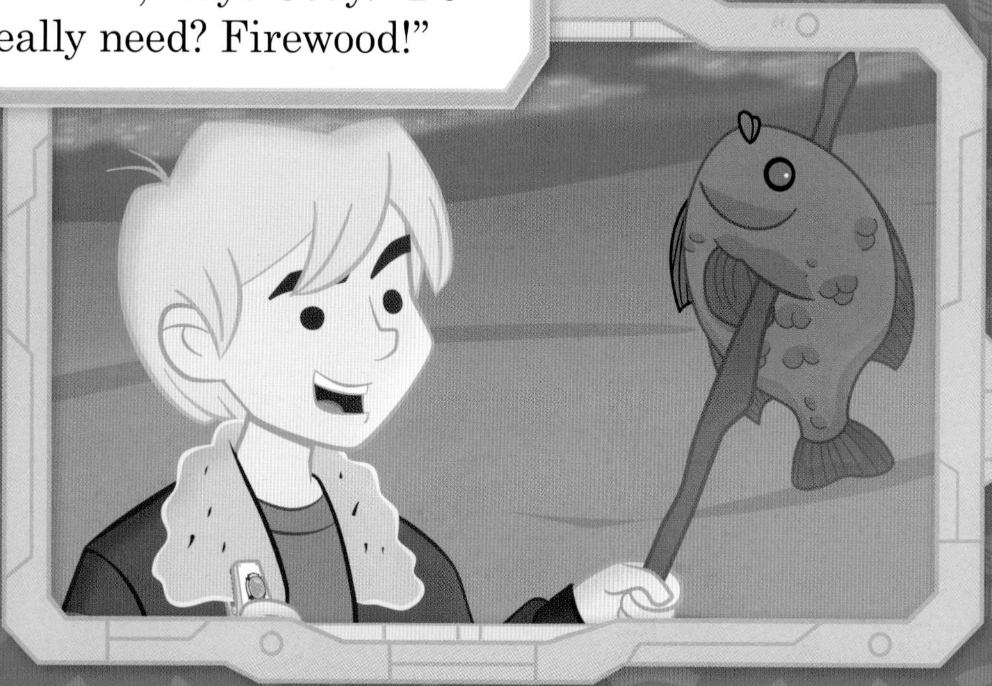

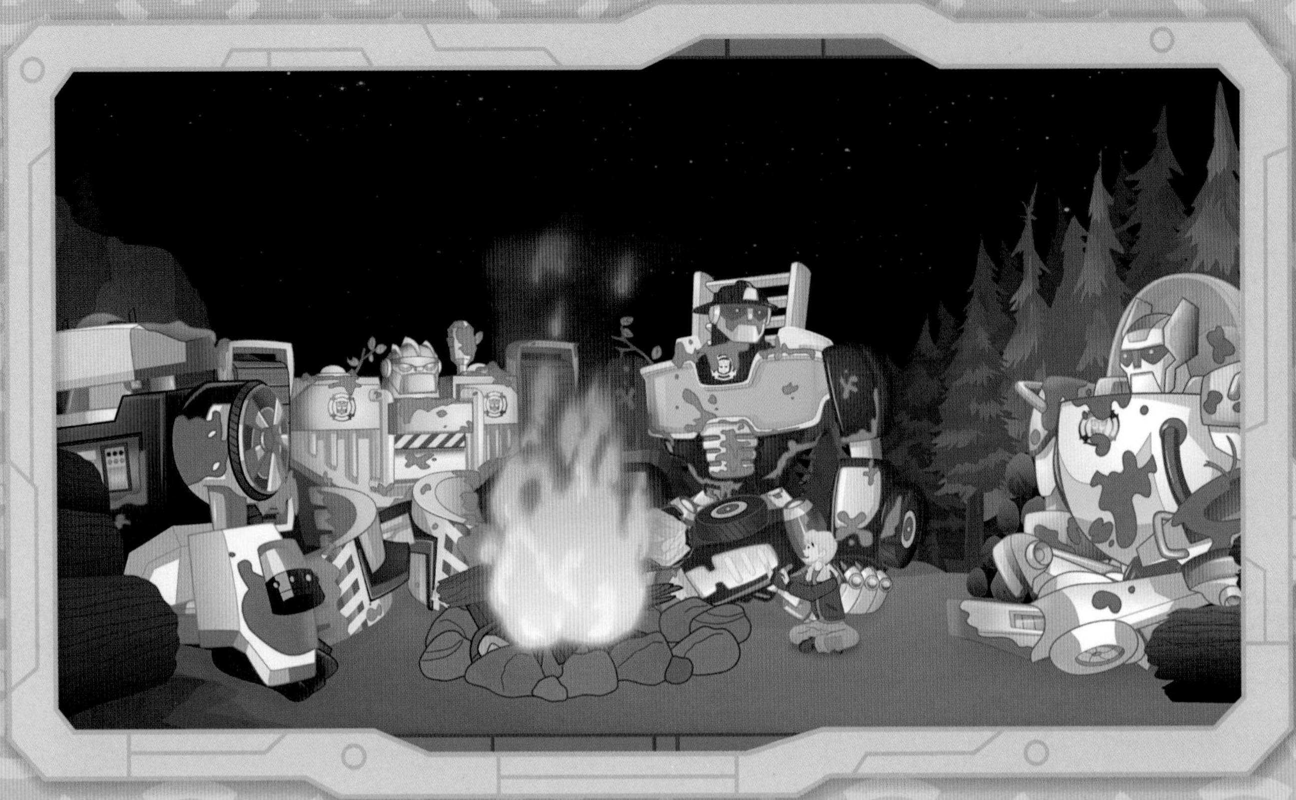

Once again, the Bots roll into action. They gather lots of wood and use it to make an enormous fire.

"So what's next?" asks Boulder.

"We could tell spooky stories," Cody says. "I know a good one. Five friends are in a dark and creepy forest...."

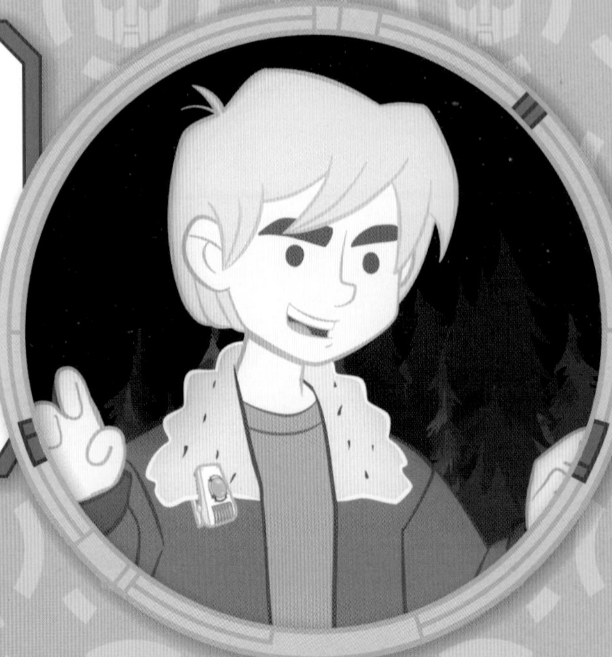

This is enough to scare Blades. He jumps up and shouts, "The fire needs more fuel!" as he lifts a large chunk of wood.

"Wait!" Cody exclaims. "Something is carved into that. It's a crow! Like the figurehead on the pirate ship!"

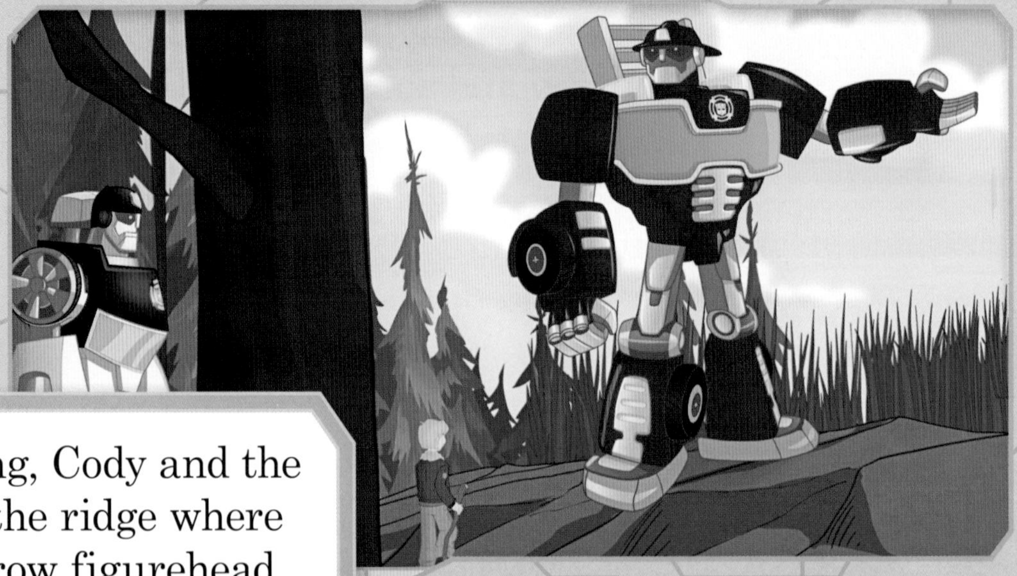

The next morning, Cody and the Rescue Bots go to the ridge where Blades found the crow figurehead.

The group looks for more pirate artifacts. Suddenly, they fall to the bottom of a dimly lit cavern!

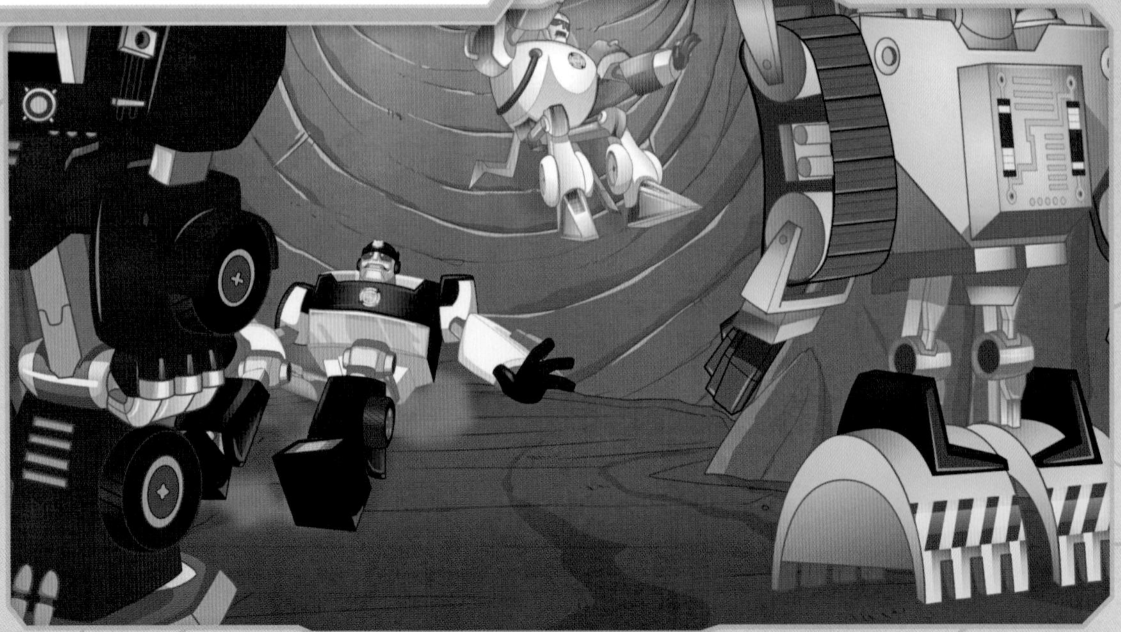

“What did we just fall through?” Chase asks.

“A secret hatchway!” Cody announces after some exploring. “And you will never believe what we just found!”

Cody leads the Bots around a bend to reveal the *Oaken Crow* pirate ship floating in a large grotto!

“Astonishing,” Chase gasps.

“Looks like it came through there,” Boulder says, pointing to an opening blocked by rocks.

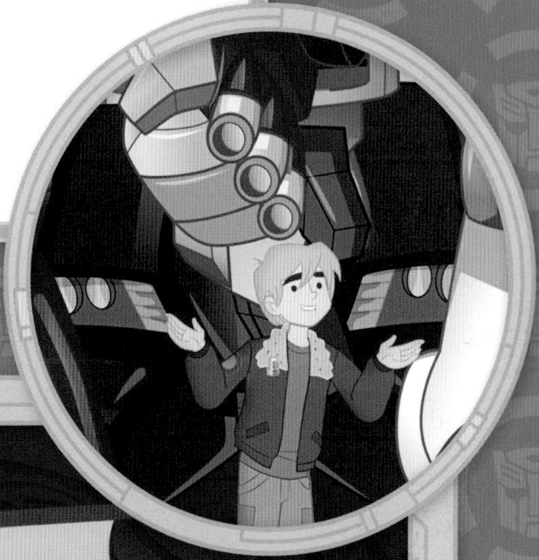

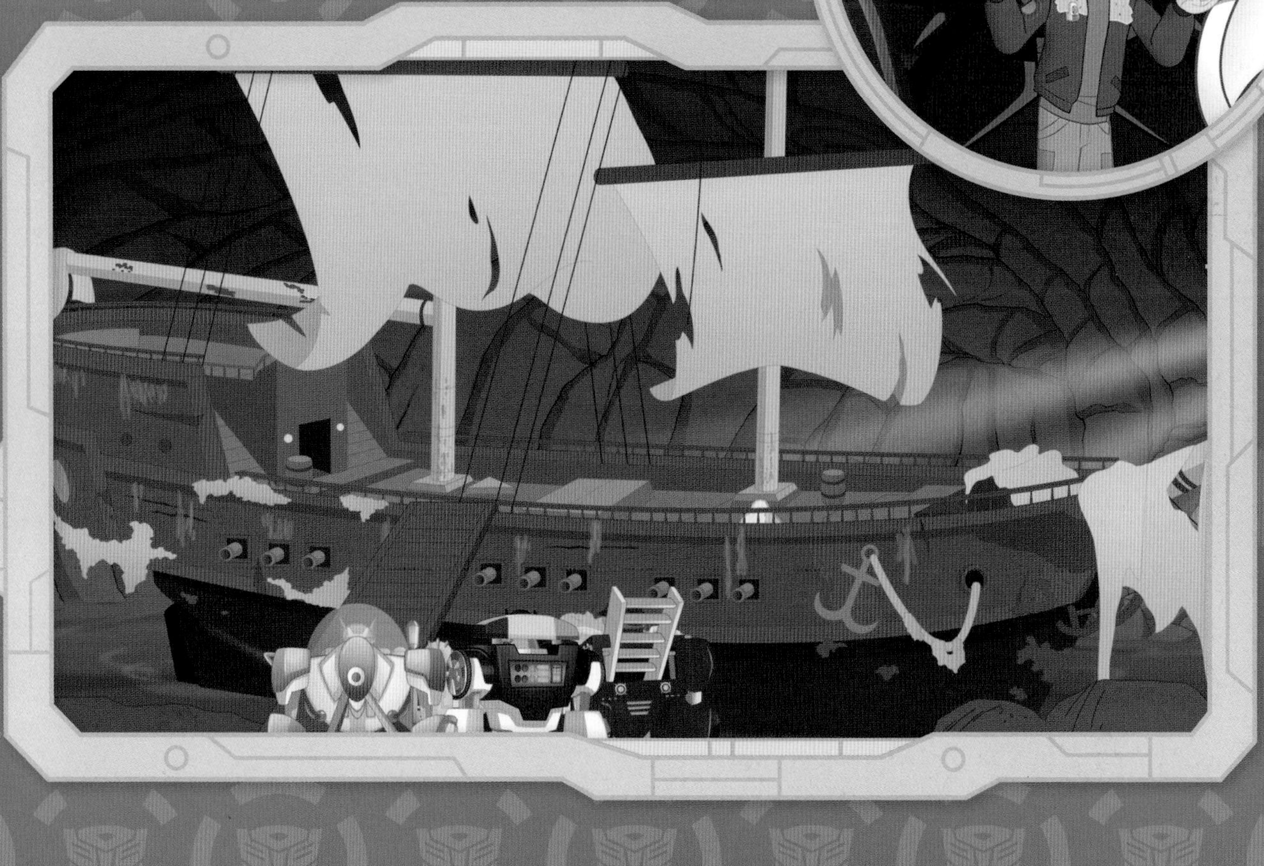

“C’mon! Let’s see what’s on board!” Cody exclaims.

Cody sprints up the gangplank and leaps on board. The Rescue Bots follow close behind him. There, on the deck of the ship, is the long-lost Settlers’ Bell!

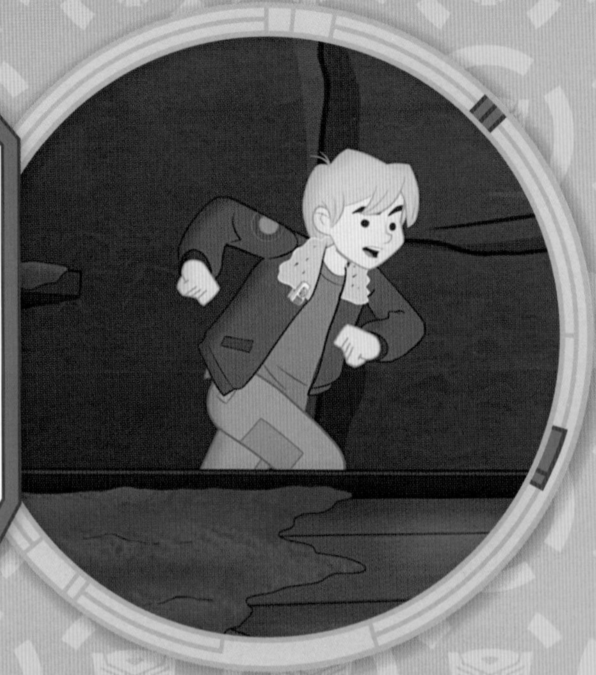

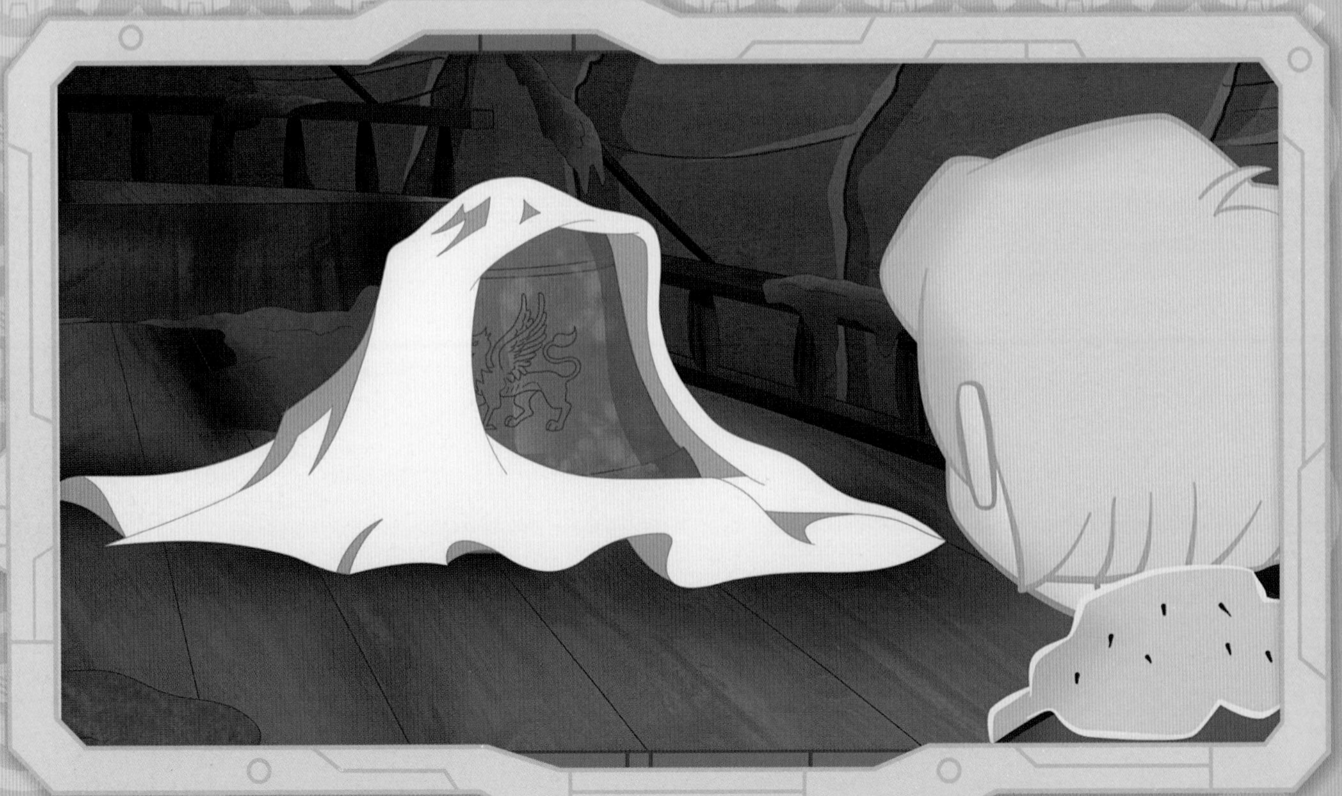

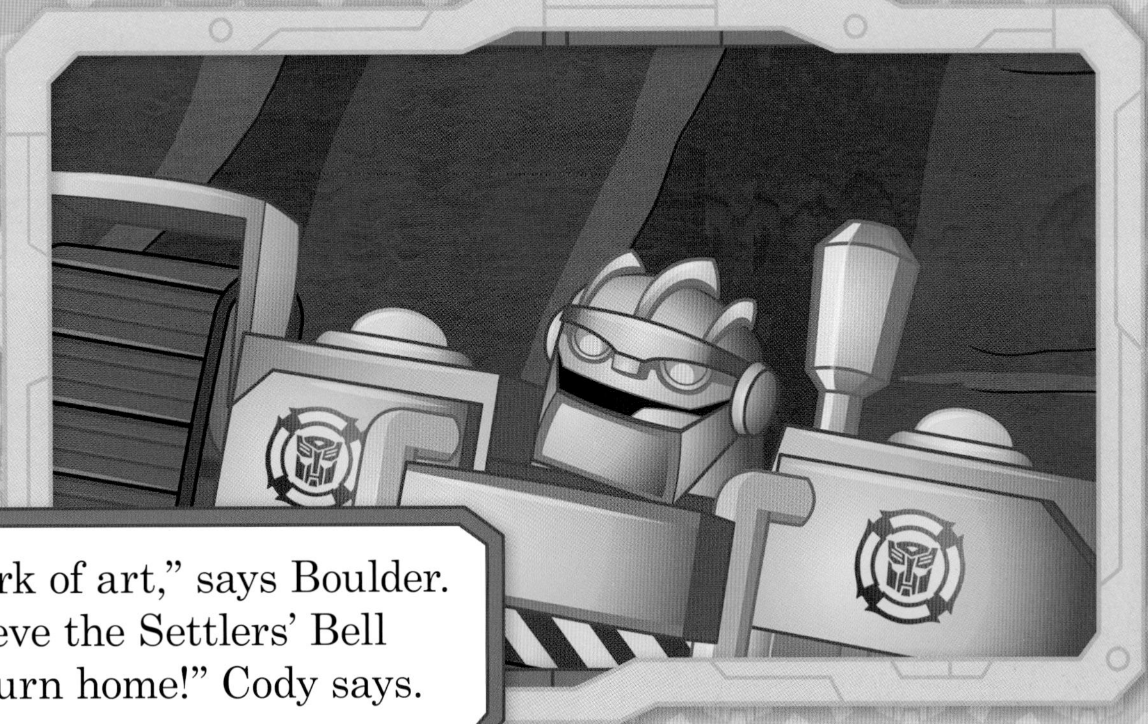

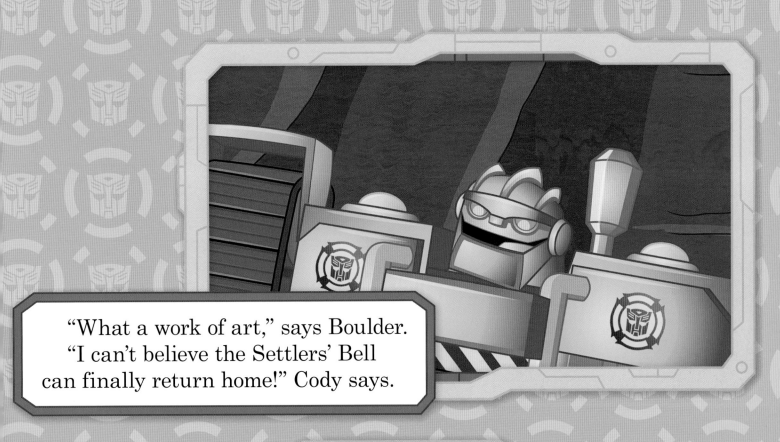

“What a work of art,” says Boulder.
“I can’t believe the Settlers’ Bell
can finally return home!” Cody says.

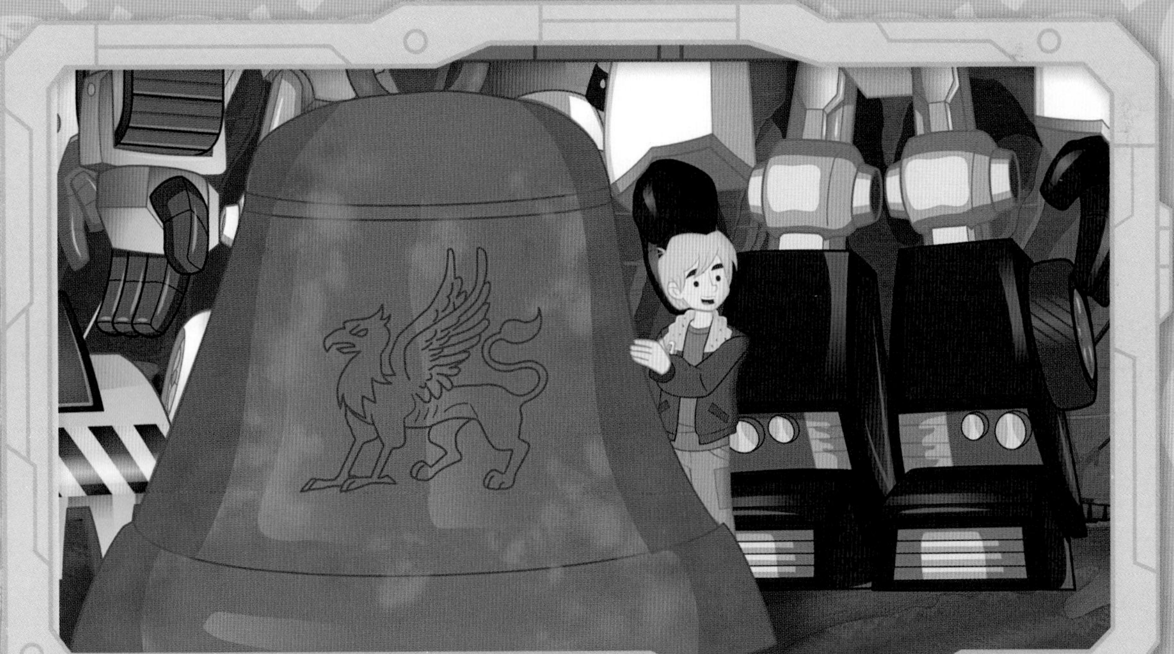

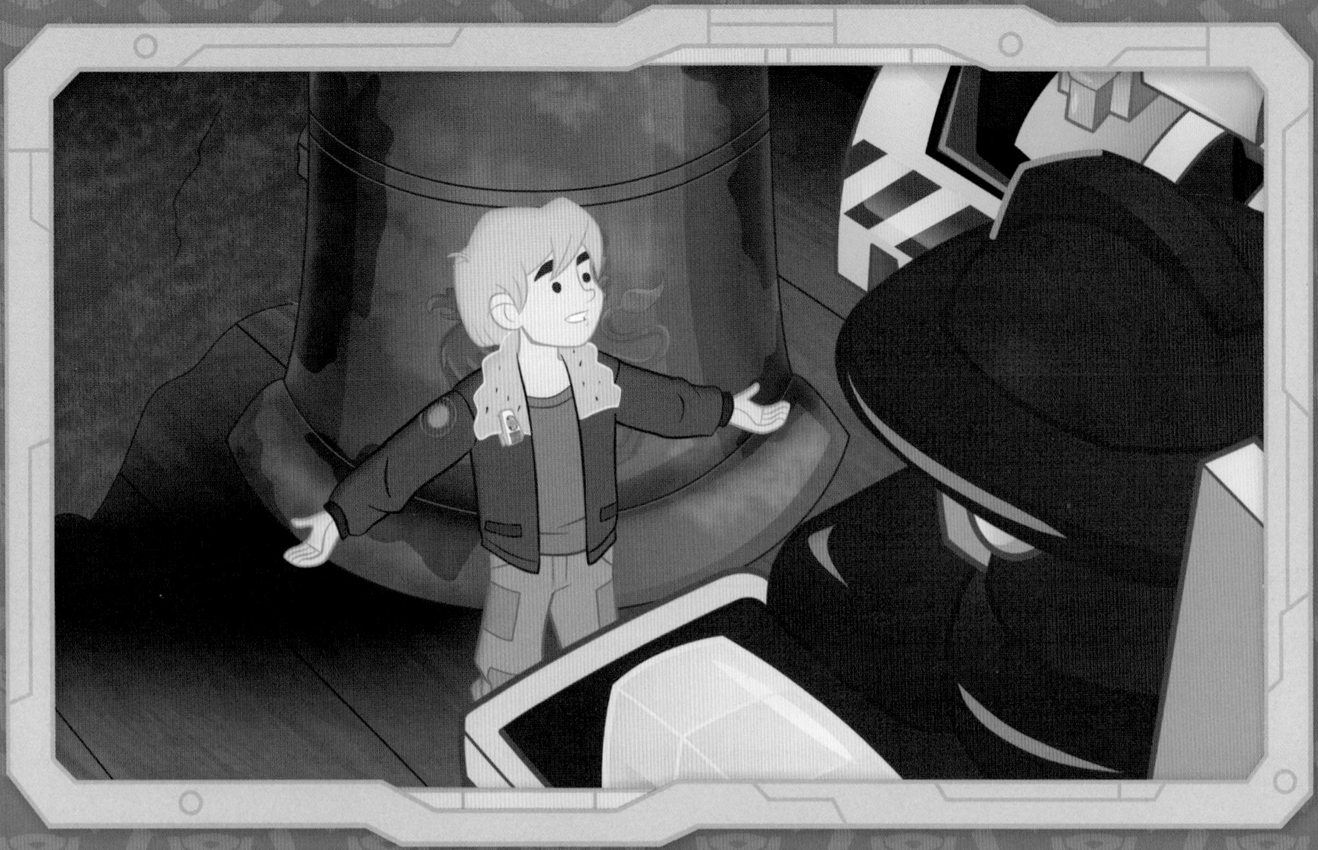

Cody quickly realizes that the ship has been stuck down there for centuries. How will they get it out?

"While knowing how things were done in the past is helpful, nothing beats a state-of-the-art Rescue Bot," says Chase.

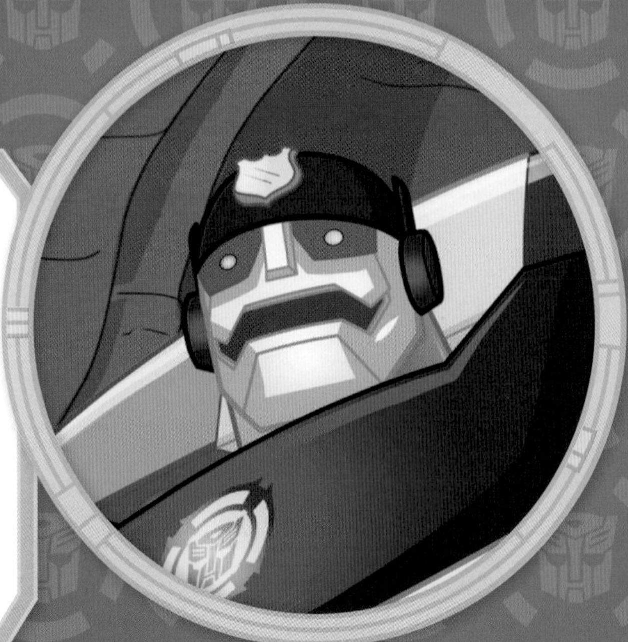

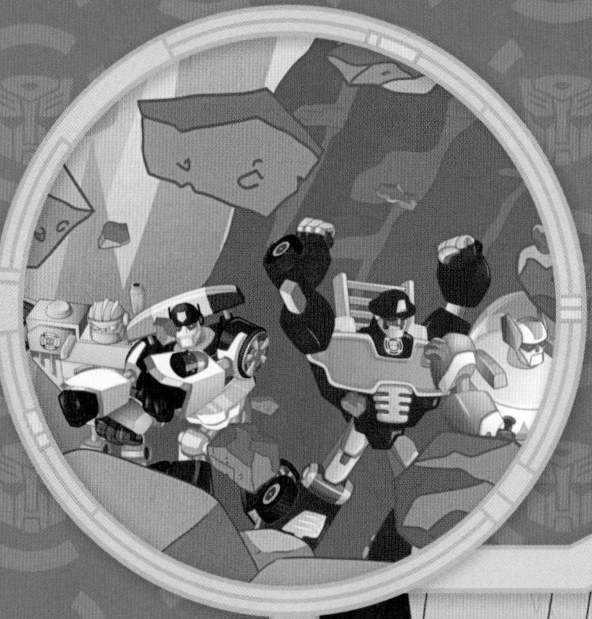

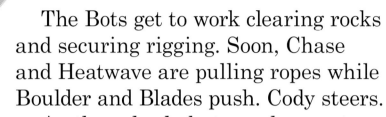

The Bots get to work clearing rocks and securing rigging. Soon, Chase and Heatwave are pulling ropes while Boulder and Blades push. Cody steers.

As they slowly but surely emerge from the cavern, the whole team cheers!

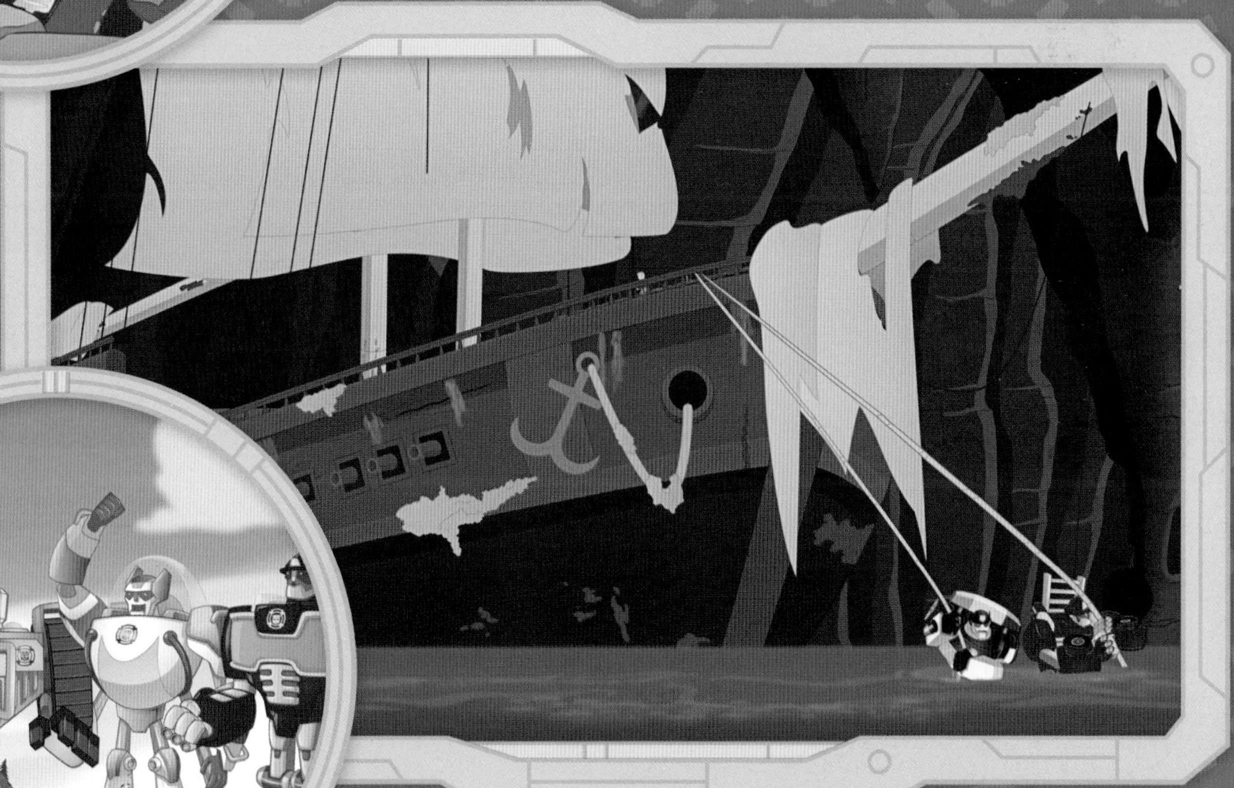

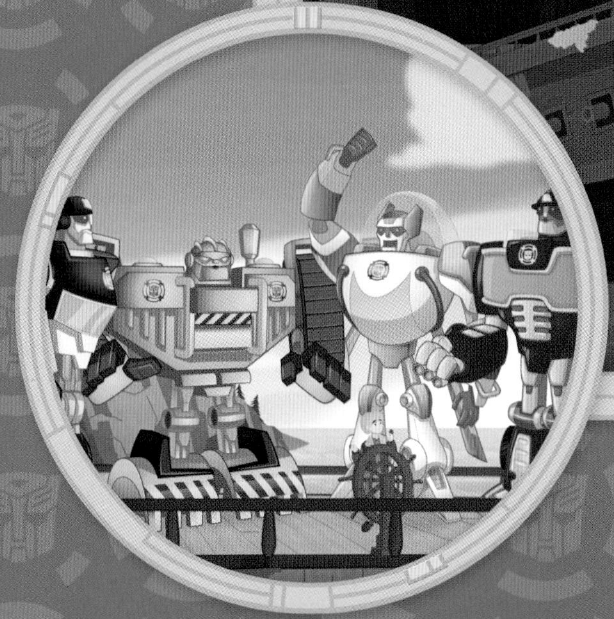

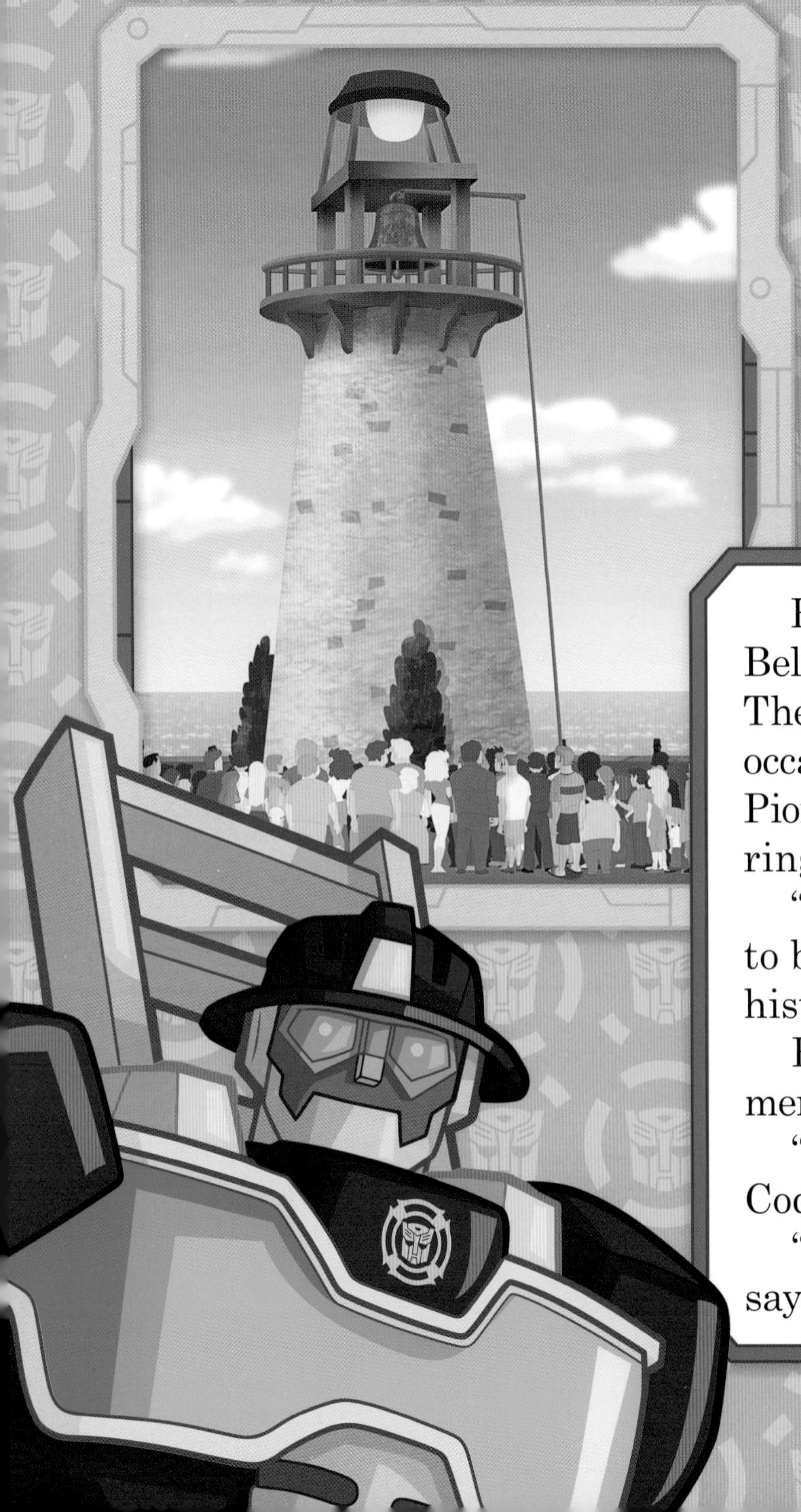

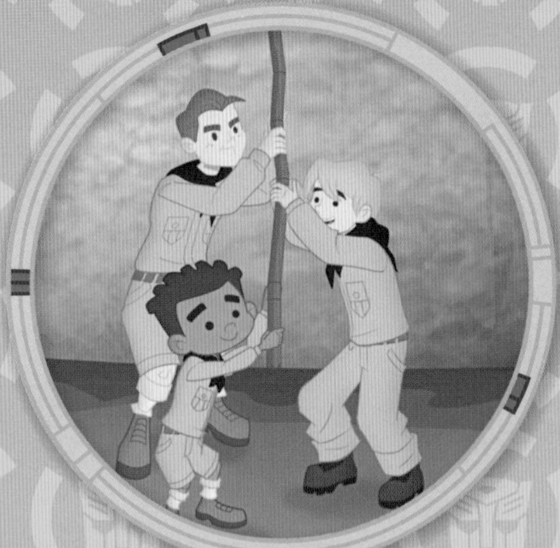

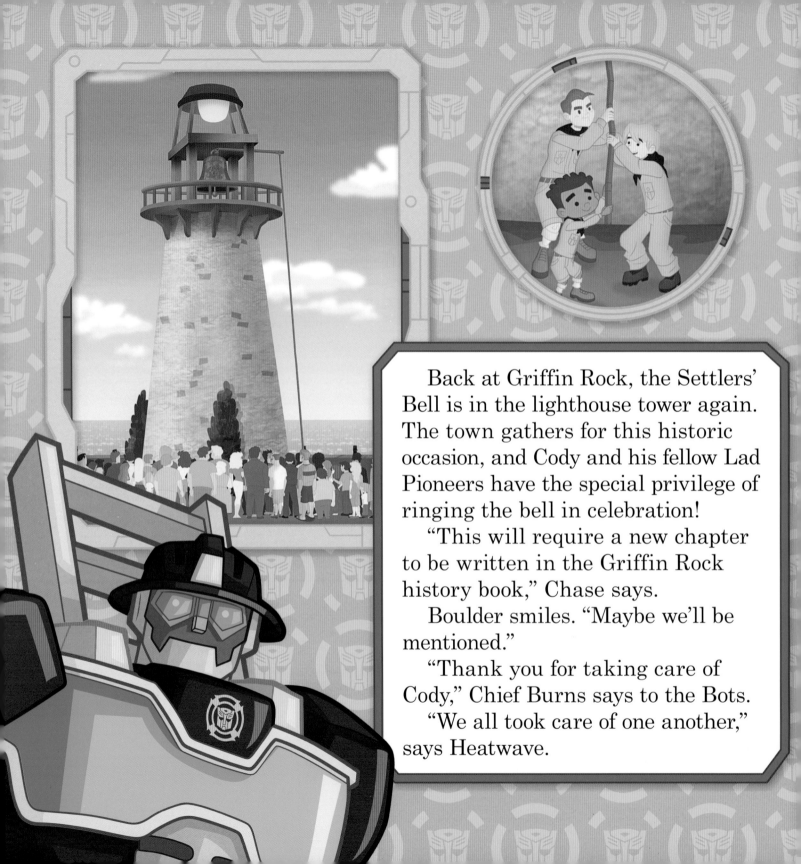

Back at Griffin Rock, the Settlers' Bell is in the lighthouse tower again. The town gathers for this historic occasion, and Cody and his fellow Lad Pioneers have the special privilege of ringing the bell in celebration!

"This will require a new chapter to be written in the Griffin Rock history book," Chase says.

Boulder smiles. "Maybe we'll be mentioned."

"Thank you for taking care of Cody," Chief Burns says to the Bots.

"We all took care of one another," says Heatwave.

TRANSFORMERS RESCUE BOTS

Return of the Dino Bot

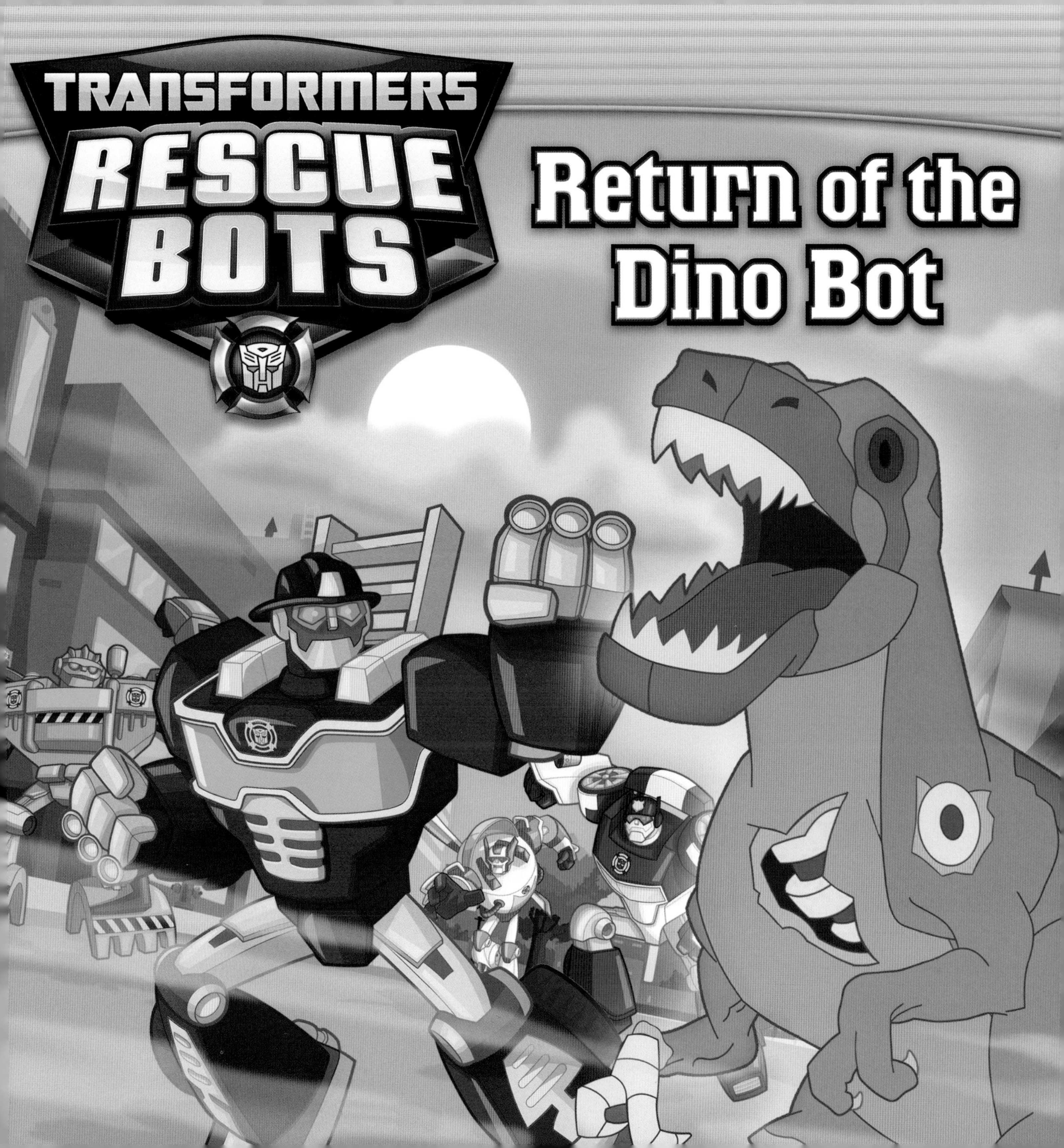

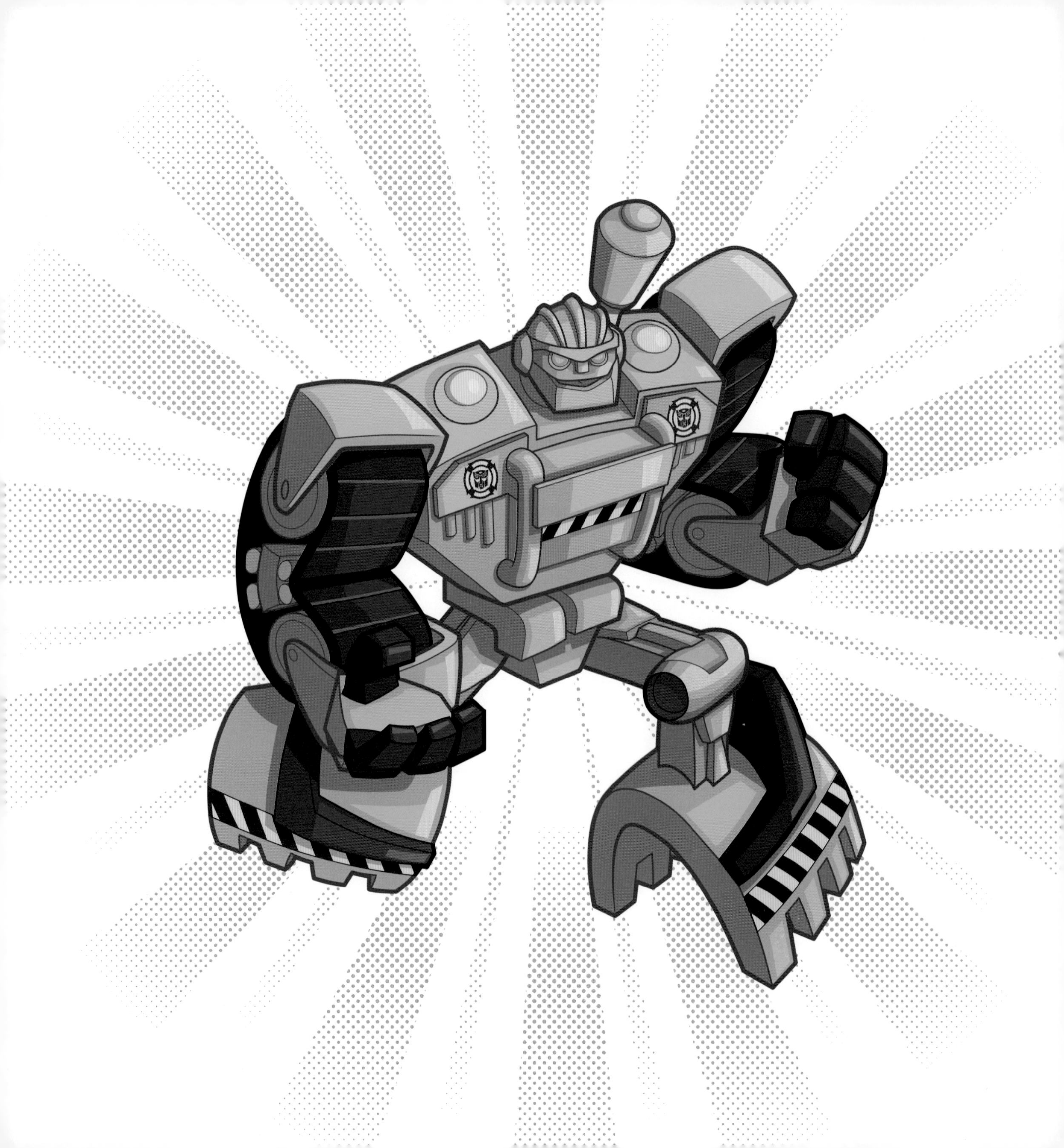

Return of the Dino Bot

TRANSFORMERS RESCUE BOTS

Adapted by John Sazaklis
Based on the episode "Return of the Dino Bot"
written by Luke McMullen

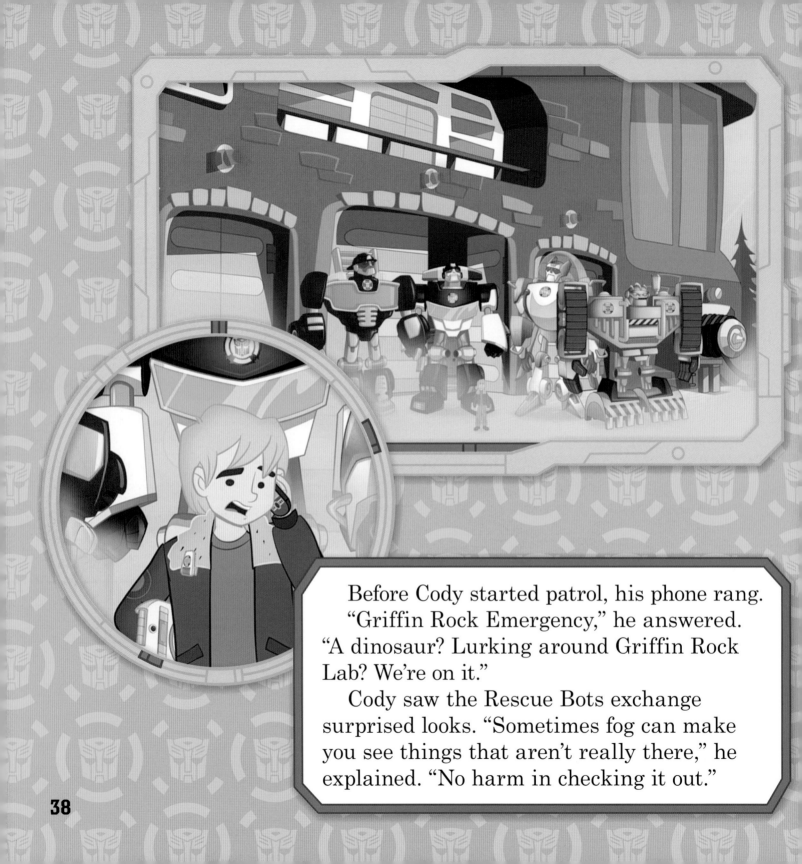

Before Cody started patrol, his phone rang.

"Griffin Rock Emergency," he answered. "A dinosaur? Lurking around Griffin Rock Lab? We're on it."

Cody saw the Rescue Bots exchange surprised looks. "Sometimes fog can make you see things that aren't really there," he explained. "No harm in checking it out."

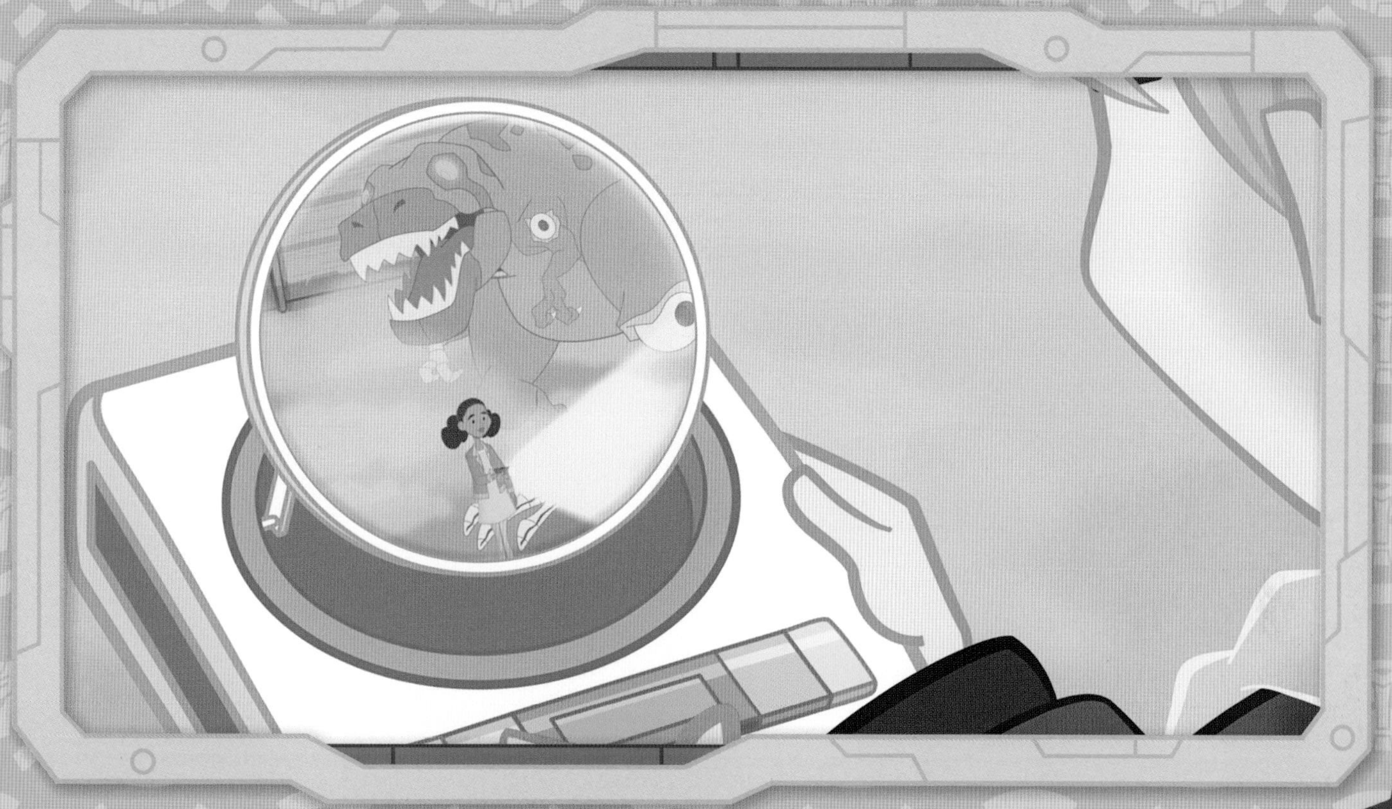

Cody used his Com-Link to view the lab. The screen showed Francine, Doc Greene's daughter, searching the perimeter.

"Frankie's a little older than me, but she's no dinosaur," Cody joked. Suddenly, a large creature appeared behind her.

"The Dino Bot has returned!" said Blades.

Heatwave stood tall and said, "Rescue Bots, roll to the rescue!"

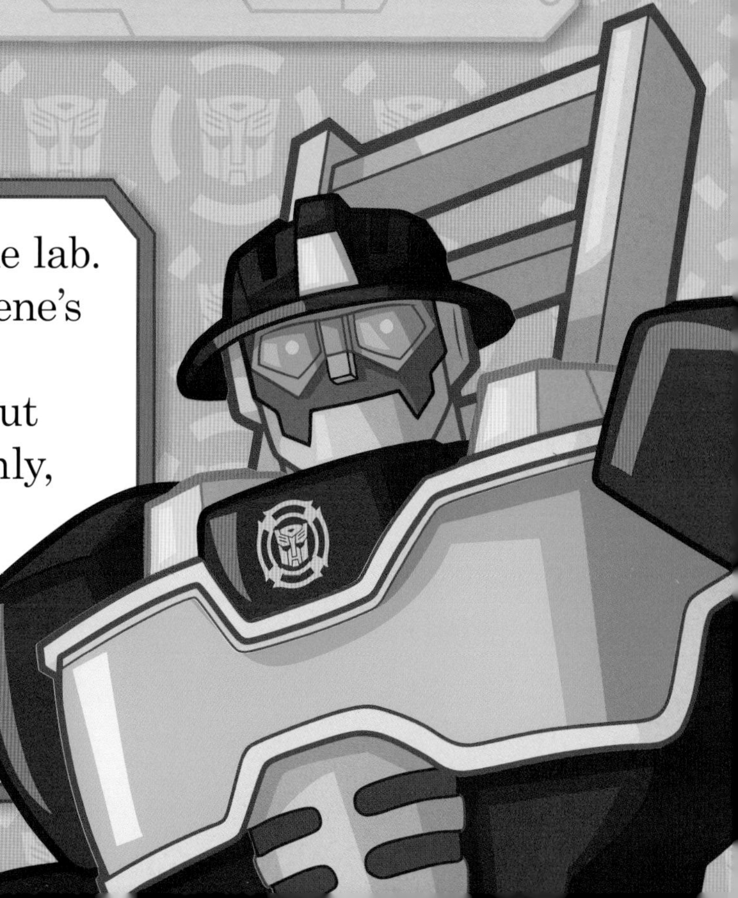

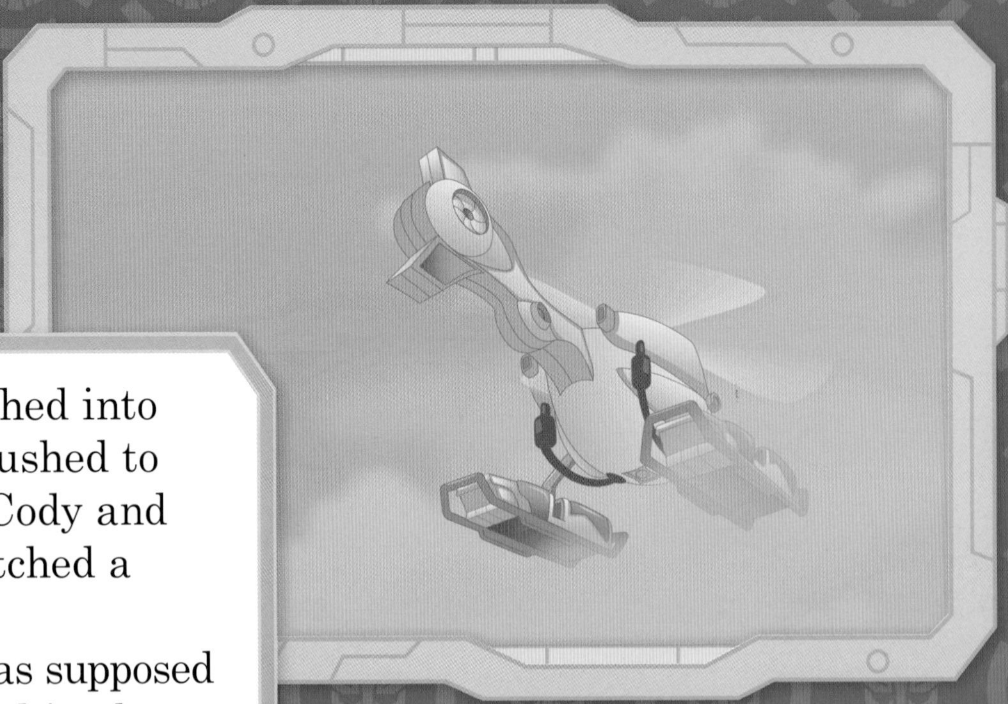

The robots switched into vehicle mode and rushed to Griffin Rock Lab. Cody and his sister, Dani, hitched a ride inside Blades.

"The Dino Bot was supposed to be shut down and in the museum," Dani said. "Are you sure that's what you saw?"

"Yes, and it was stalking Frankie!" replied Cody. "Look, there they are!"

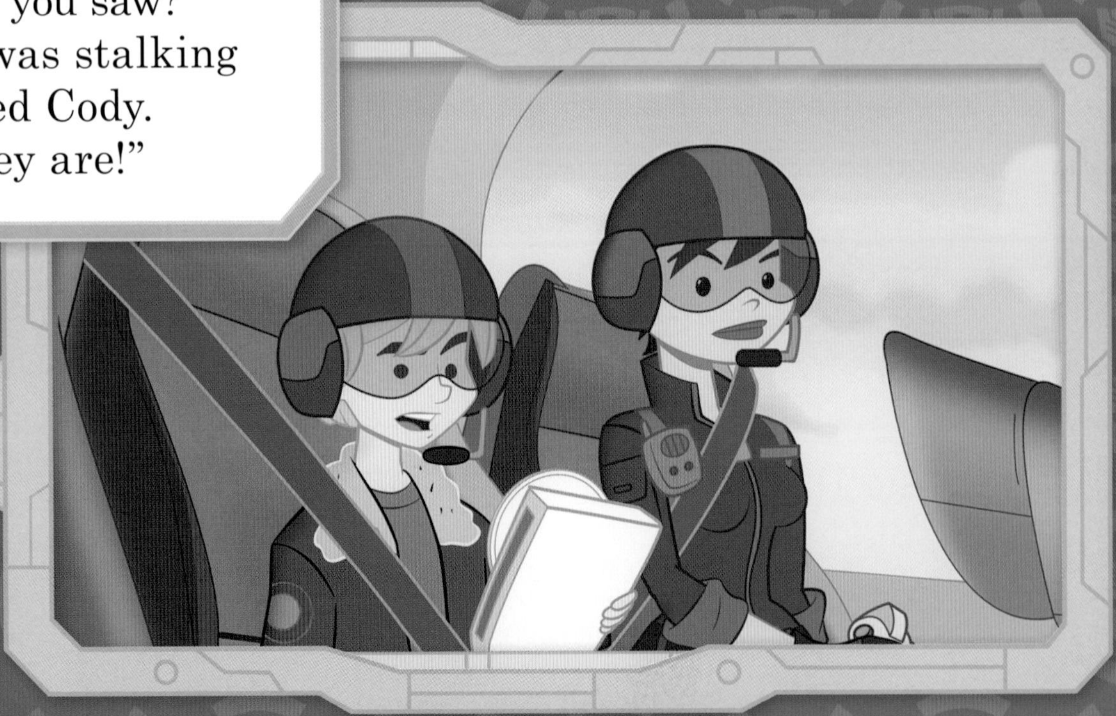

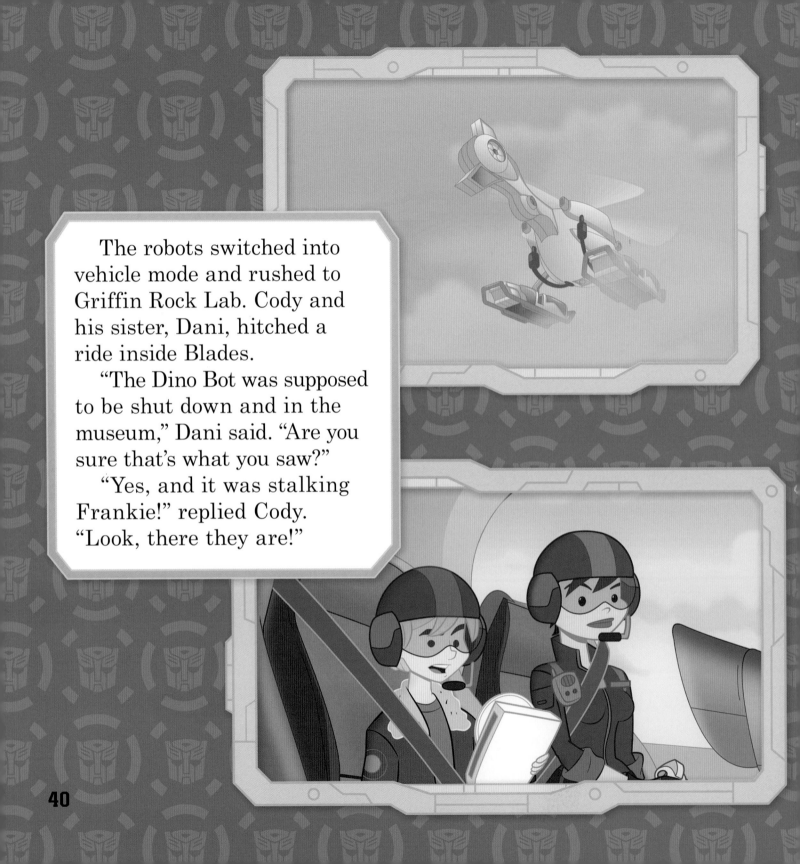

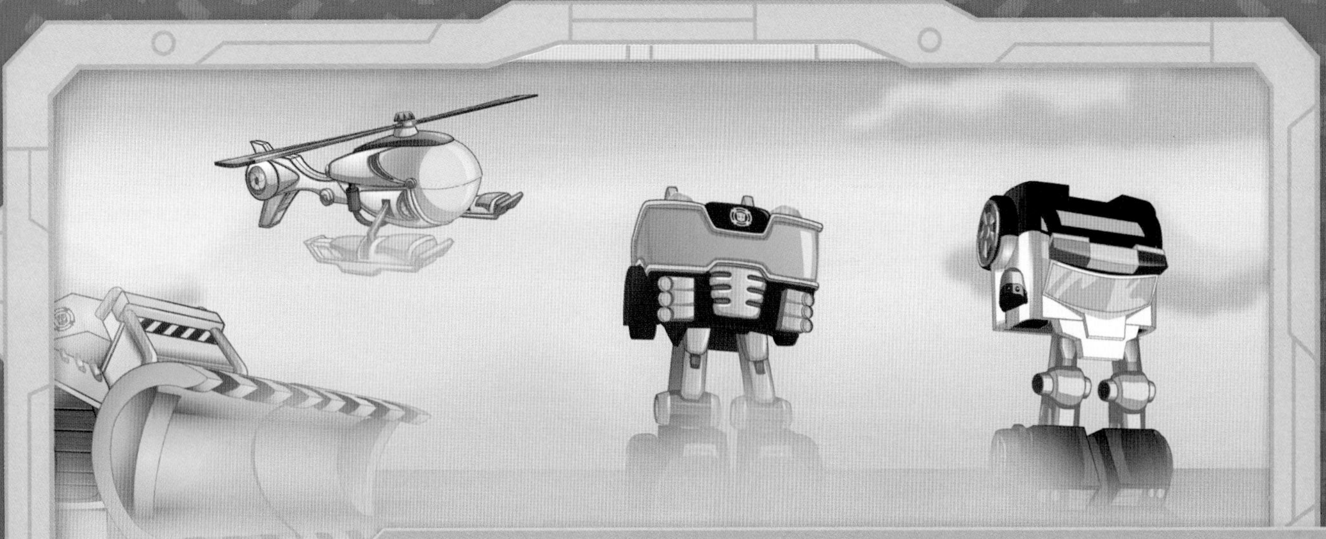

Blades landed near his teammates Boulder, Heatwave, and Chase. They all changed forms and surrounded the mechanical menace.

"Attention, human! Take cover!" Heatwave said to Frankie. He aimed his water blasters at the Dino Bot and prepared to fire.

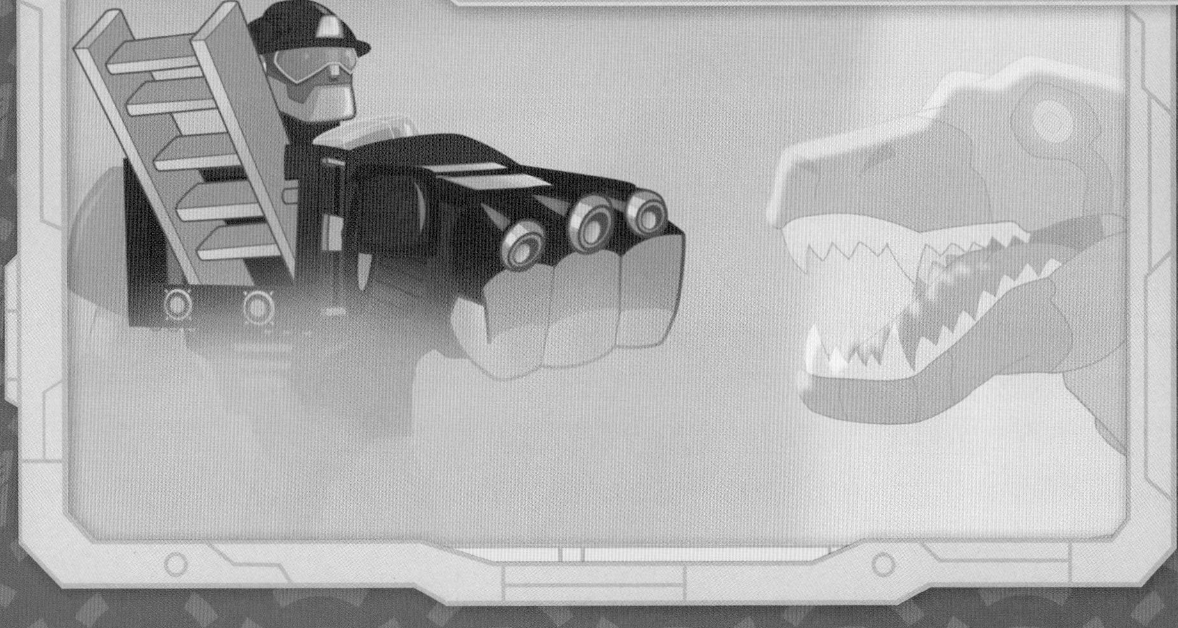

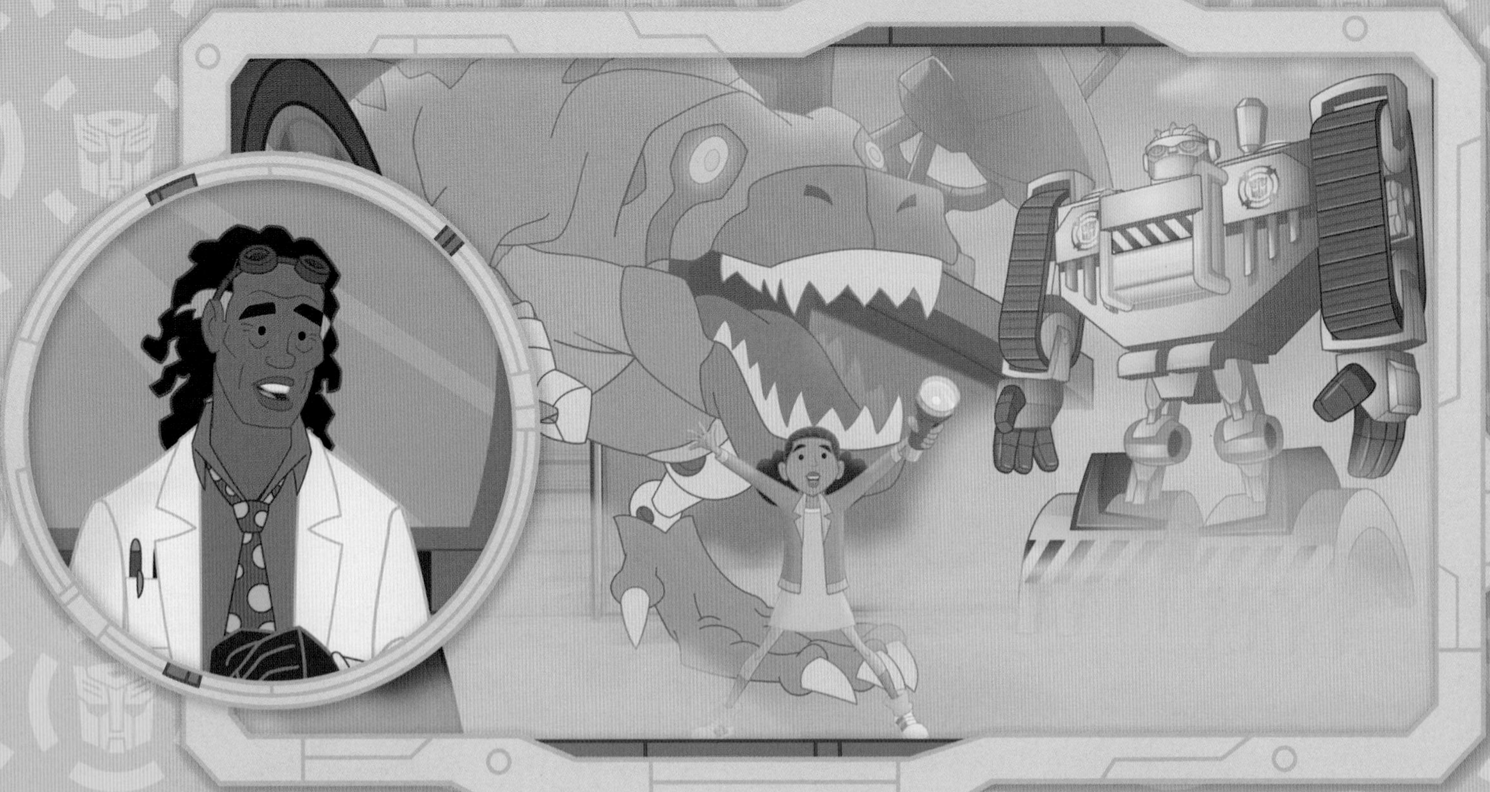

Frankie ran between Heatwave and the Dino Bot. “Wait!” she cried, waving her arms. “He’s friendly now. His name is Trex!”

Heatwave lowered his blasters. He and the other Rescue Bots were confused.

“That’s right,” Doc Greene said. “I’ve reprogrammed the Dino Bot to protect our lab. The other day, an intruder tried to break into our computer system.”

“Yikes!” replied Graham, one of Cody’s brothers. “A hacker could control everything automated in town!”

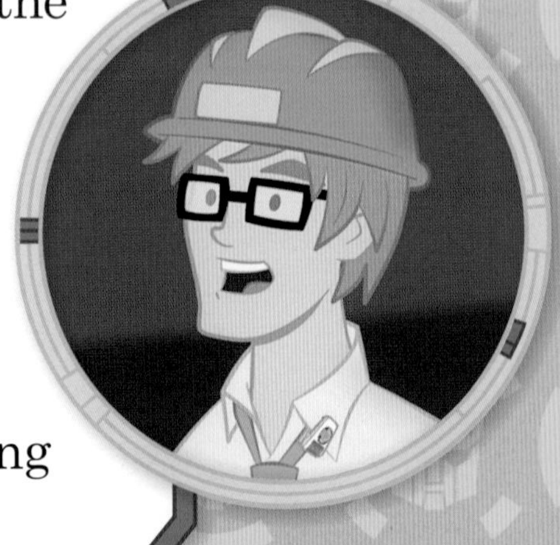

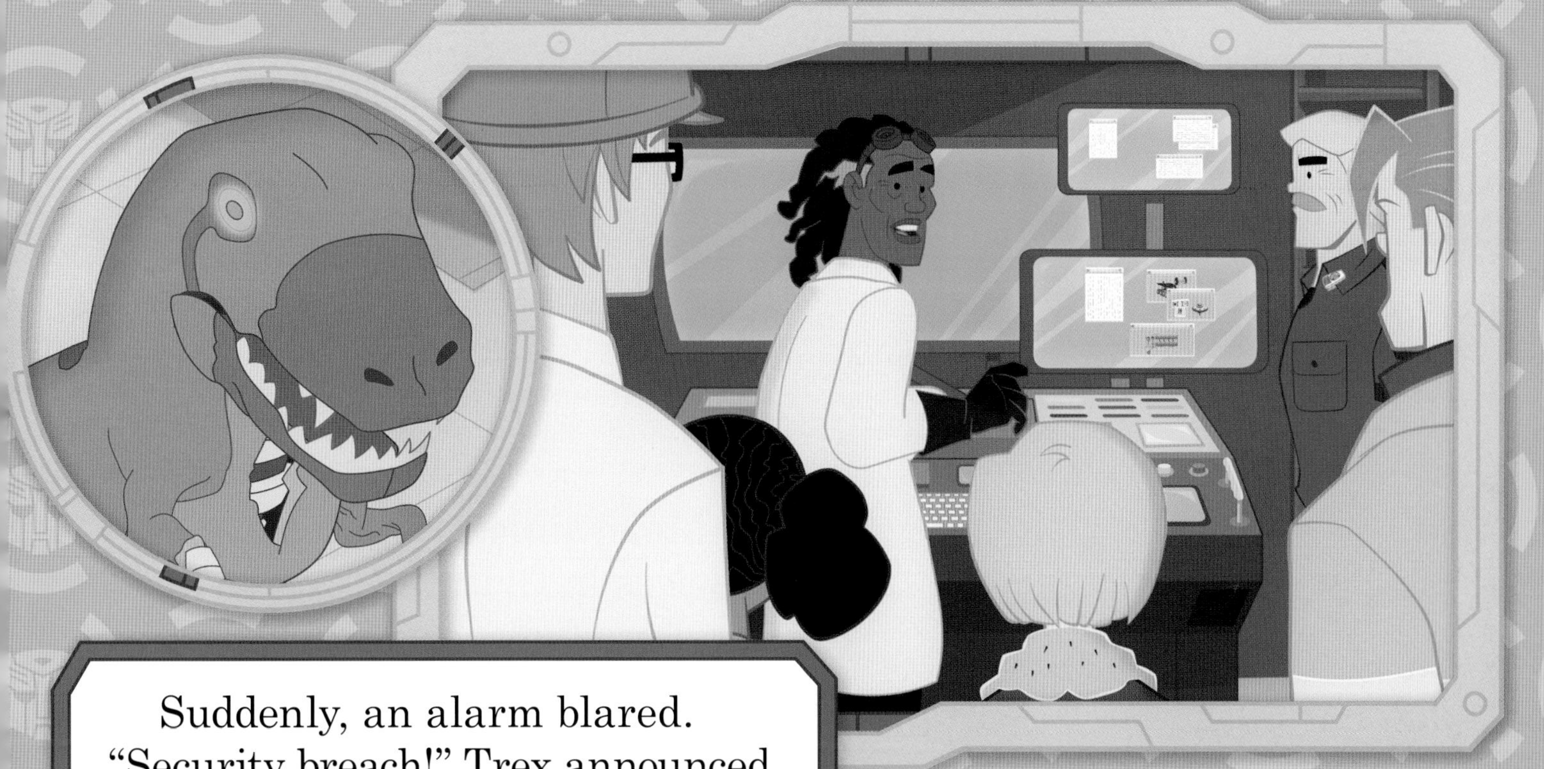

Suddenly, an alarm blared.
"Security breach!" Trex announced.
"Threat: maximum!"
"Oh no!" Doc Greene shouted.
The friends gathered around a large monitor. There was chaos in the city. The Rescue Bots changed into vehicles again and zoomed off.

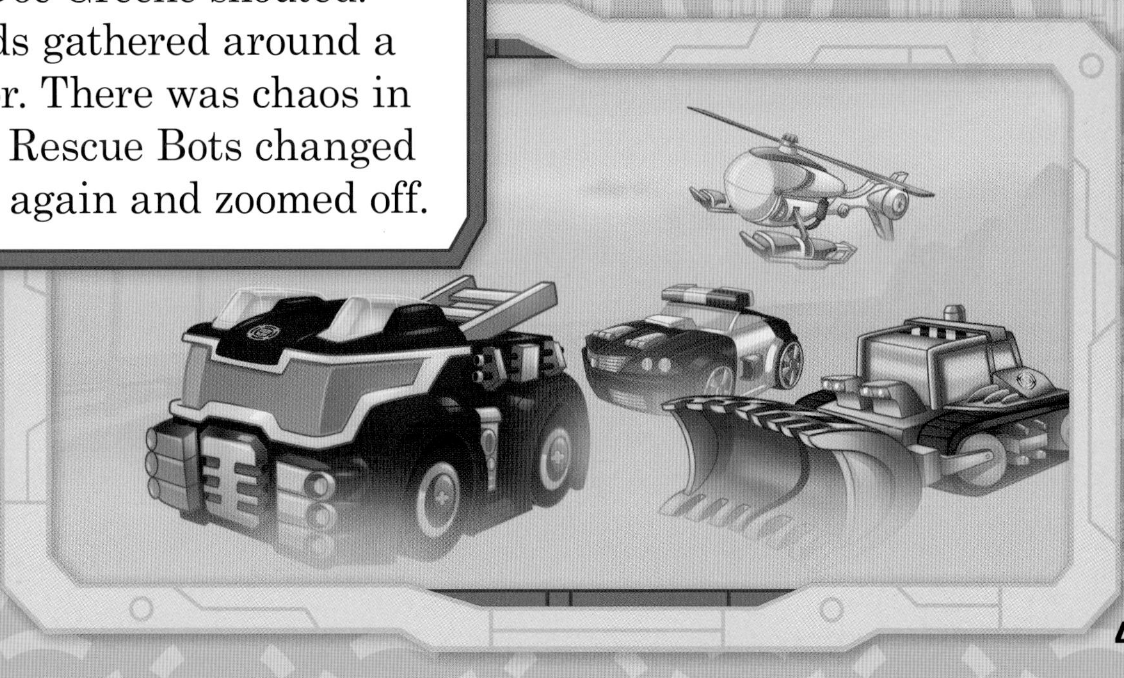

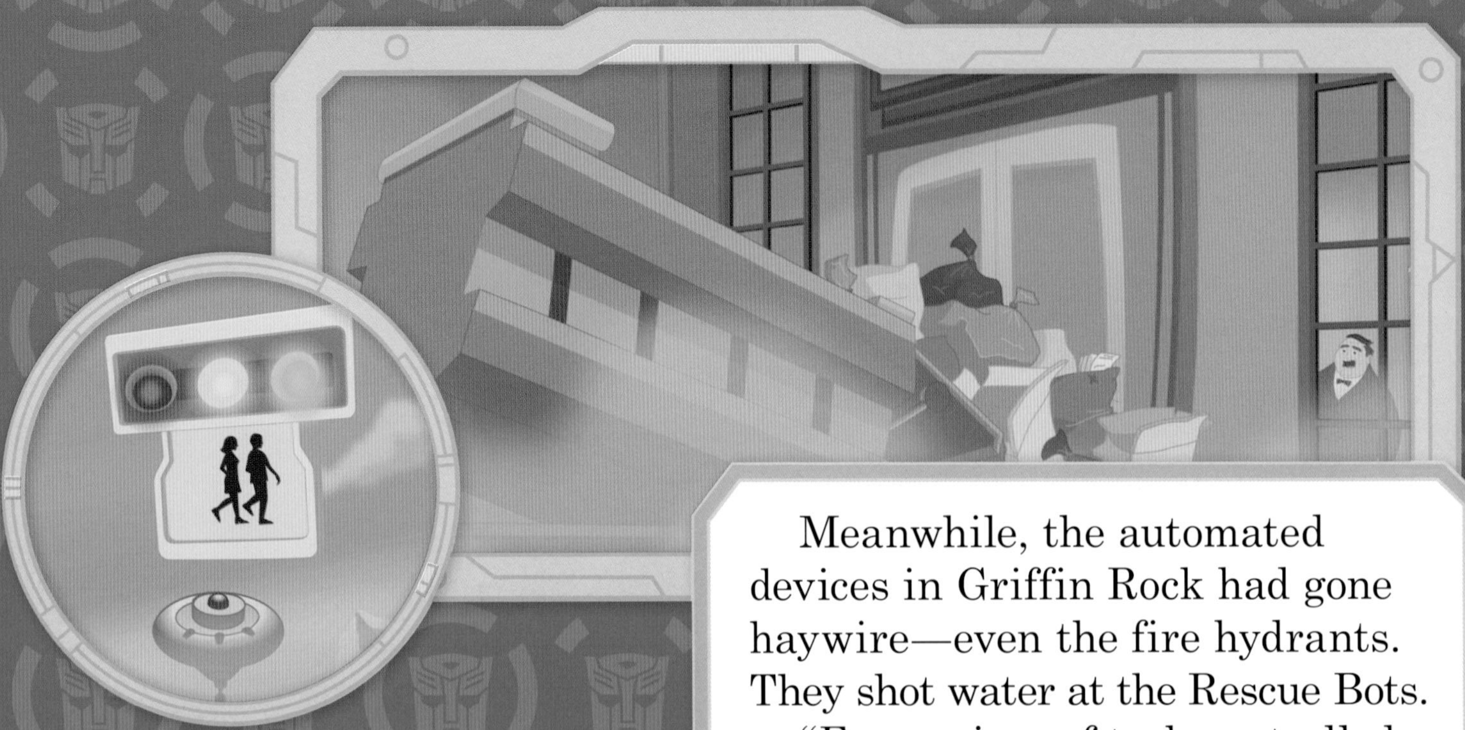

Meanwhile, the automated devices in Griffin Rock had gone haywire—even the fire hydrants. They shot water at the Rescue Bots.

"Every piece of tech controlled by the city's mainframe has gone berserk!" Heatwave cried.

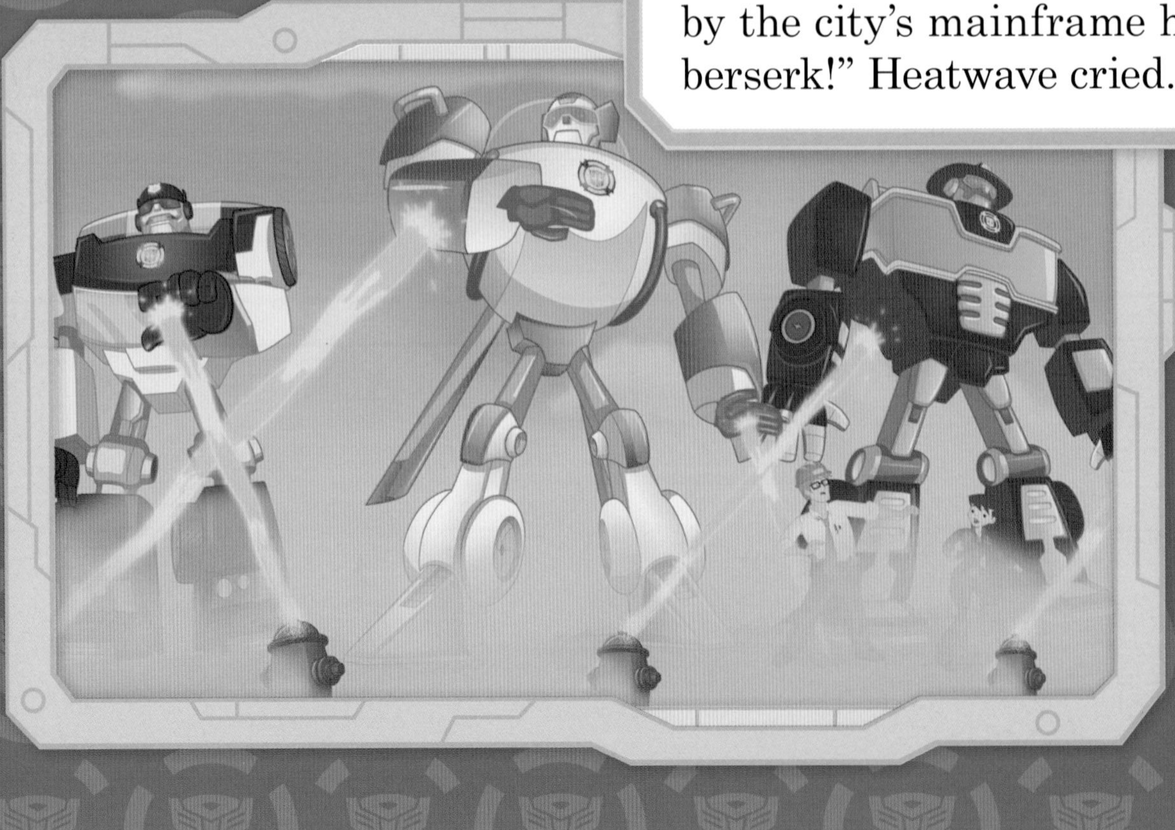

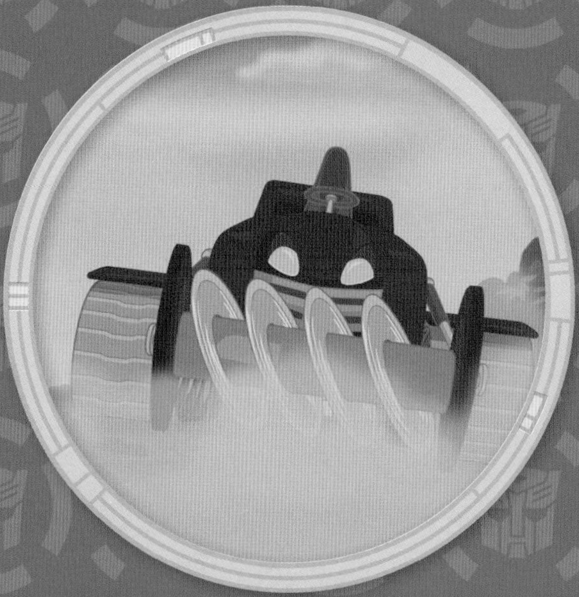

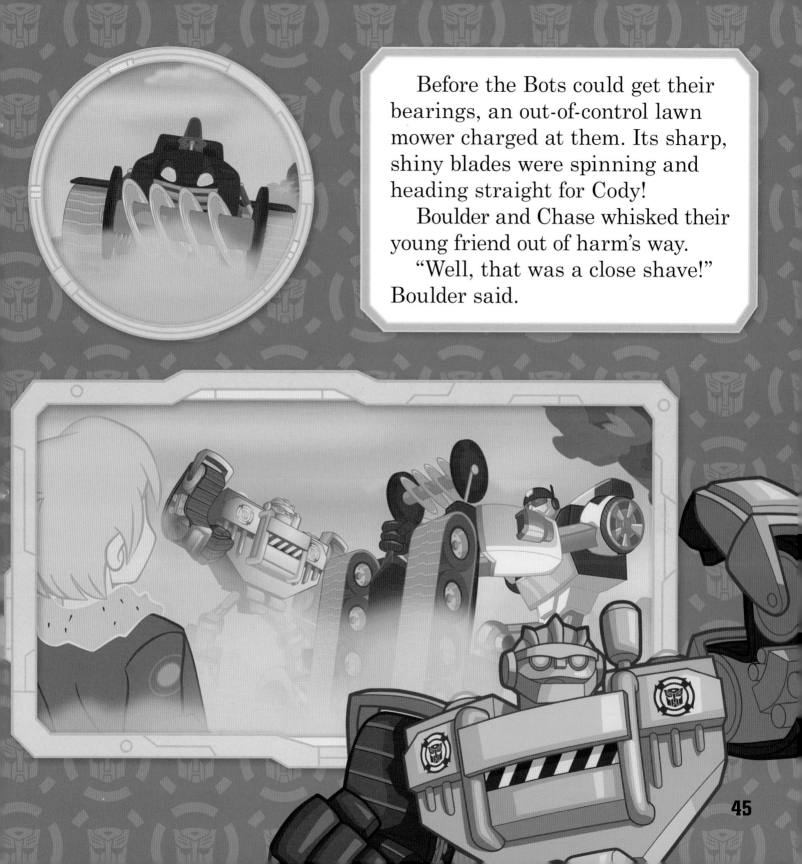

Before the Bots could get their bearings, an out-of-control lawn mower charged at them. Its sharp, shiny blades were spinning and heading straight for Cody!

Boulder and Chase whisked their young friend out of harm's way.

"Well, that was a close shave!" Boulder said.

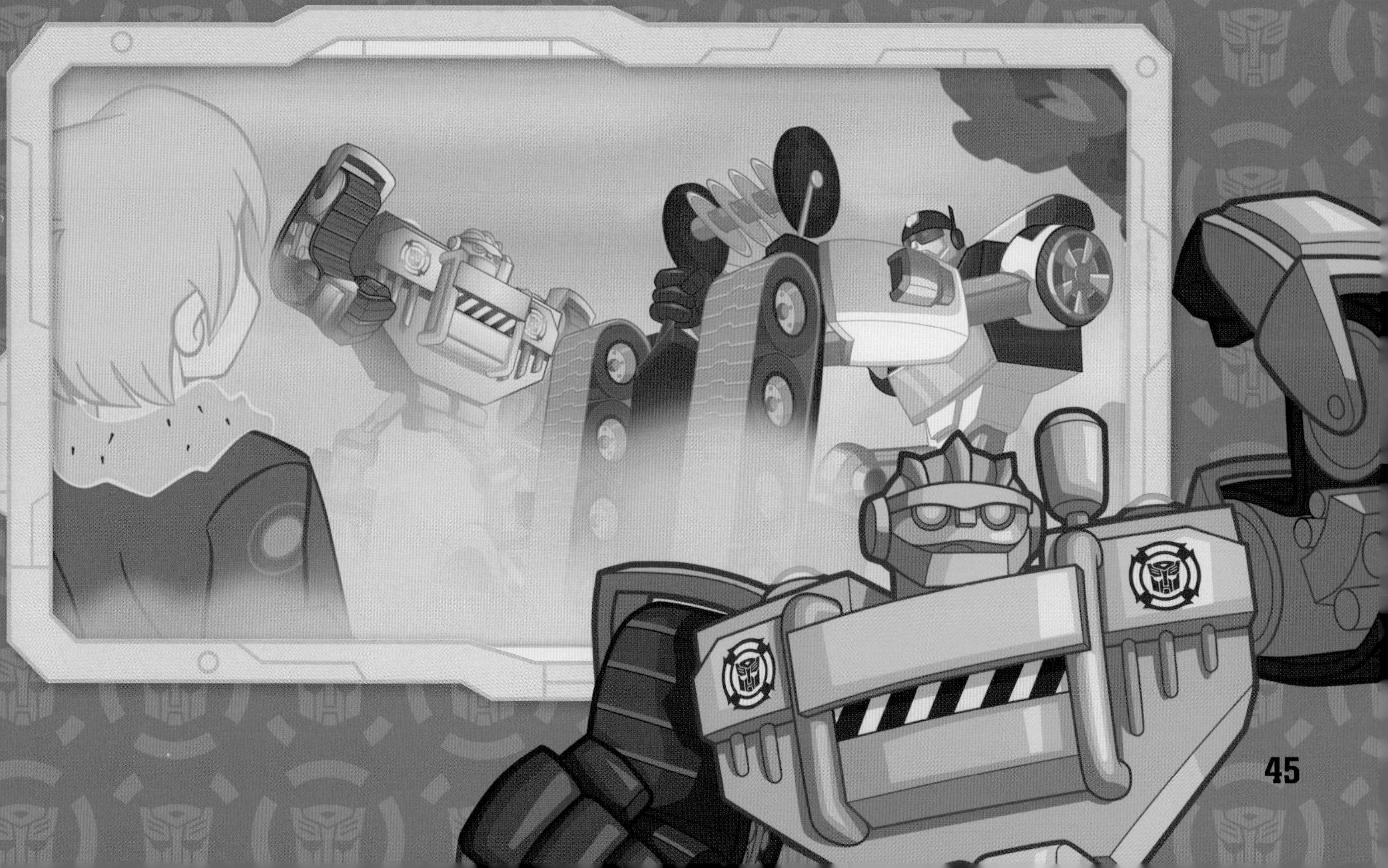

At the lab, Doc Greene and Frankie discovered that the cause of the chaos was a computer virus. It had reprogrammed the Dino Bot from harmless guard dog to predator. Trex's first instruction was to destroy the humans!

"We must plug my laptop into the mainframe," Doc Greene said as they ran from Trex. "It's the only computer not affected."

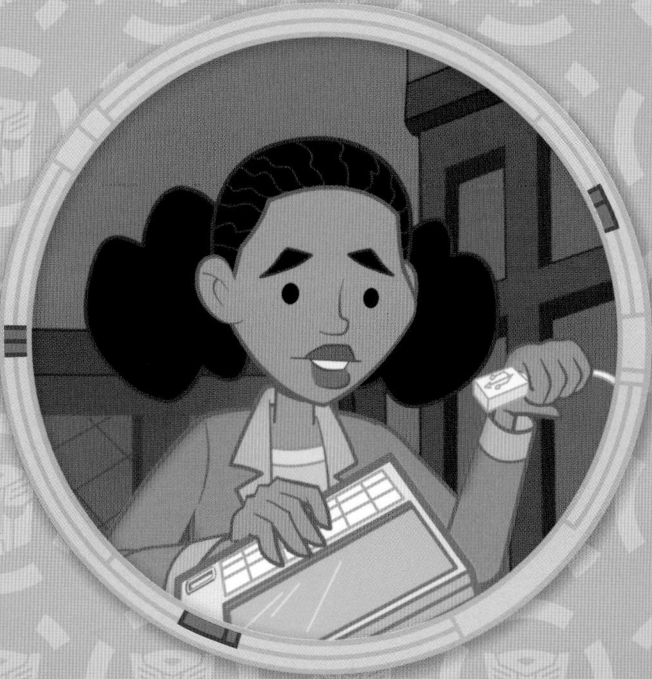

Thinking quickly, Doc Greene lured the Dino Bot to the other side of the lab. This gave Frankie time to upload the software needed to remove the virus.

Before the upload was complete, Trex screeched and ran out of the lab, disappearing into the fog.

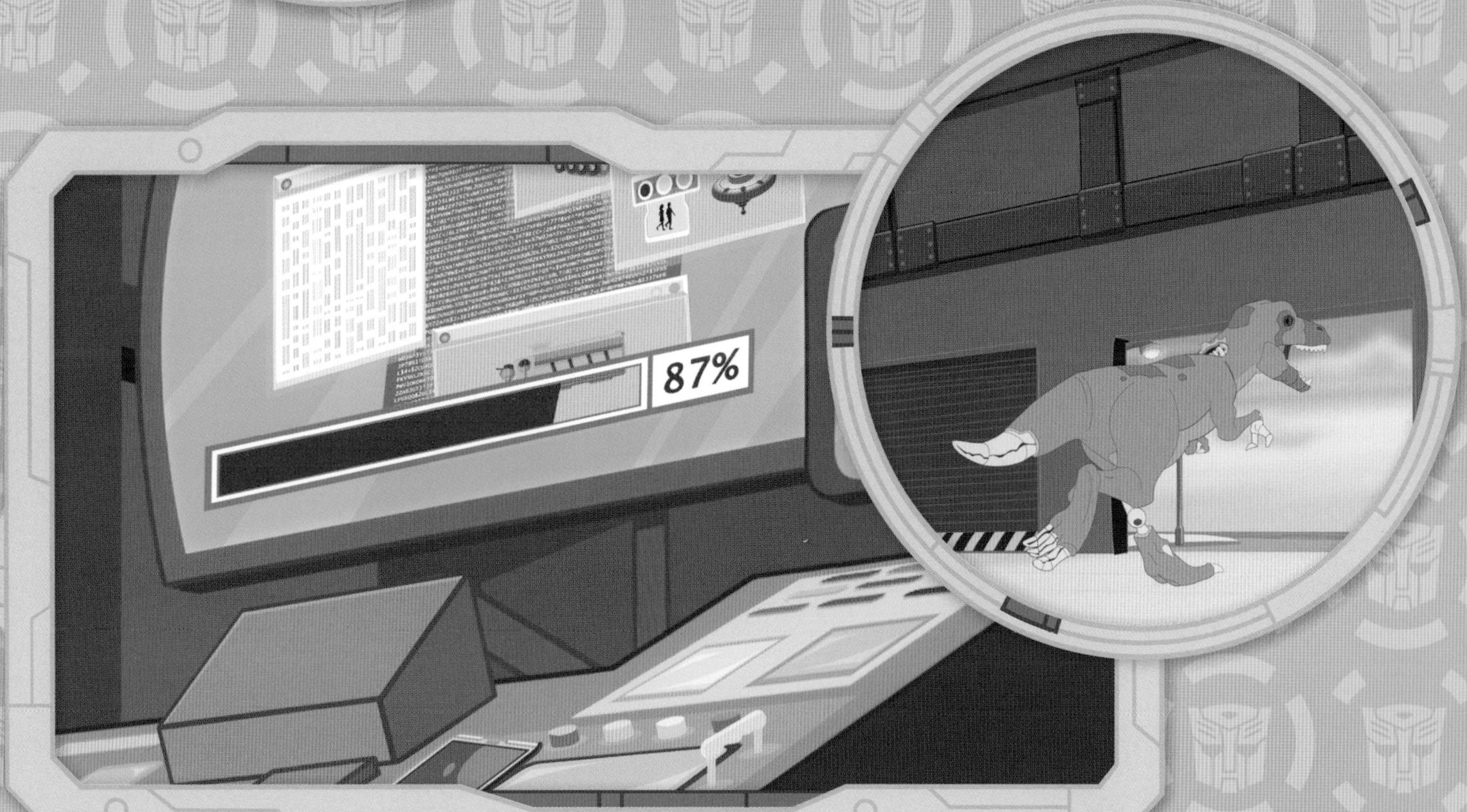
87%

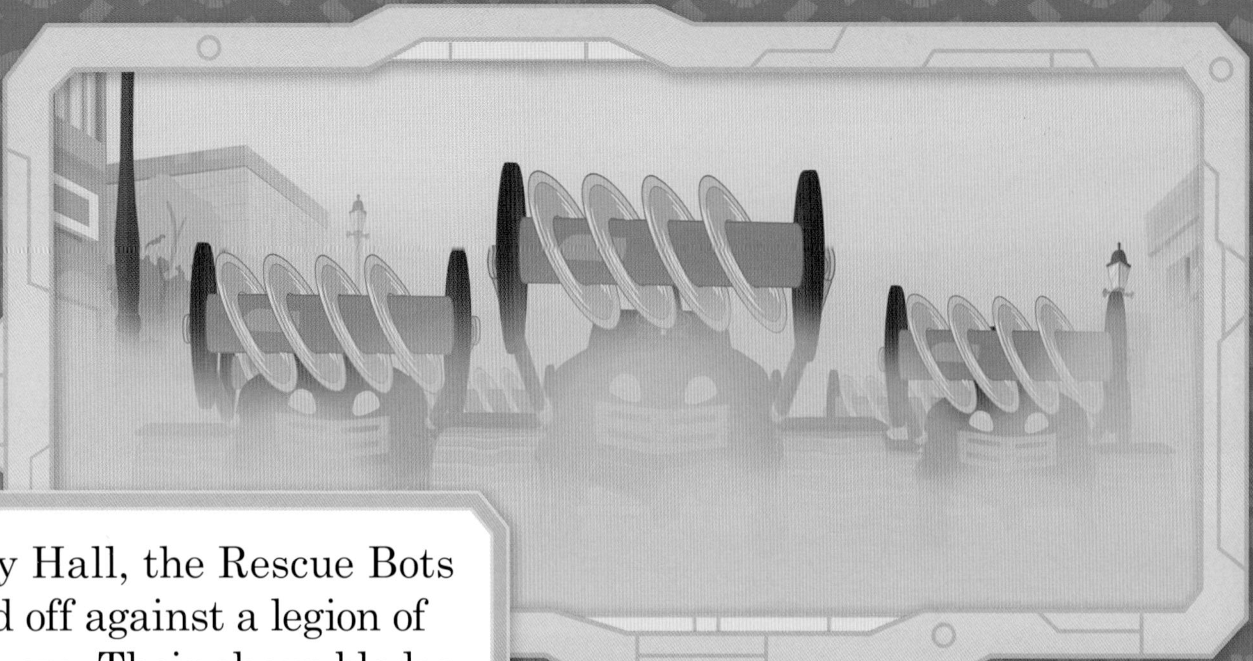

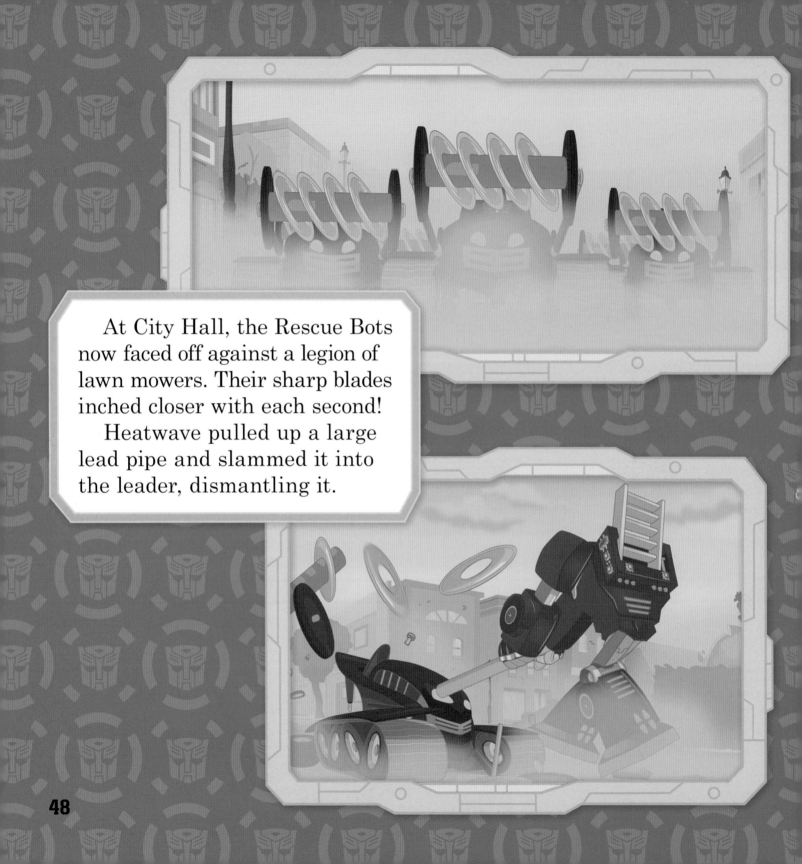

At City Hall, the Rescue Bots now faced off against a legion of lawn mowers. Their sharp blades inched closer with each second!

Heatwave pulled up a large lead pipe and slammed it into the leader, dismantling it.

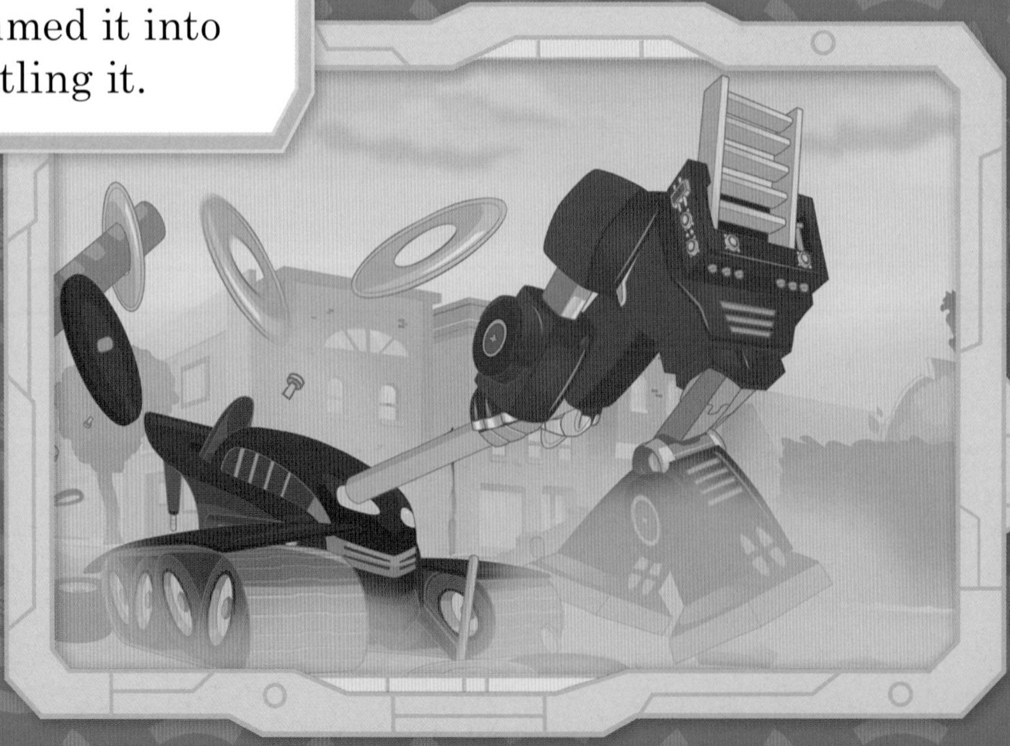

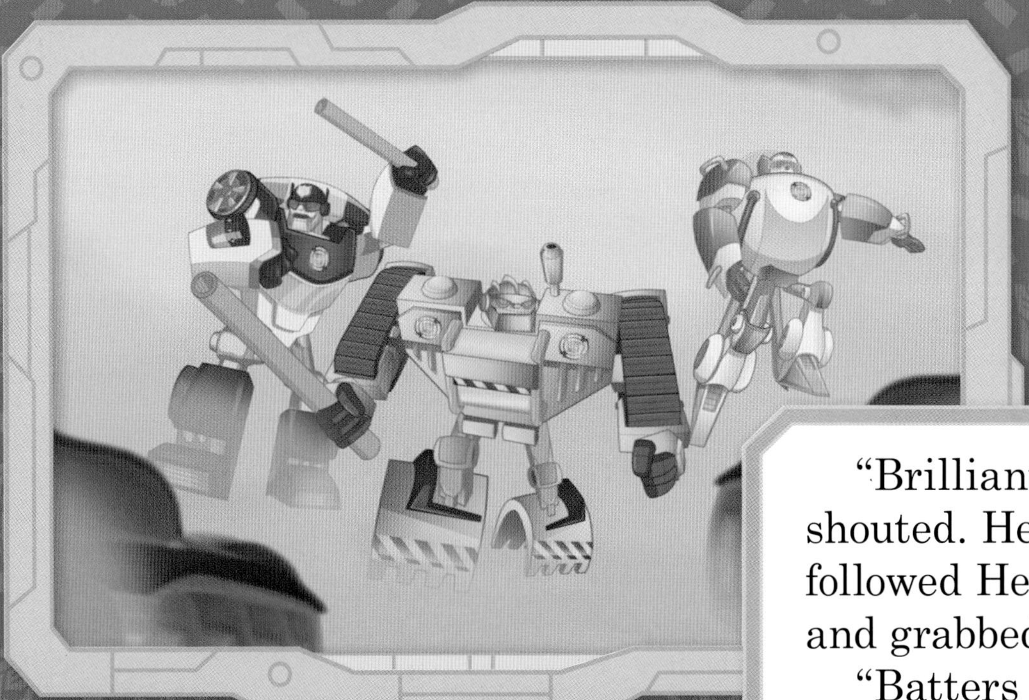

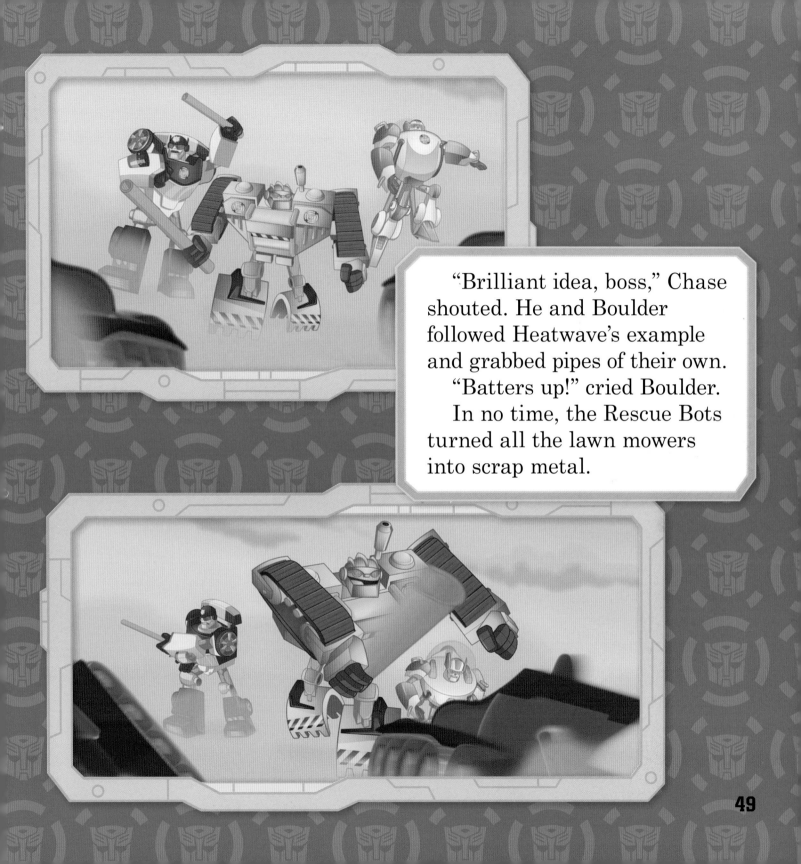

“Brilliant idea, boss,” Chase shouted. He and Boulder followed Heatwave’s example and grabbed pipes of their own.

“Batters up!” cried Boulder.

In no time, the Rescue Bots turned all the lawn mowers into scrap metal.

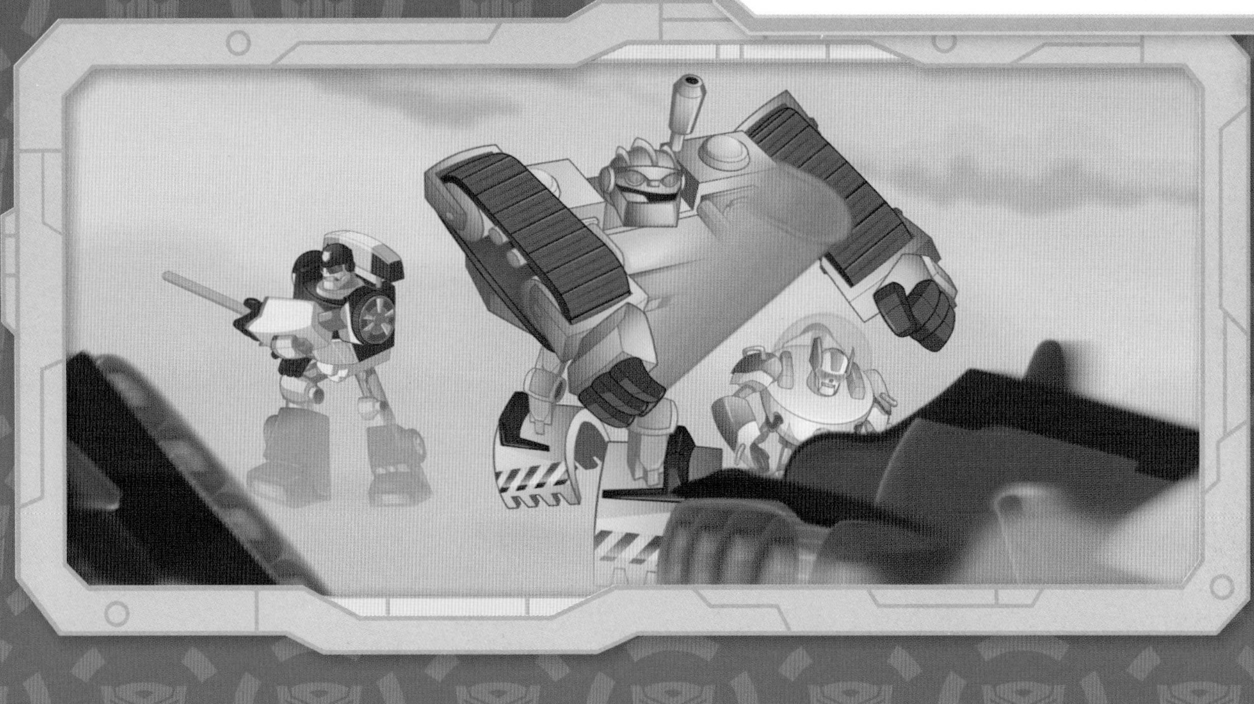

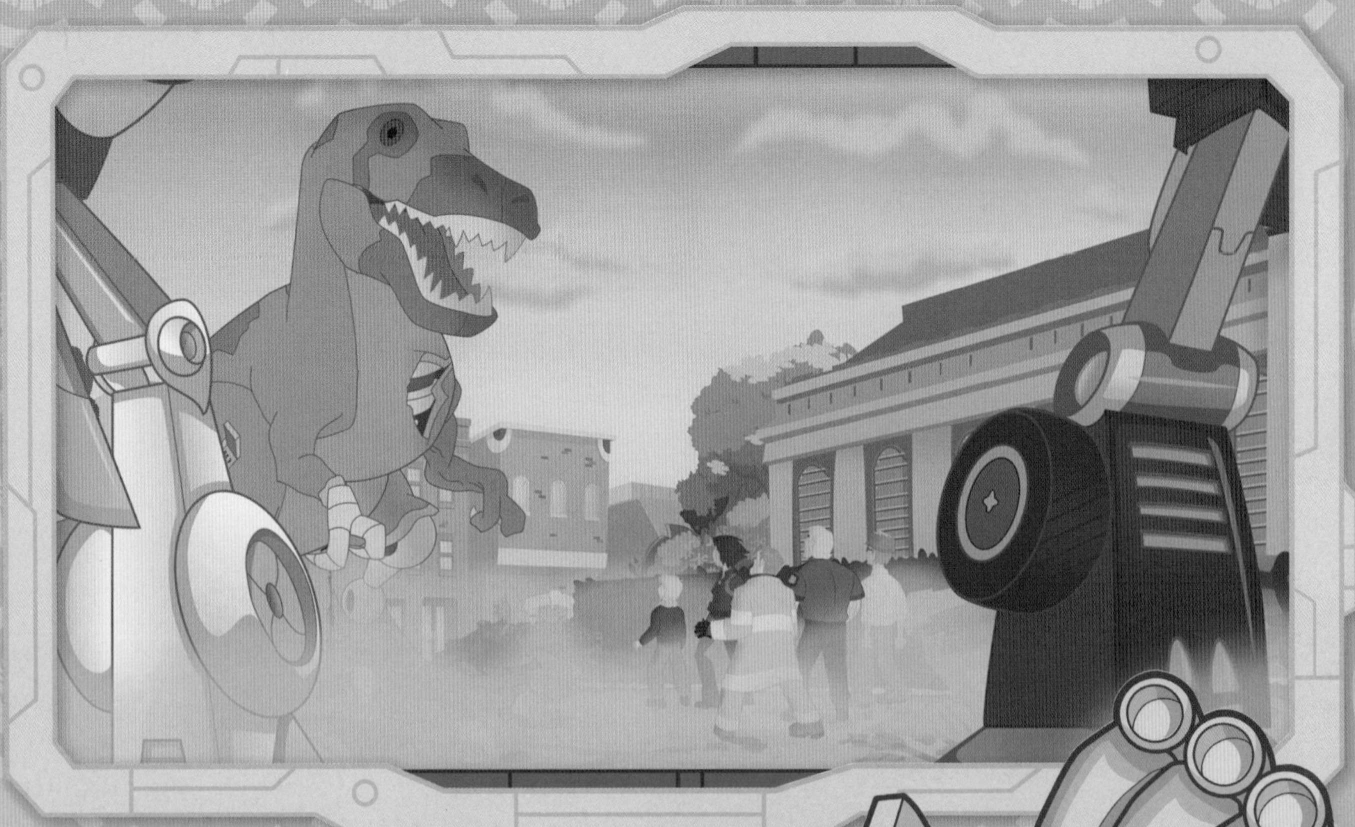

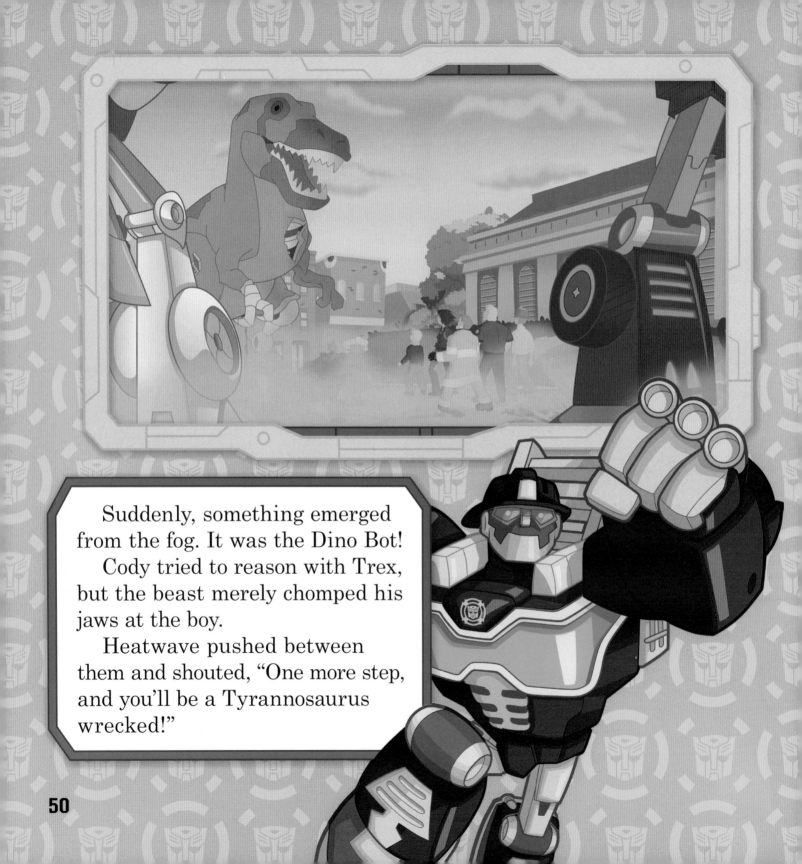

Suddenly, something emerged from the fog. It was the Dino Bot!

Cody tried to reason with Trex, but the beast merely chomped his jaws at the boy.

Heatwave pushed between them and shouted, “One more step, and you’ll be a Tyrannosaurus wrecked!”

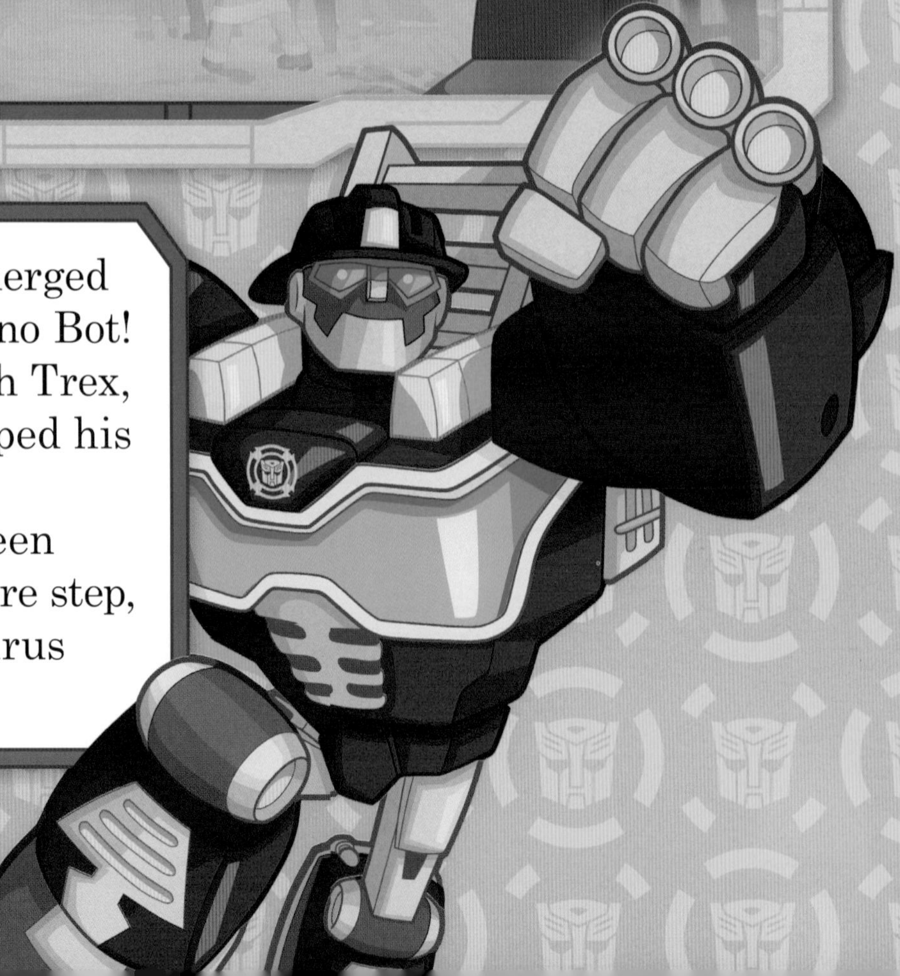

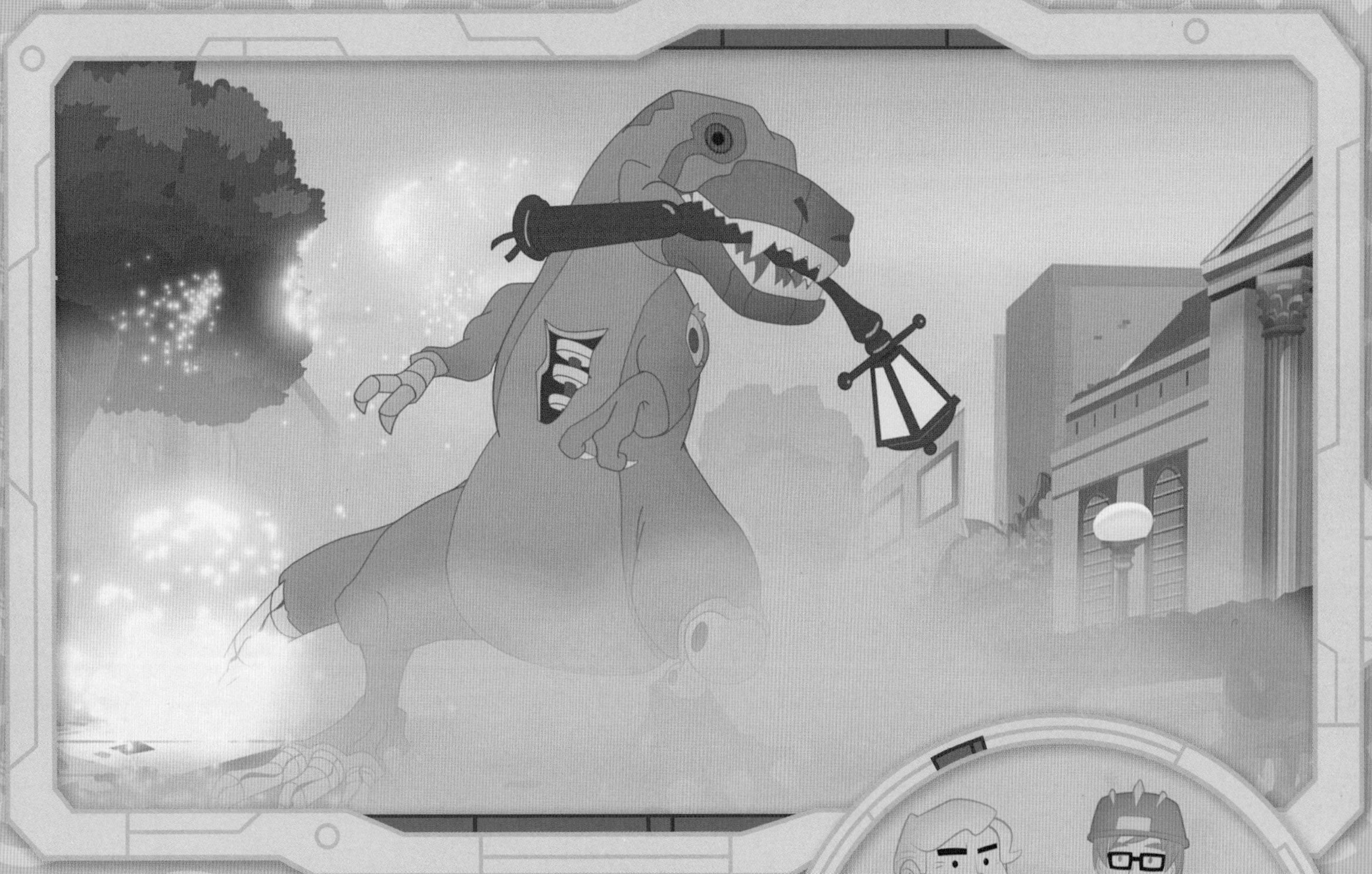

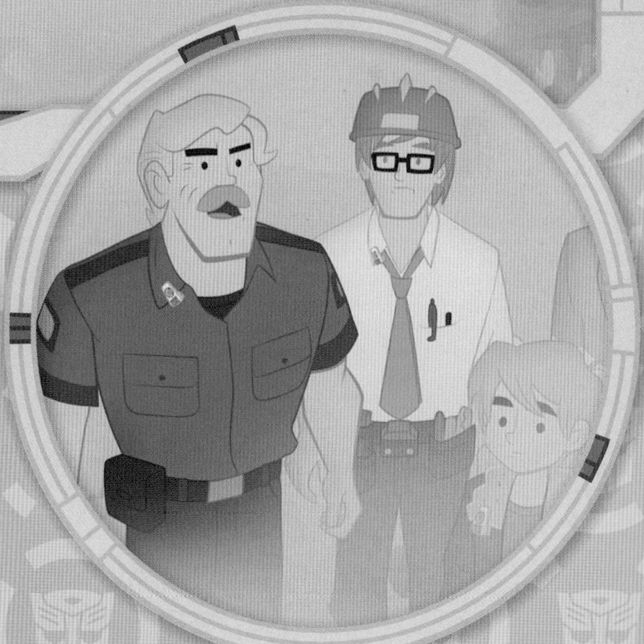

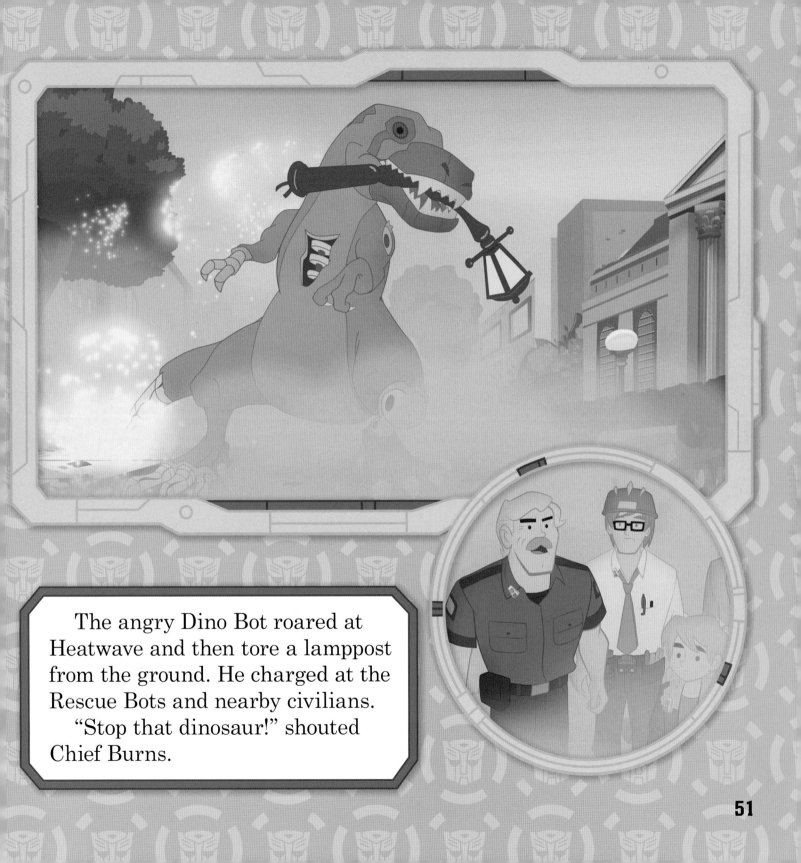

The angry Dino Bot roared at Heatwave and then tore a lamppost from the ground. He charged at the Rescue Bots and nearby civilians.

"Stop that dinosaur!" shouted Chief Burns.

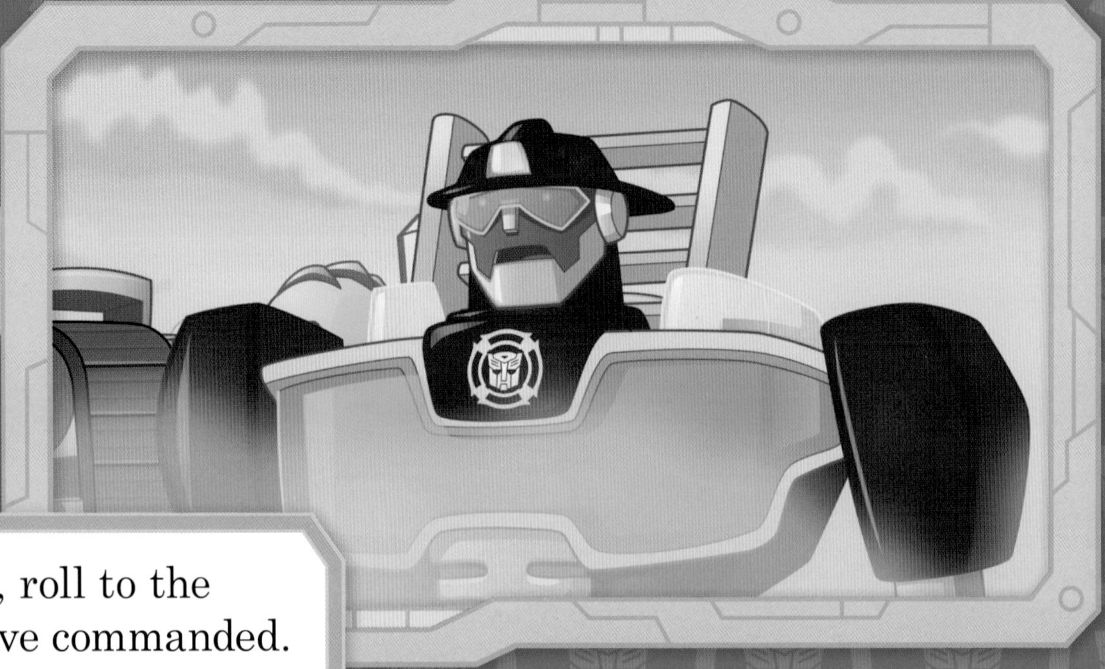

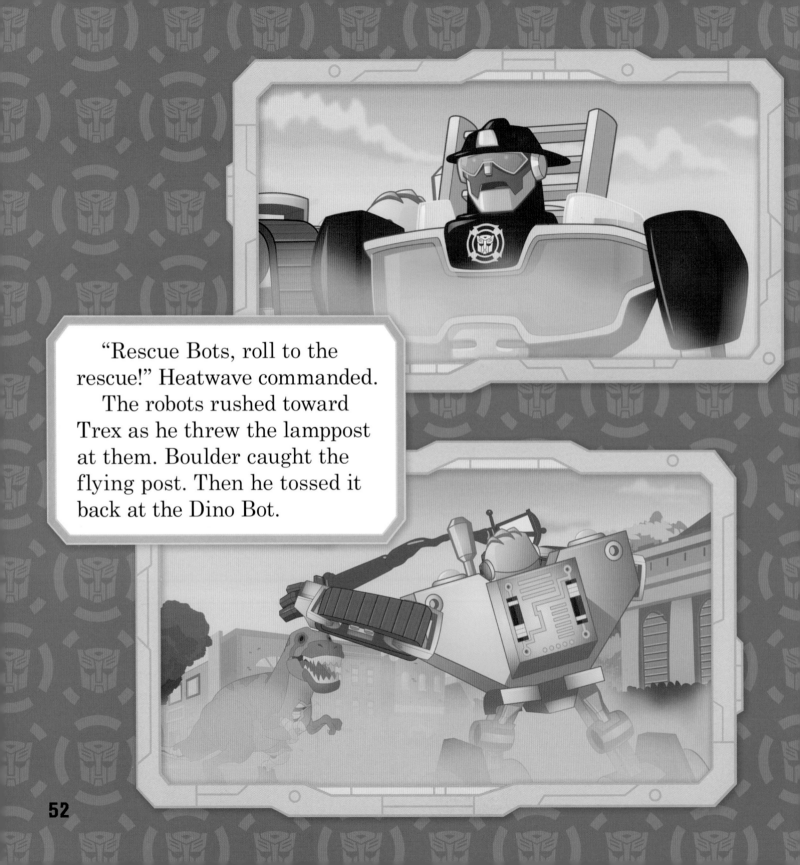

"Rescue Bots, roll to the rescue!" Heatwave commanded.

The robots rushed toward Trex as he threw the lamppost at them. Boulder caught the flying post. Then he tossed it back at the Dino Bot.

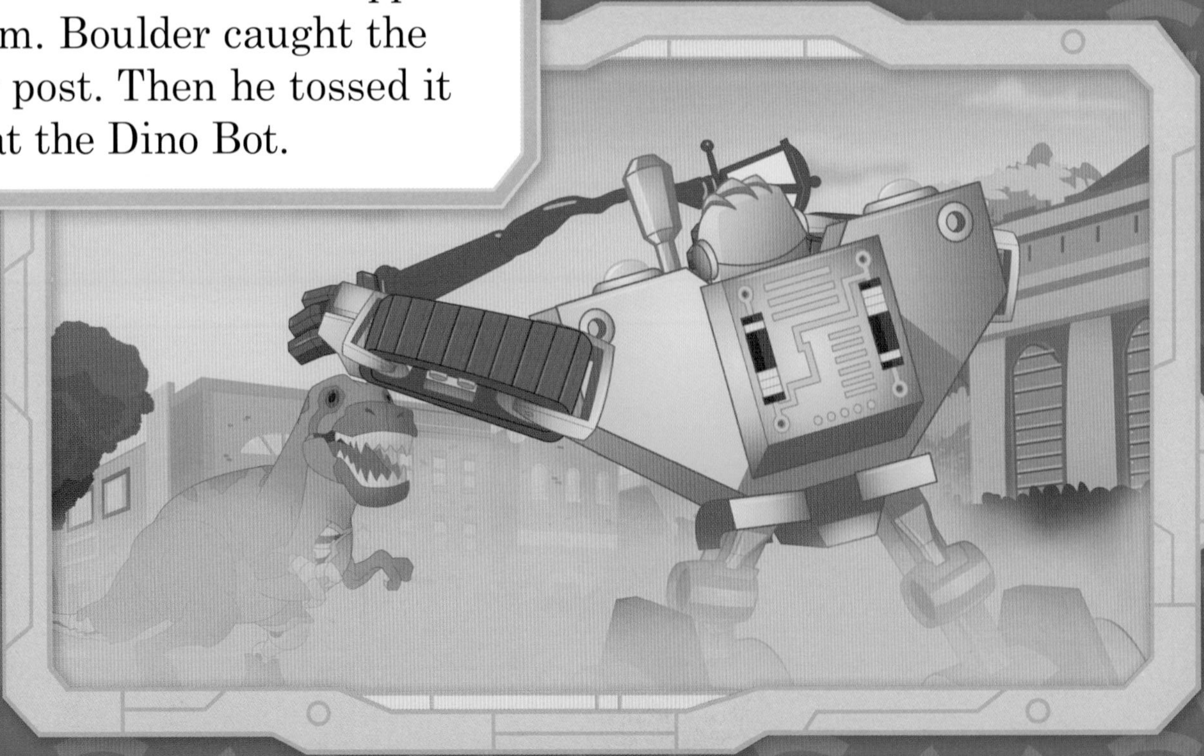

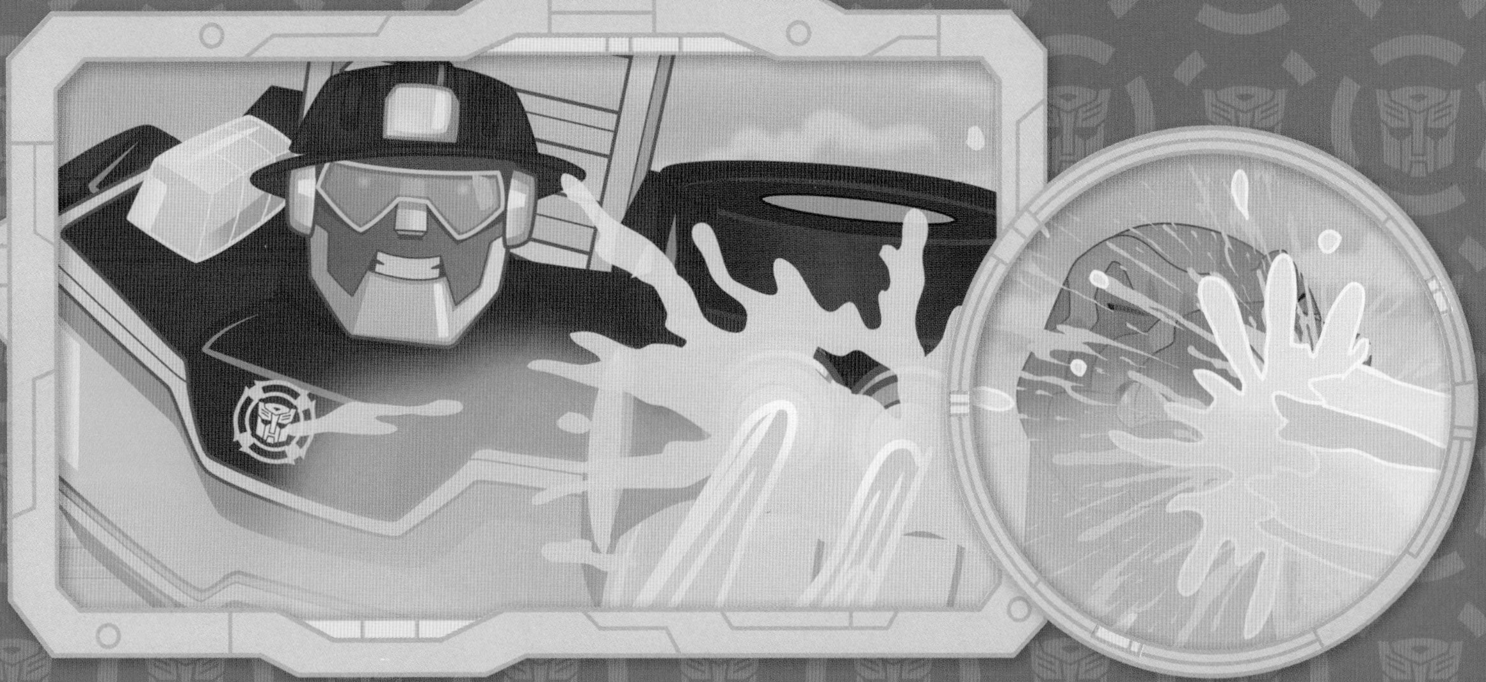

Heatwave attacked Trex with his water blasters. Disoriented, the creature spun in circles and swatted Heatwave with his tail!

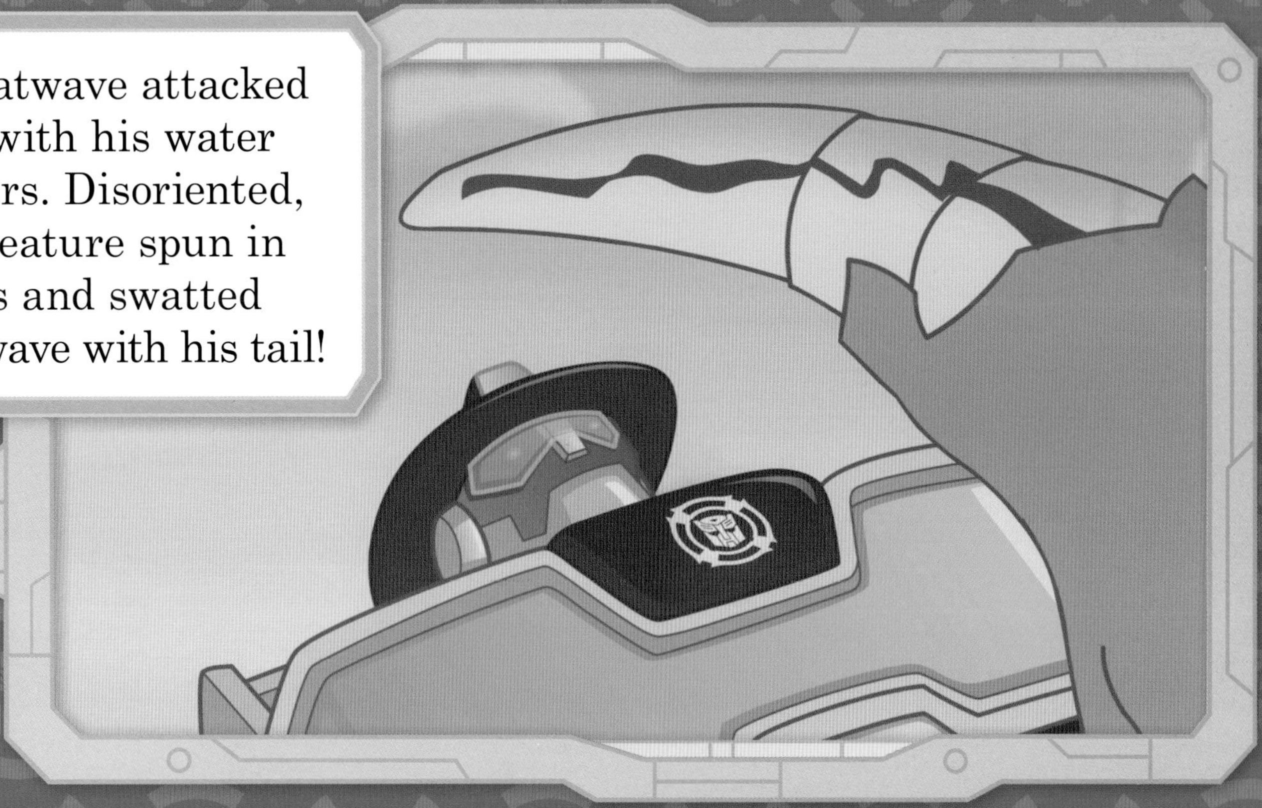

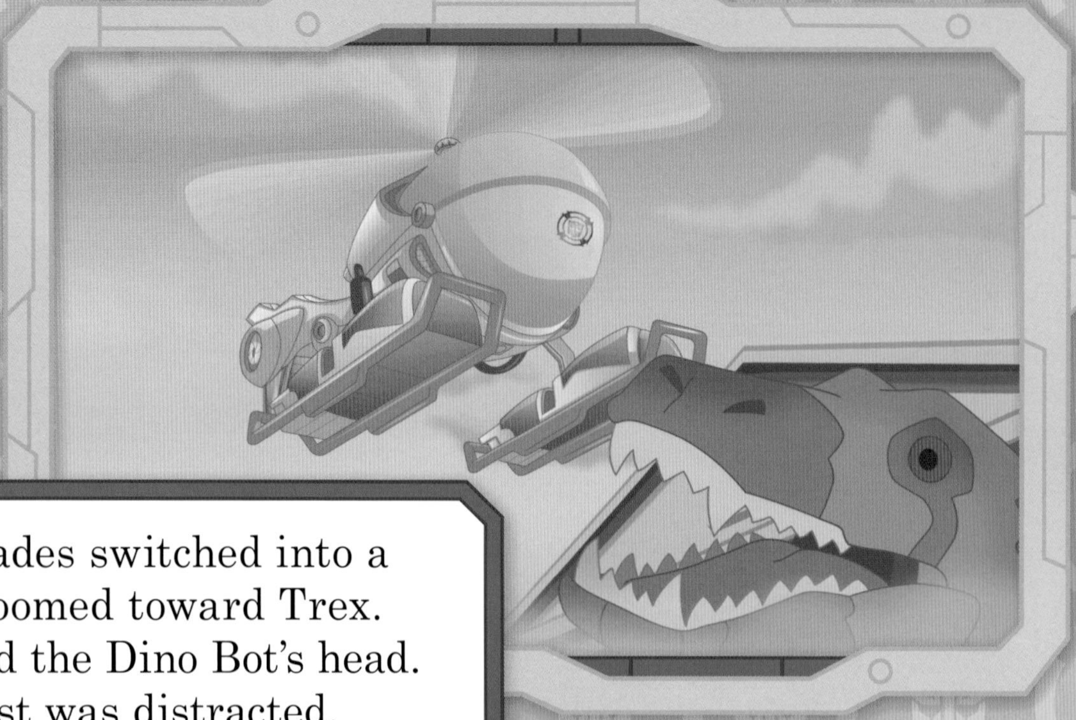

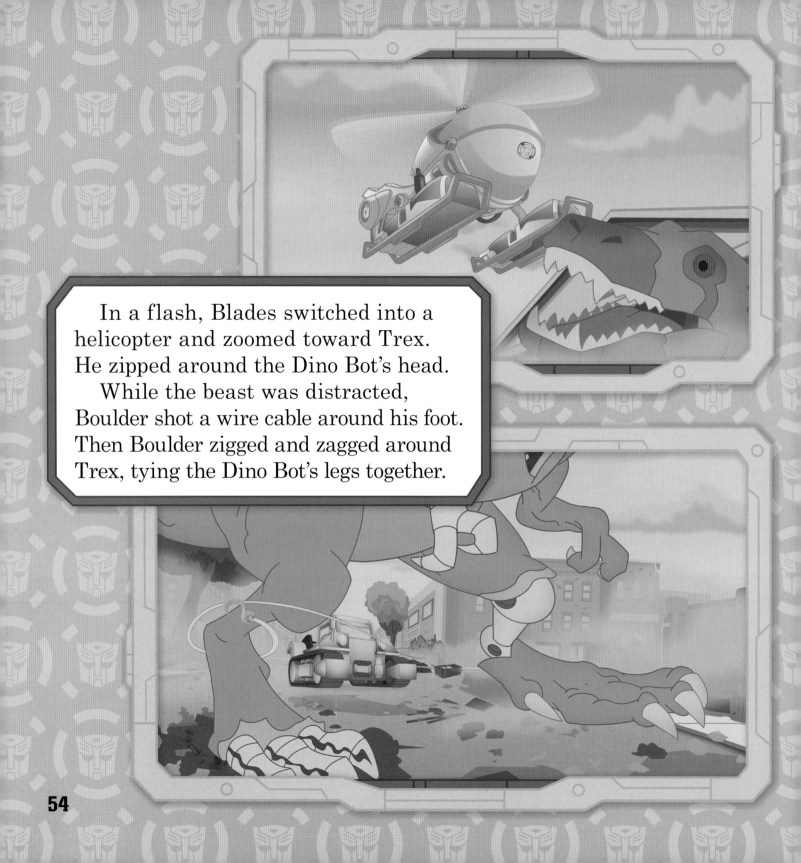

In a flash, Blades switched into a helicopter and zoomed toward Trex. He zipped around the Dino Bot's head.

While the beast was distracted, Boulder shot a wire cable around his foot. Then Boulder zigged and zagged around Trex, tying the Dino Bot's legs together.

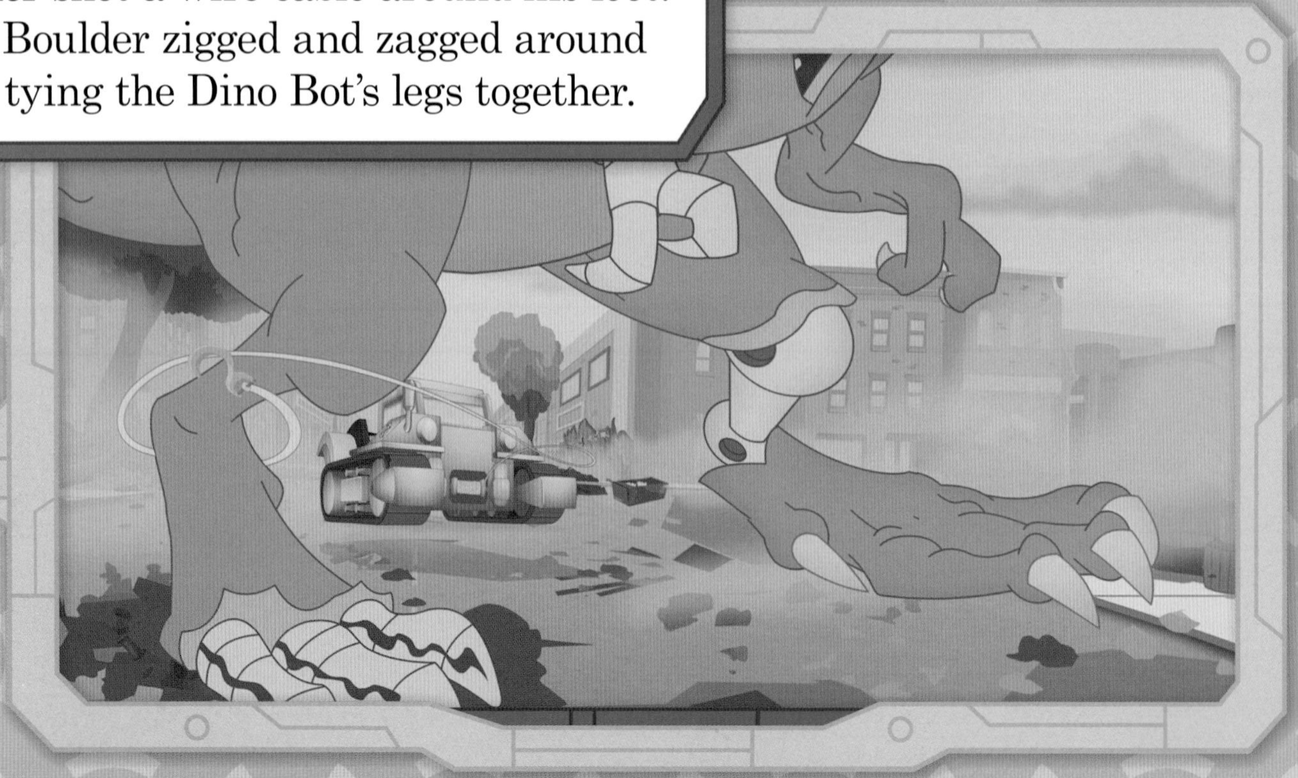

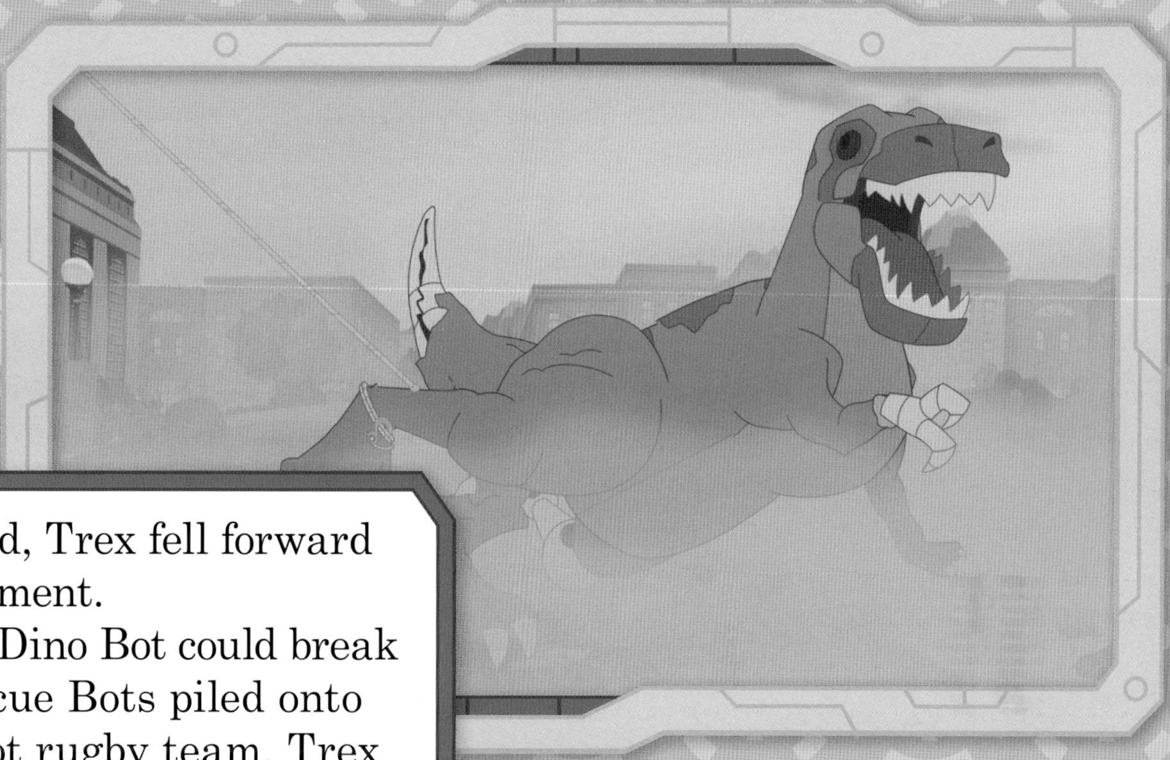

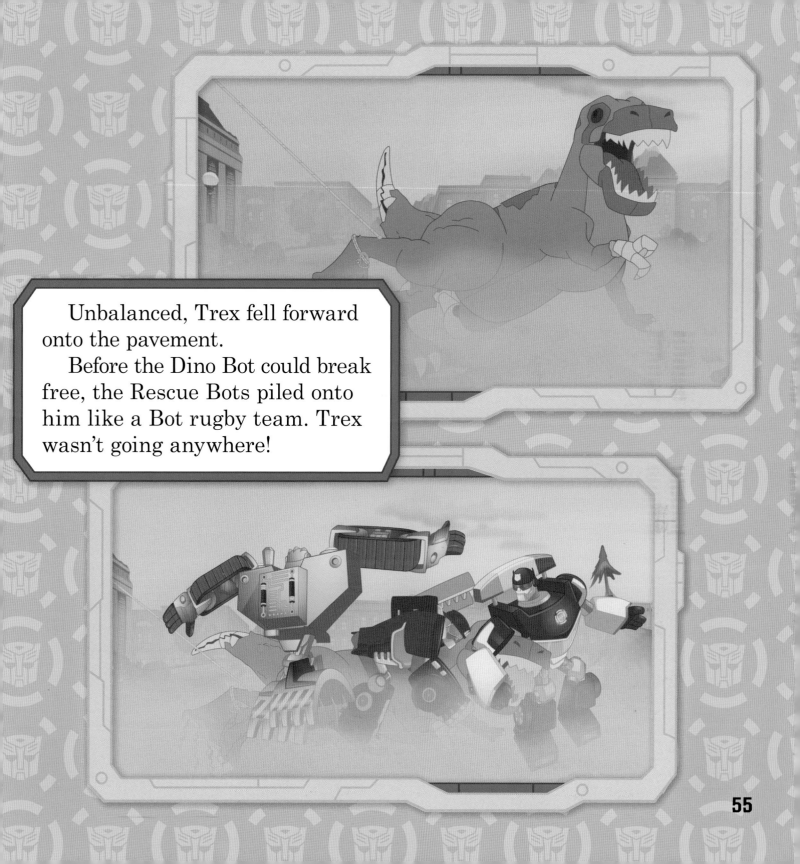

Unbalanced, Trex fell forward onto the pavement.

Before the Dino Bot could break free, the Rescue Bots piled onto him like a Bot rugby team. Trex wasn't going anywhere!

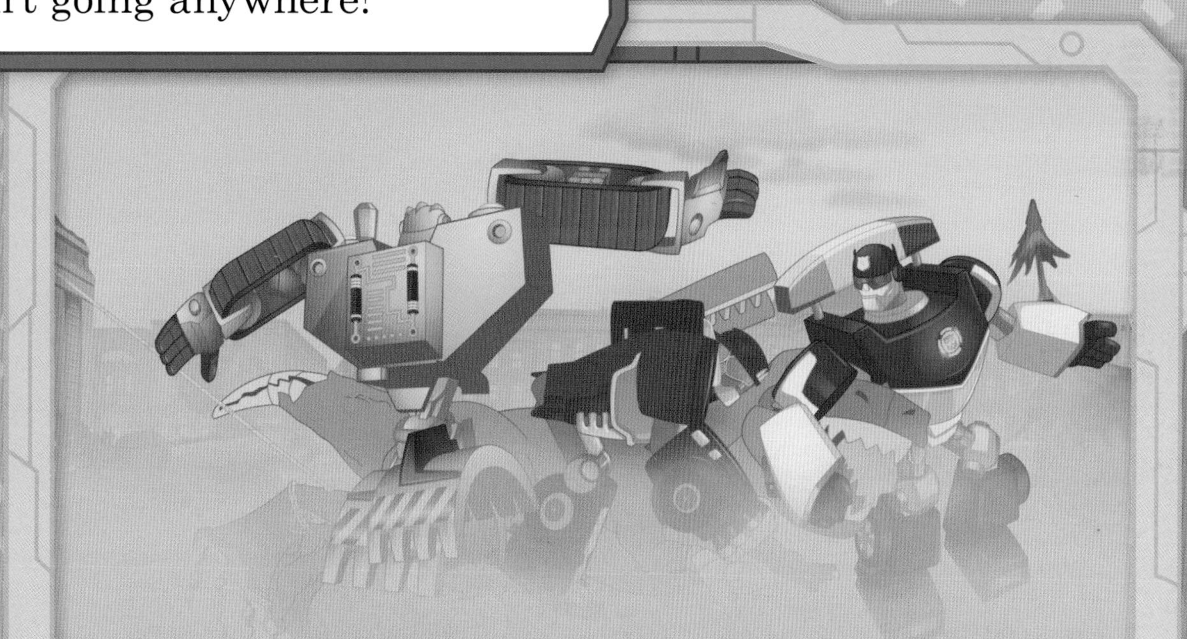

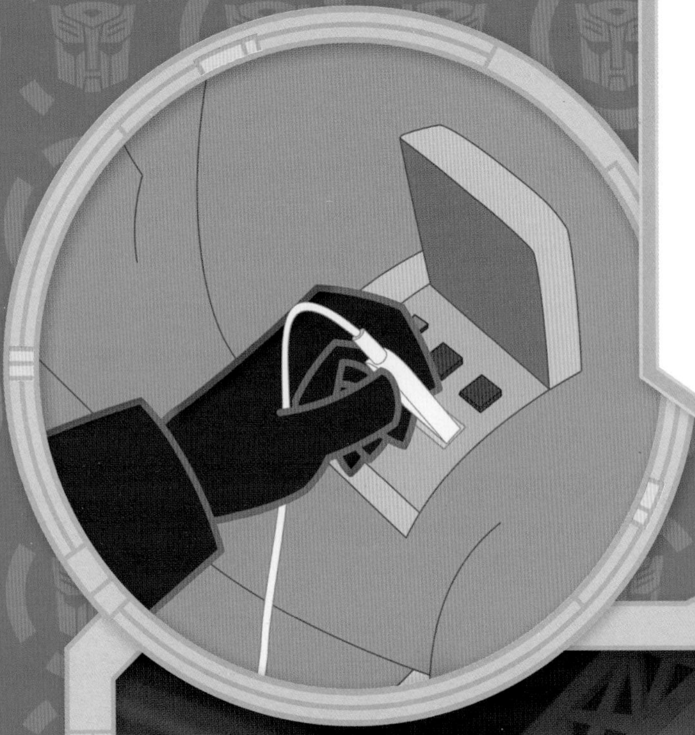

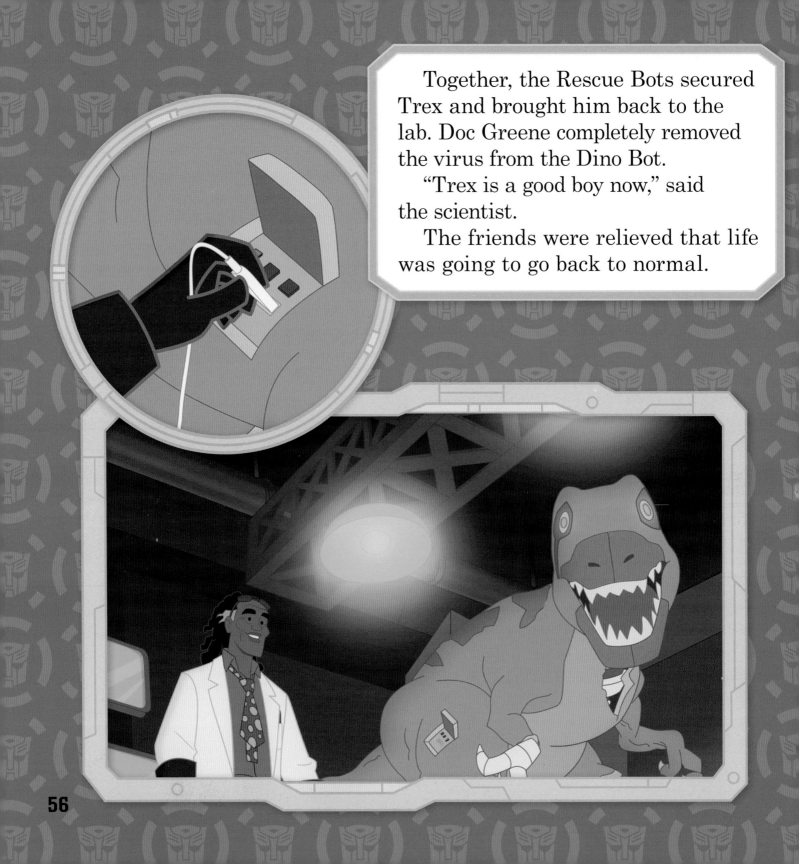

Together, the Rescue Bots secured Trex and brought him back to the lab. Doc Greene completely removed the virus from the Dino Bot.

"Trex is a good boy now," said the scientist.

The friends were relieved that life was going to go back to normal.

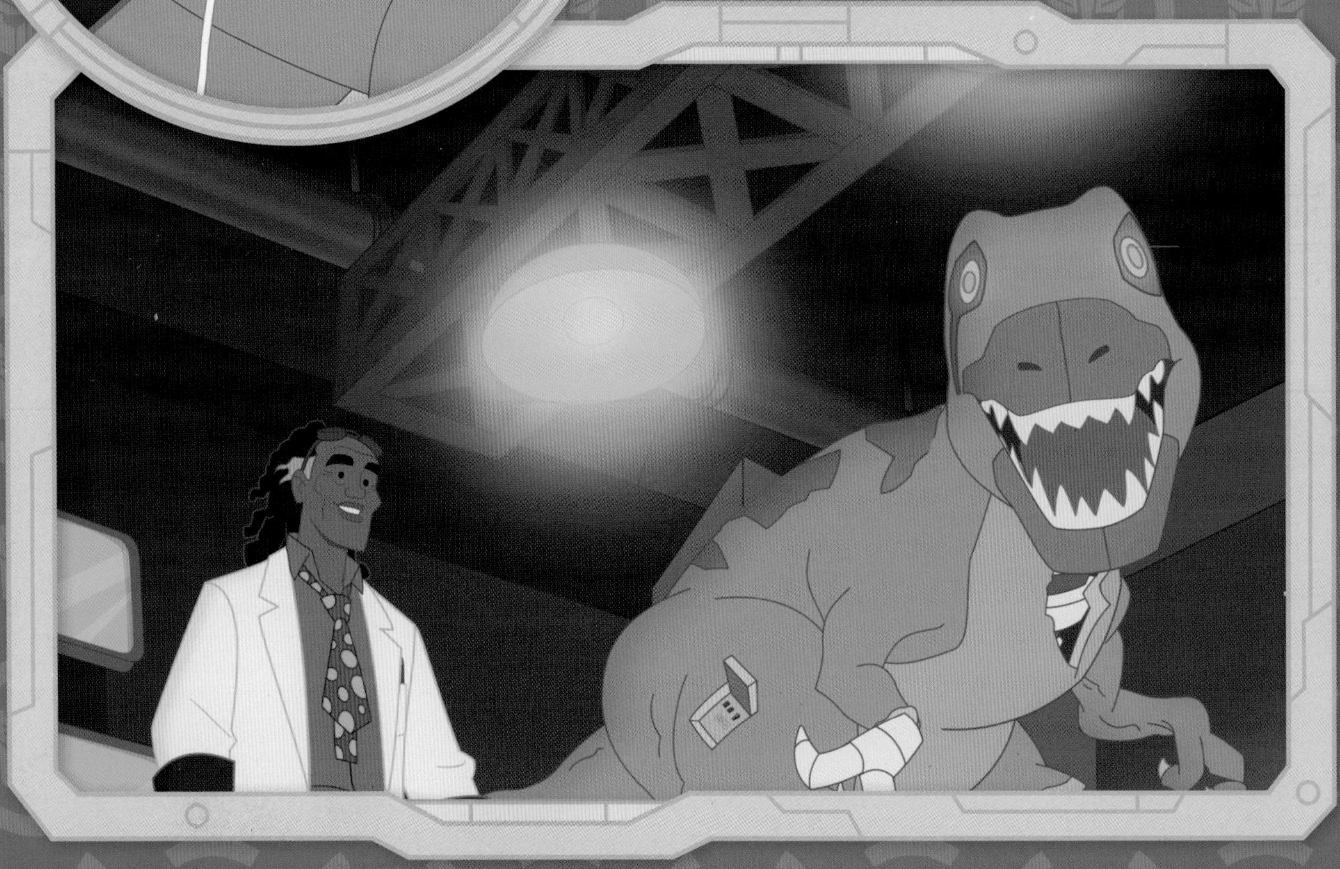

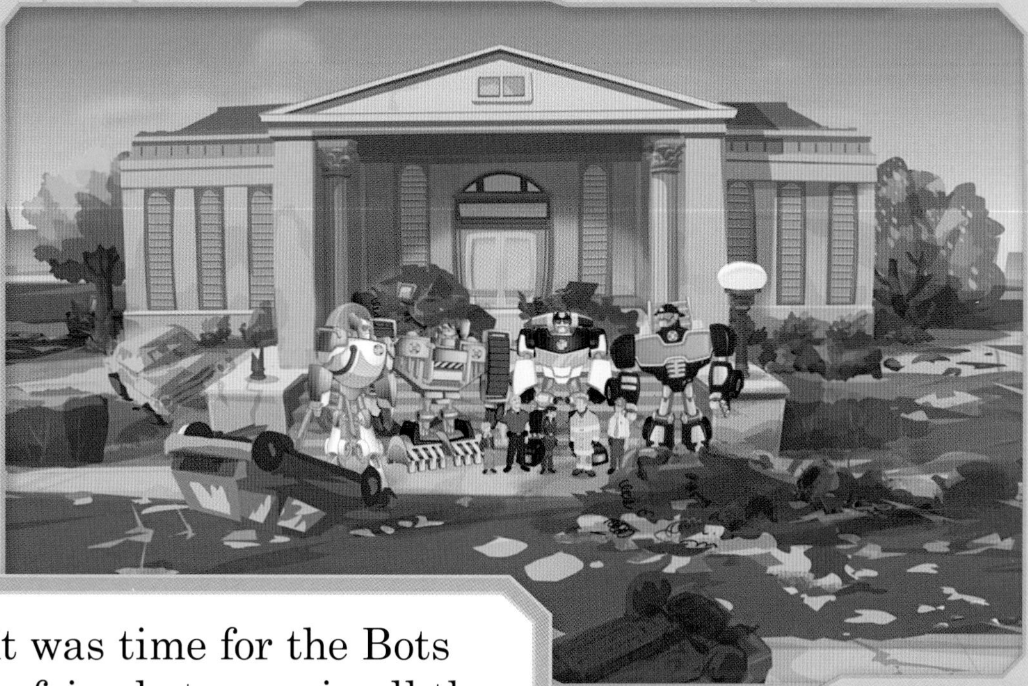

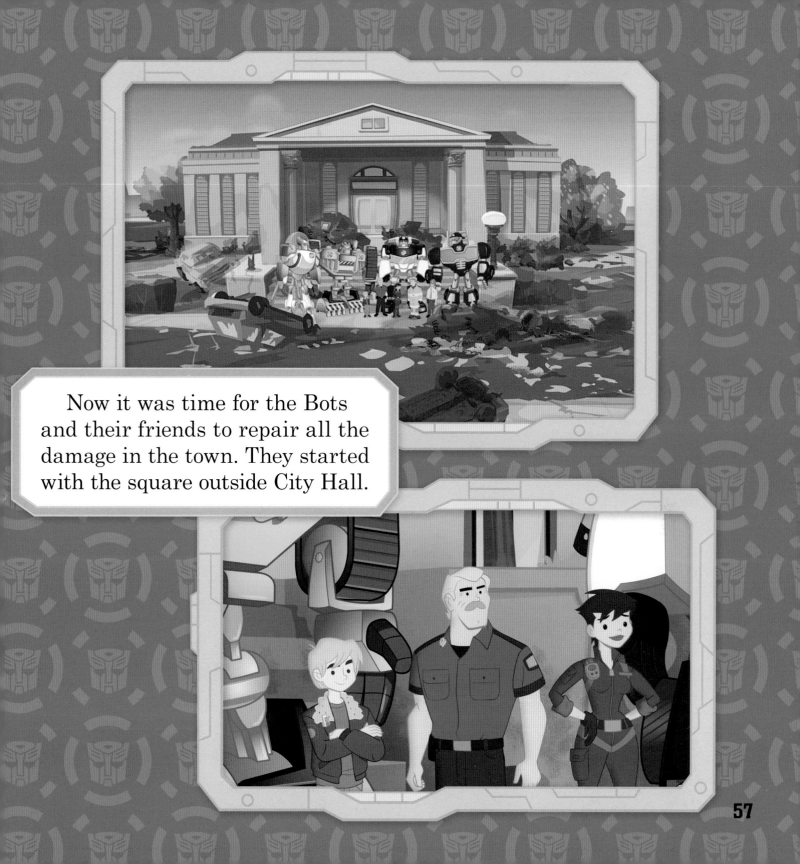

Now it was time for the Bots and their friends to repair all the damage in the town. They started with the square outside City Hall.

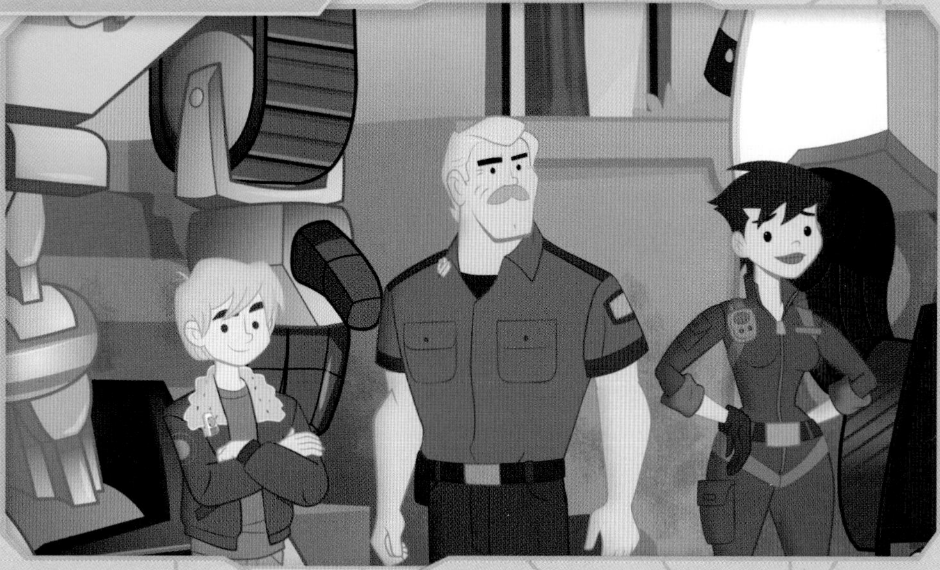

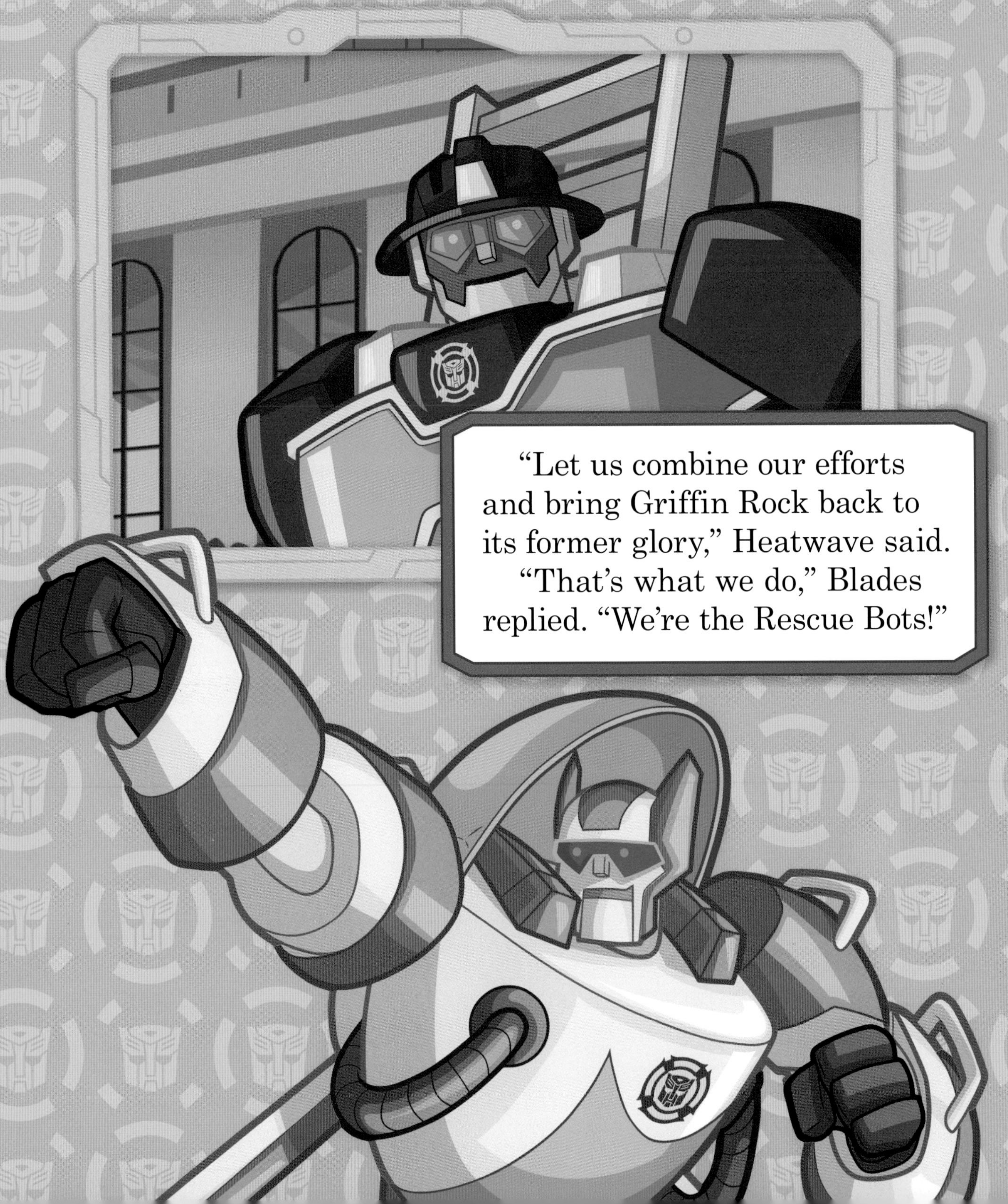

"Let us combine our efforts and bring Griffin Rock back to its former glory," Heatwave said.

"That's what we do," Blades replied. "We're the Rescue Bots!"

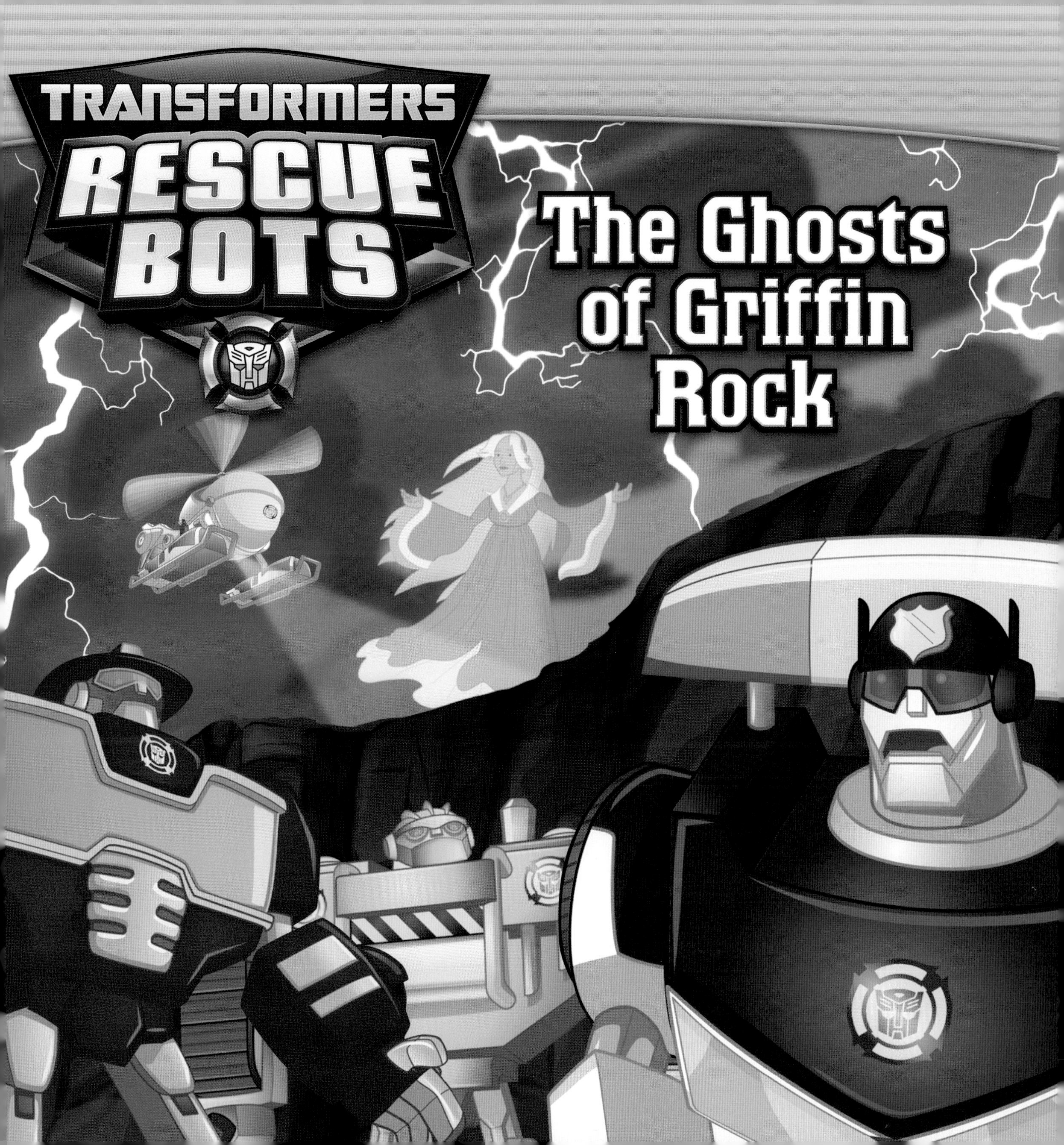
TRANSFORMERS
RESCUE BOTS
The Ghosts of Griffin Rock

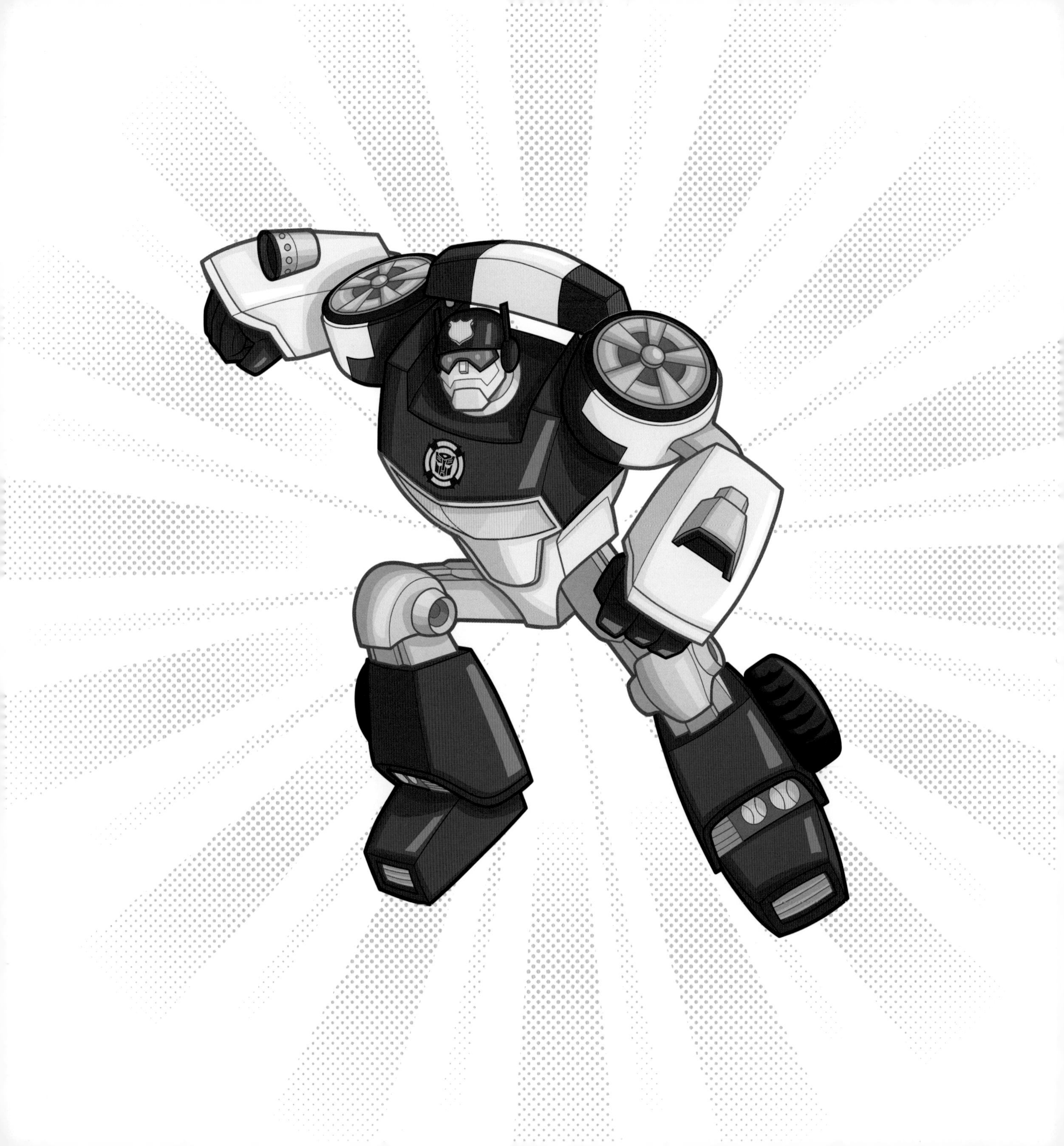

TRANSFORMERS RESCUE BOTS

The Ghosts of Griffin Rock

Adapted by John Sazaklis
Based on the episode "The Haunting of Griffin Rock"
written by Steve Aranguren

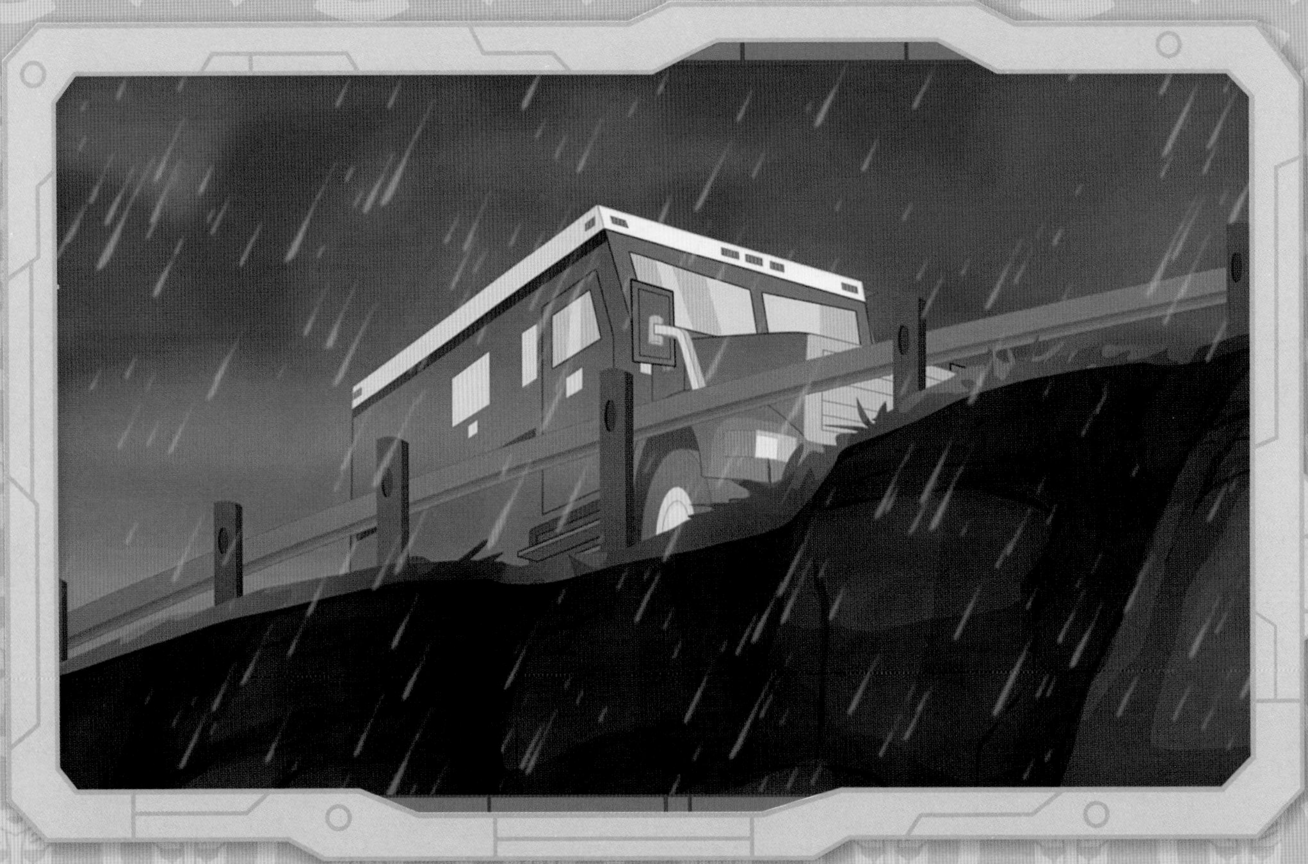

It is a dark and stormy night. Jerry is driving an armored truck full of money down a winding road along the edge of a cliff. With a crash of thunder and a flash of lightning, the glowing figure of a woman appears!

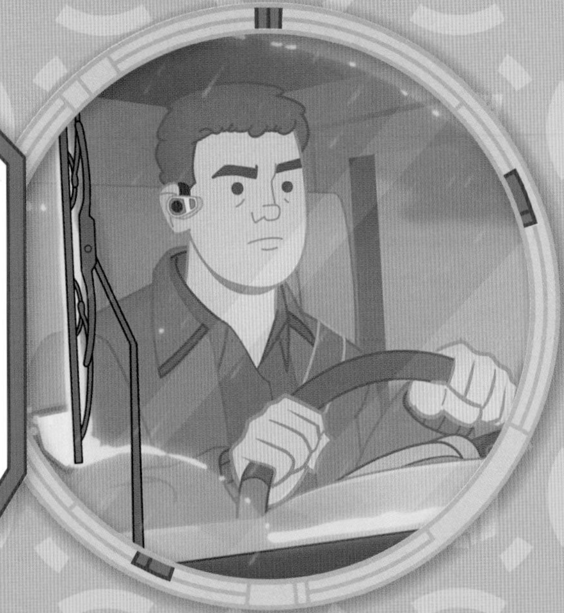

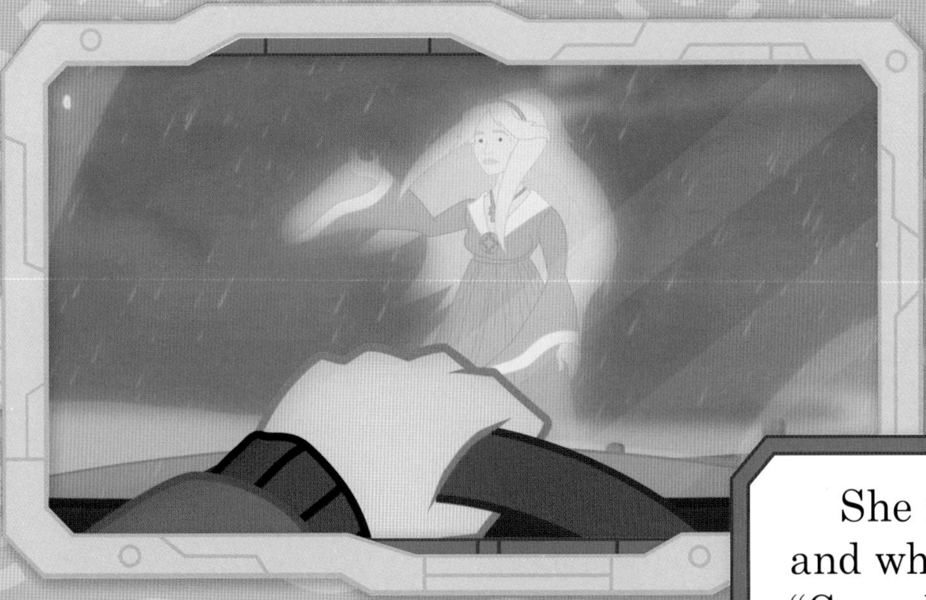

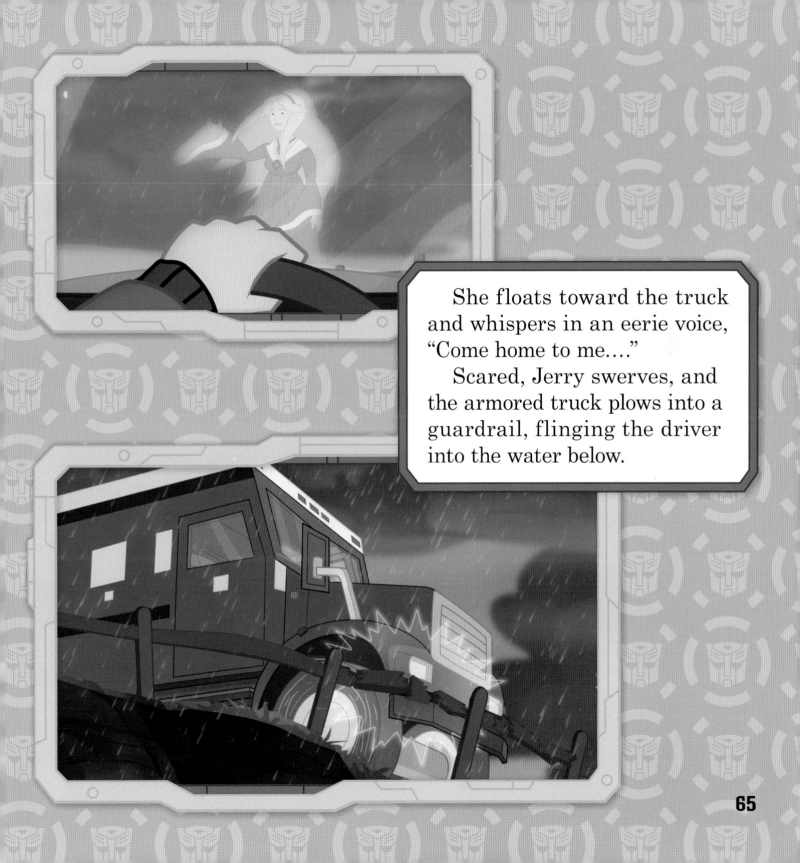

She floats toward the truck and whispers in an eerie voice, “Come home to me....”

Scared, Jerry swerves, and the armored truck plows into a guardrail, flinging the driver into the water below.

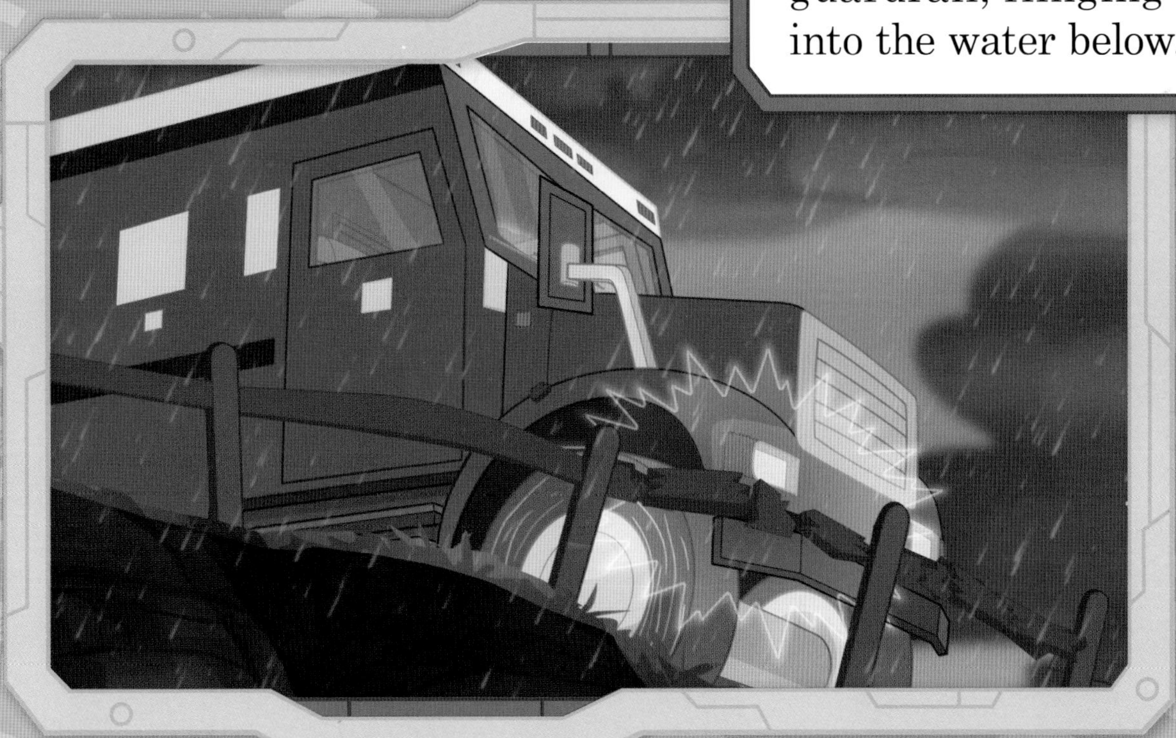

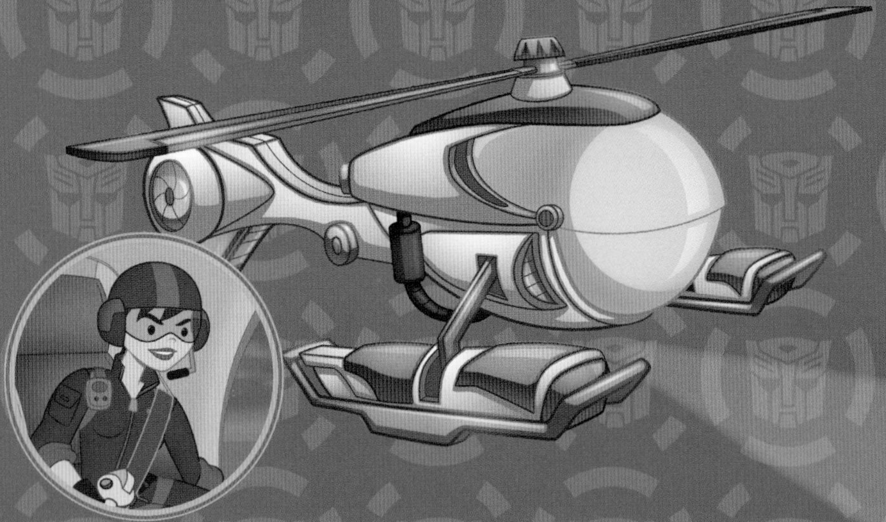

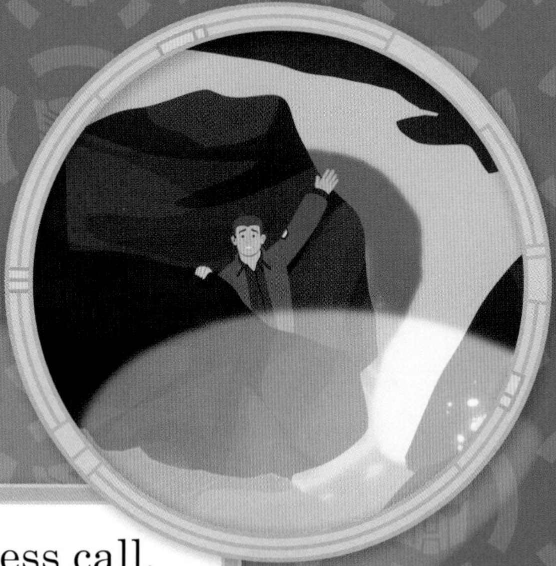

The Rescue Bots respond to Jerry's distress call. Dani and Blades find the driver clinging to a rock on the surf. They carry him to safety.

"Can you tell us what happened?" Chief Burns asks.

"It was the Lady of Griffin Rock!" Jerry exclaims.

Kade scoffs and says, "Have you had your eyes checked lately?"

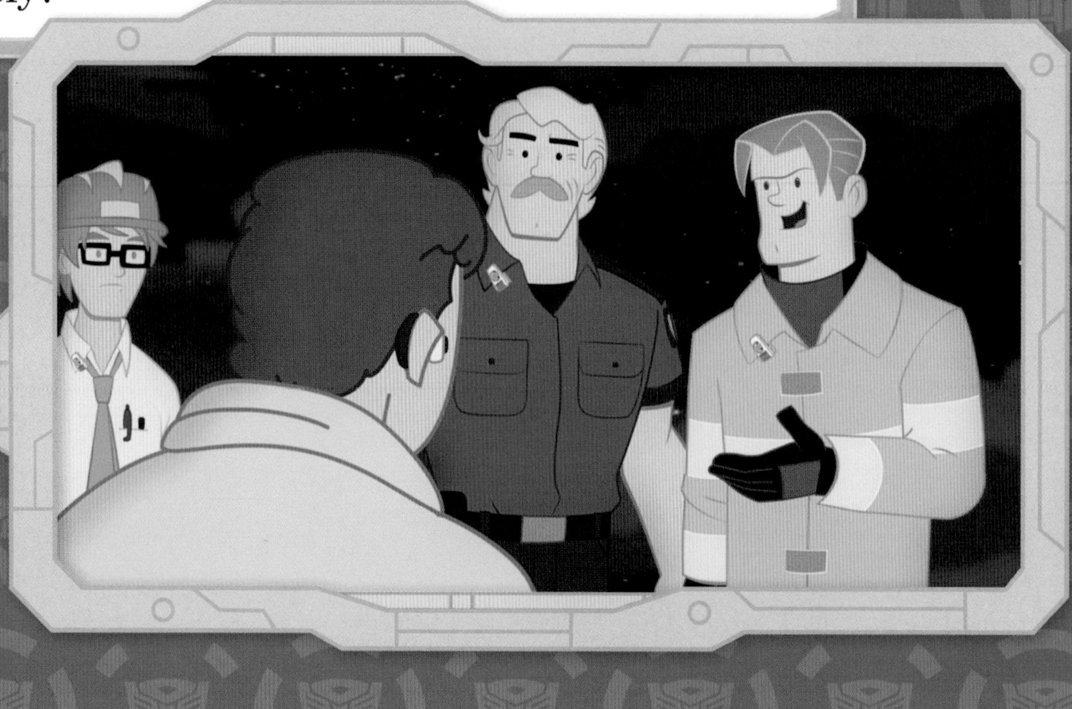

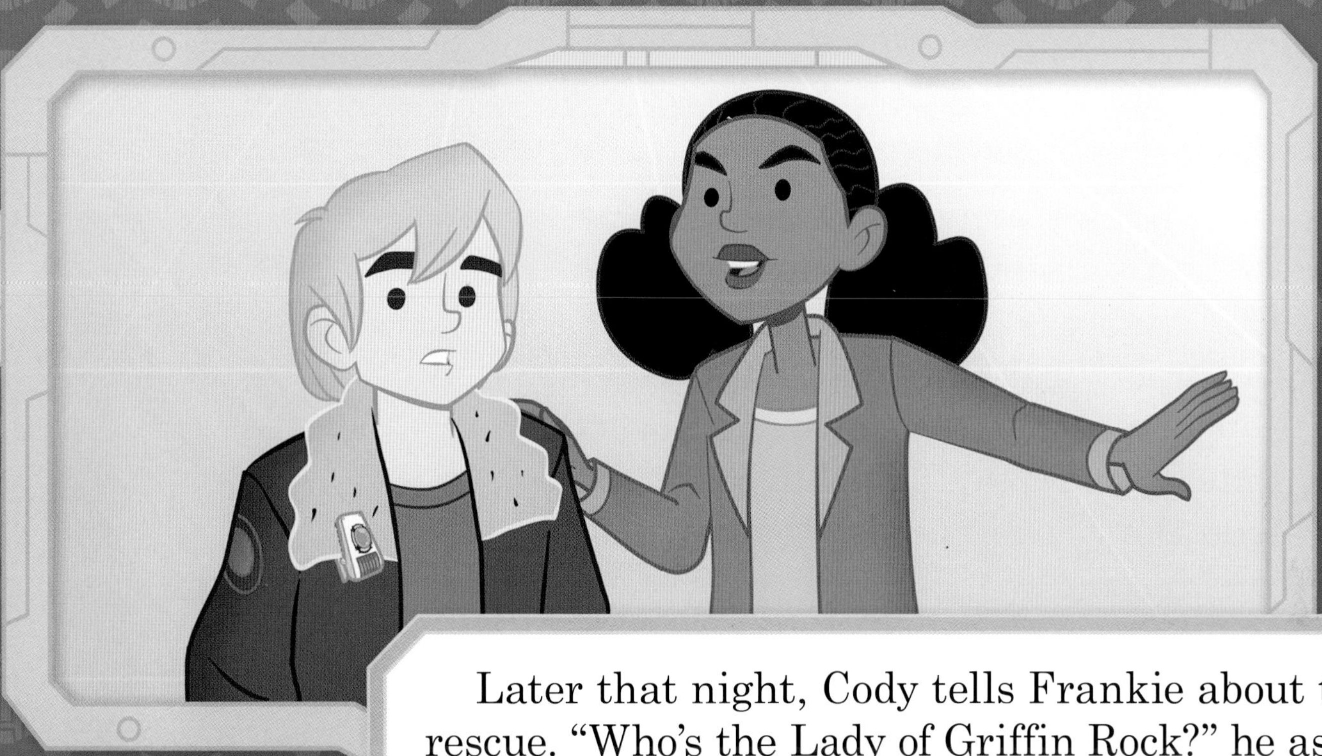

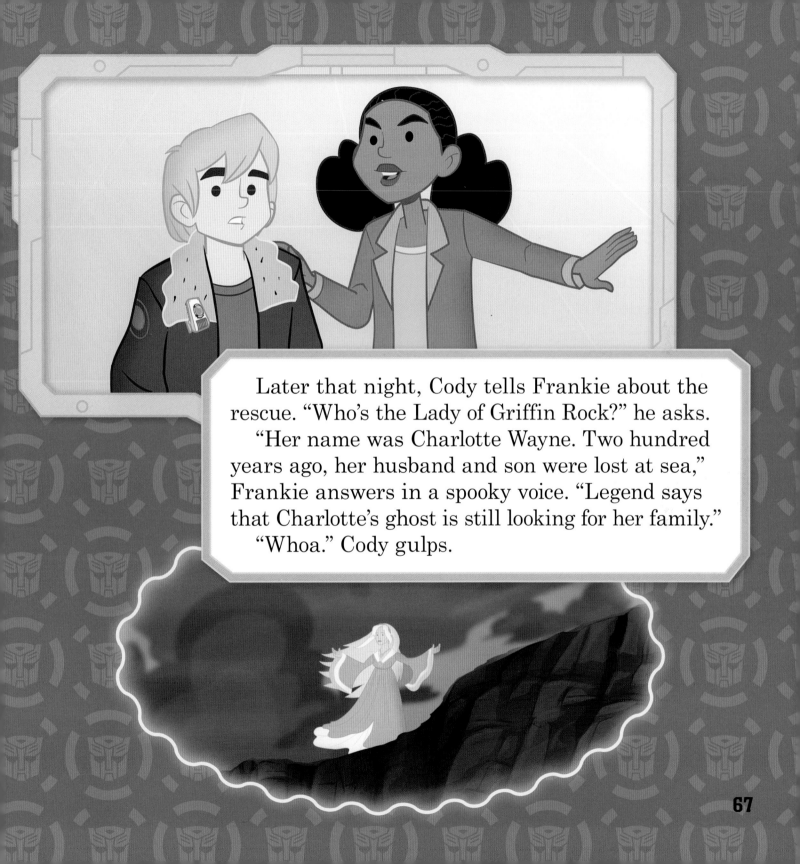

Later that night, Cody tells Frankie about the rescue. “Who’s the Lady of Griffin Rock?” he asks.

“Her name was Charlotte Wayne. Two hundred years ago, her husband and son were lost at sea,” Frankie answers in a spooky voice. “Legend says that Charlotte’s ghost is still looking for her family.”

“Whoa.” Cody gulps.

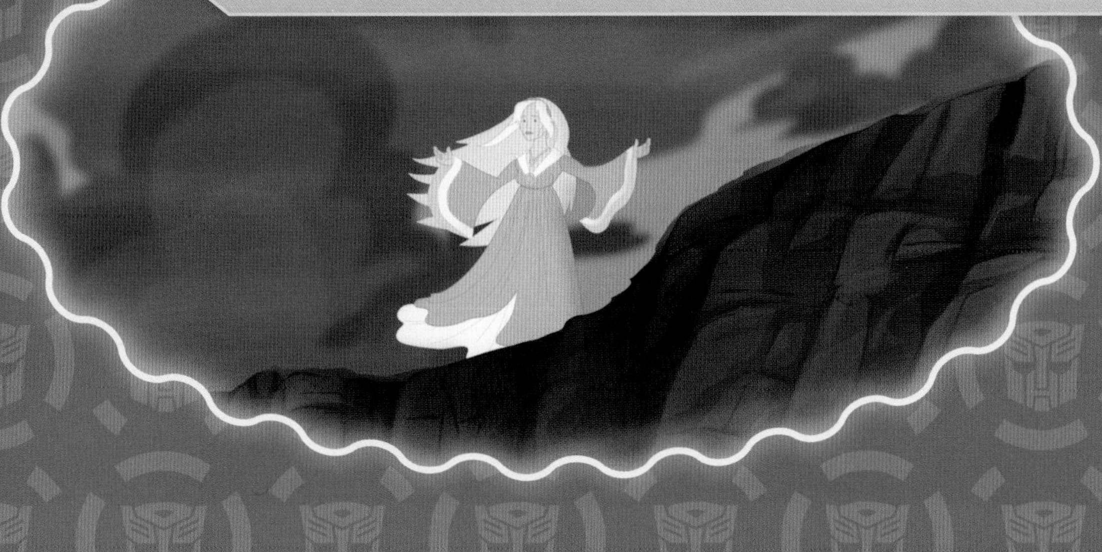

The next day, the emergency line rings. Chief Burns answers it, then says, "There's a ghost at the bank scaring away the customers."

The team exchanges concerned looks. Something spooky is happening in Griffin Rock.

"That's great!" Frankie exclaims. "It's the perfect opportunity to test my dad's Spectral Vapor Filters. They're designed to catch ghosts!"

"Rescue Bots," commands Heatwave, "roll to the rescue!"

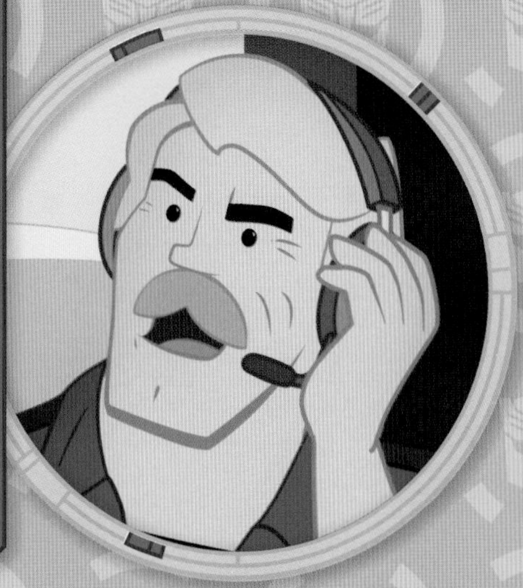

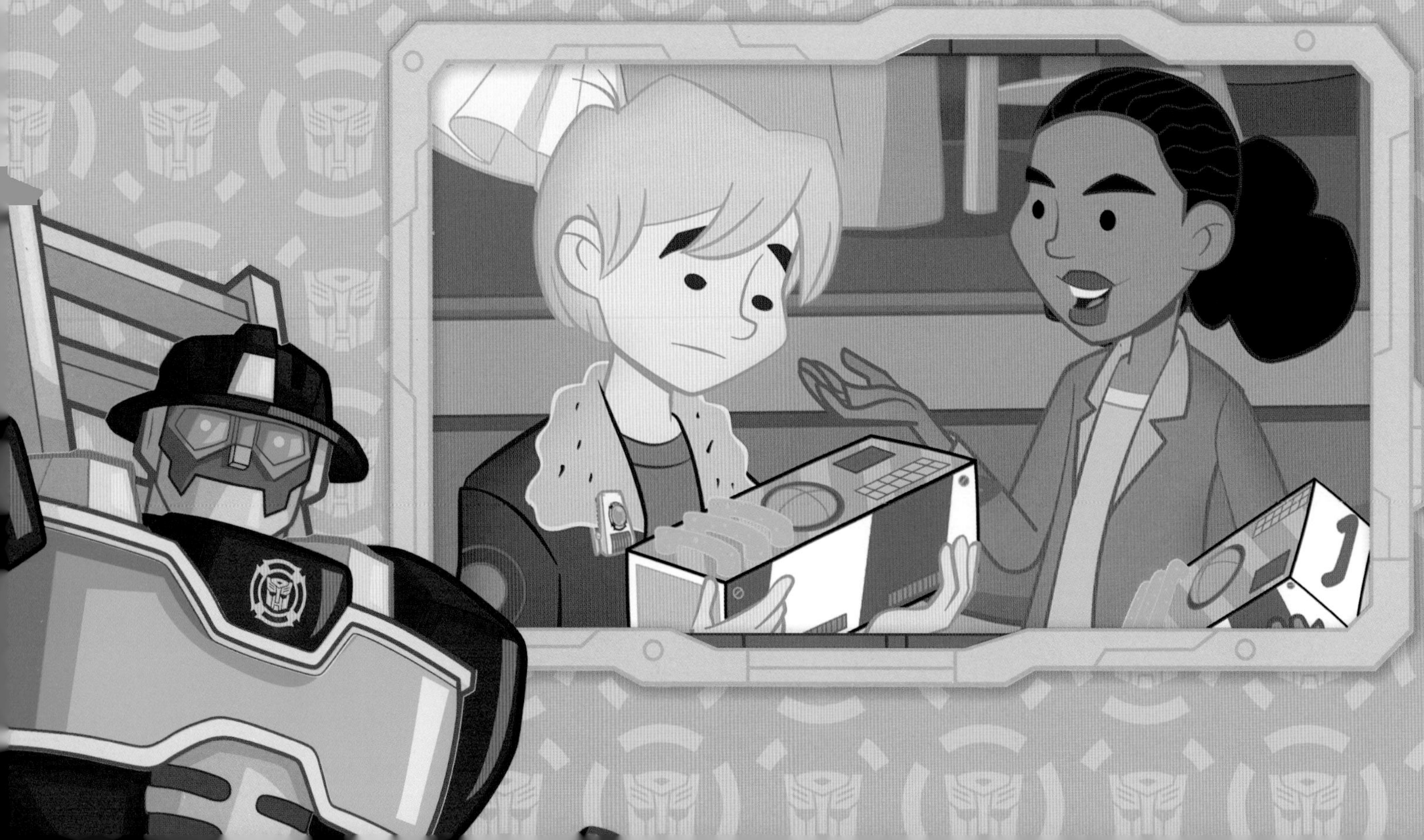

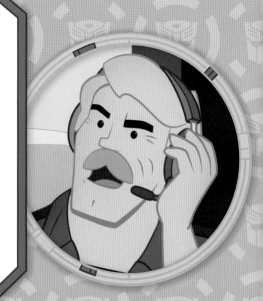

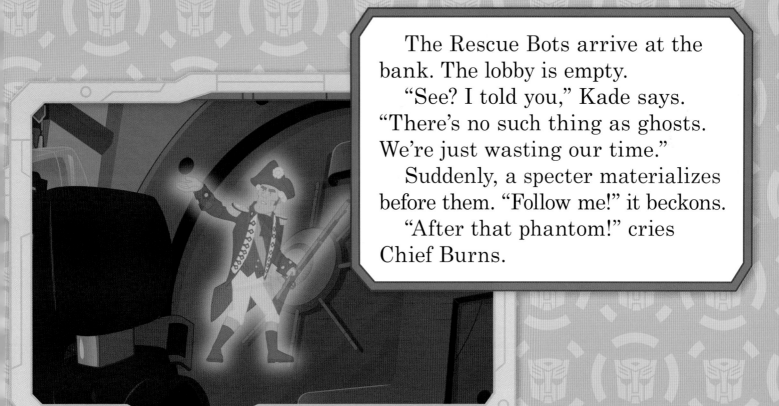

The Rescue Bots arrive at the bank. The lobby is empty.

"See? I told you," Kade says. "There's no such thing as ghosts. We're just wasting our time."

Suddenly, a specter materializes before them. "Follow me!" it beckons.

"After that phantom!" cries Chief Burns.

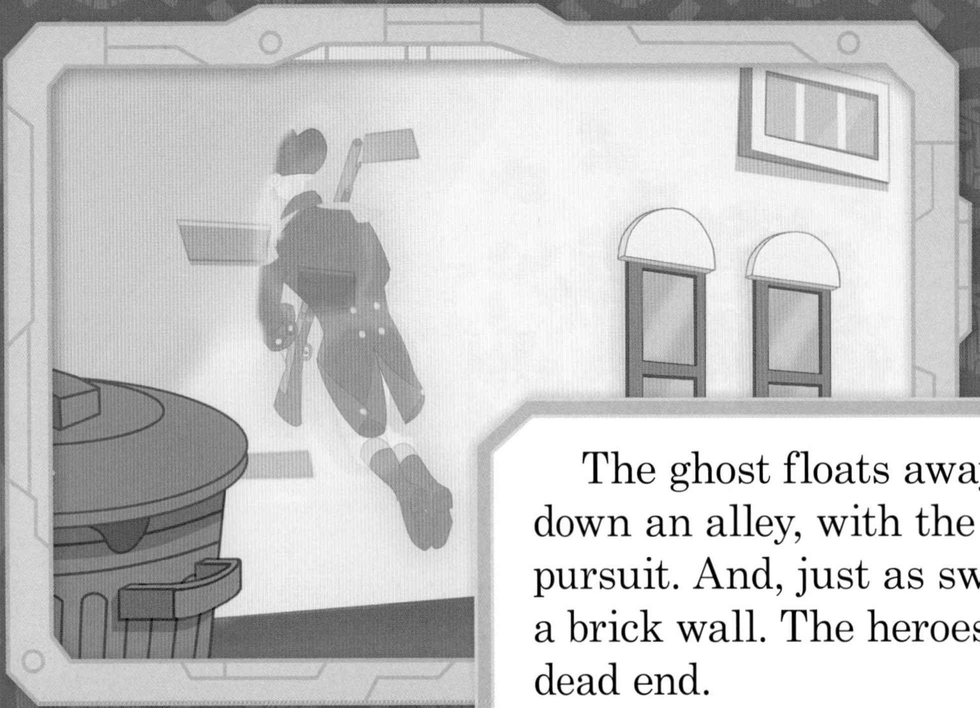

The ghost floats away from the bank and down an alley, with the Rescue Team in pursuit. And, just as swiftly, it passes through a brick wall. The heroes find themselves at a dead end.

Suddenly, the bank alarm goes off.

"Everyone, back inside!" yells Chief Burns.

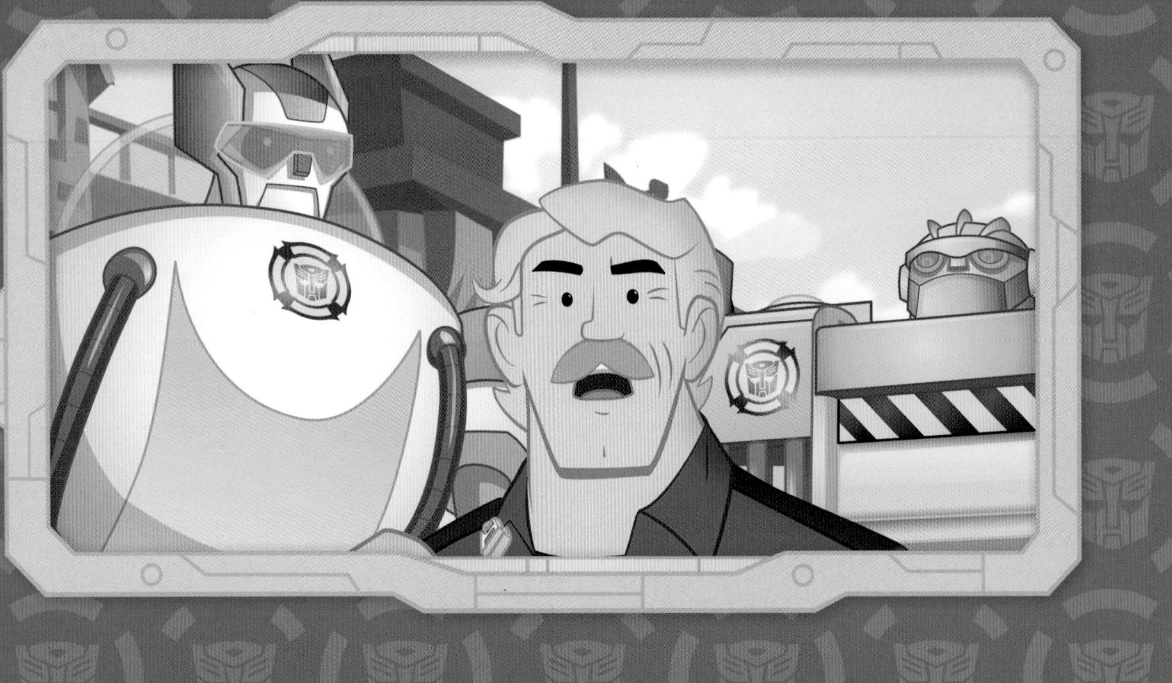

Chief Burns and his team race to the large vault. The contents have been completely cleared!

"How did that ghost empty the vault?" Boulder asks. "We were right behind it!"

"It didn't," answers the chief. "Ghosts can't steal."

The team deduces that the ghost was really a distraction, but they still don't know who, or what, the actual culprit is.

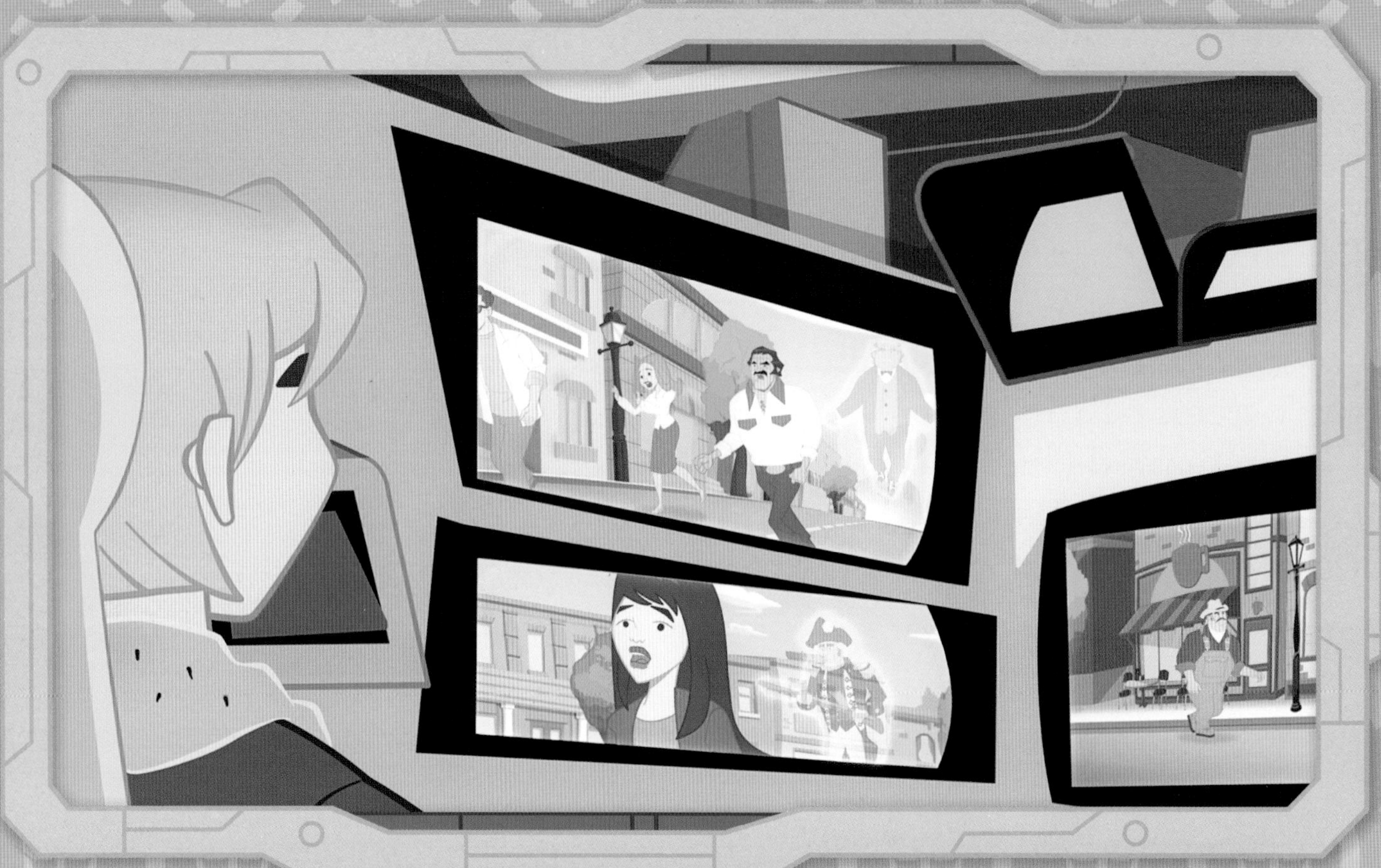

Cody's voice crackles over the Com-Link. "Guys, there are a lot of weird calls coming in," he says.

"Tell me it's not another ghost," replies Dani.

"Okay," says Cody. "It's a whole *lot* of other ghosts!"

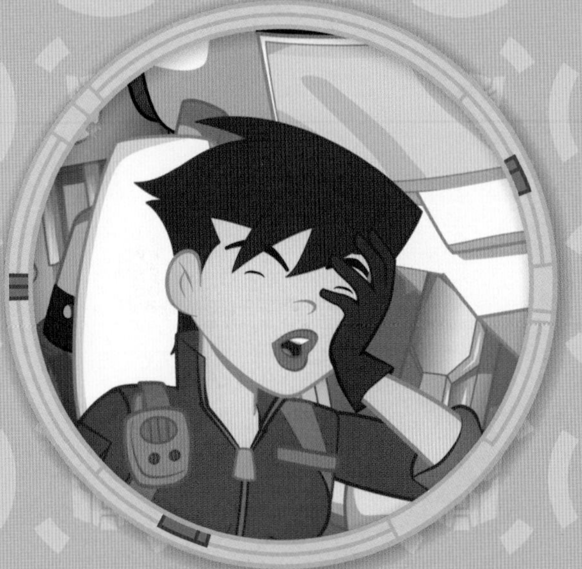

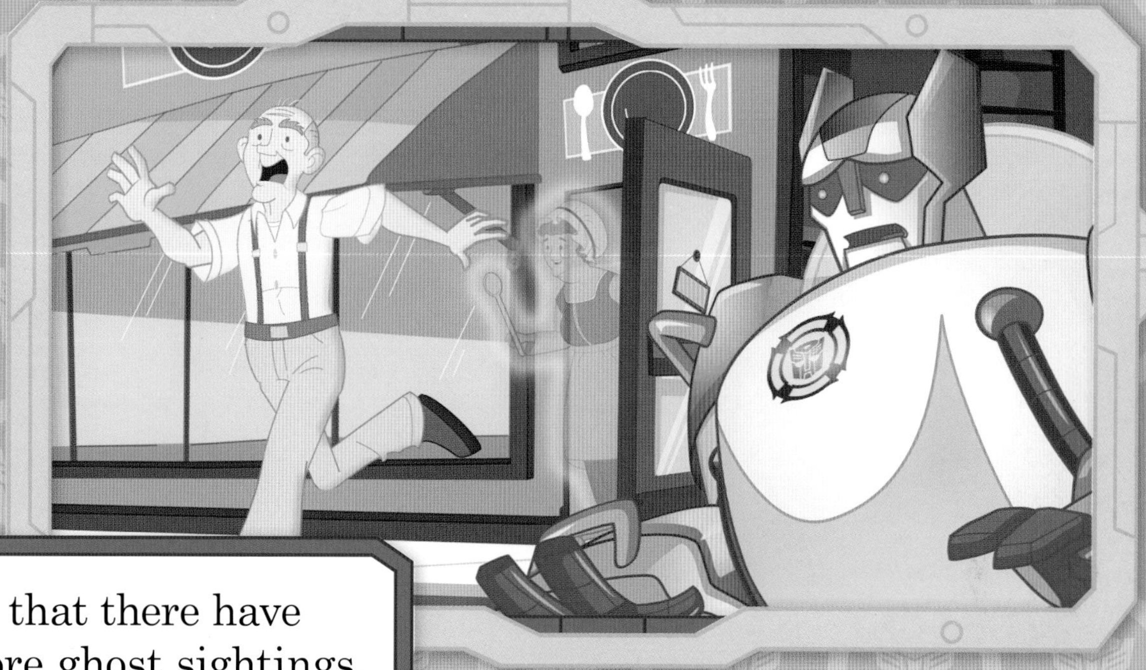

Cody relays that there have been many more ghost sightings. Citizens are fleeing for their lives!

Chief Burns and the Rescue Bots are seeing ghosts, too, but they still can’t believe their eyes!

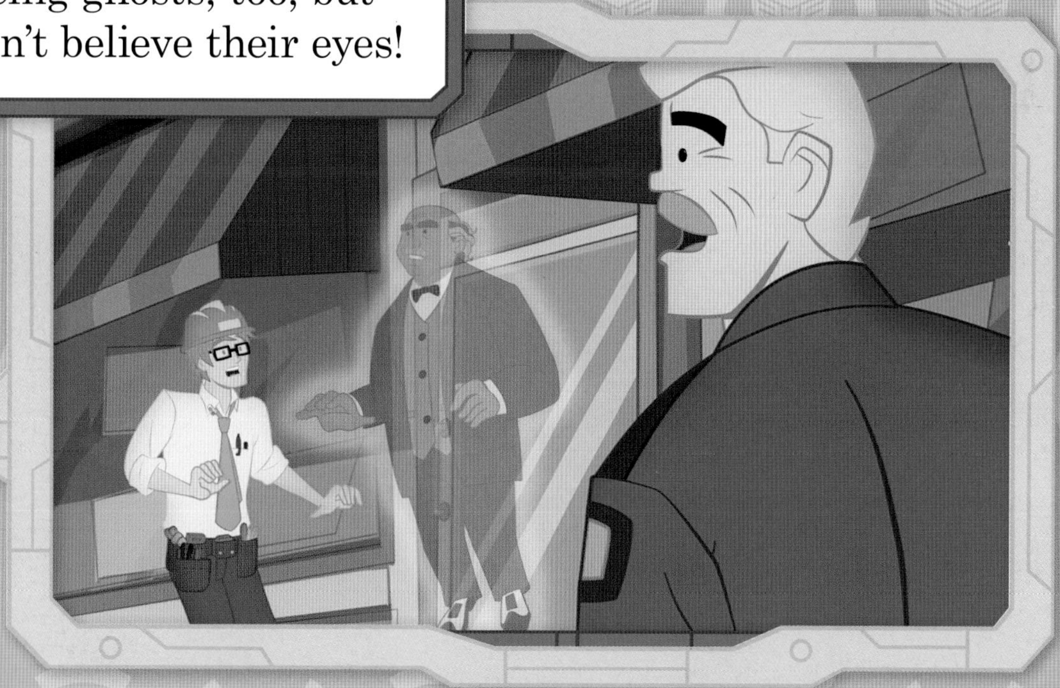

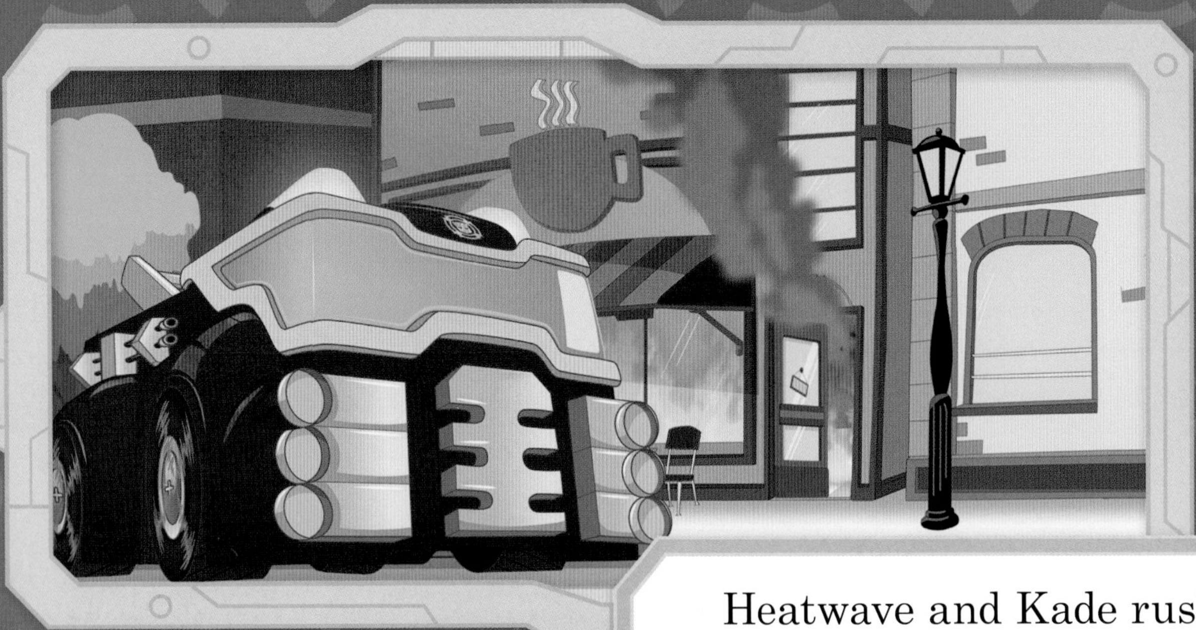

Heatwave and Kade rush to a restaurant that has gone up in flames.

"Finally," says Kade. "An emergency I know how to handle!"

Kade grabs a nearby hose and blasts the blaze until the fire is out.

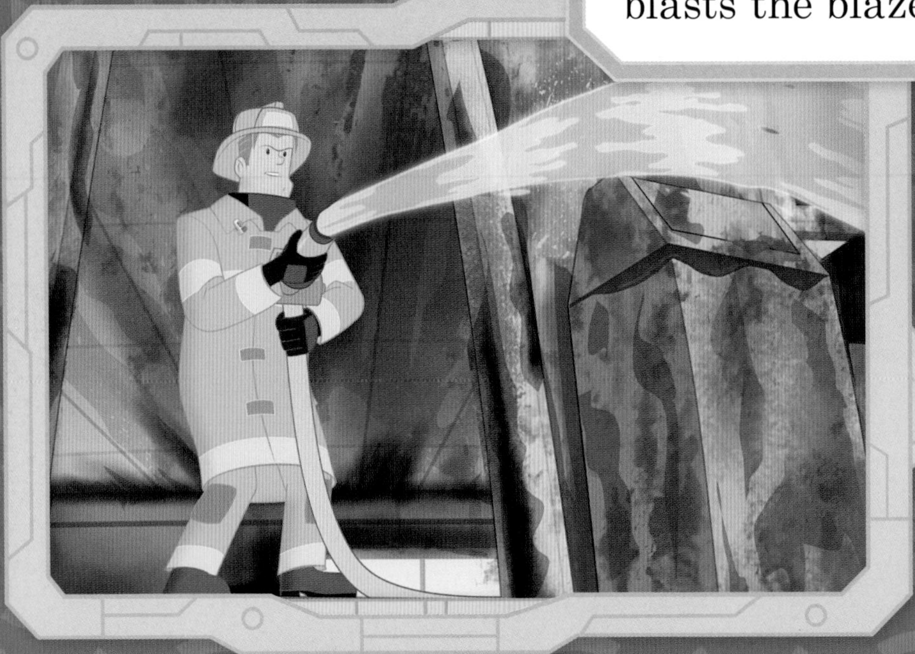

The firefighter and the Autobot enter the restaurant and make a discovery. "Fire's out, but the register has been robbed," Kade says into his Com-Link.

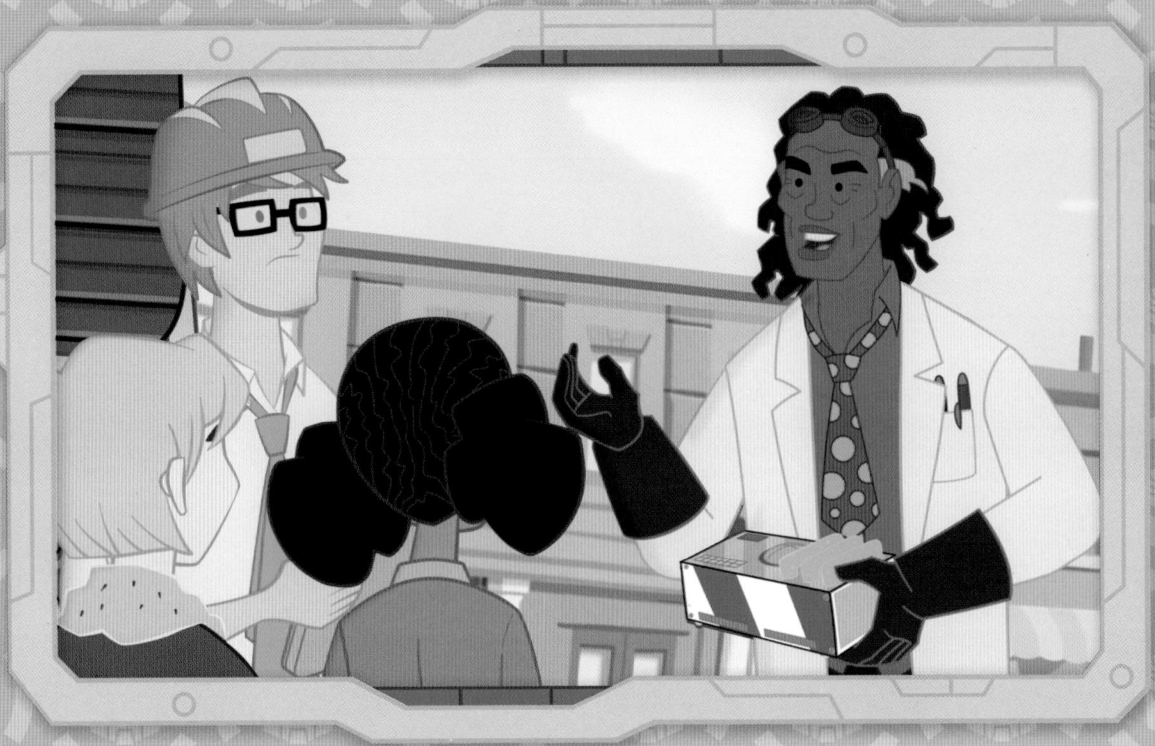

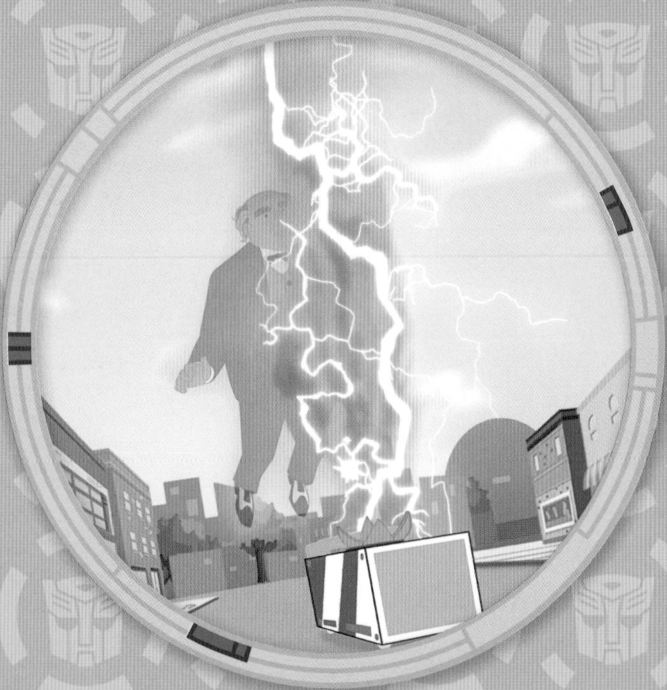

At that moment, Doc Greene arrives downtown with Cody and Frankie. “How do we stop the ghosts?” Graham asks.

“Allow me,” Doc Greene replies. He pulls out his Spectral Vapor Filter and activates it. An energy field zaps one of the ghosts, causing it to fizzle and fade.

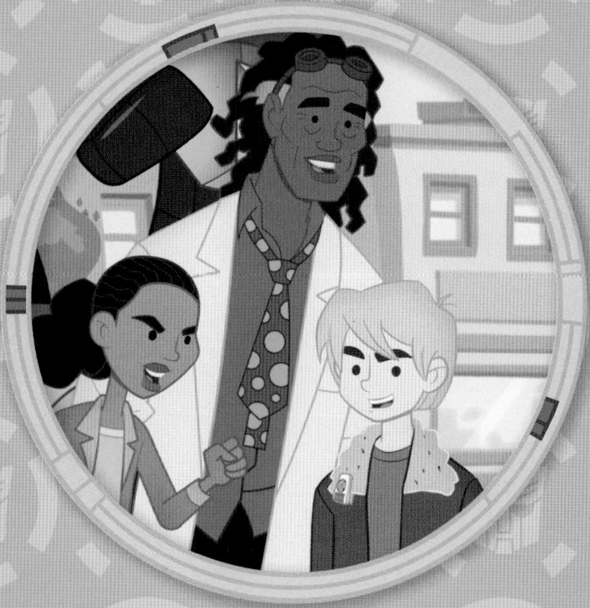

“That ghost is toast!” Frankie cheers.

But the victory is short-lived because the ghost reappears.

“Hmm,” says Doc Greene. “My readings show that this is not a ghost—it’s a hologram!”

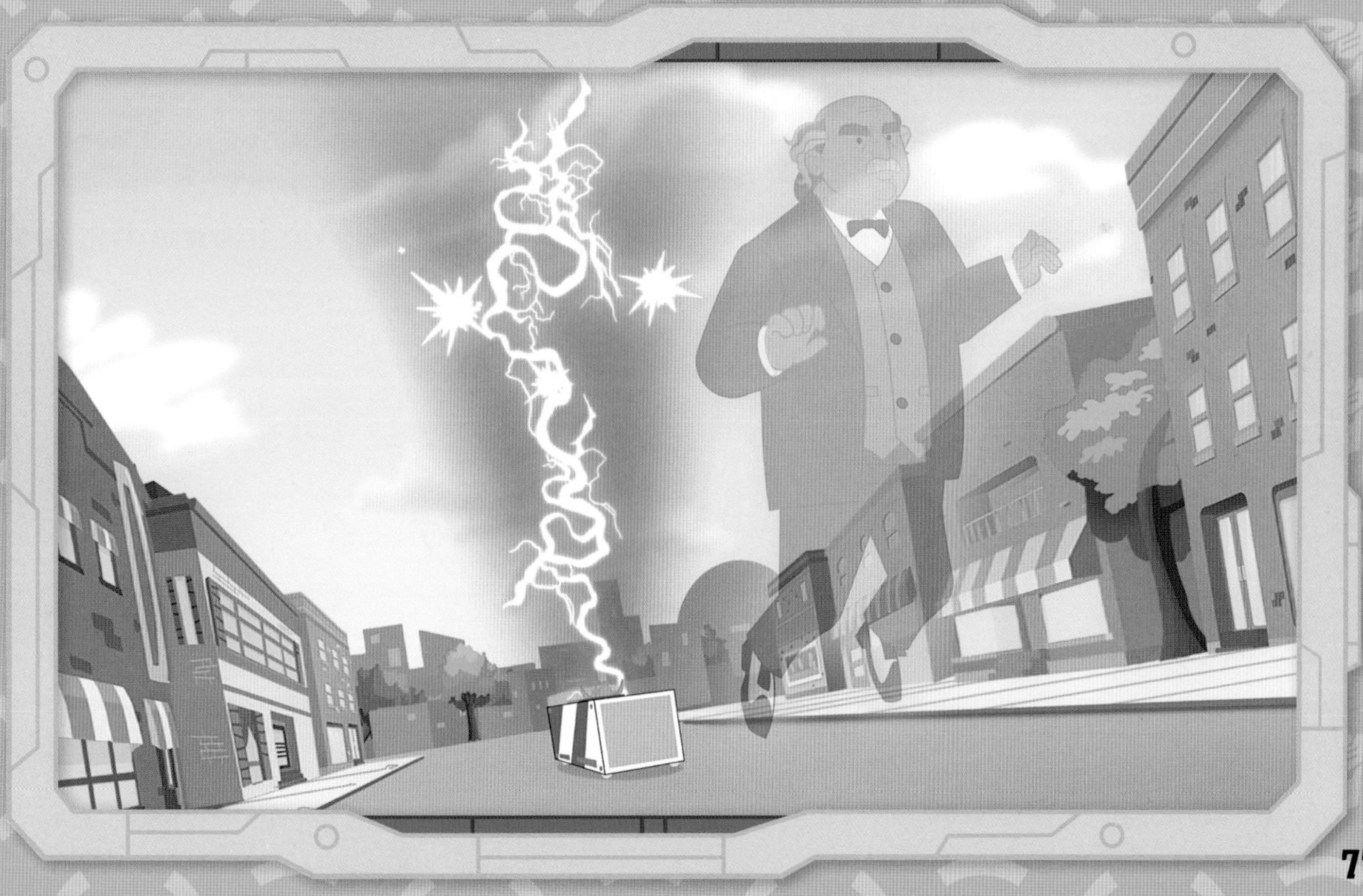

The team goes to Doc Greene's lab. After some quick research, they learn that the holograms are coming from different projectors throughout the city.

"The signal is originating from the jail," the scientist says.

On the screen is an image of brothers Evan and Myles. "Ghosts can't steal," Cody says, "but those two do it for a living!"

Chief Burns heads to the police station and finds the two prisoners inside their cell. They are pacing back and forth, but the chief notices they haven't touched their food. As he enters, one of the prisoners passes right through him.

"The brothers must have escaped and hacked into the computer system," cries Chief Burns. "They built holograms of themselves to fool us!"

Another alarm blares.

Now a jewelry store is the target. Chief Burns contacts his team and tells them where the burglars are striking.

"It's time to put an end to this ghost story!" he says.

The Rescue Bots roll out to the scene of the crime.

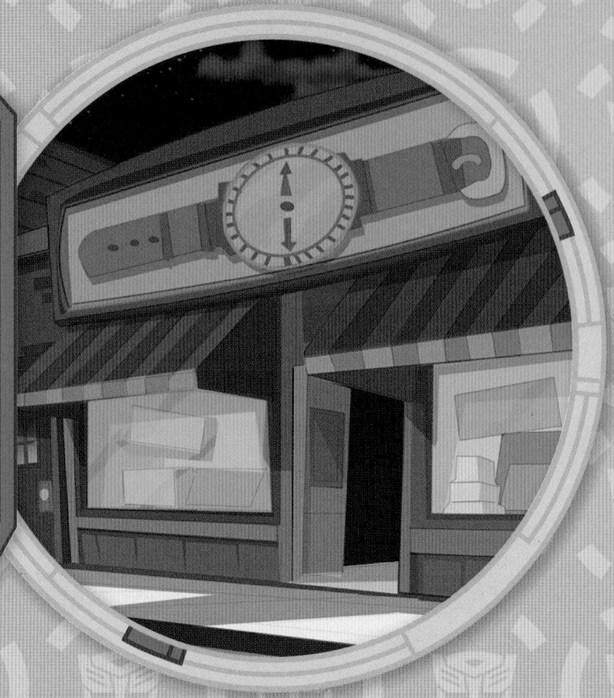

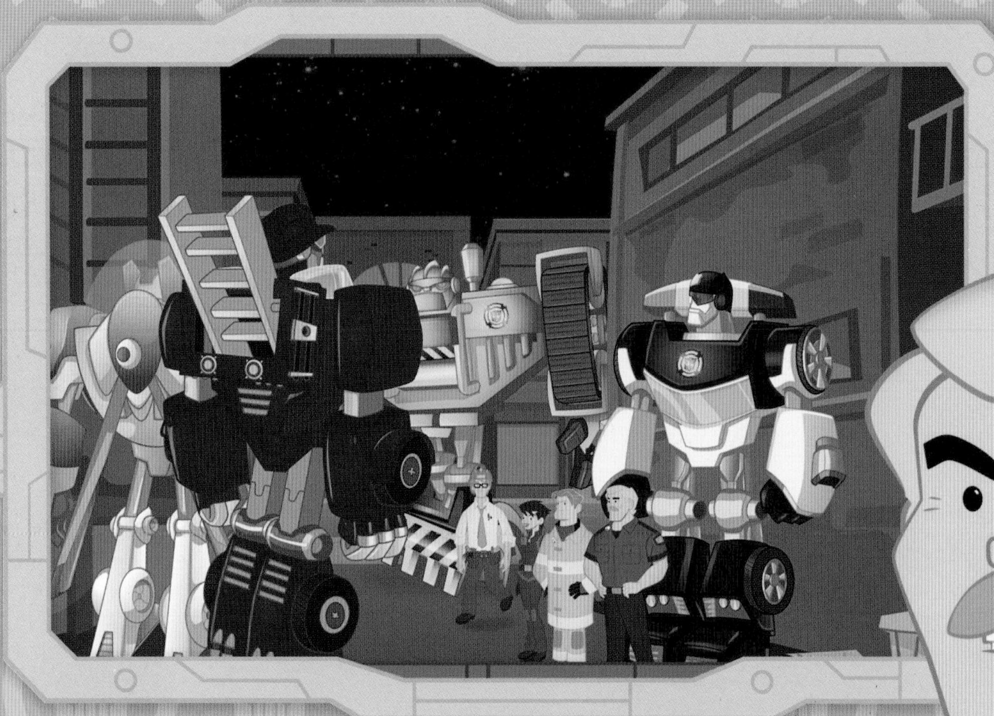

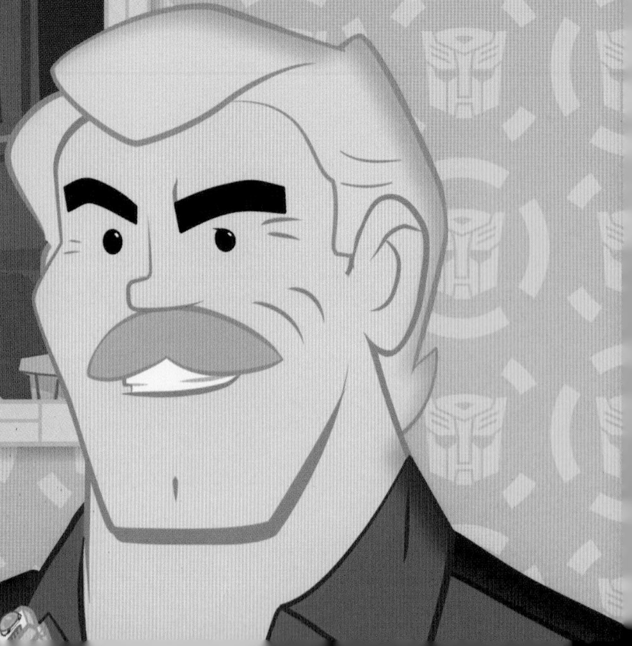

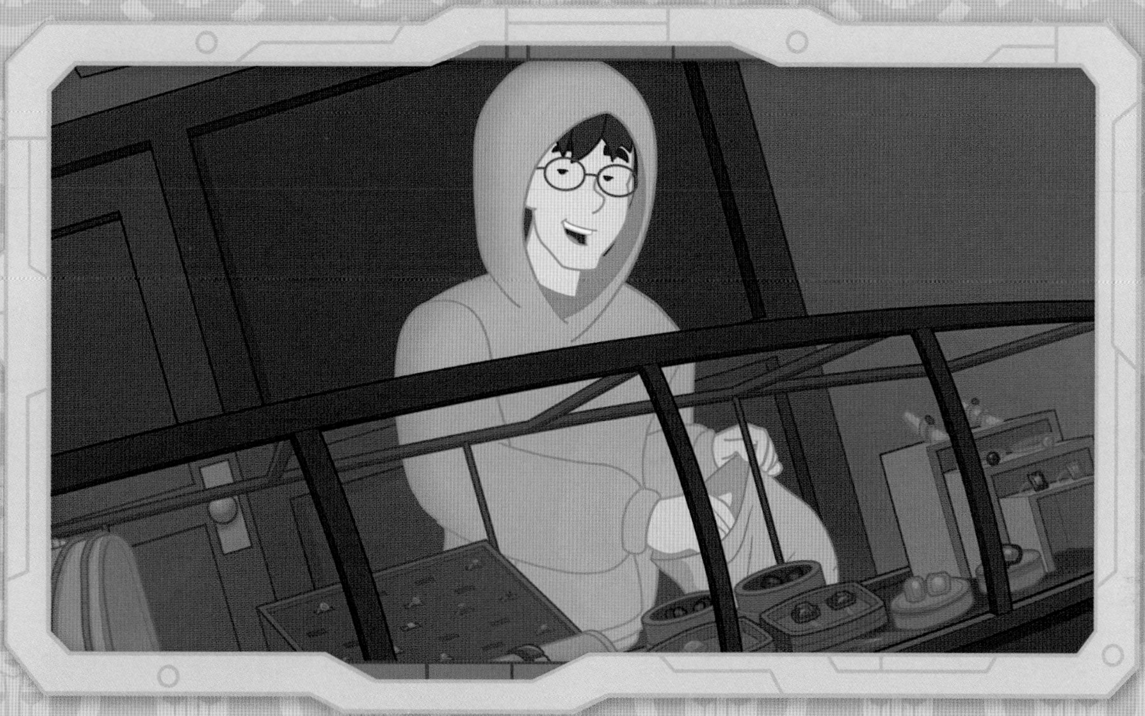

Meanwhile, the two brothers are in the jewelry store filling up their burlap bags with expensive items.

"That police chief and his team of tin cans aren't as smart as we are." Evan laughs.

"Yeah," Myles agrees. "Thanks to our dirty little trick, we're picking this city clean."

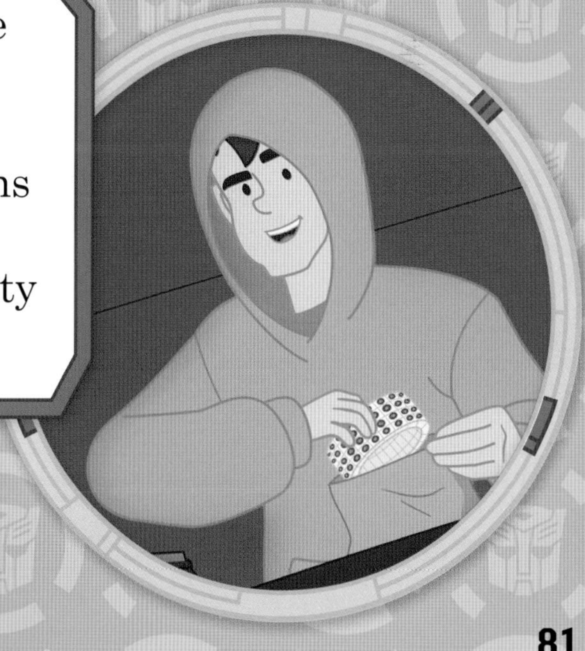

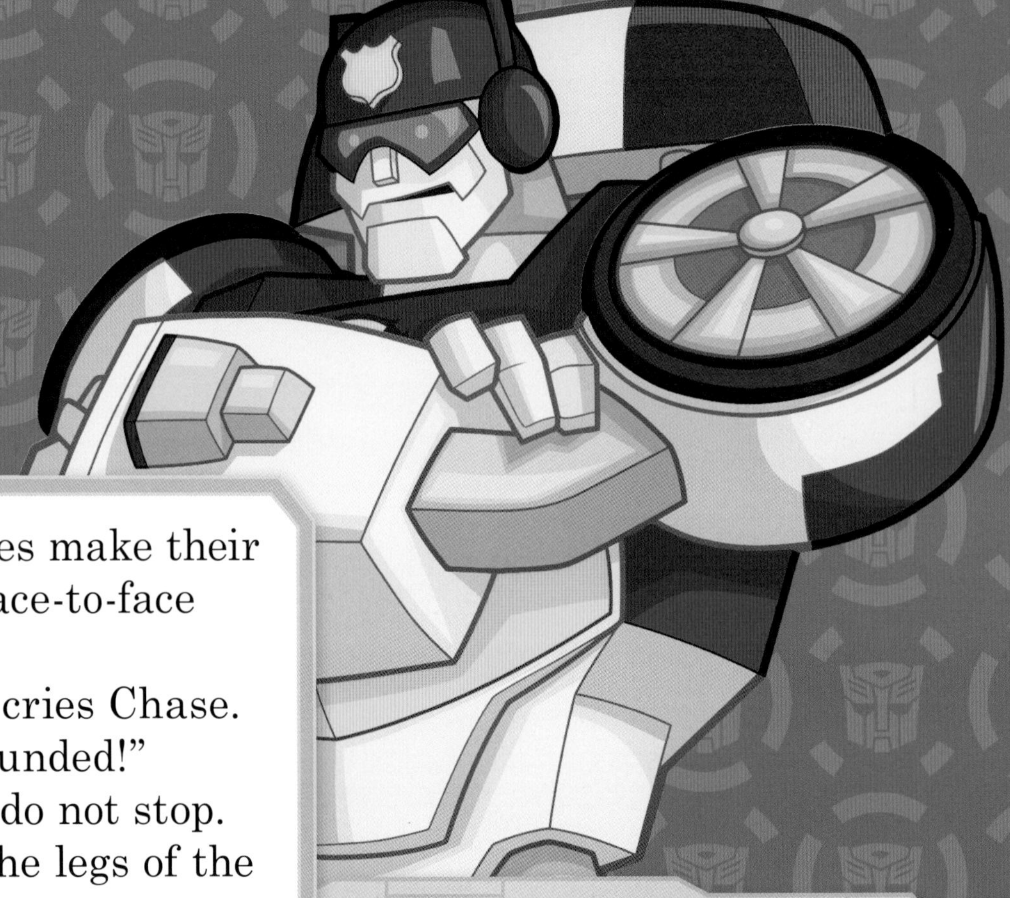

As Evan and Myles make their escape, they come face-to-face with the law.

"Halt, burglars," cries Chase. "We have you surrounded!"

But the brothers do not stop. They run through the legs of the robots as fast as they can.

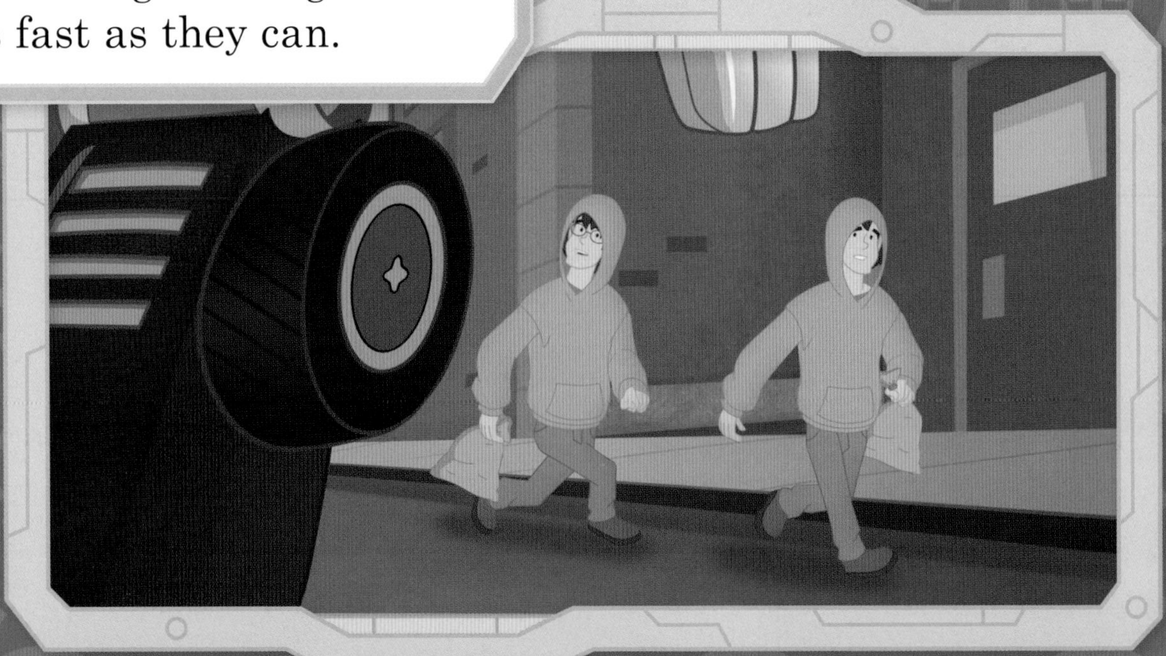

Heatwave leaps into action and swings through the air. He lands in front of Evan and Myles, blocking their path. In a flash, the Autobot blasts the brothers with his water cannons.

"Your criminal career is all washed up!" Heatwave says.

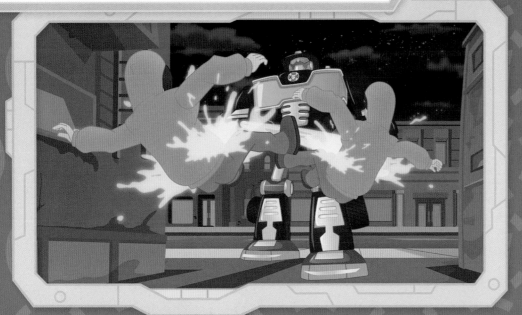

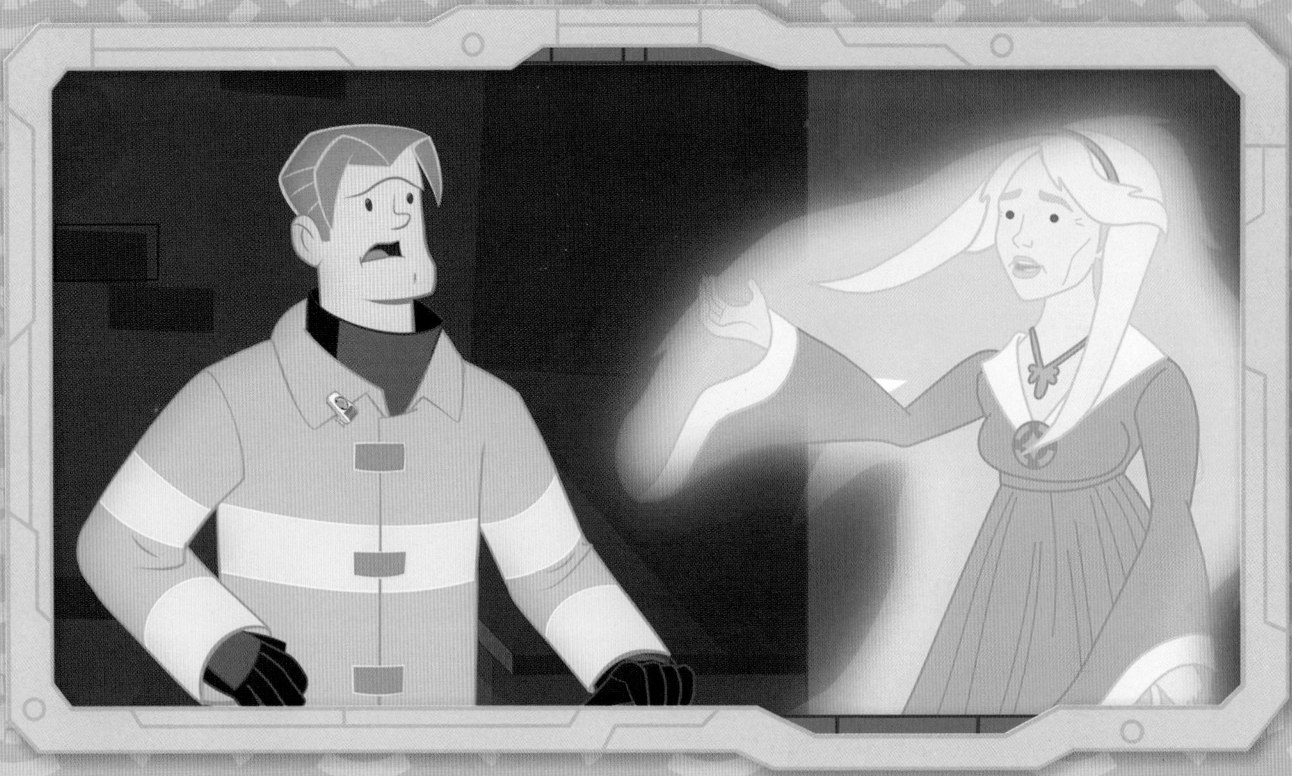

While Chase and Chief Burns take the brothers back to jail, Kade turns to the others and says, "Looks like the hauntings were a hoax after all."

Suddenly, the Lady of Griffin Rock appears and cries, "Come home to me!"

Kade jumps with fright. "Was that a hologram or a ghost?!"

Cody smiles and says, "We'll never know!"

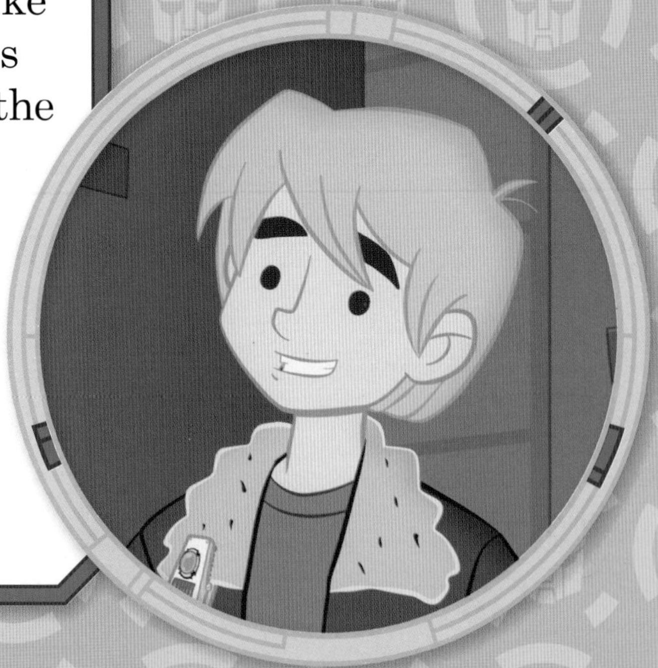

TRANSFORMERS RESCUE BOTS

Land Before Prime

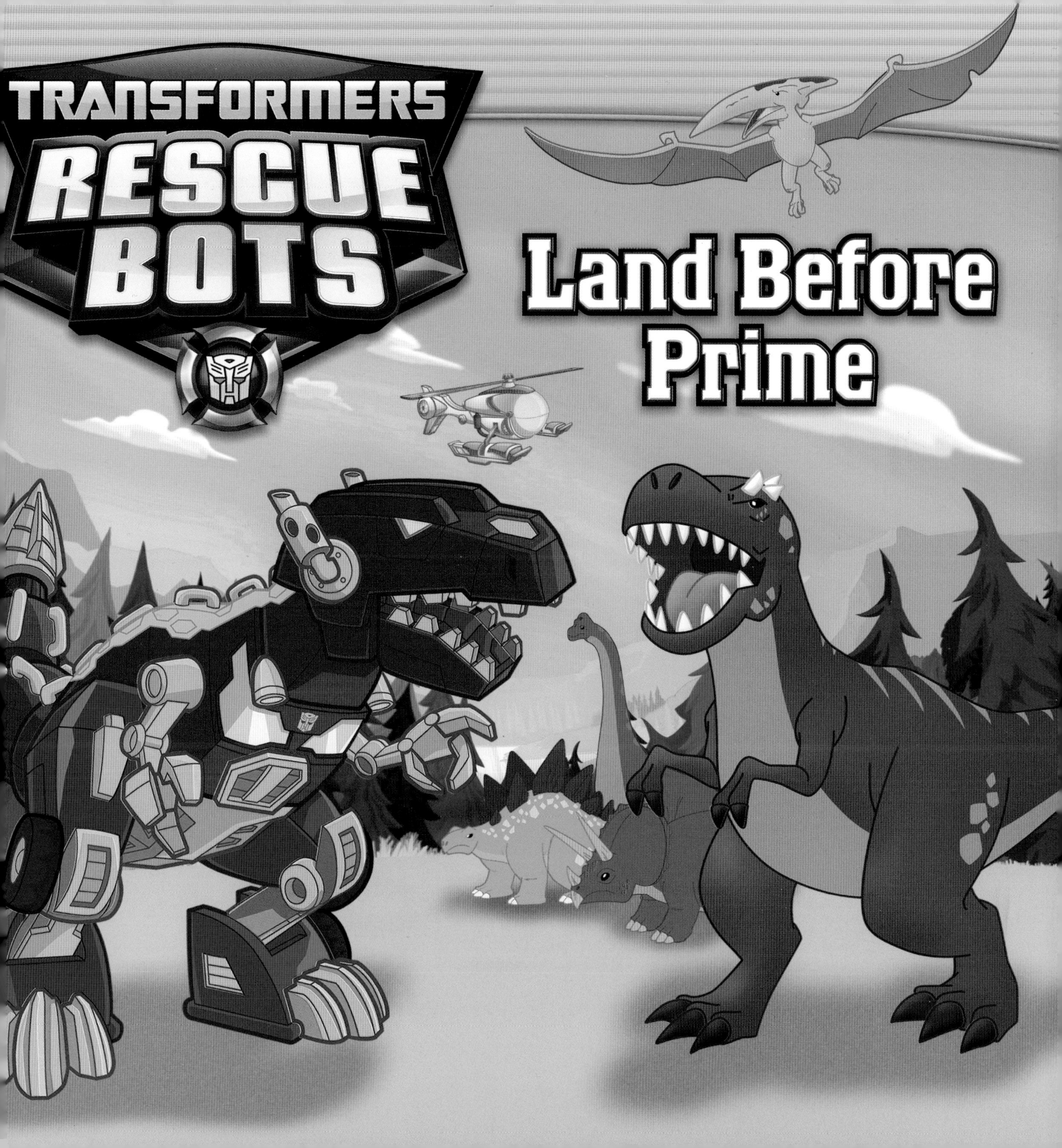

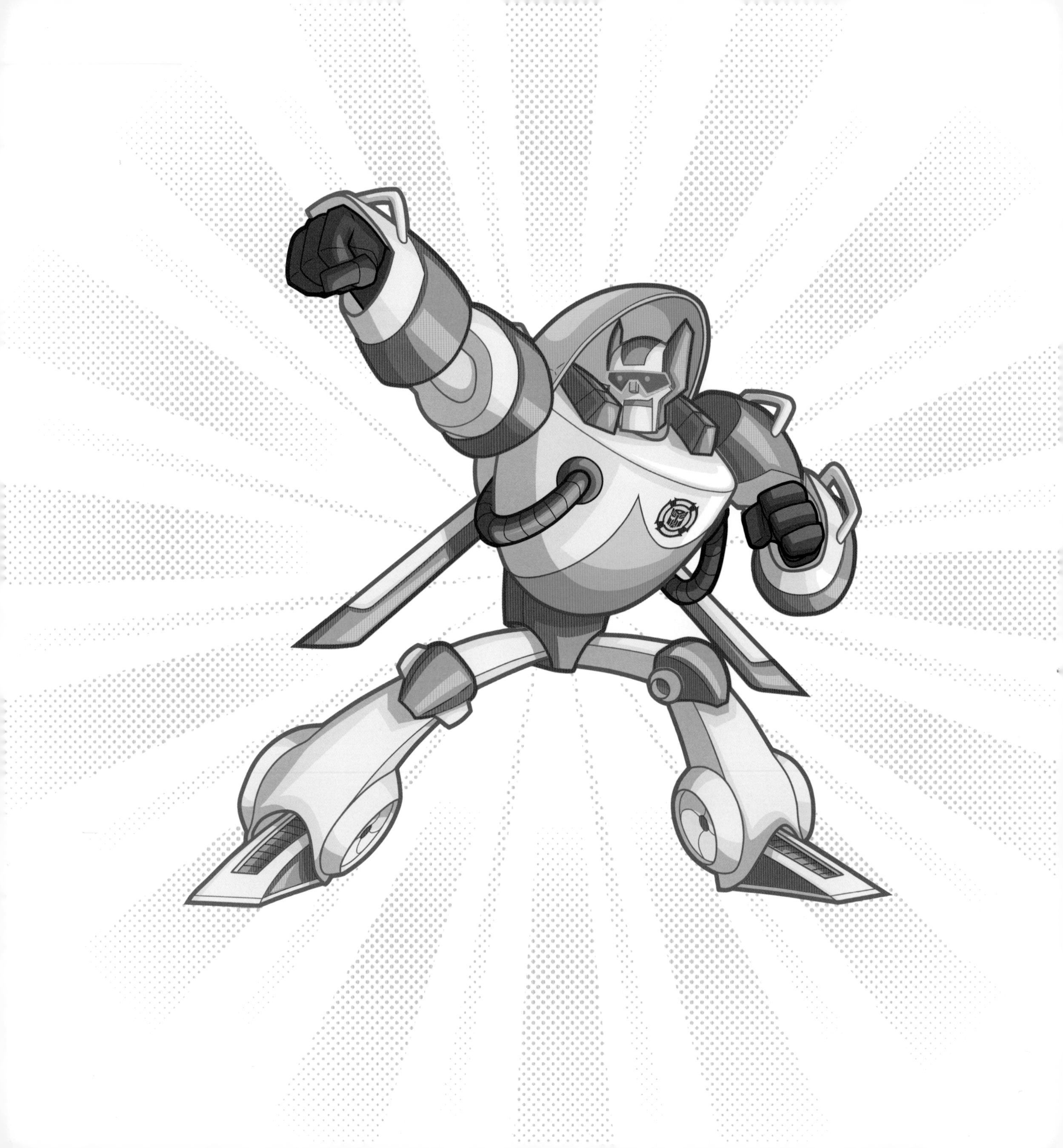

TRANSFORMERS RESCUE BOTS

Land Before Prime

Adapted by John Sazaklis
Based on the episode "Land Before Prime"
written by Nicole Dubuc

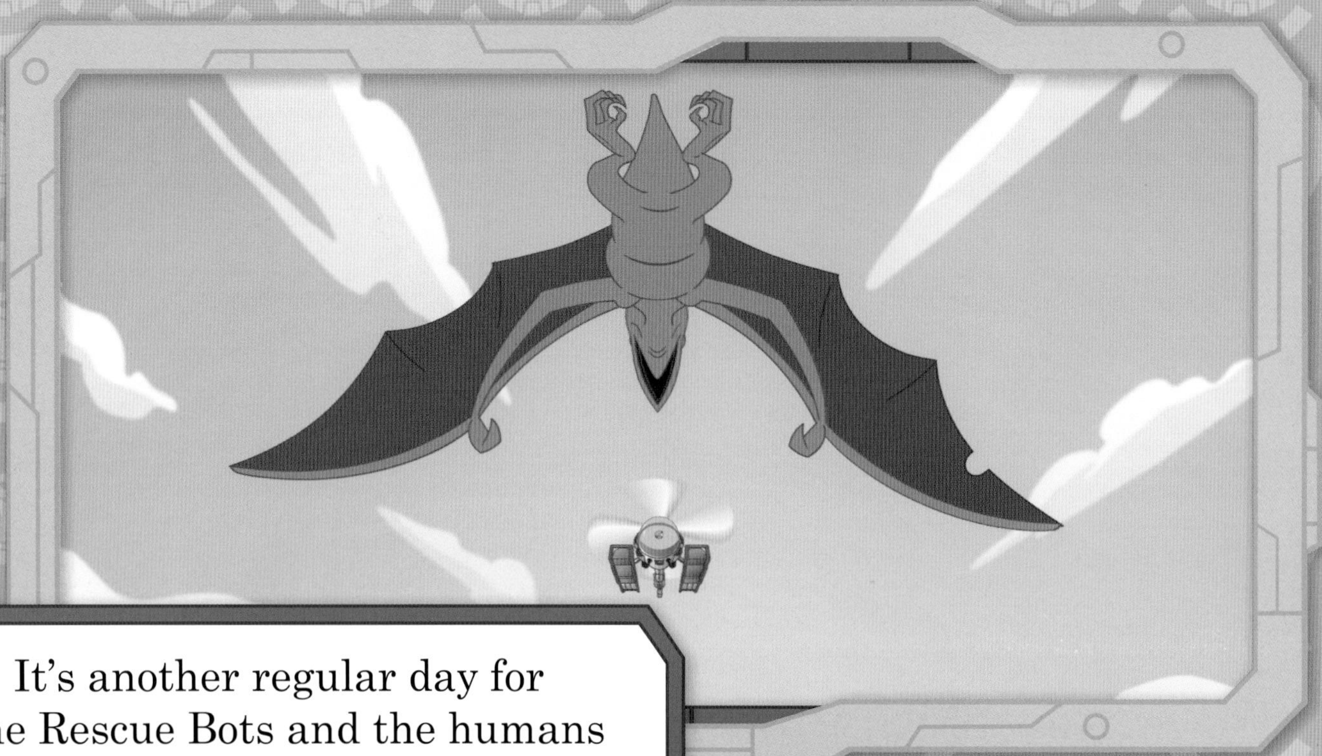

It’s another regular day for the Rescue Bots and the humans patrolling Griffin Rock. Blades and Dani are scanning the skies when they come across something very strange—a pterodactyl!

“Aaaaah!” Blades cries. “Is that what I think it is?”

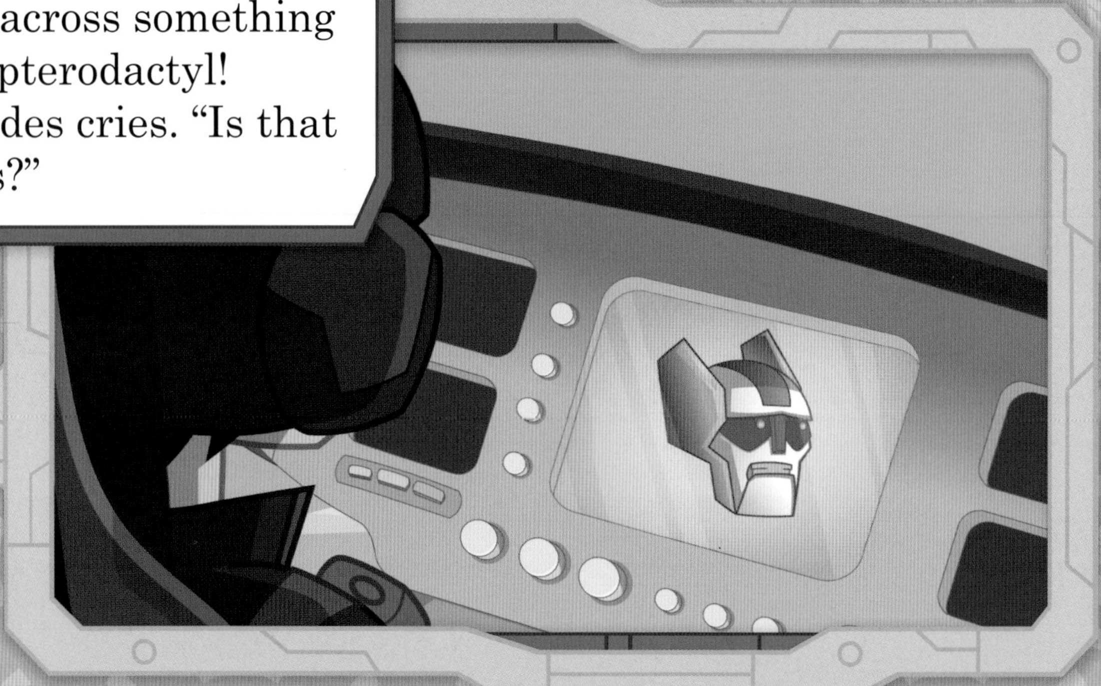

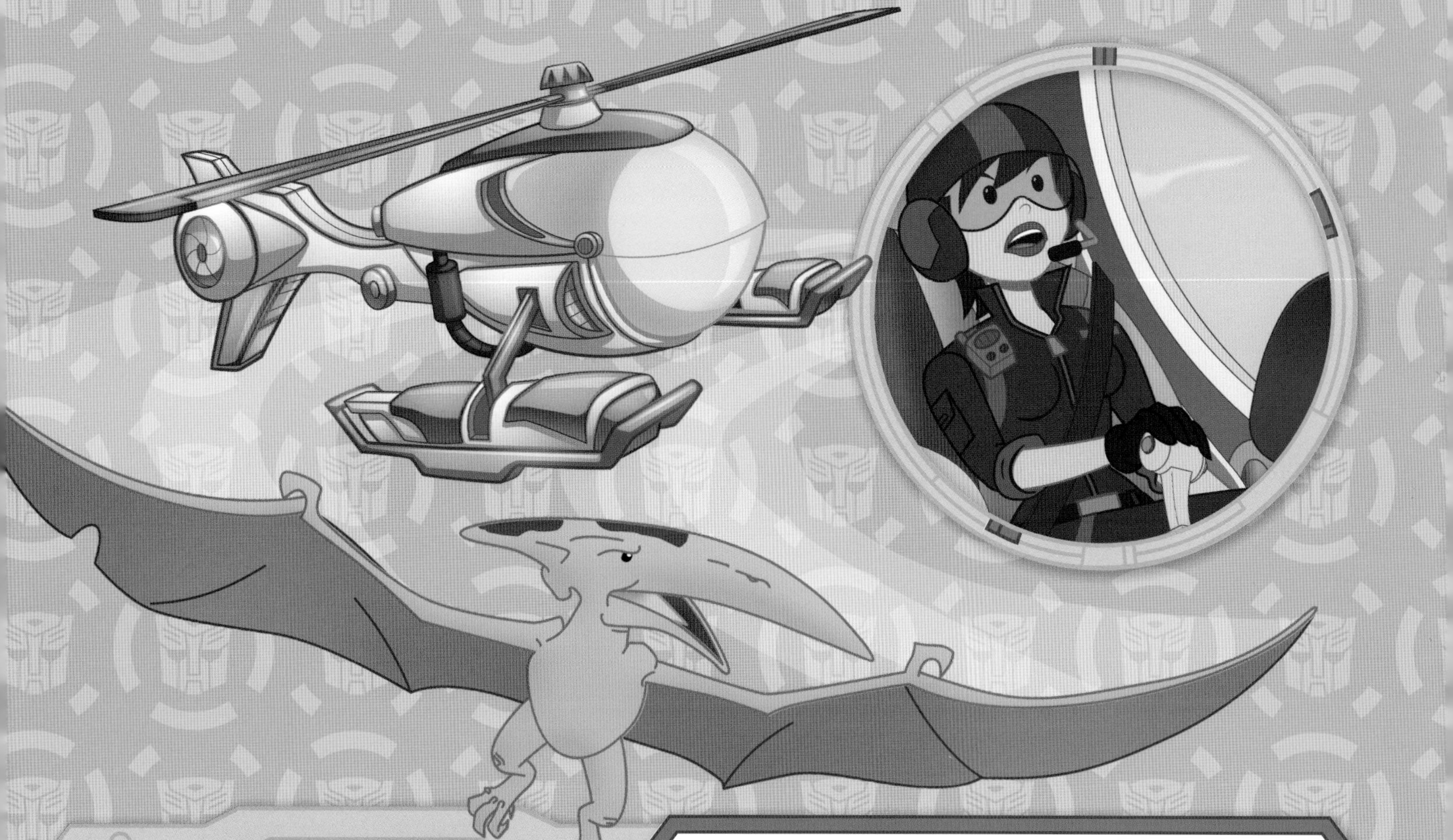

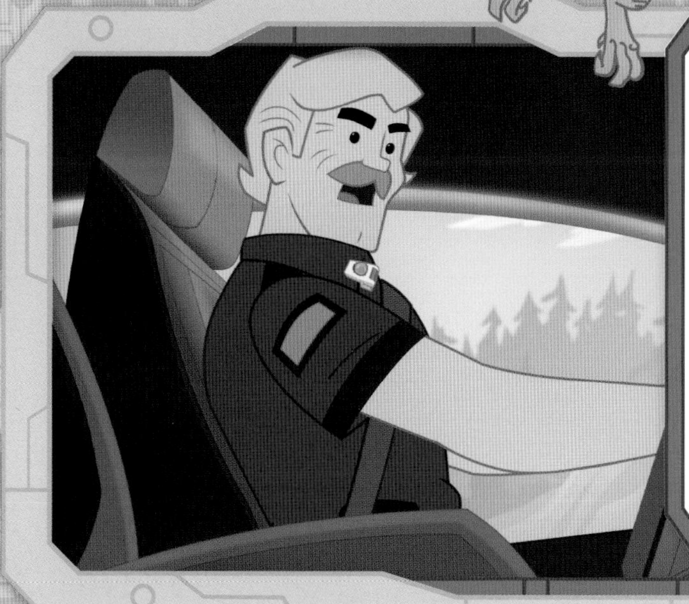

The creature screeches and flies toward them. Dani weaves out of its path and watches as it perches on Mount Griffin.

Dani calls Chief Burns and says, "Dad, we just saw a pterodactyl!"

"Hmm," Chief Burns replies. "Guess it doesn't know it's extinct. I'll call Doc Greene."

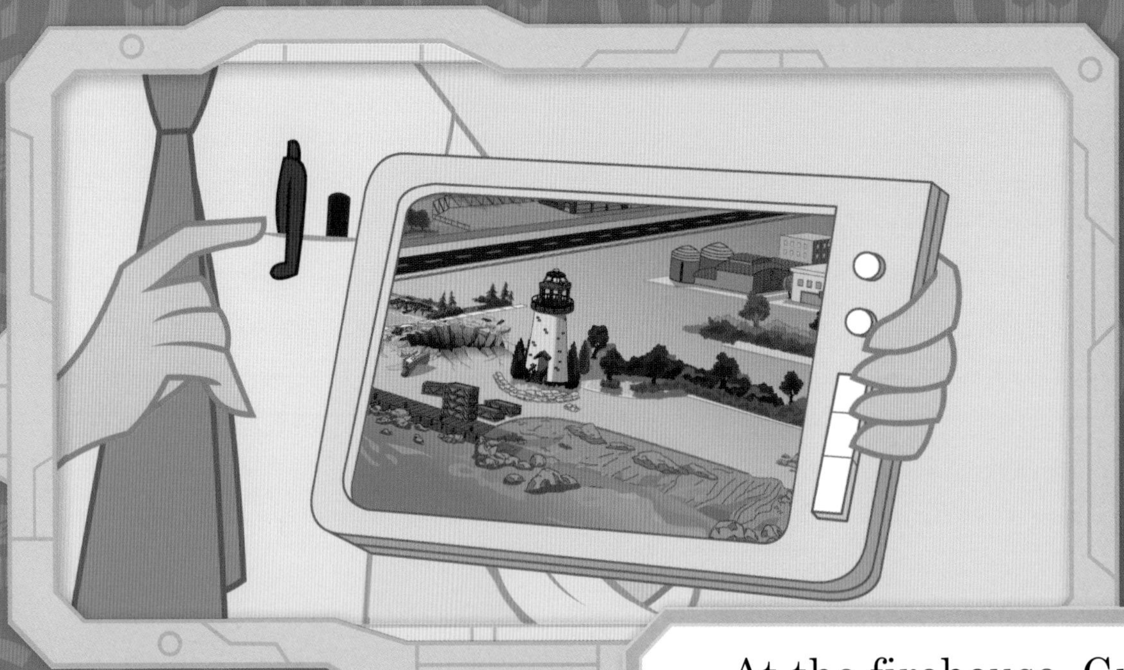

At the firehouse, Graham explains where the winged reptile came from. “A chain of explosions opened deep sinkholes beneath Griffin Rock,” he says. “It’s possible one of them reached as far down as the prehistoric caverns. There must be life within!”

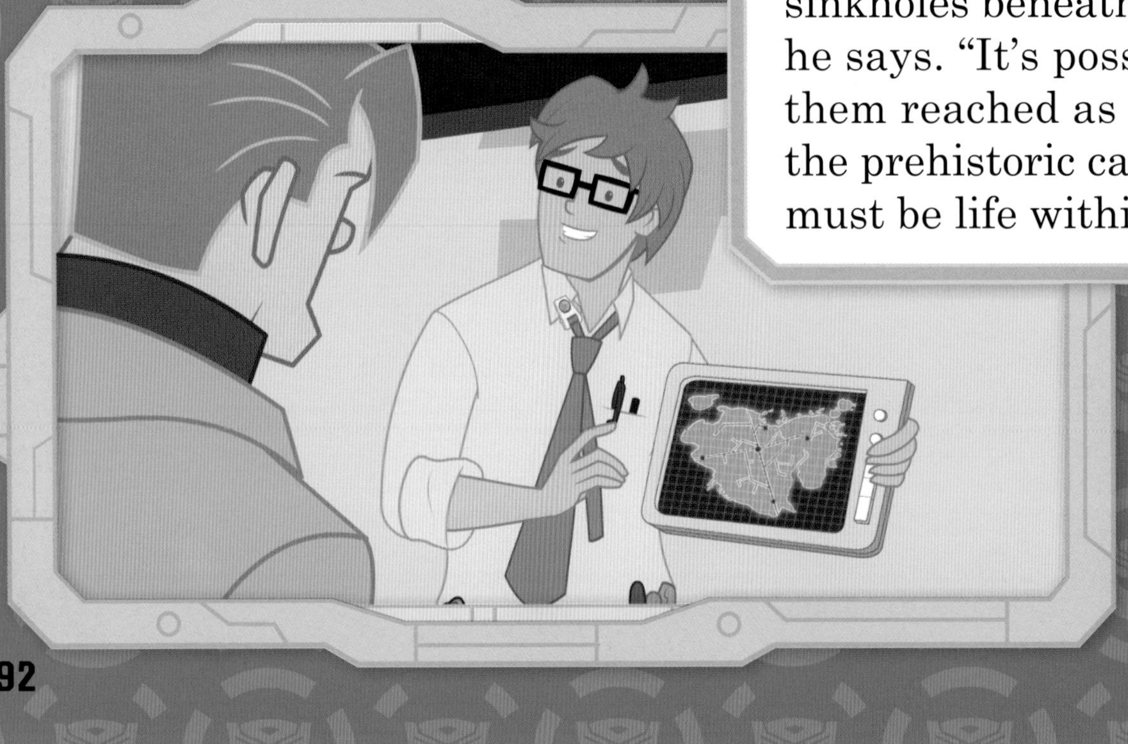

The Com-Link beeps with an incoming message. It's Doc Greene. He is flying alongside the pterodactyl with a hang glider!

"This is amazing!" he exclaims. "I've never imagined seeing one of these up close!"

"When I said to observe that thing, I meant with a telescope!" Chief Burns says. "So, what's the plan?"

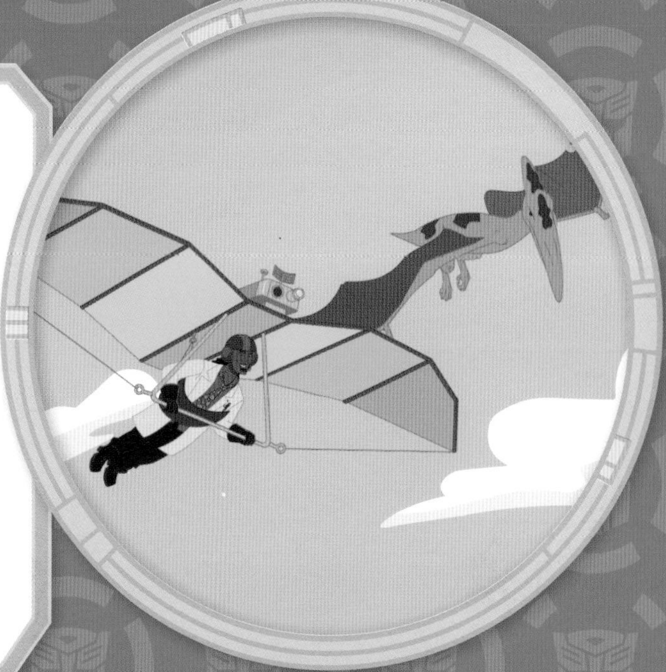

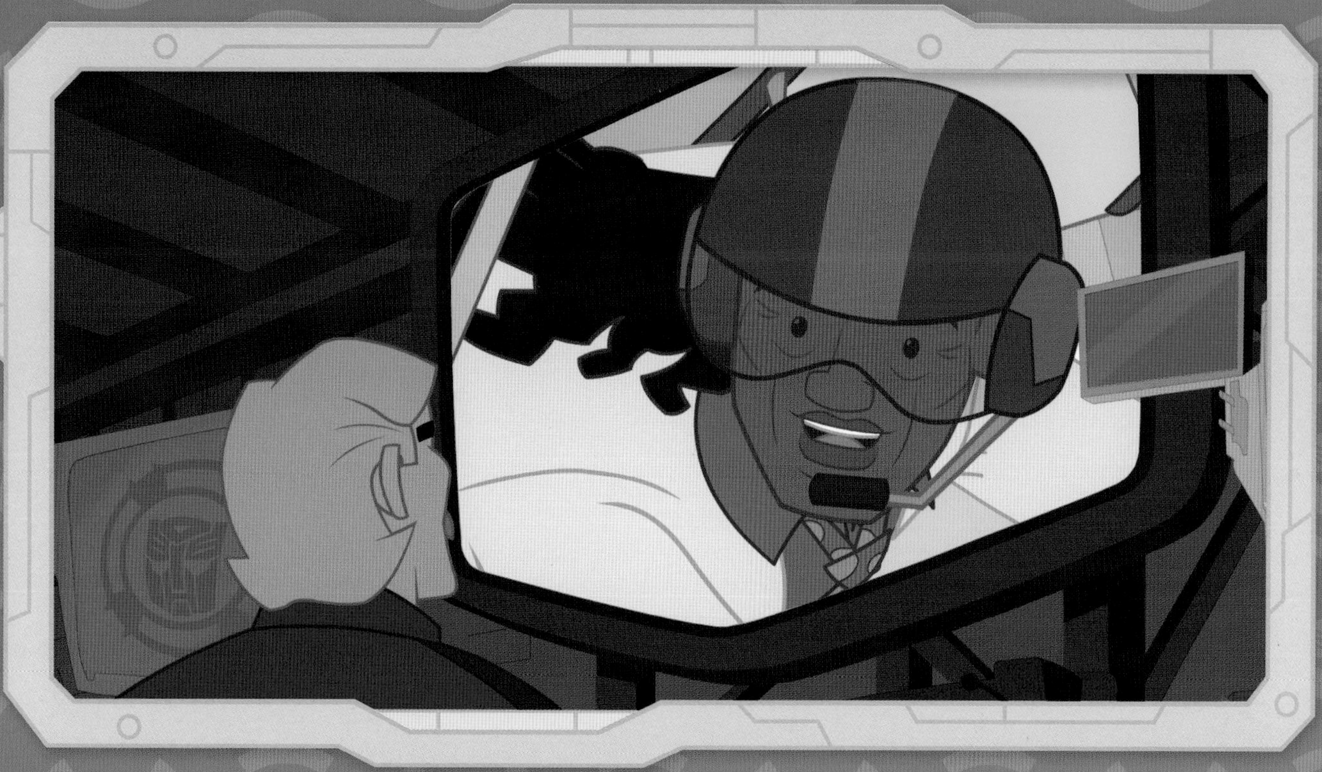

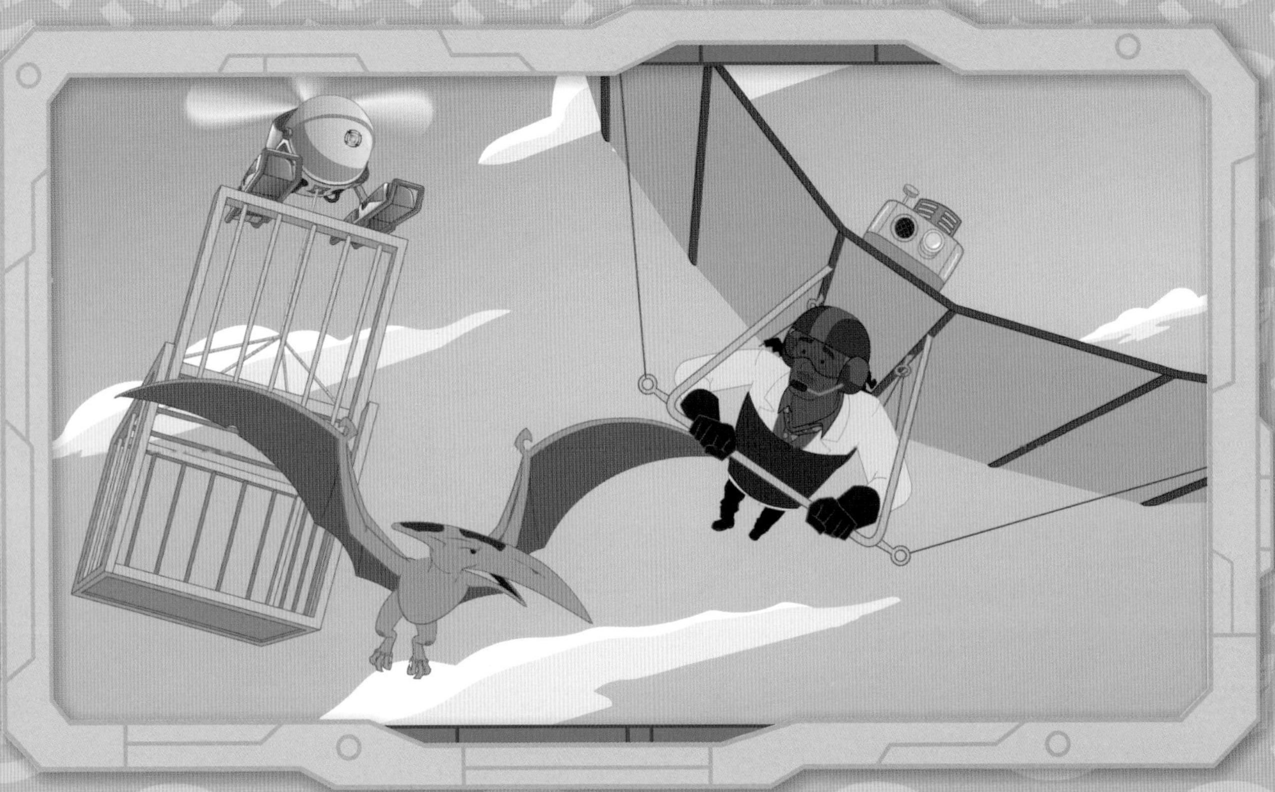

“We’ll cage the pterodactyl long enough to place a tracker on her,” Doc Greene says. “After she’s released, we can follow her and make sure she gets home safely. My guess is that she’s nesting.”

The Rescue Bots follow the scientist’s orders. They meet Doc Greene at Mount Griffin. Blades has a cage dangling from his winch. He drops it over the creature.

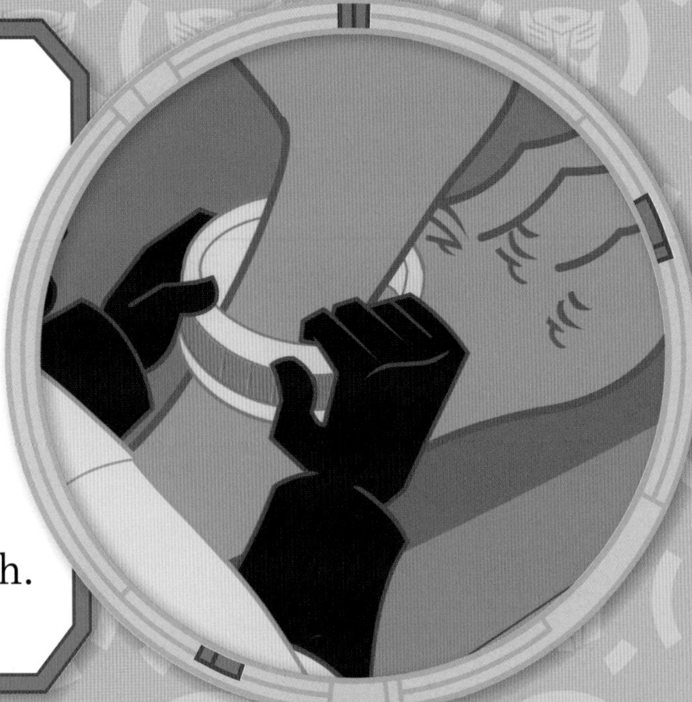

After putting a tracking device on the pterodactyl, they free her from the cage. “She’s headed toward Wayward Island. That’s where the subterranean rift must be located,” says Graham.

“I would be happy to search for the passage myself,” Doc Greene says.

“It’s dangerous, Doc,” Chief Burns says.

“I’ll take Trex with me. What’s a more logical bodyguard than a robotic dinosaur?”

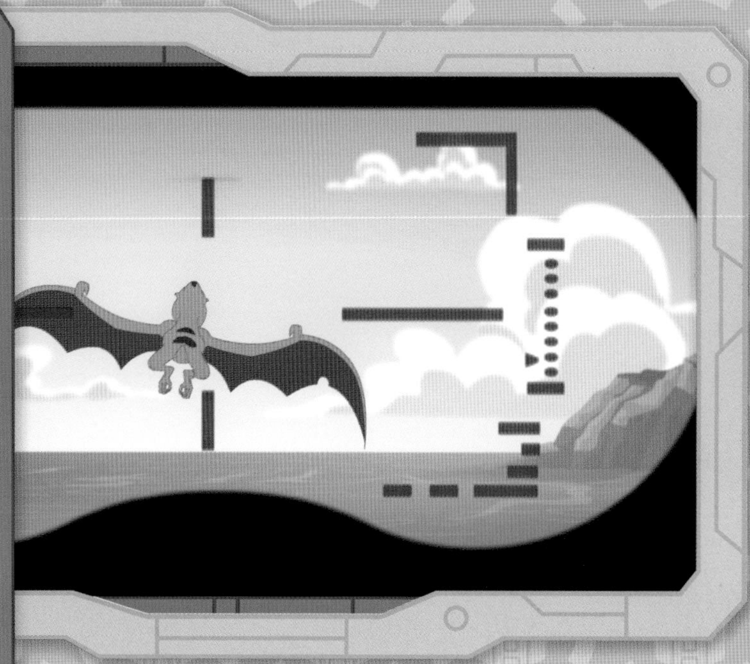

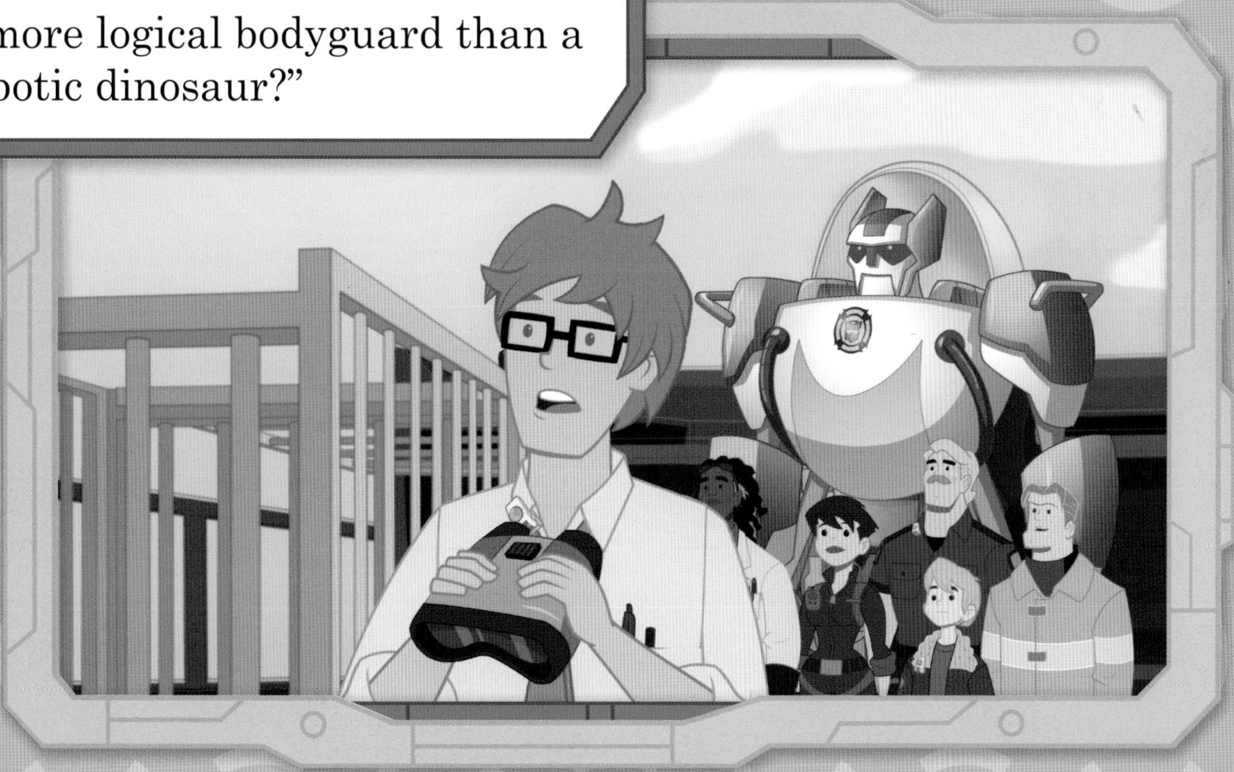

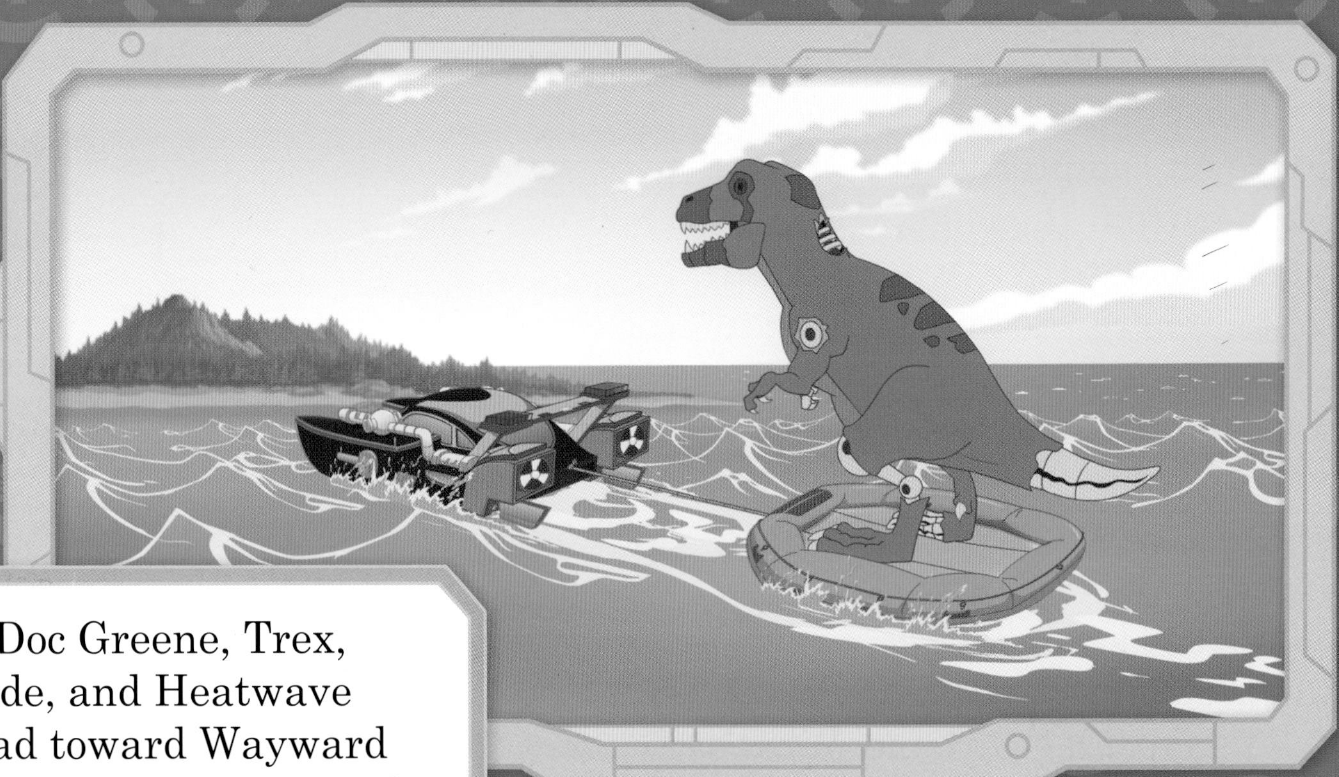

Doc Greene, Trex, Kade, and Heatwave head toward Wayward Island. They soon reach the coast and pull up to the shore.

"I wonder if there really are dinosaurs on the island," Kade says.

"Only one way to find out," says Doc Greene. "We'll be back soon."

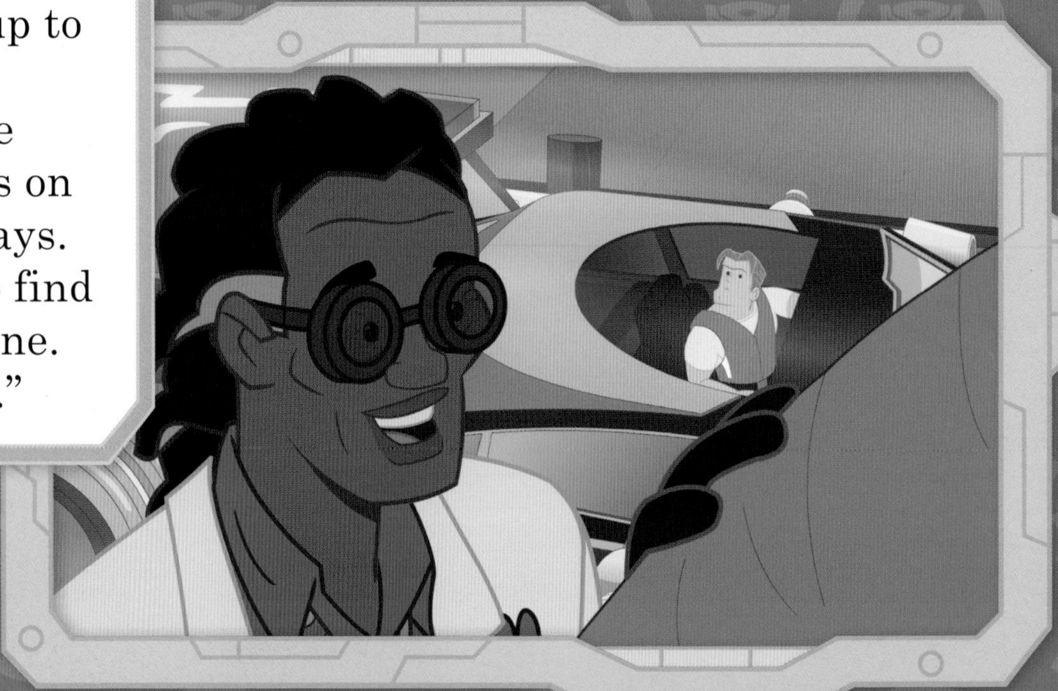

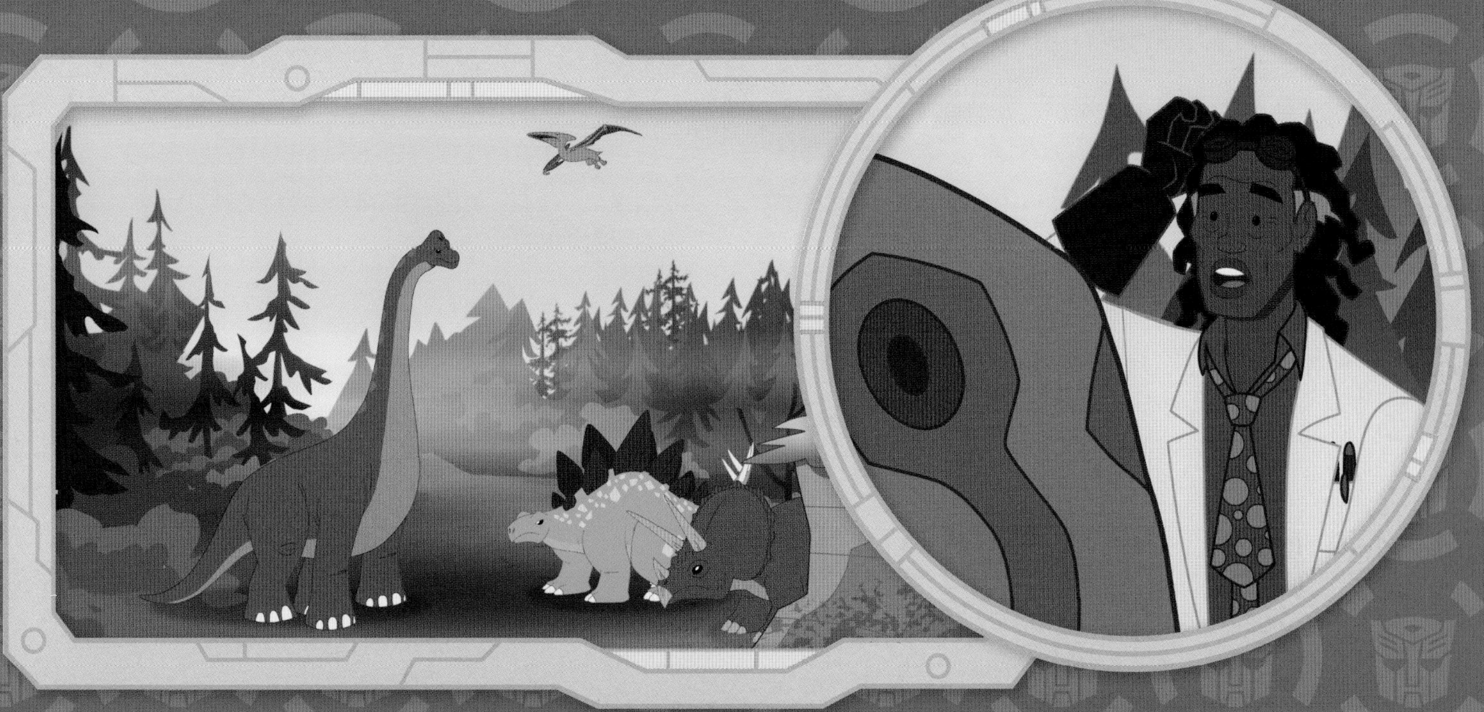

The doctor and the Dino Bot head deep into the dense jungle. When they reach a clearing, they see an astounding sight—real live dinosaurs!

"Great thunder lizards!" shouts Doc Greene.

A large tyrannosaur sees Doc Greene and charges at him! Trex tries to help but gets trapped by falling rocks!

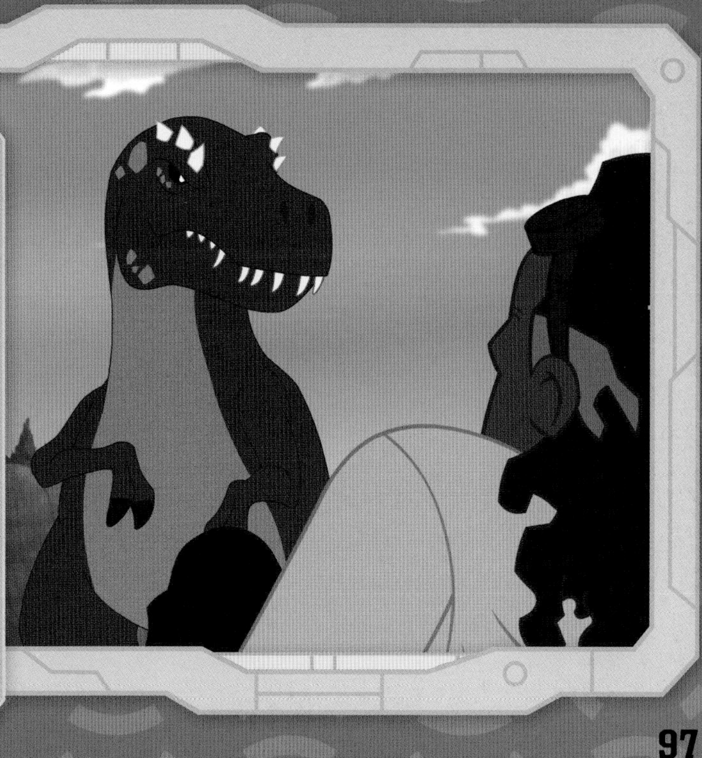

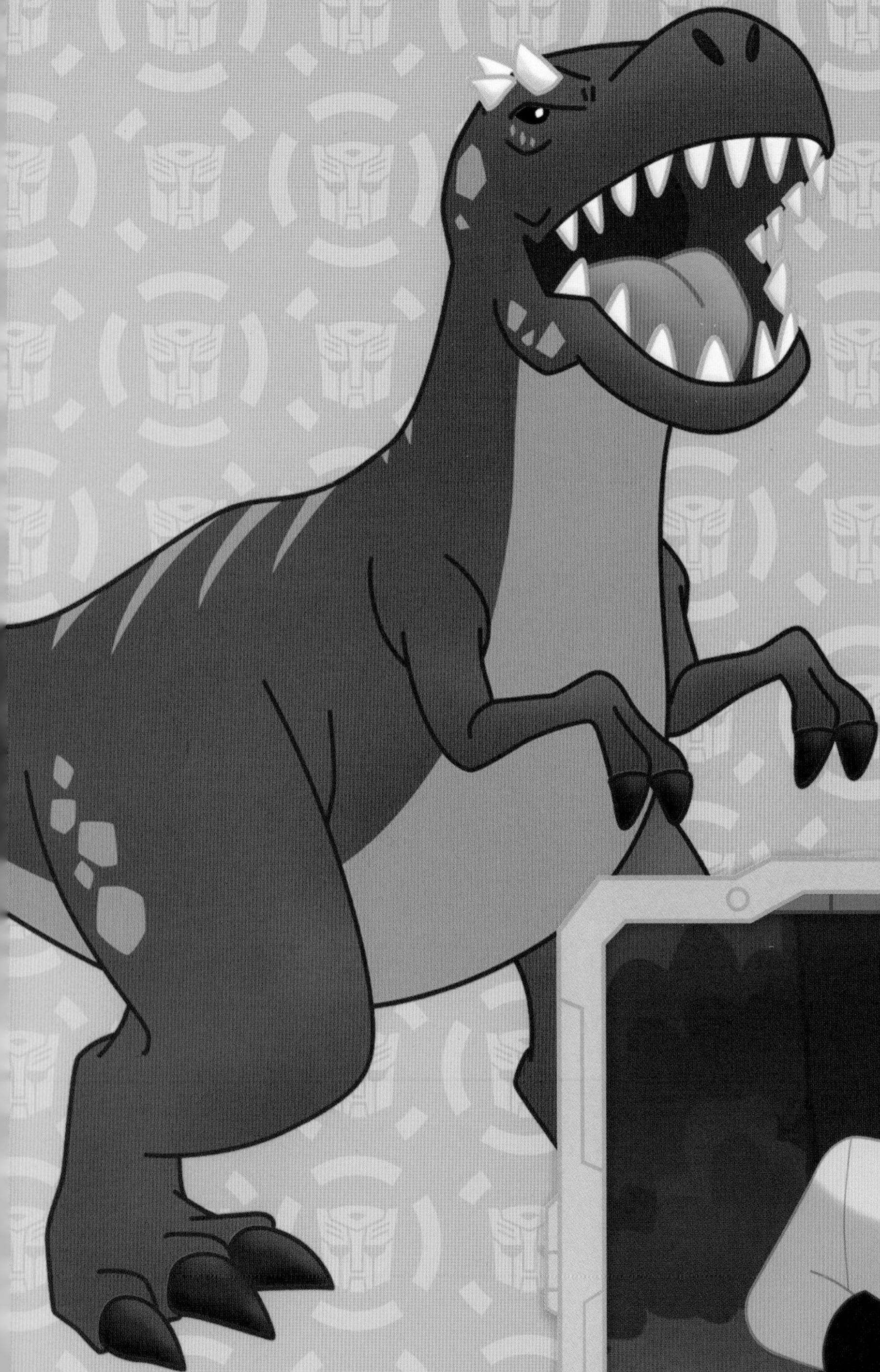

While running away, Doc Greene gets lost in the jungle-like plants. He stops to catch his breath and hears a sound among the trees.

At first, he thinks Trex has escaped from the rockslide. But it's the real tyrannosaur roaring with rage!

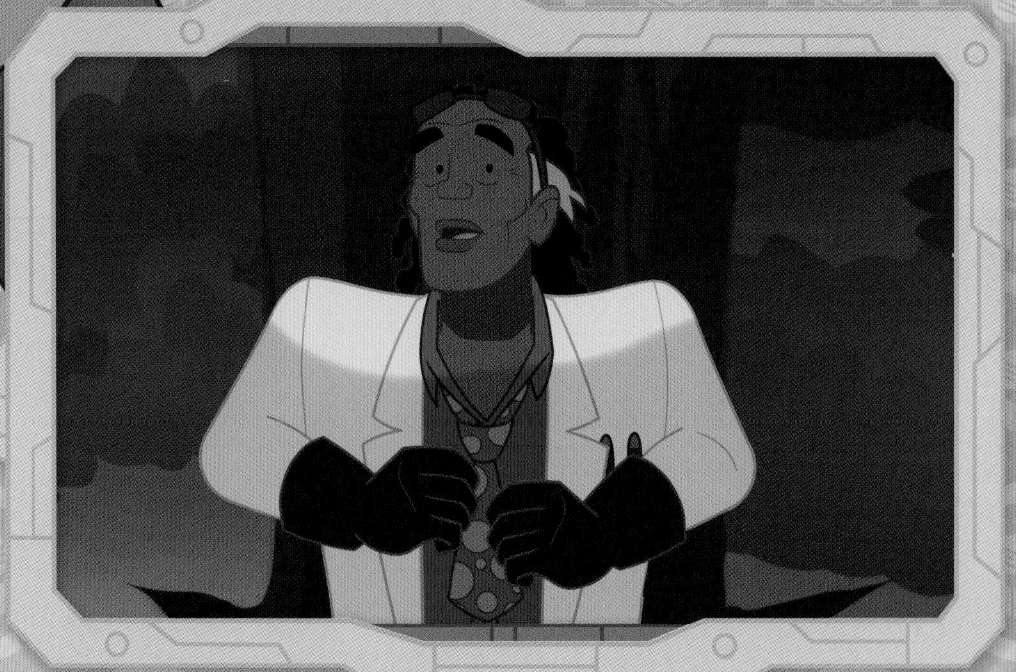

Heatwave springs into action and sprays the dinosaur with his water blasters. “Back off, scaly!” he shouts.

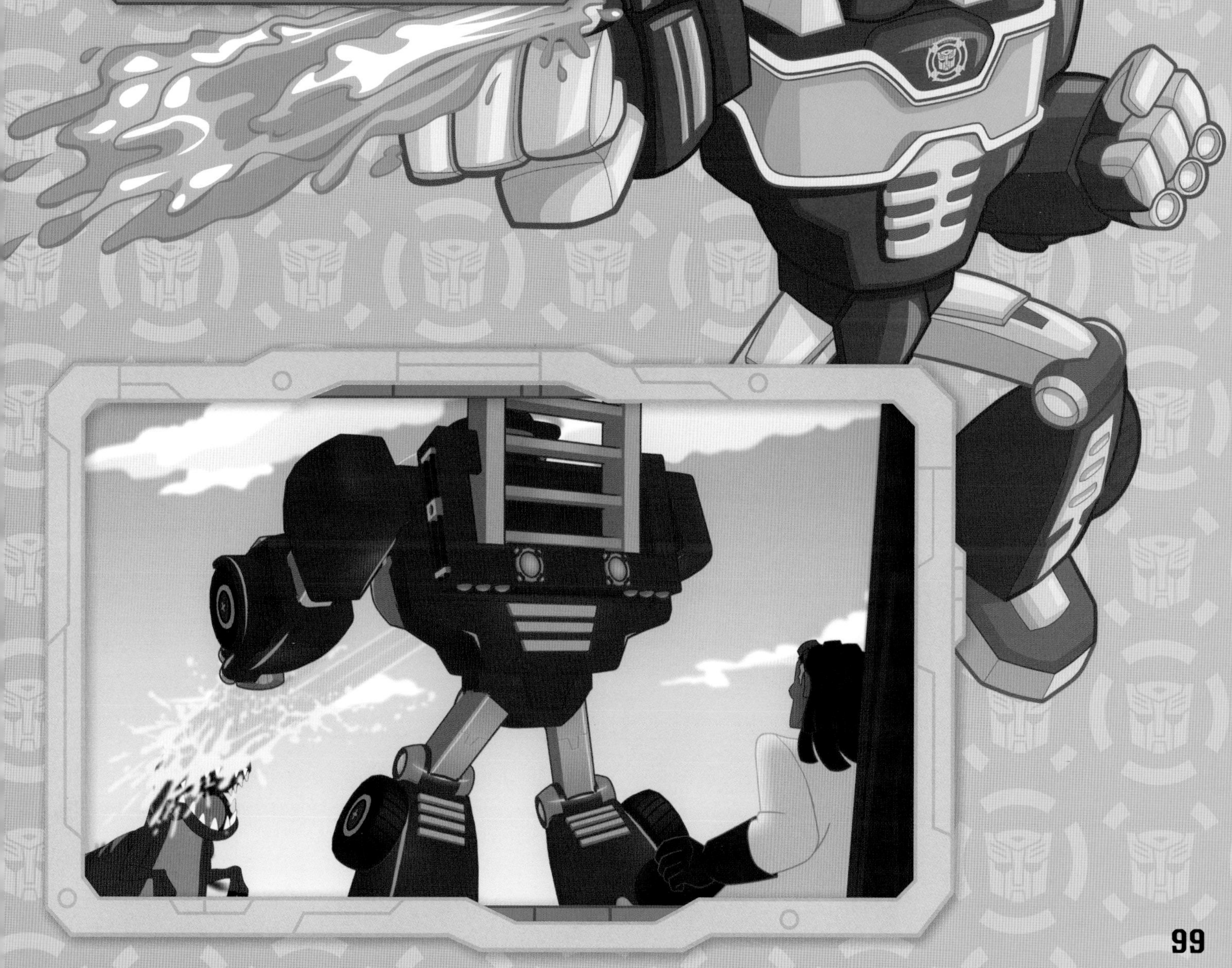

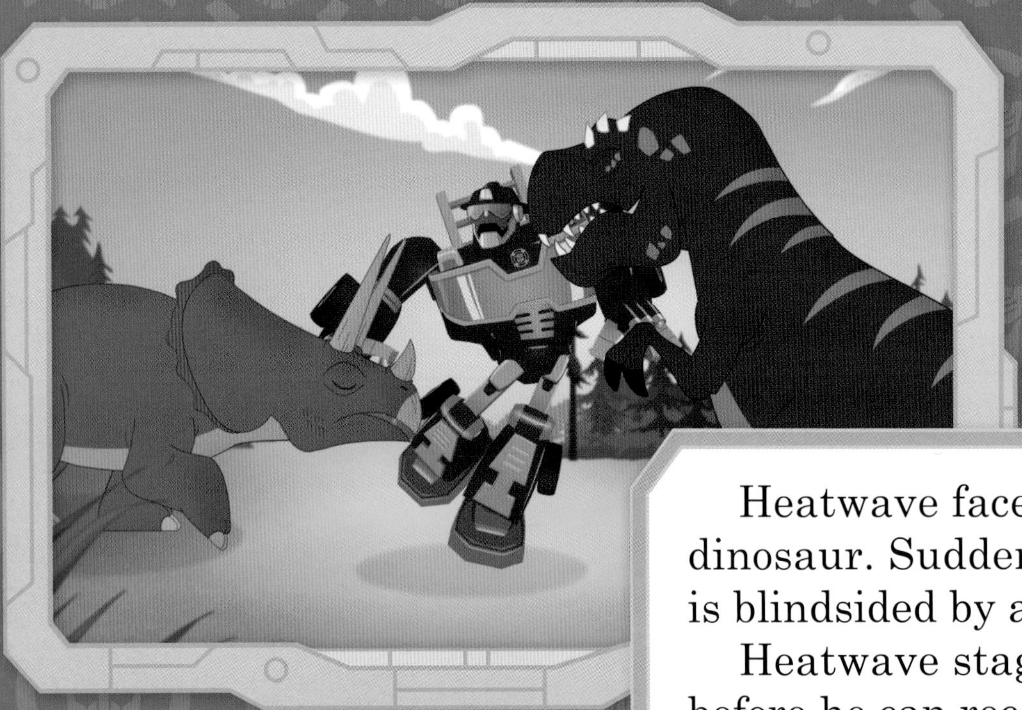

Heatwave faces off against the dinosaur. Suddenly, the Rescue Bot is blindsided by a triceratops. *Wham!*

Heatwave staggers back, and before he can recover, he is ambushed by a stegosaur! It lashes Heatwave with its tail. *Bam!*

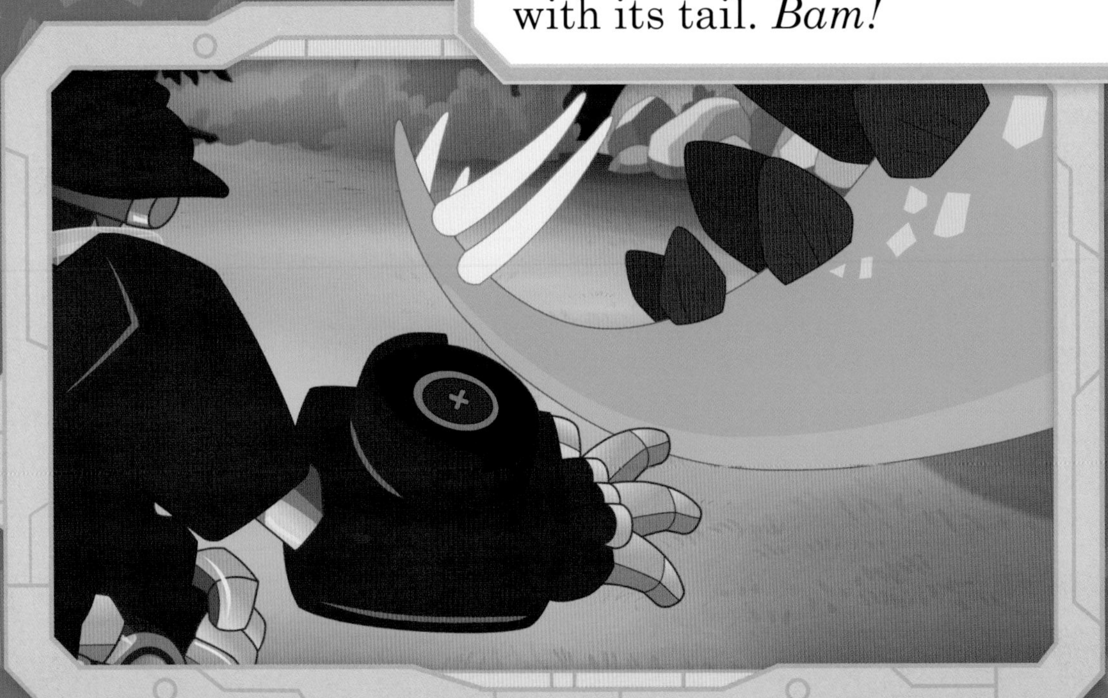

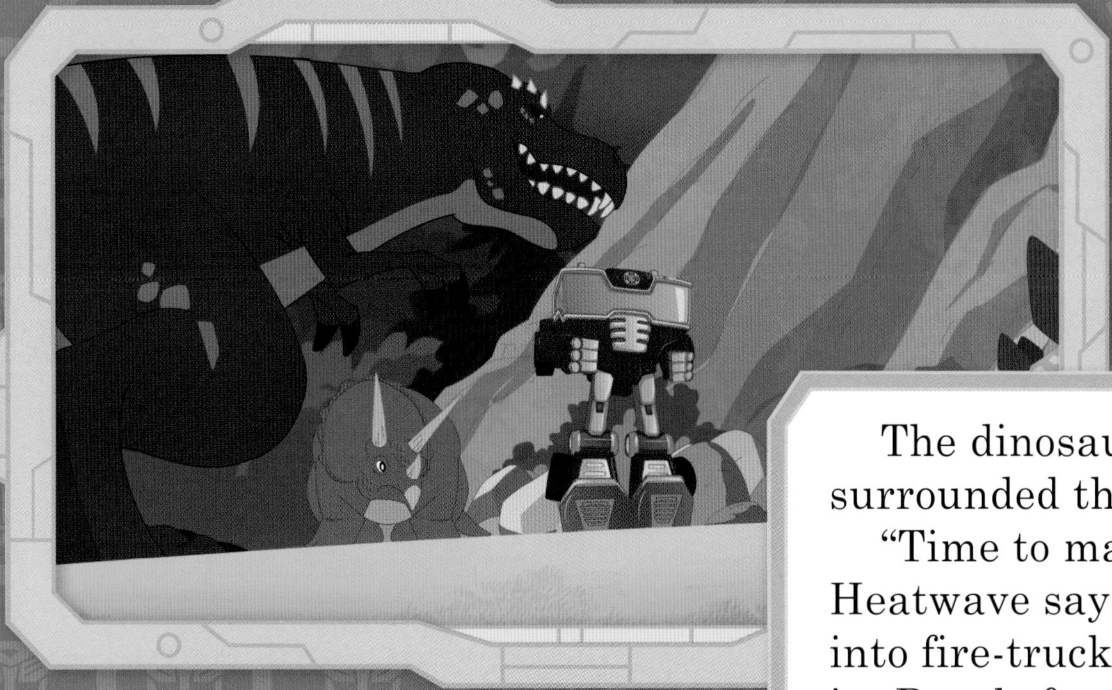

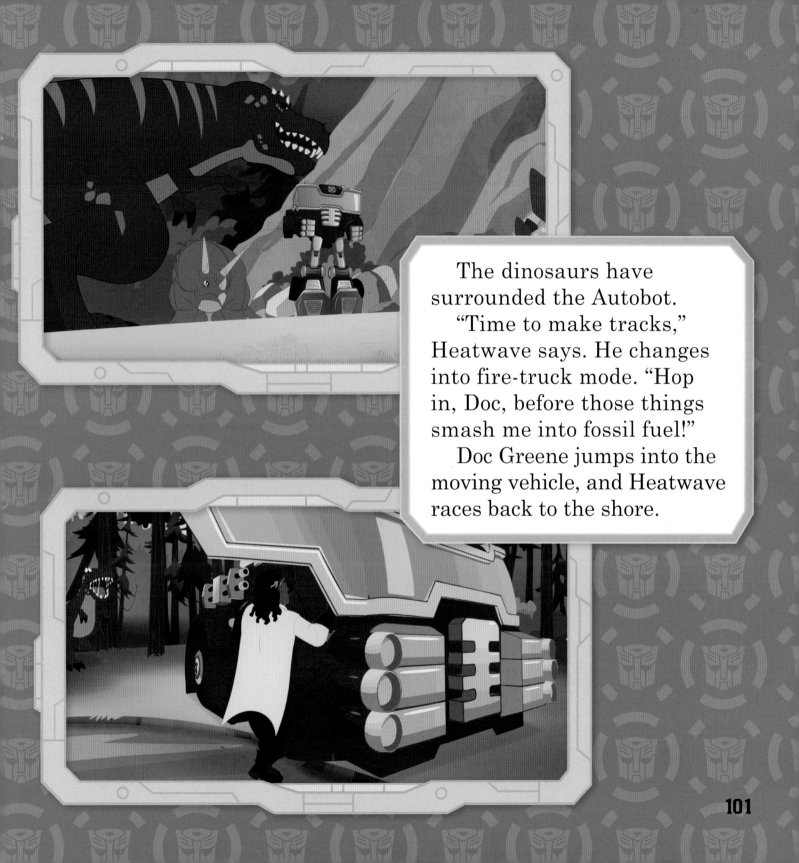

The dinosaurs have surrounded the Autobot.

"Time to make tracks," Heatwave says. He changes into fire-truck mode. "Hop in, Doc, before those things smash me into fossil fuel!"

Doc Greene jumps into the moving vehicle, and Heatwave races back to the shore.

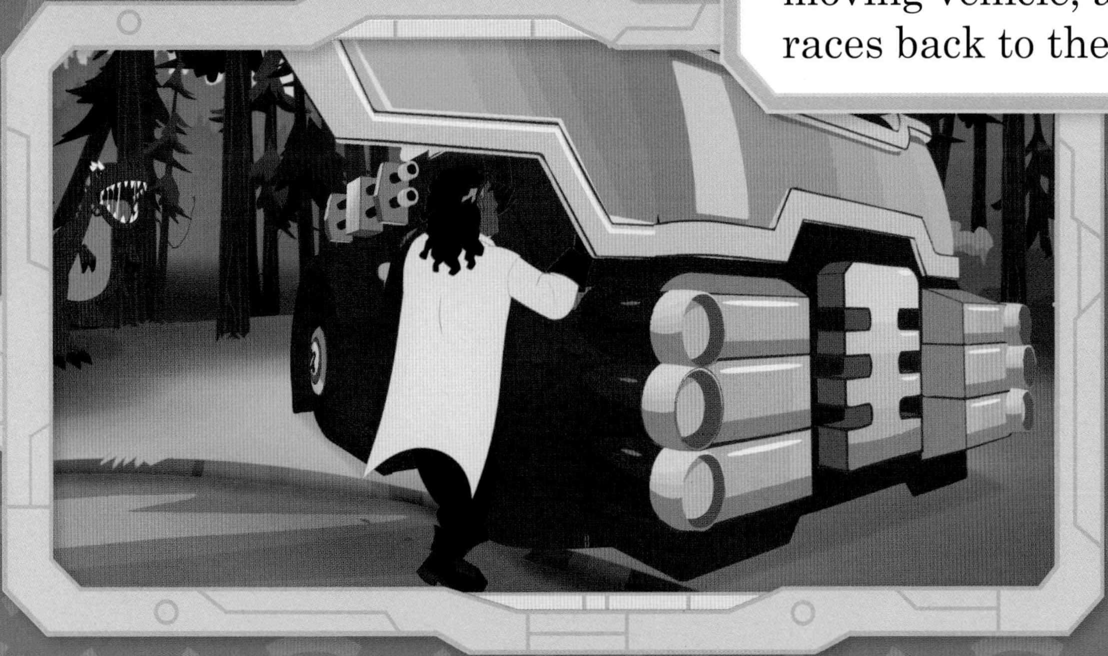

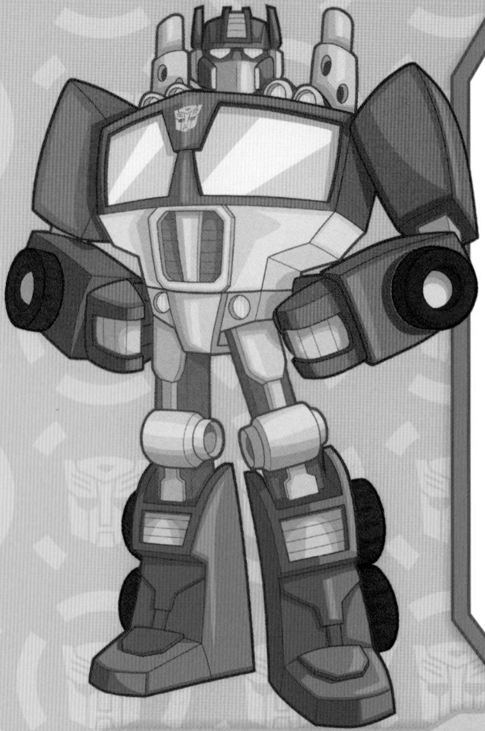

Meanwhile, Optimus Prime arrives at headquarters. “I heard about the subterranean passage and came to oversee the mission,” he says. “Those dinosaurs could have been living underground for millions of years!”

All of a sudden, a distress call from Kade comes in. “The dinosaurs are acting up, and we’re in trouble!” he says.

Optimus Prime deploys the rest of the team. “Rescue Bots, roll to the rescue!” he commands. Only he and Cody stay behind.

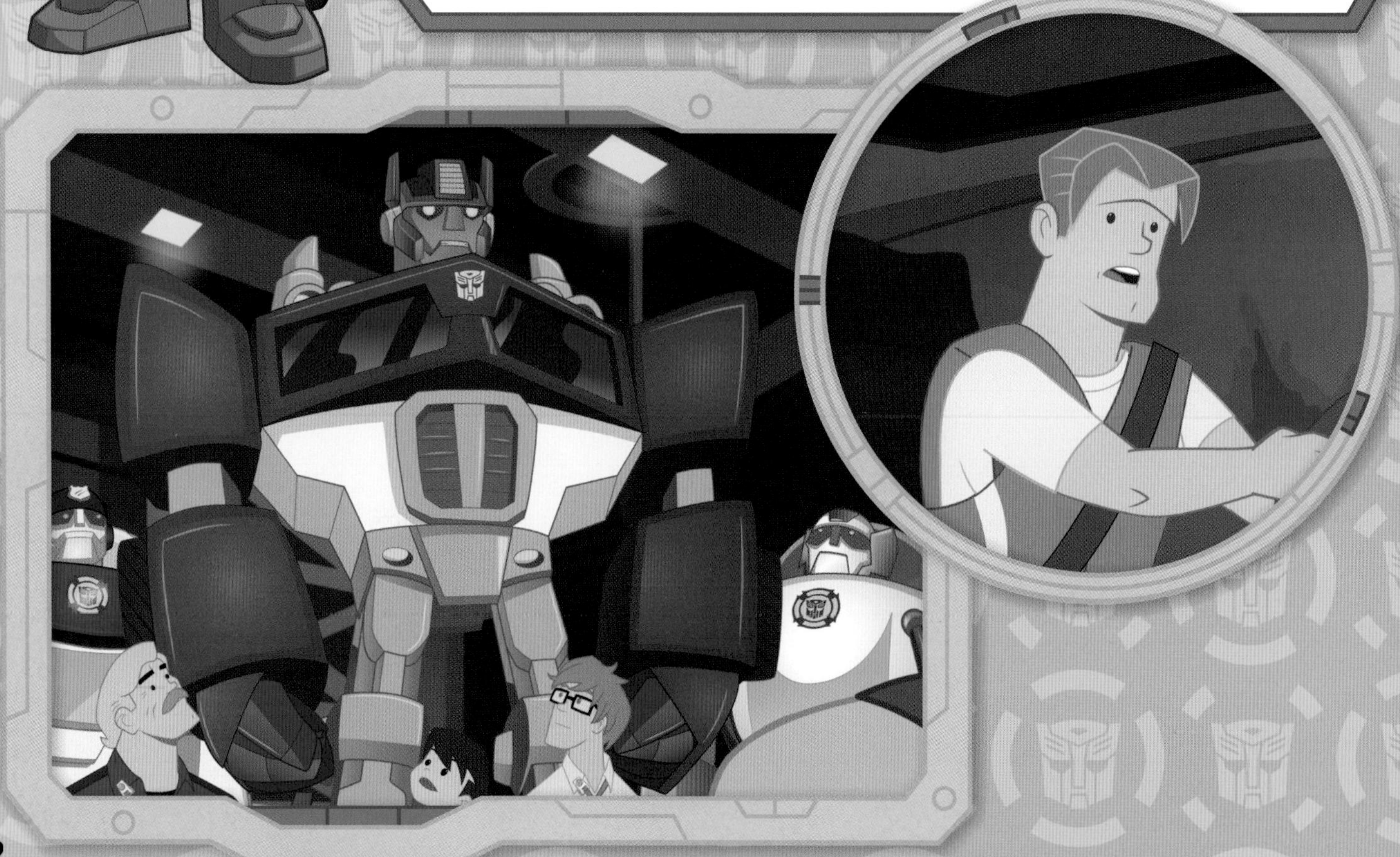

Once the entire team arrives at Wayward Island, Heatwave and Doc Greene lead them into the jungle.

"The dinosaurs tried to enter the passage, but a rockslide occurred," says Doc Greene. "Trex is trapped under some boulders. We have to save him and help the dinosaurs get home!"

The heroes find Trex, but as soon as they approach, they hear a terrible roar!

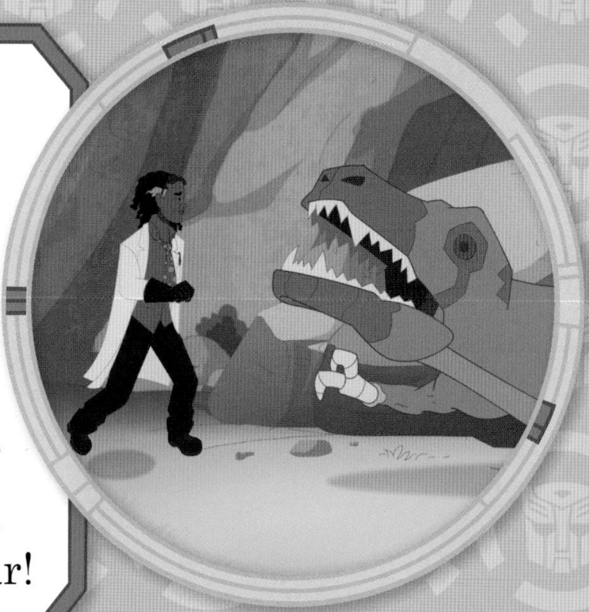

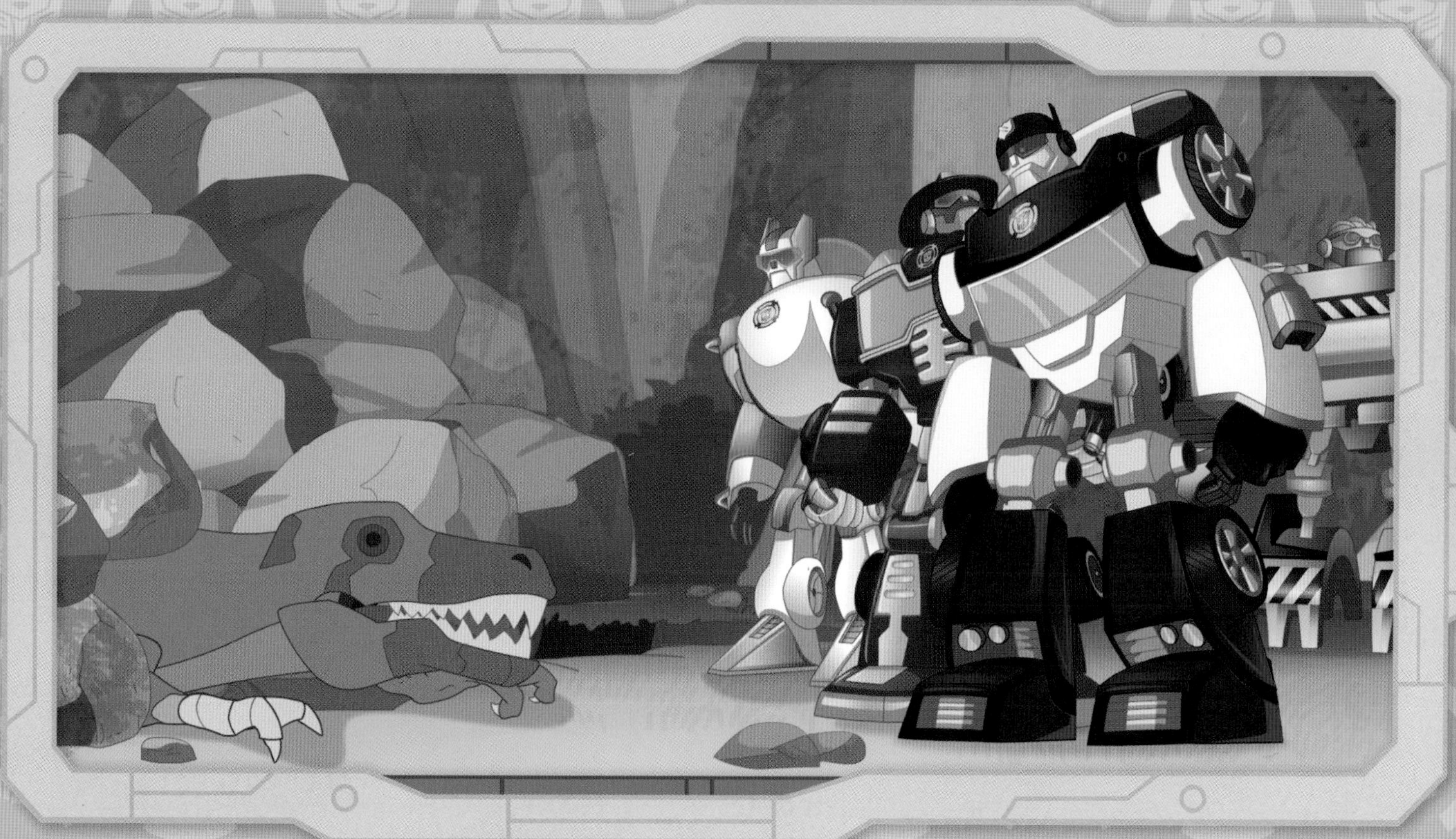

The tyrannosaur has returned, and he's brought his friends along for another fight!

"Stop! We're trying to help you!" cries Heatwave as a brachiosaur slams him into the ground. A triceratops locks its horns with Boulder, a stegosaur gets ready to slam Chase, and the pterodactyl stalks Blades.

"Fall back and regroup!" Heatwave shouts. The Rescue Bots change into vehicles and retreat from the rumble.

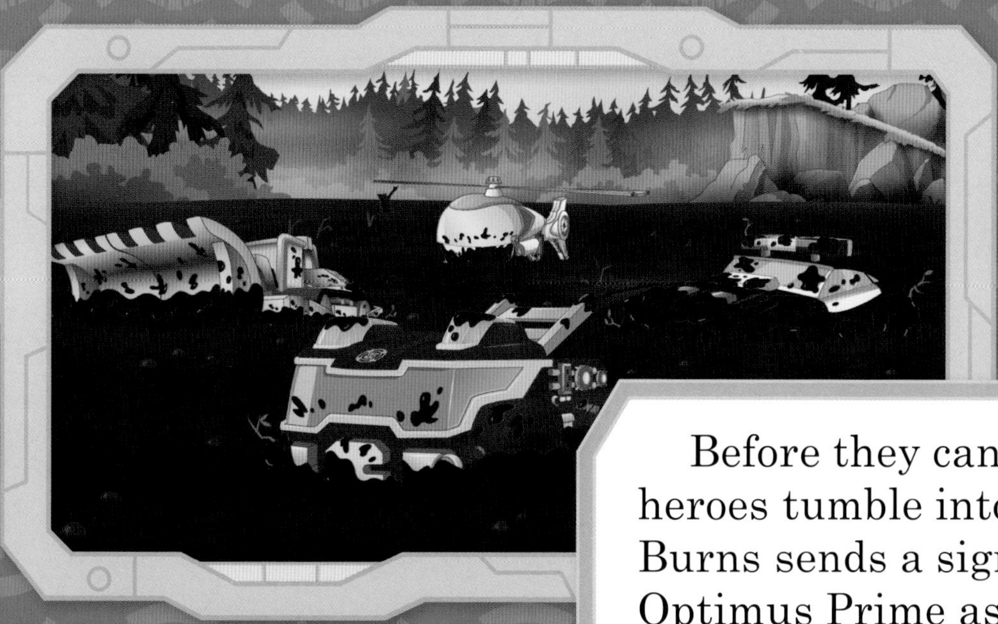

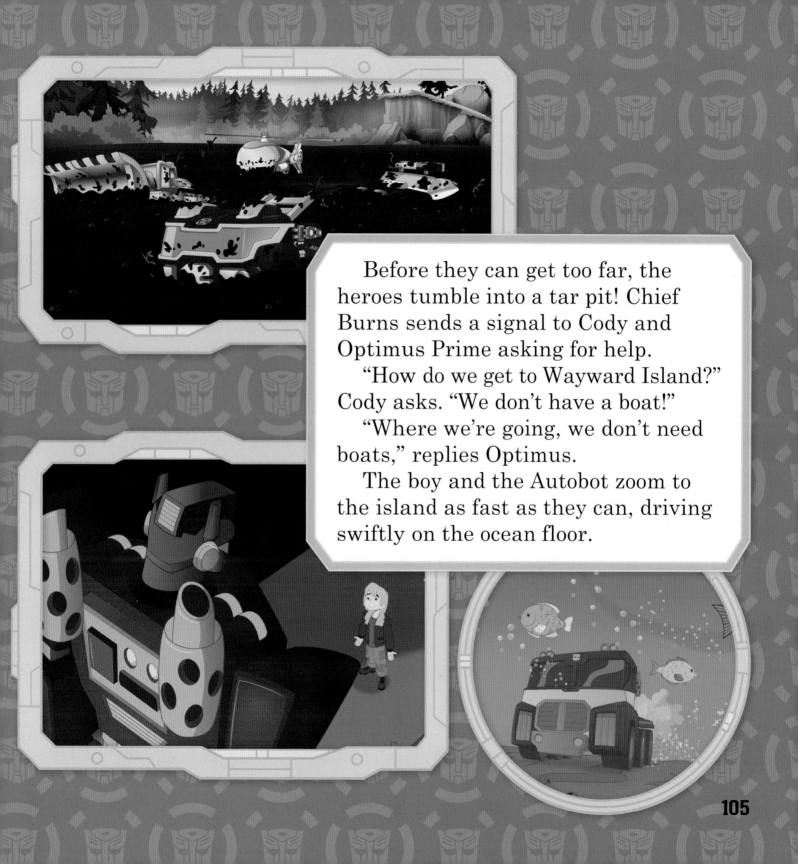

Before they can get too far, the heroes tumble into a tar pit! Chief Burns sends a signal to Cody and Optimus Prime asking for help.

"How do we get to Wayward Island?" Cody asks. "We don't have a boat!"

"Where we're going, we don't need boats," replies Optimus.

The boy and the Autobot zoom to the island as fast as they can, driving swiftly on the ocean floor.

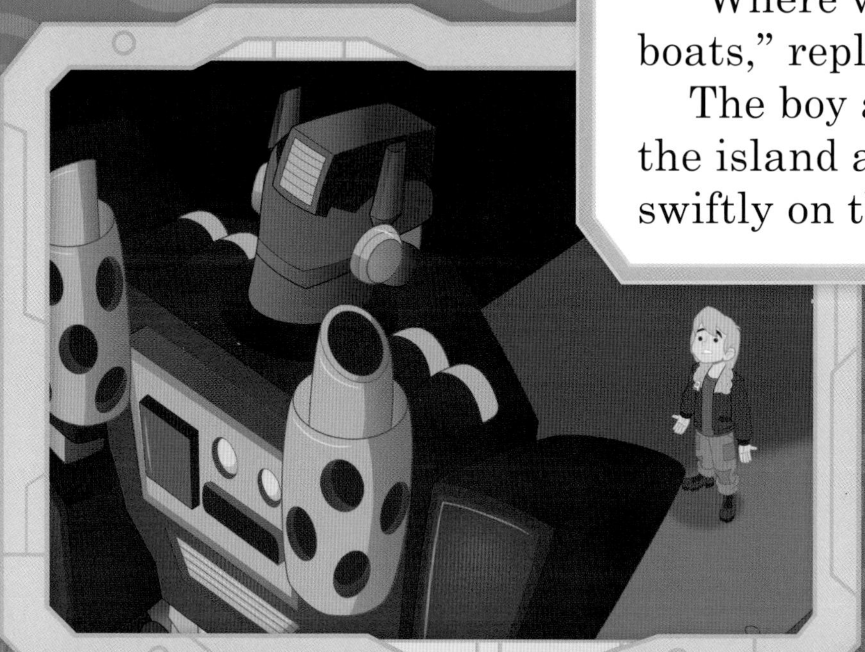

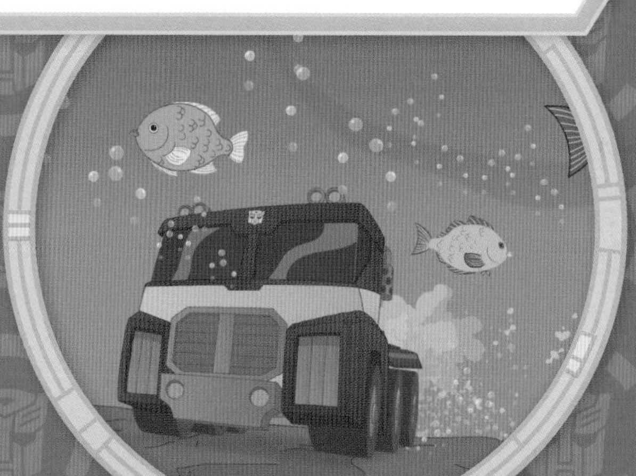

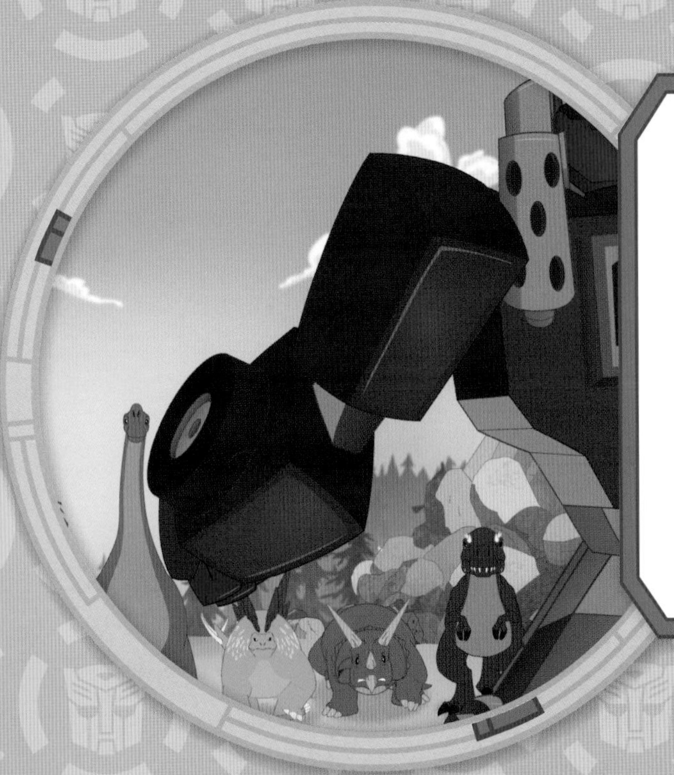

When Cody and Optimus arrive, they find the team trapped in the tar pit, surrounded by dinosaurs.

"How can we help them if the dinos won't let us through?" Cody asks.

"These creatures view anything not a dinosaur as a threat," answers Optimus. Then, he has an idea. "Perhaps Trex can help *us*!"

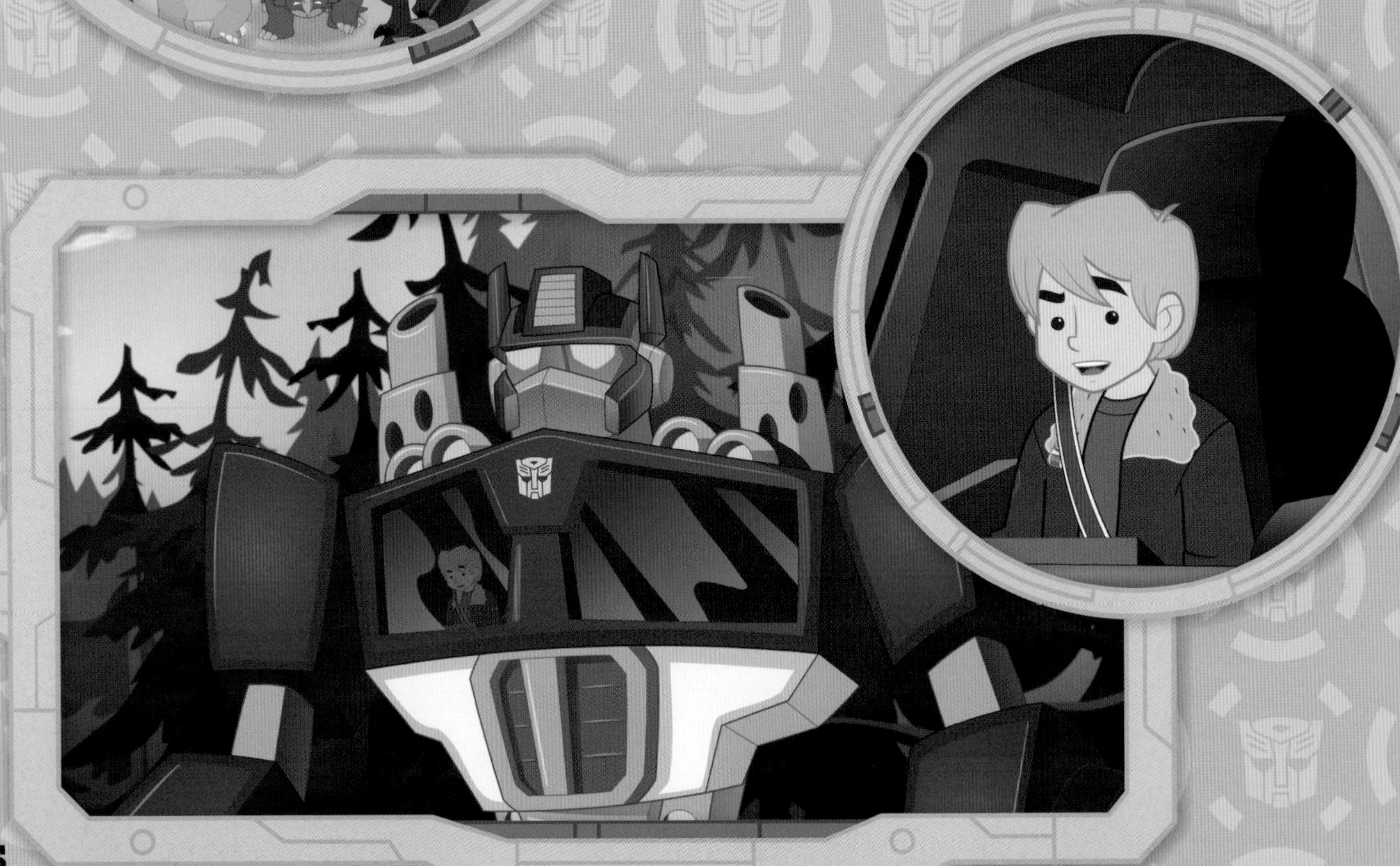

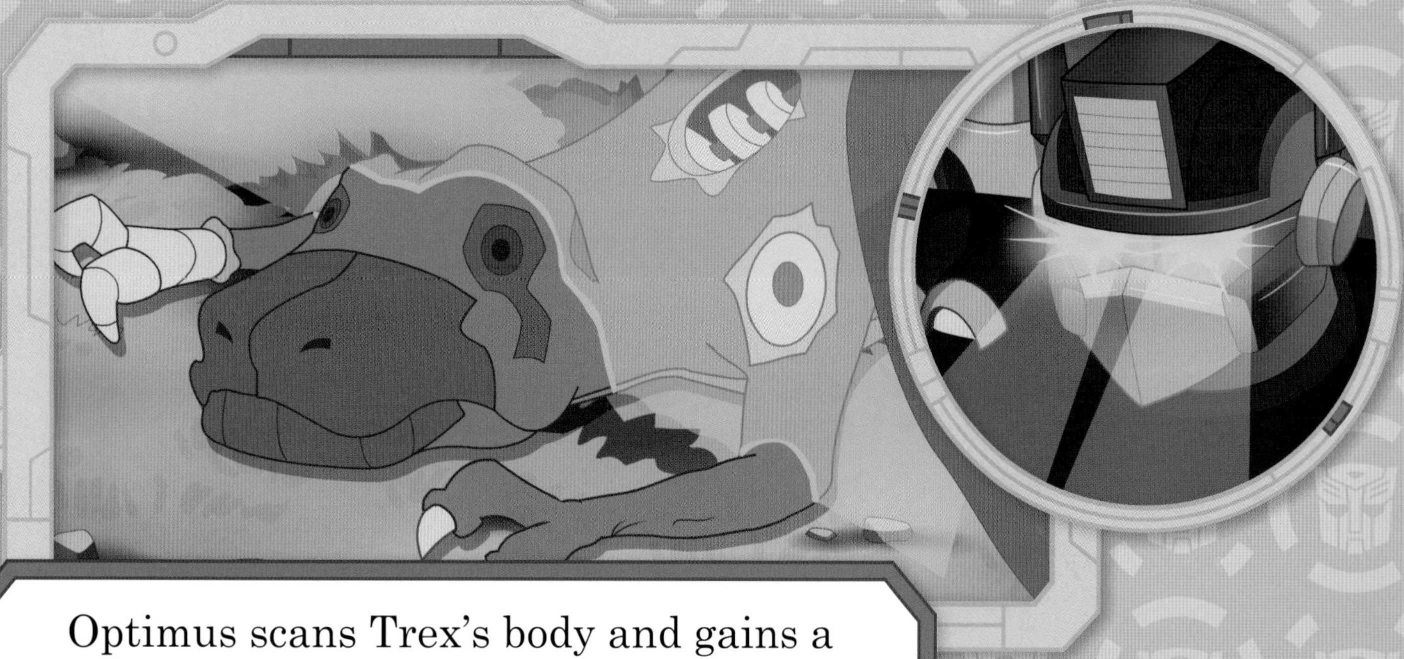

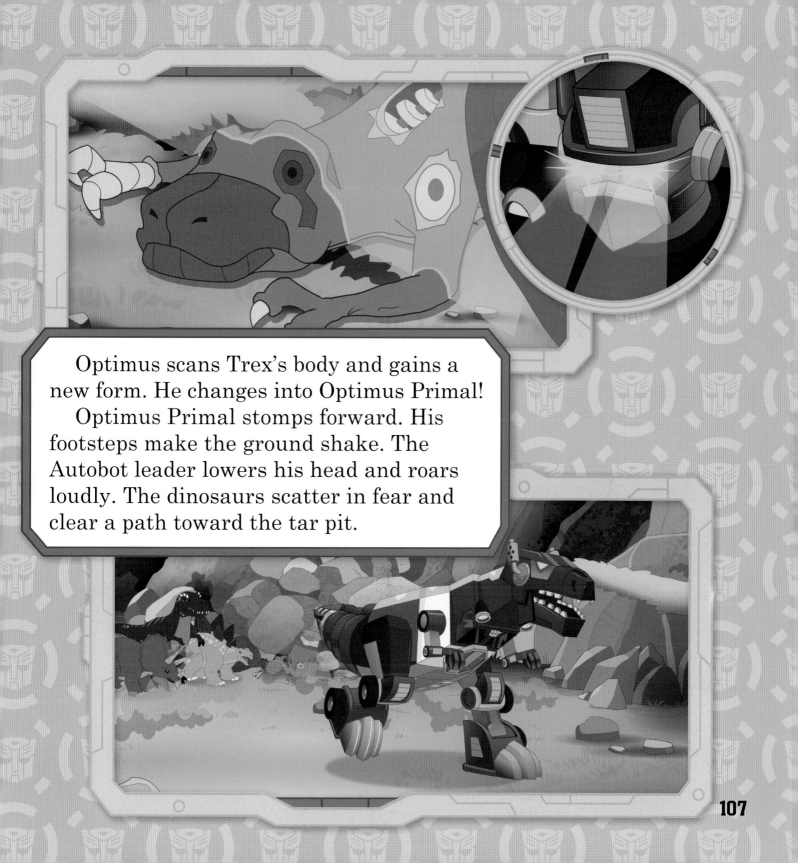

Optimus scans Trex's body and gains a new form. He changes into Optimus Primal!

Optimus Primal stomps forward. His footsteps make the ground shake. The Autobot leader lowers his head and roars loudly. The dinosaurs scatter in fear and clear a path toward the tar pit.

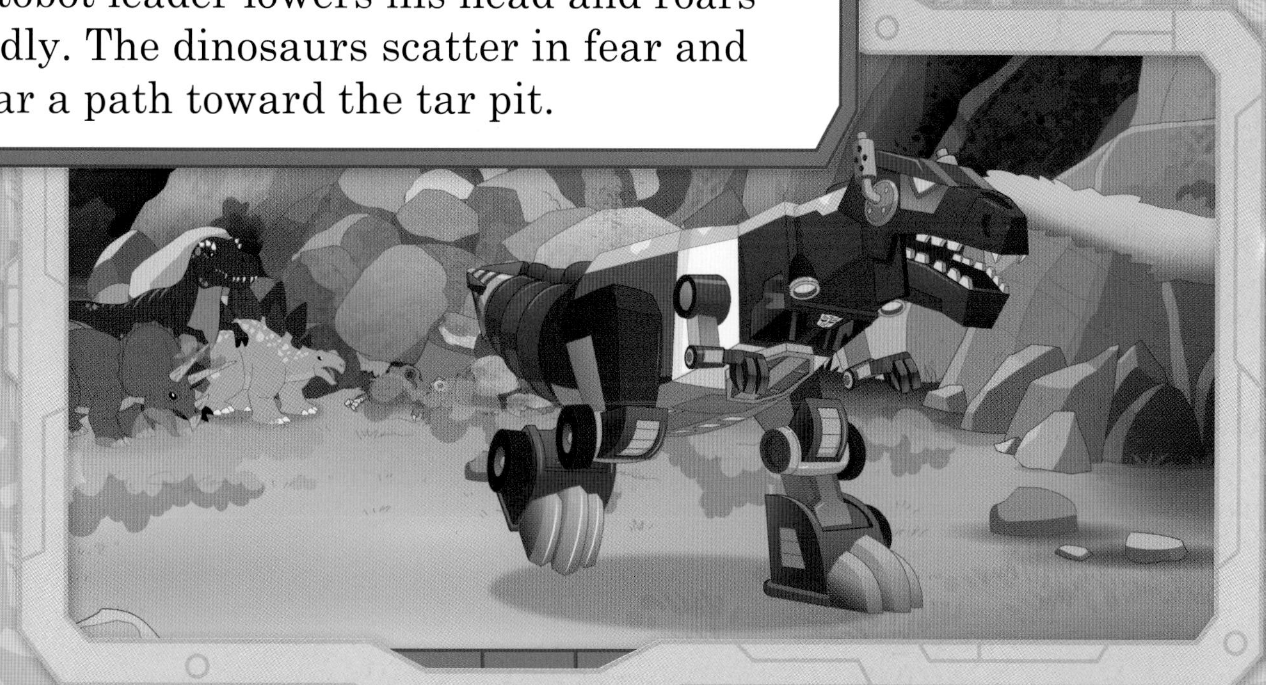

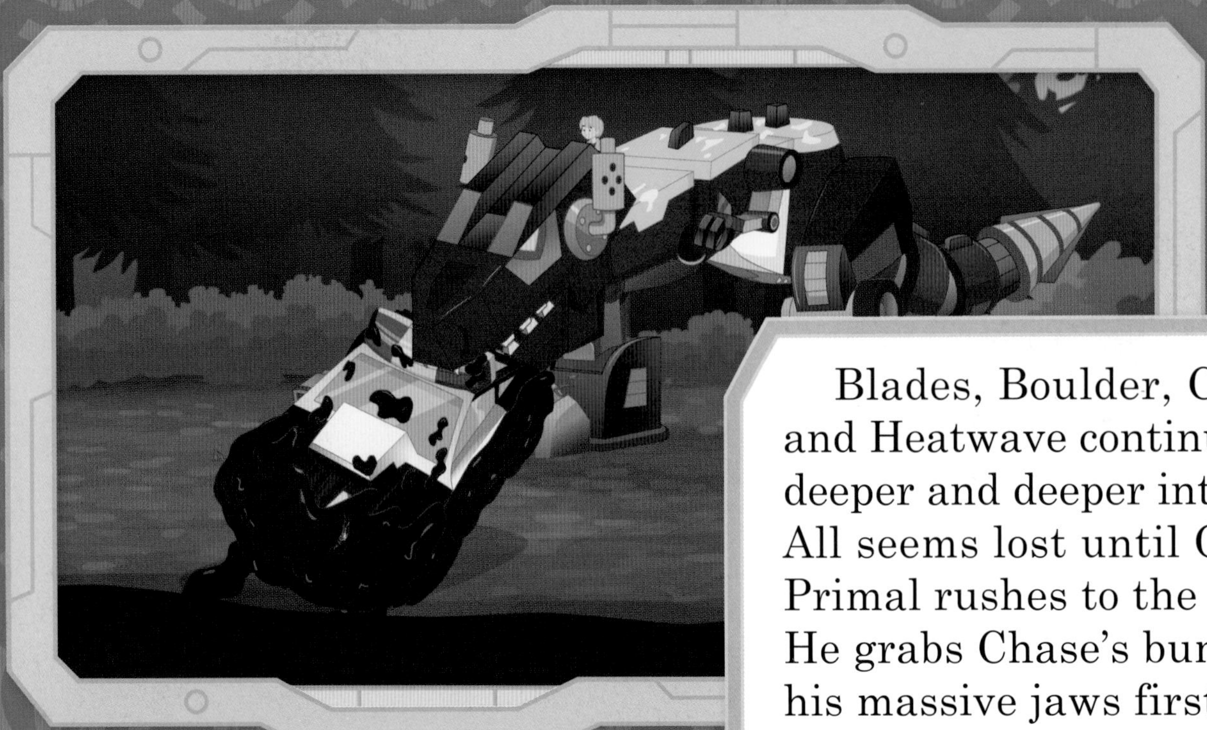

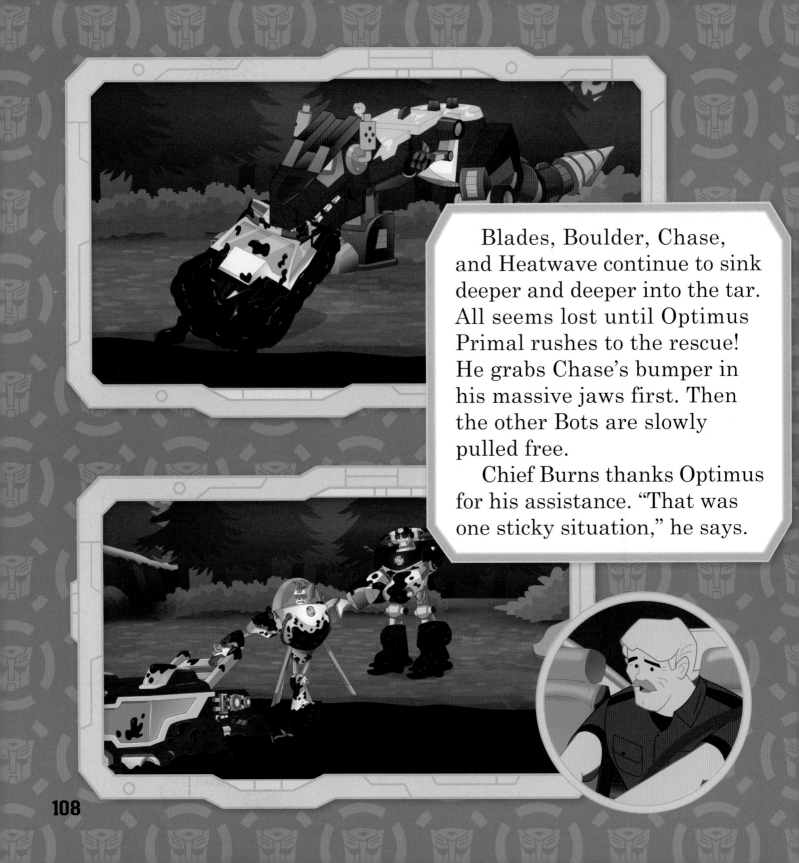

Blades, Boulder, Chase, and Heatwave continue to sink deeper and deeper into the tar. All seems lost until Optimus Primal rushes to the rescue! He grabs Chase's bumper in his massive jaws first. Then the other Bots are slowly pulled free.

Chief Burns thanks Optimus for his assistance. "That was one sticky situation," he says.

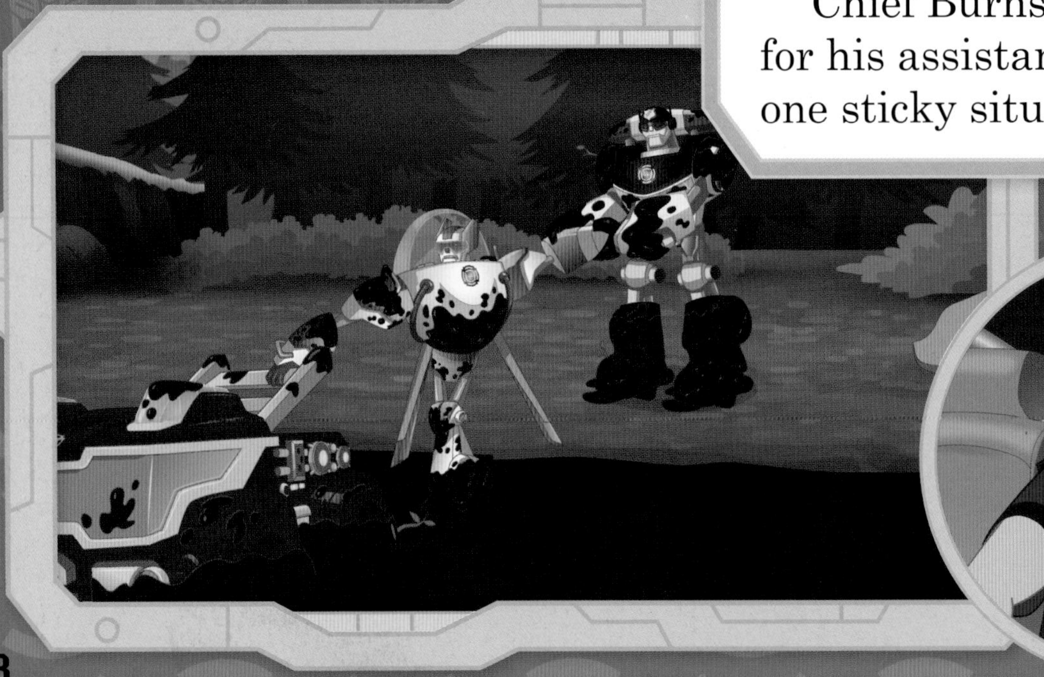

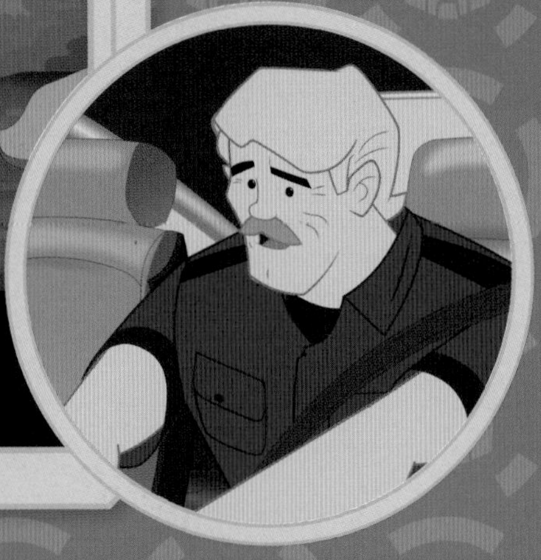

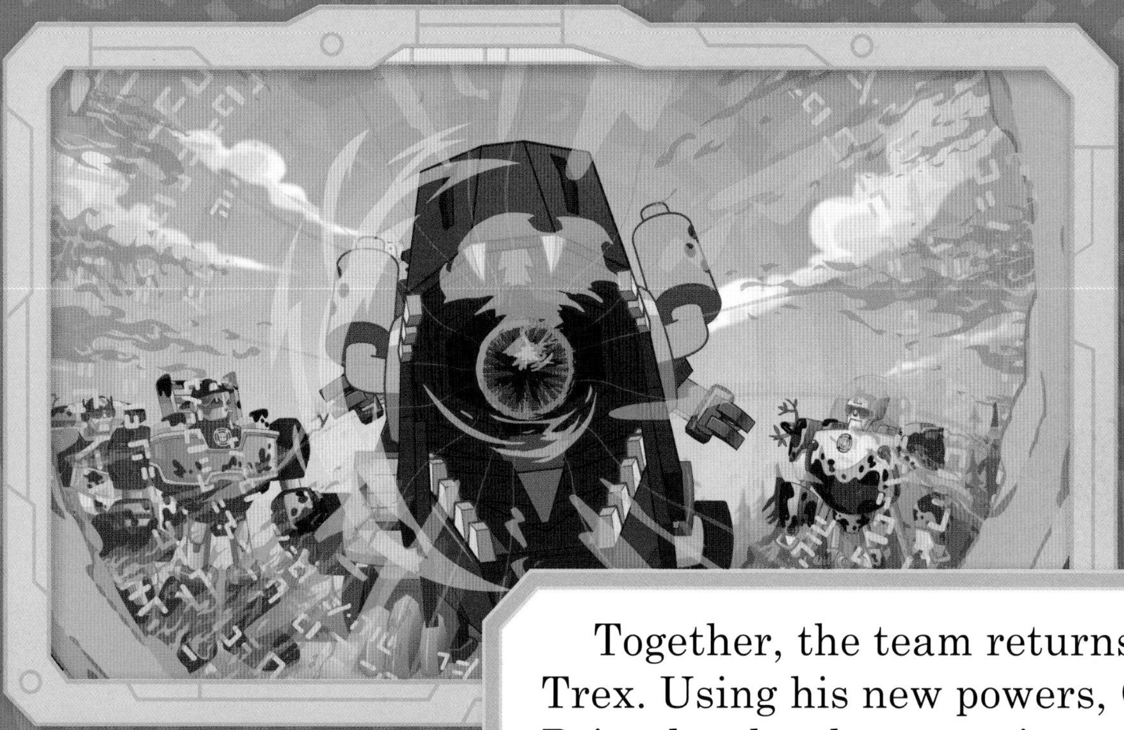

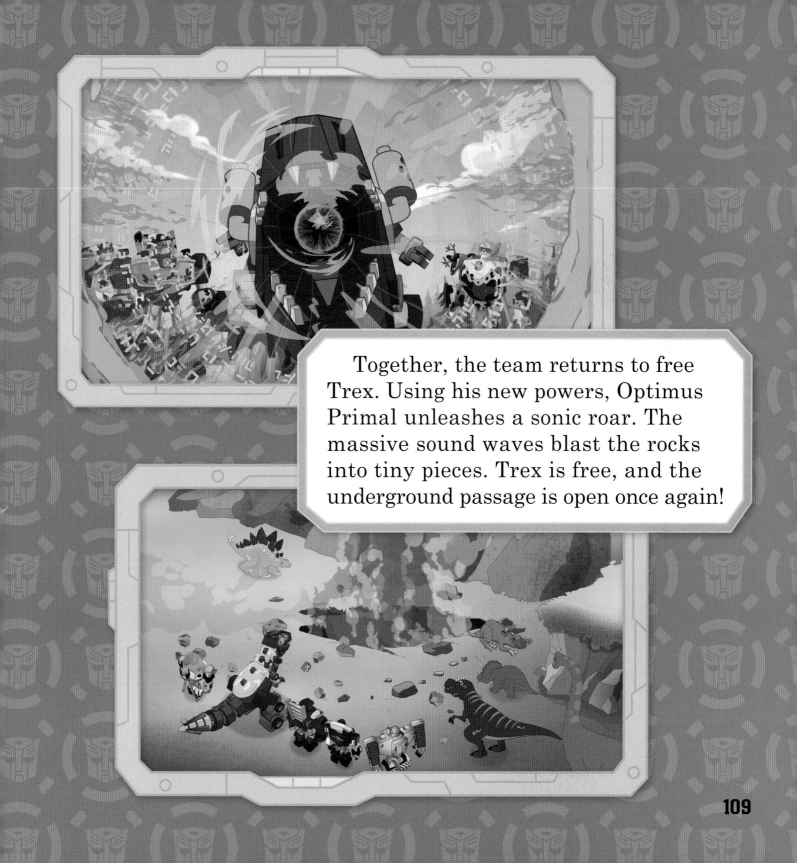

Together, the team returns to free Trex. Using his new powers, Optimus Primal unleashes a sonic roar. The massive sound waves blast the rocks into tiny pieces. Trex is free, and the underground passage is open once again!

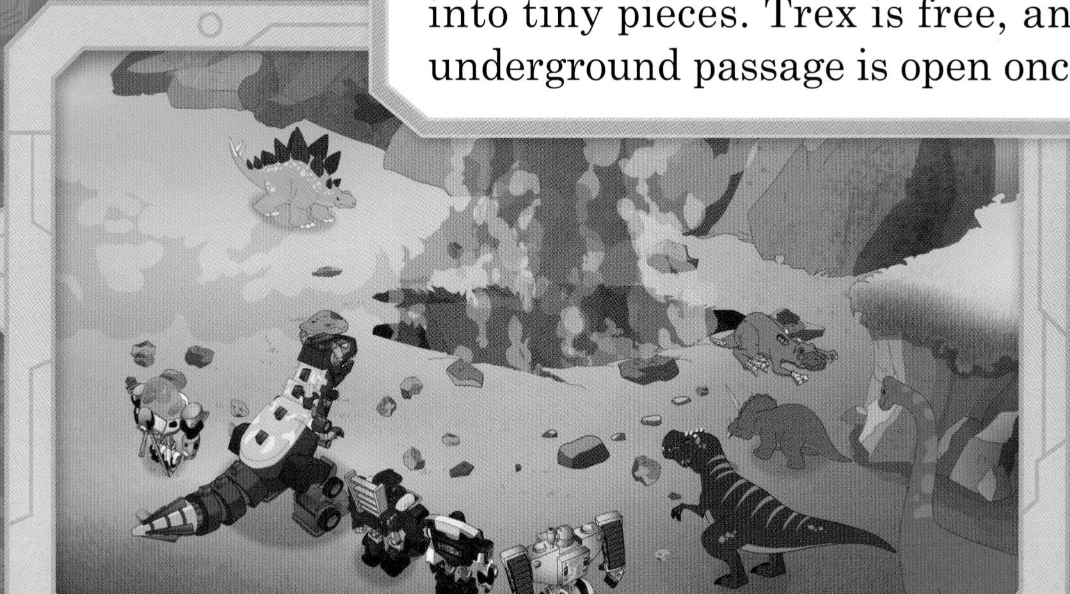

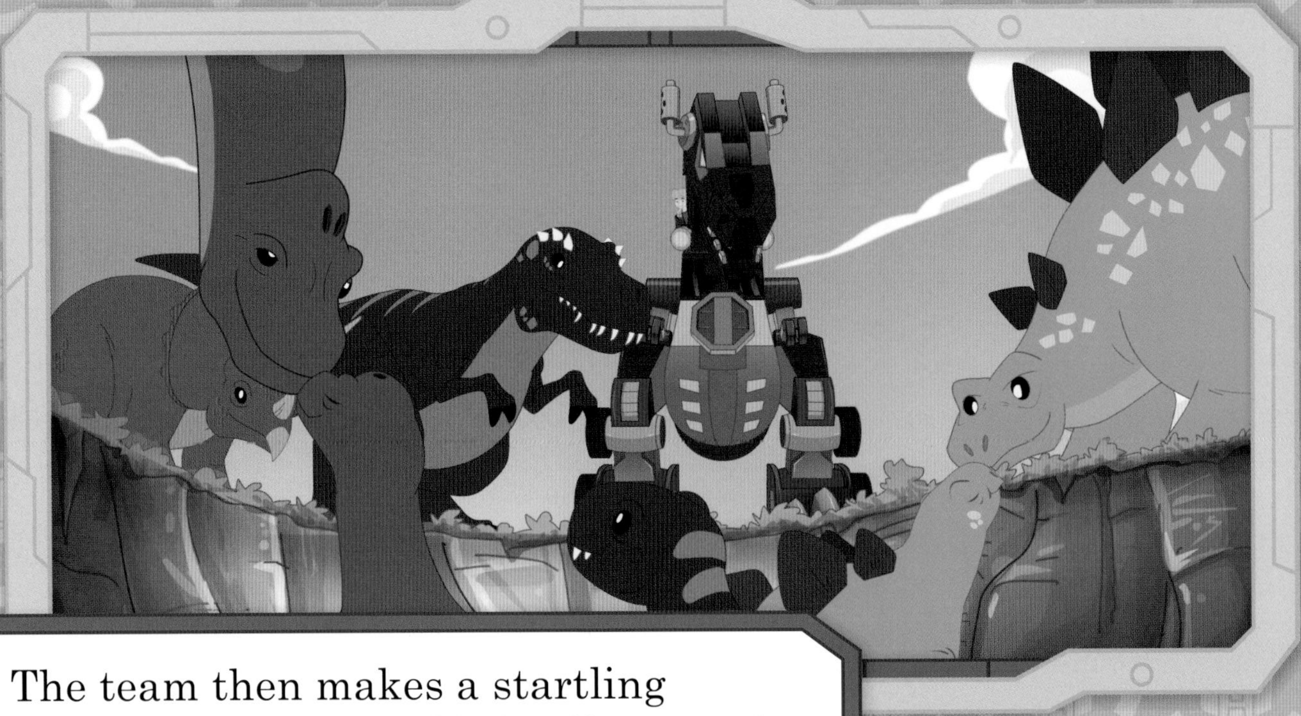

The team then makes a startling discovery—a nest full of baby dinosaurs!

"This explains why the creatures emerged," says Optimus Primal. "They were foraging for food for their young."

"They are *so* cute!" Kade squeals. "Just look at 'em!"

"Let's seal up that crack so they can stay safe underground again," Graham says. Together, the Rescue Bots and their friends move the boulders back into place.

"Everyone to the boat," says Chief Burns when they are finished. "It's time this mission became prehistory!"

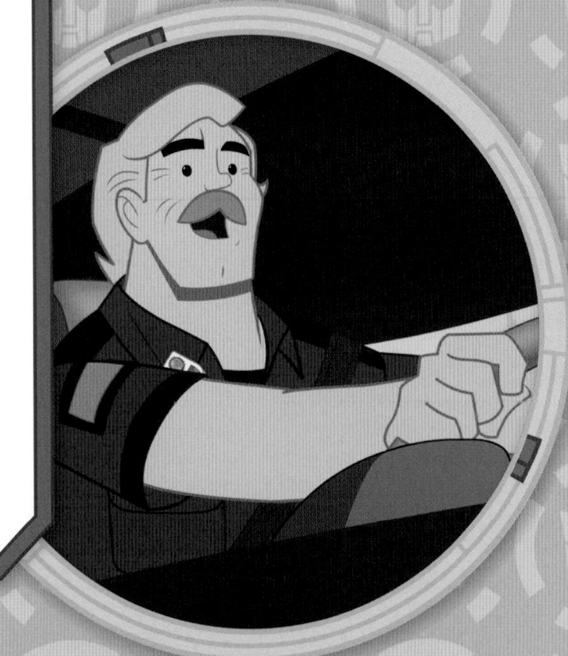

TRANSFORMERS
RESCUE BOTS

Blast Off!

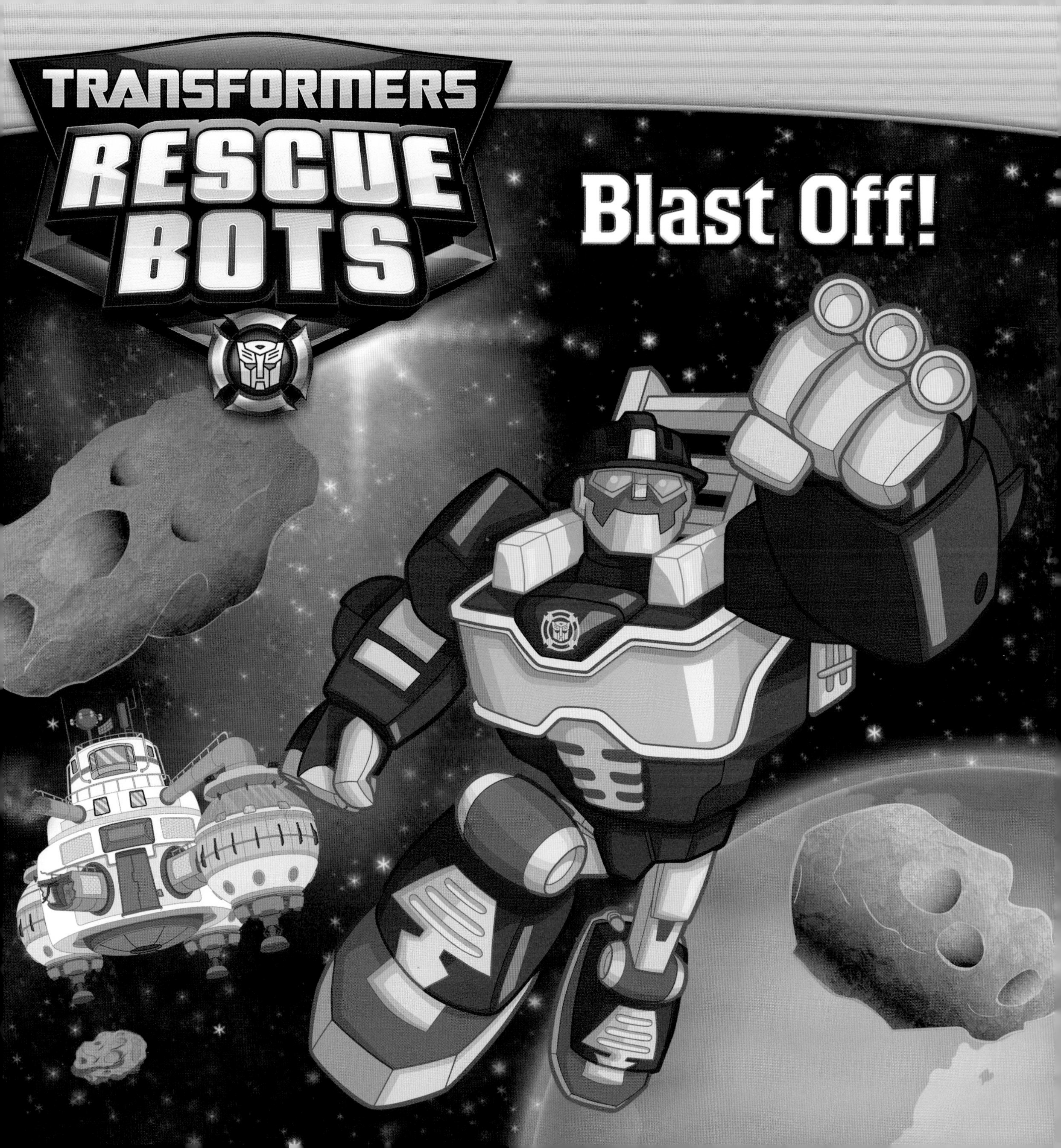

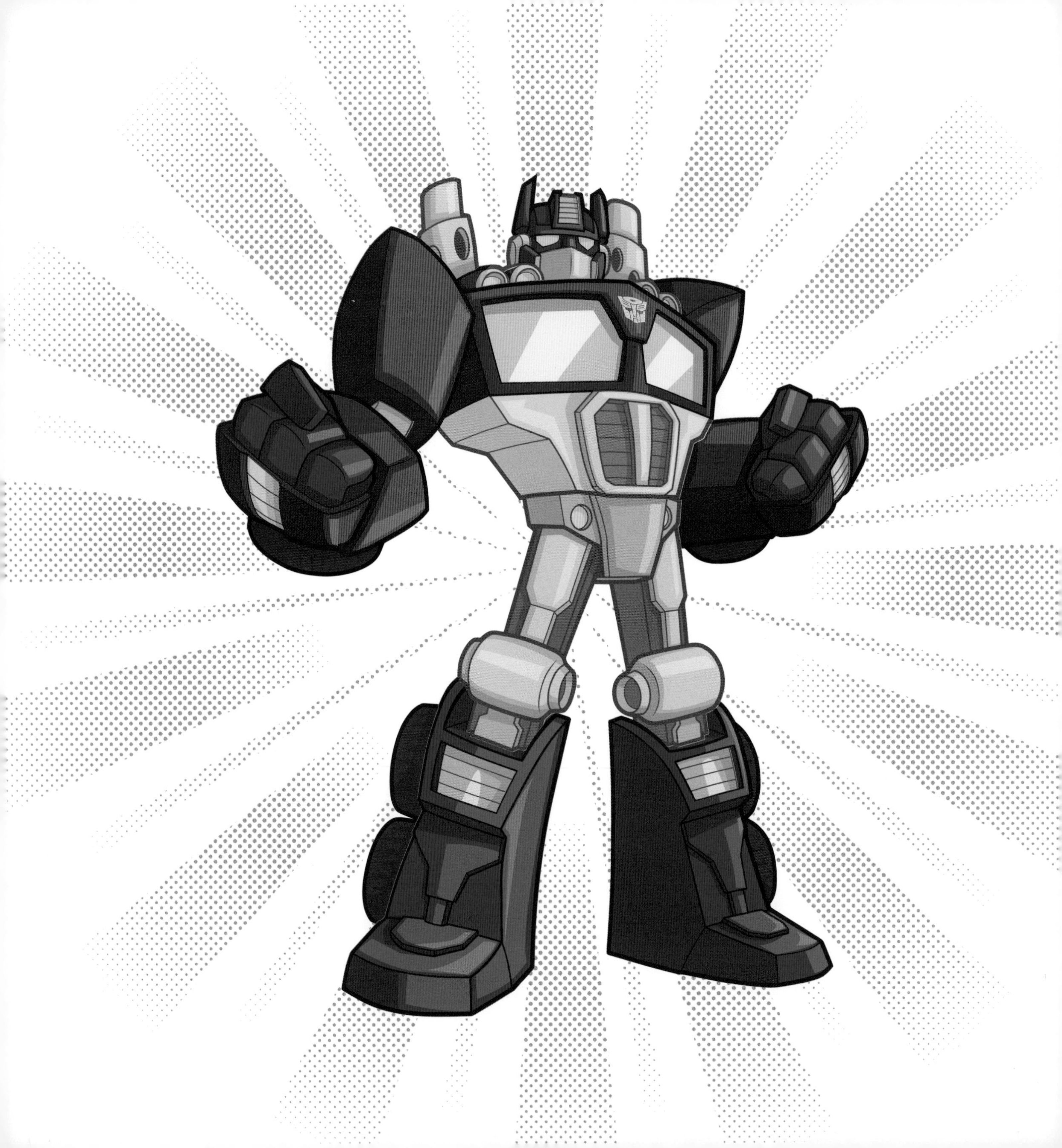

TRANSFORMERS RESCUE BOTS

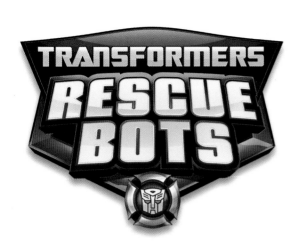

Blast Off!

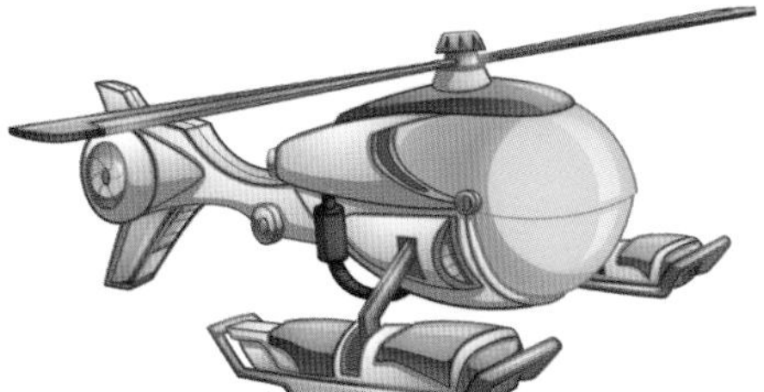

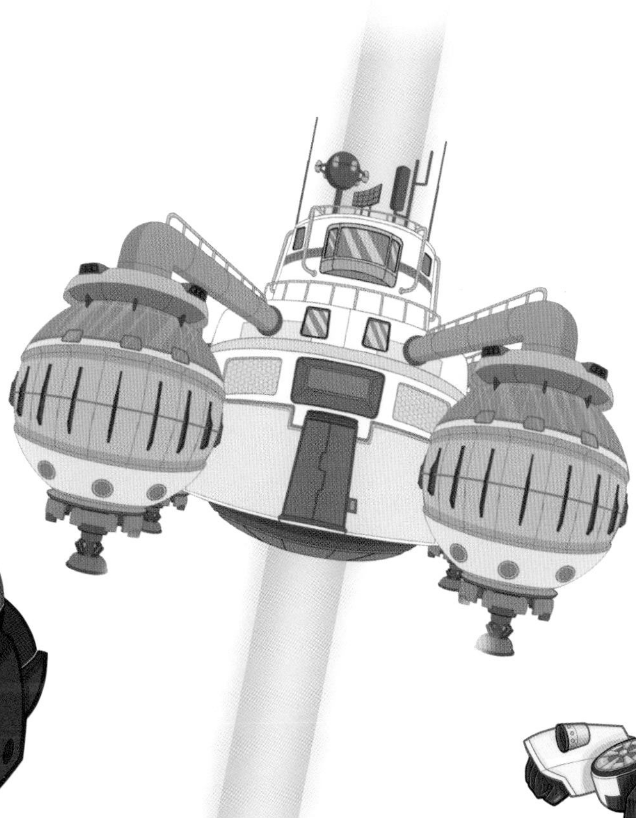

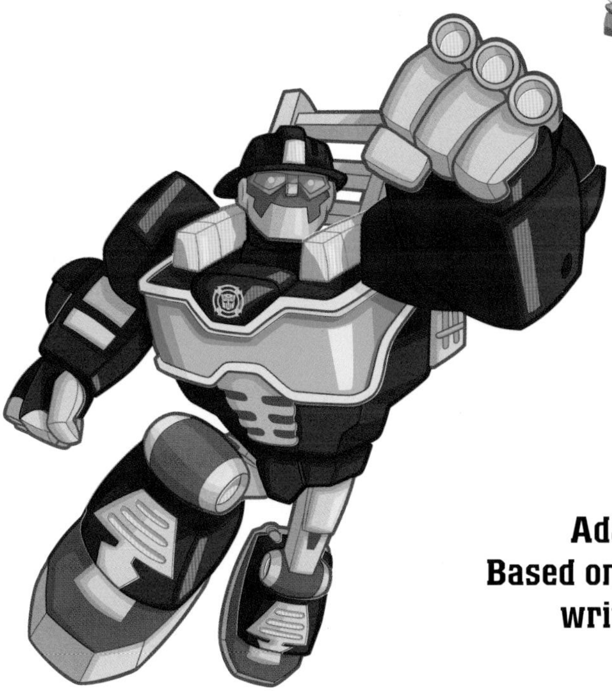

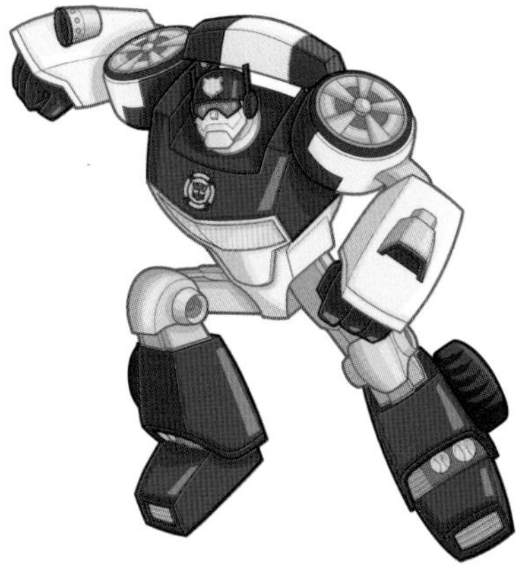

Adapted by Lucy Rosen
Based on the episode "Space Bots"
written by Greg Johnson

"Today's the big day!" Cody beams at his brother Graham. "In a few minutes, you and Doc Greene will be hurtling through space on a laser-powered elevator. Aren't you excited?"

"Sure," Graham says. "I'm excited. In a terrified sort of way."

"Come on," says Cody. "The *Asgard* is an amazing machine. You'll go straight up and come right back down. It's no big deal."

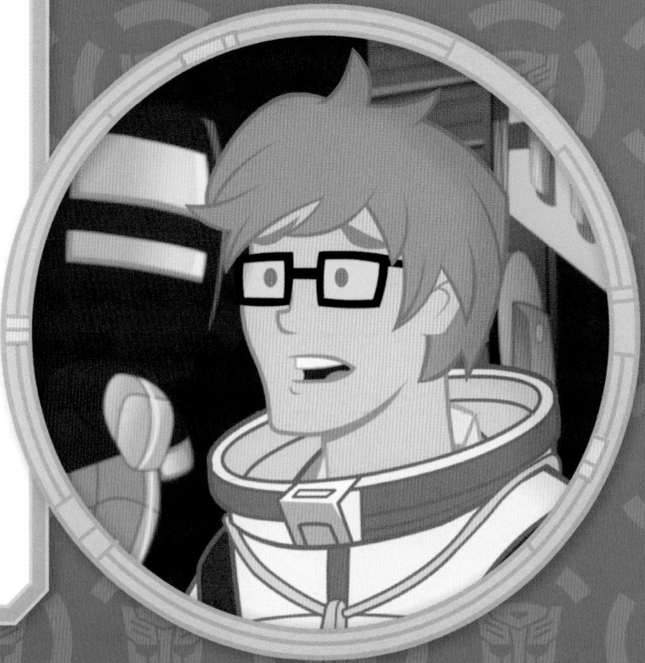

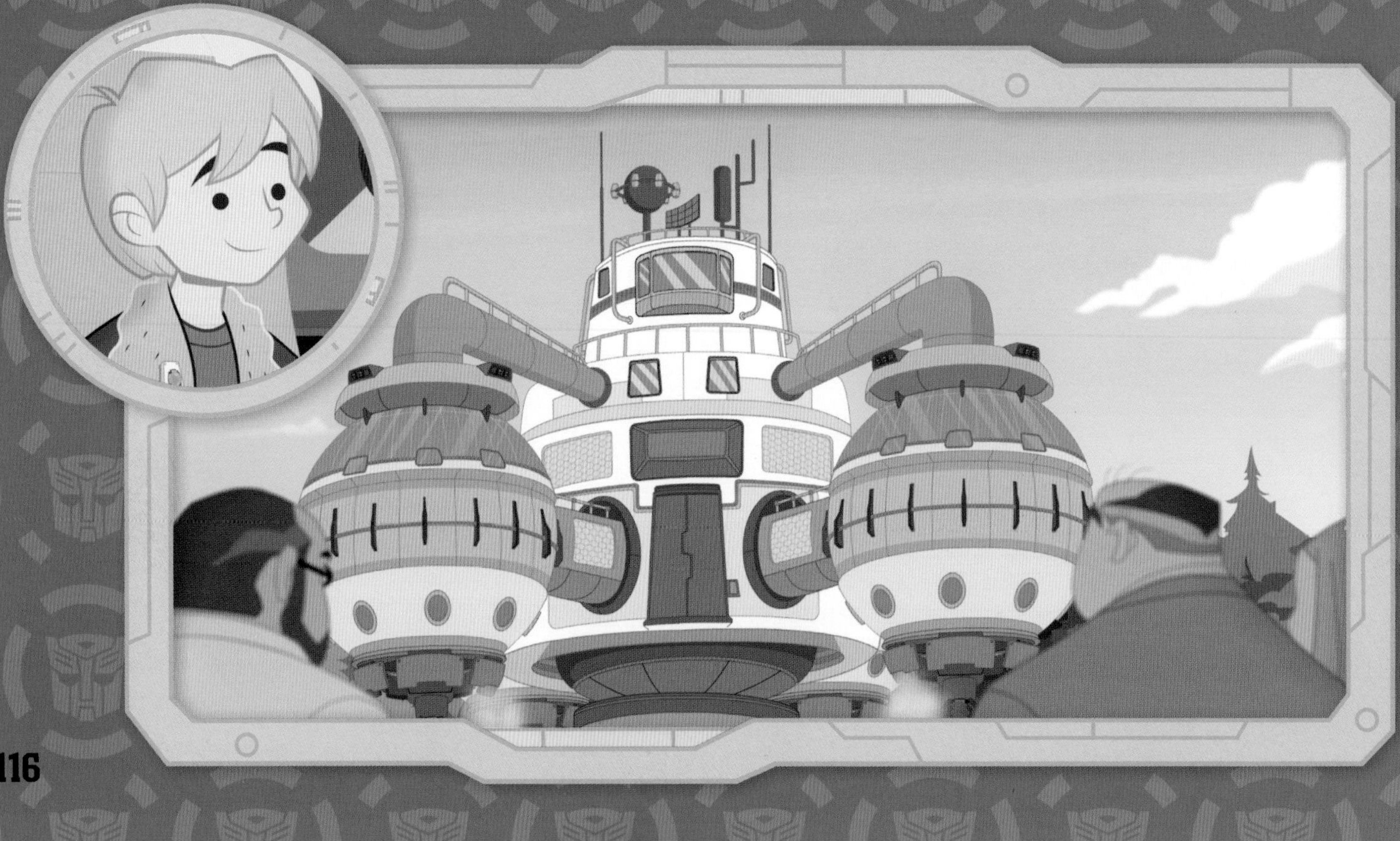

"It's time to go," says Professor Anna Baranova. She invented the *Asgard* so that scientists could easily study the galaxies from outer space. "Once you get to the top, you'll have a whole week to conduct tests and research!" she says.

Doc Greene gives his daughter, Frankie, a hug, and Graham says good-bye to the Burns family.

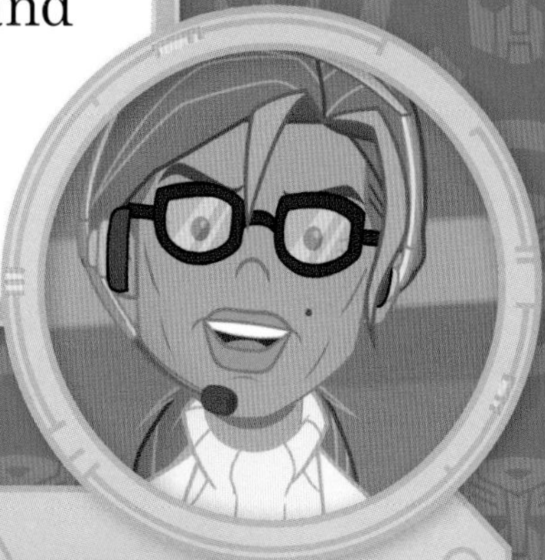

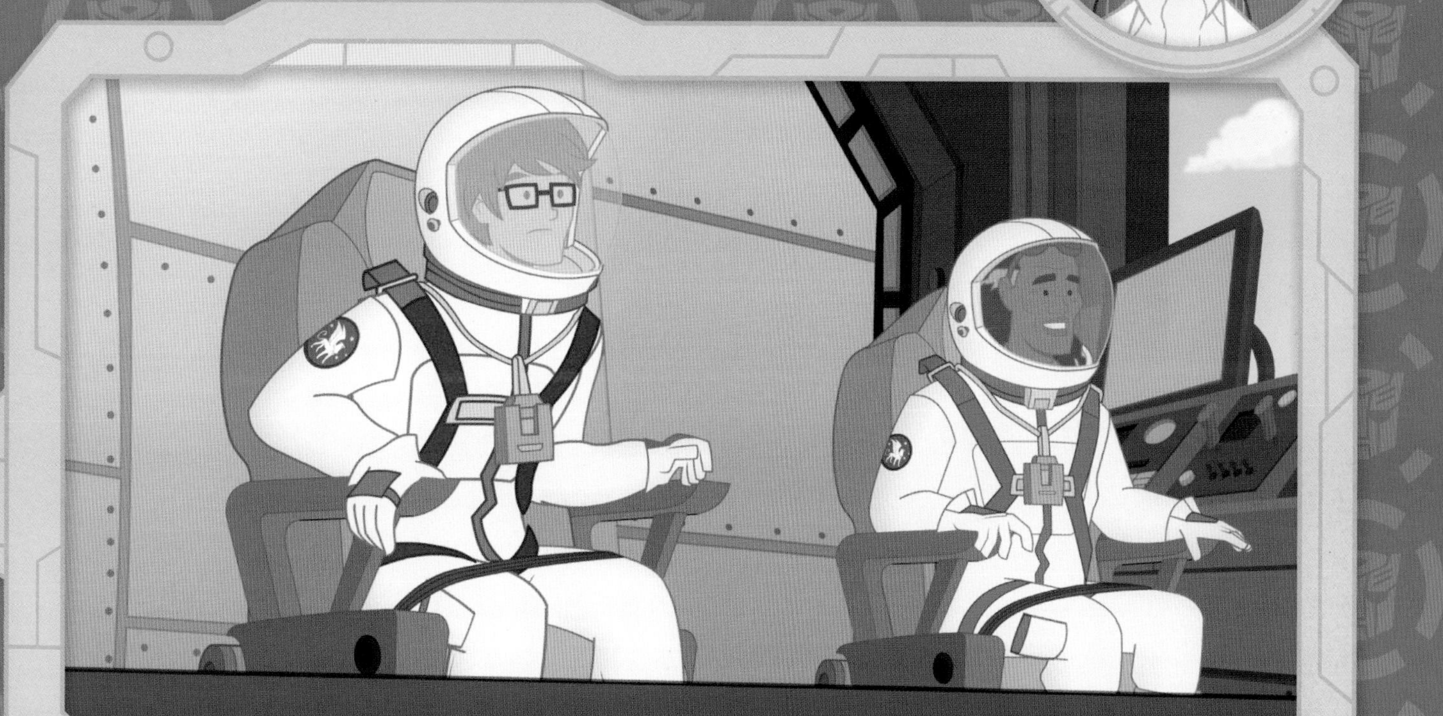

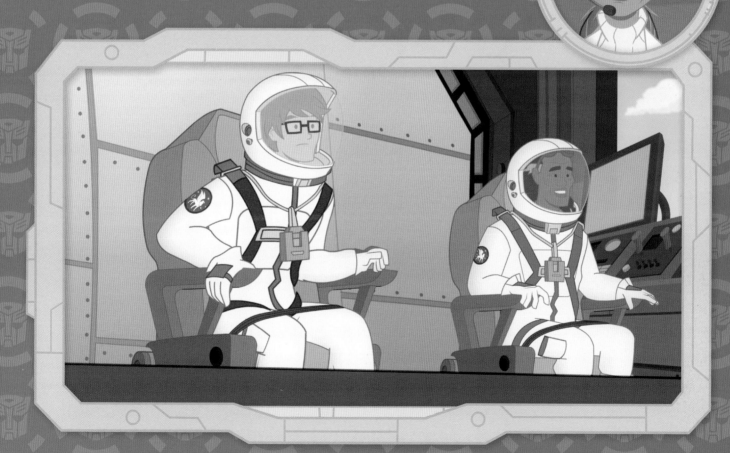

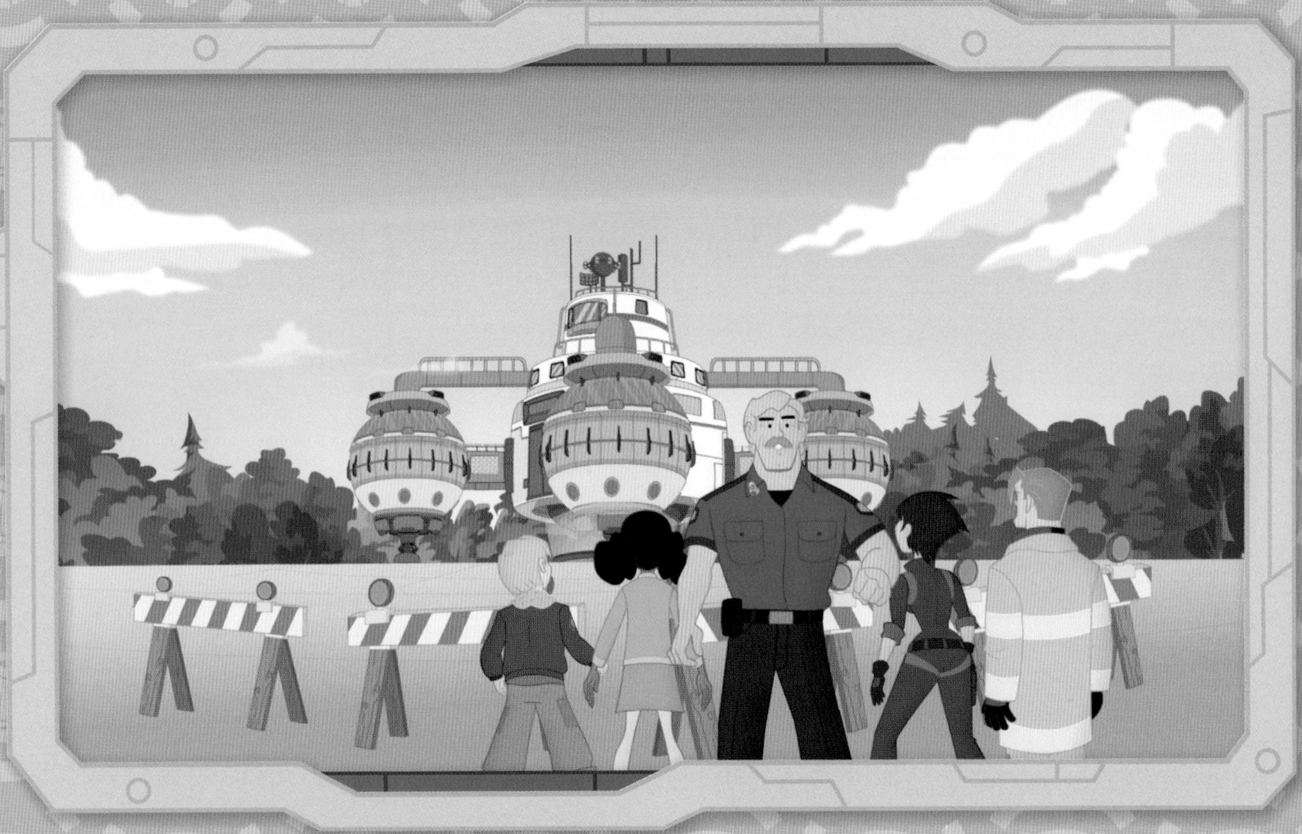

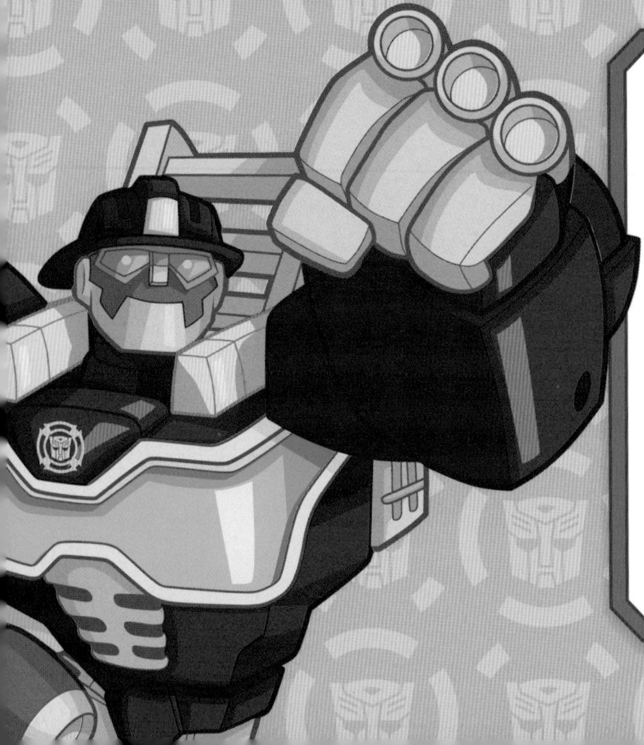

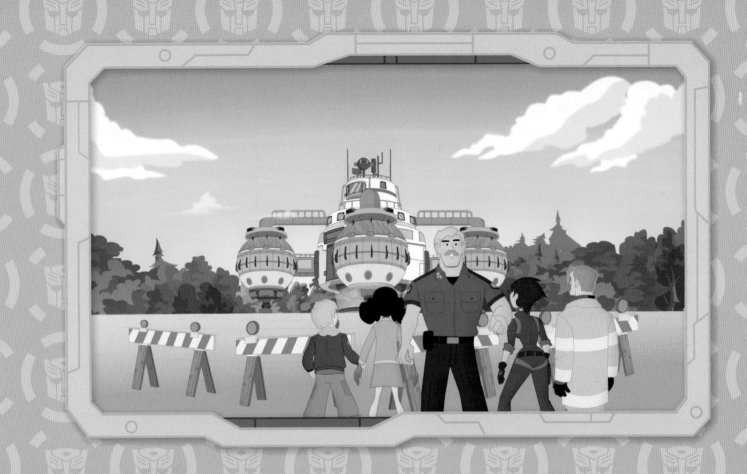

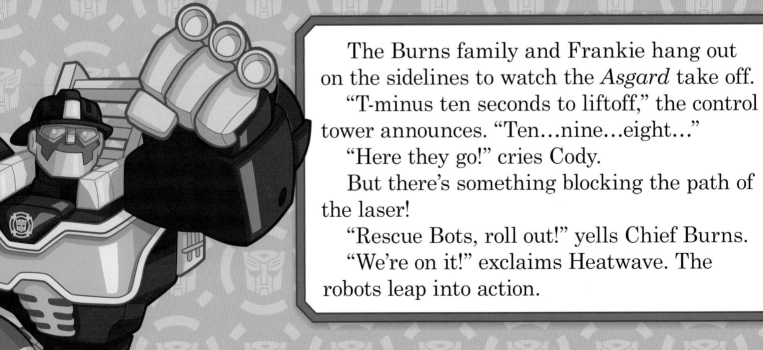

The Burns family and Frankie hang out on the sidelines to watch the *Asgard* take off.

"T-minus ten seconds to liftoff," the control tower announces. "Ten…nine…eight…"

"Here they go!" cries Cody.

But there's something blocking the path of the laser!

"Rescue Bots, roll out!" yells Chief Burns.

"We're on it!" exclaims Heatwave. The robots leap into action.

“Seven…six…five…”

Boulder, Blades, and Chase grab hold of the spacecraft and lift it off the ground.

“Four…three…two…”

“Hurry,” says Professor Baranova. “If they don’t remove the obstruction, the laser will overload!”

“One!”

With no time to lose, Heatwave leaps to swat the object out of the way.

“Blast off!”

The laser powers up and lifts the *Asgard* into the sky.

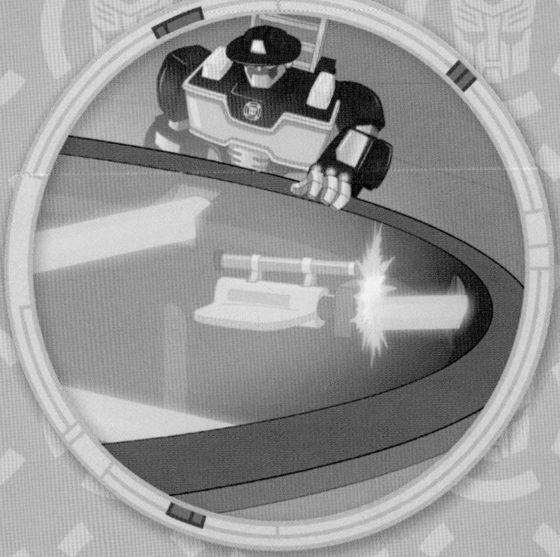

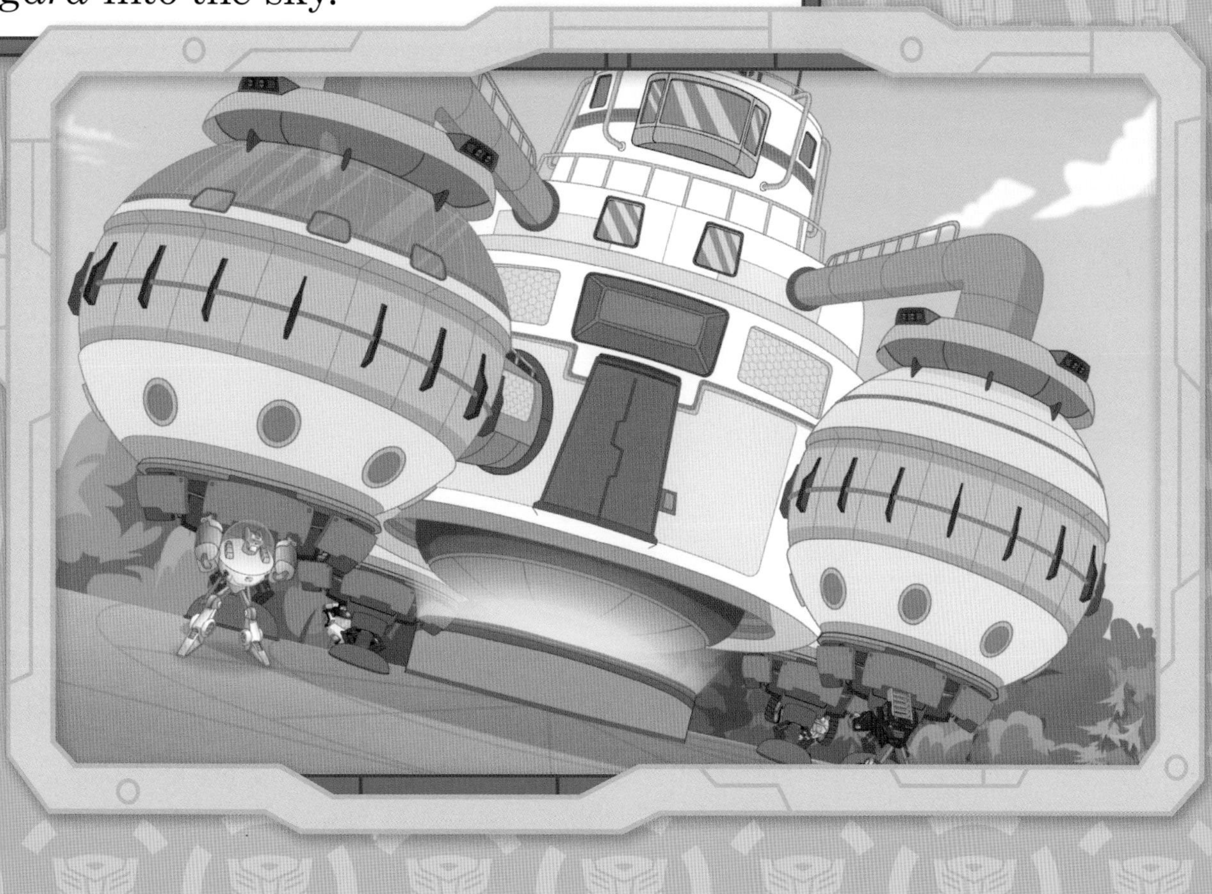

Later that night, the four Rescue Bots and Cody sit on the rooftop, while Frankie uses her telescope to search for signs of the *Asgard*.

"Maybe one of us should have gone with Doc and Graham—in case something else goes wrong," says Heatwave.

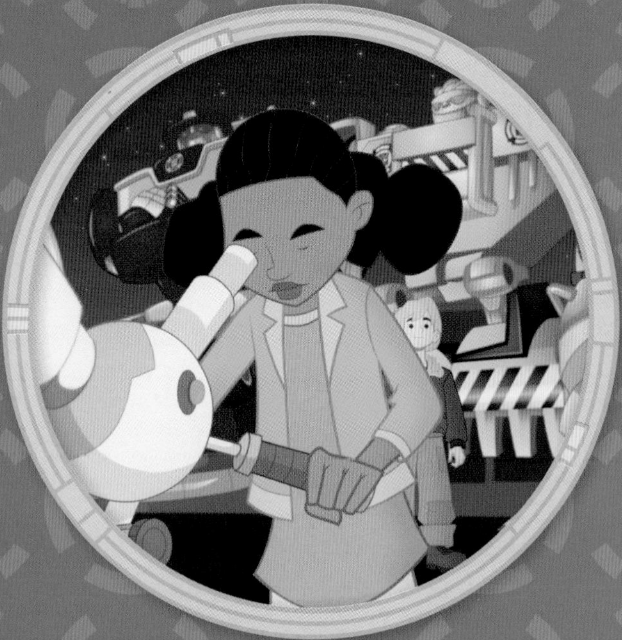

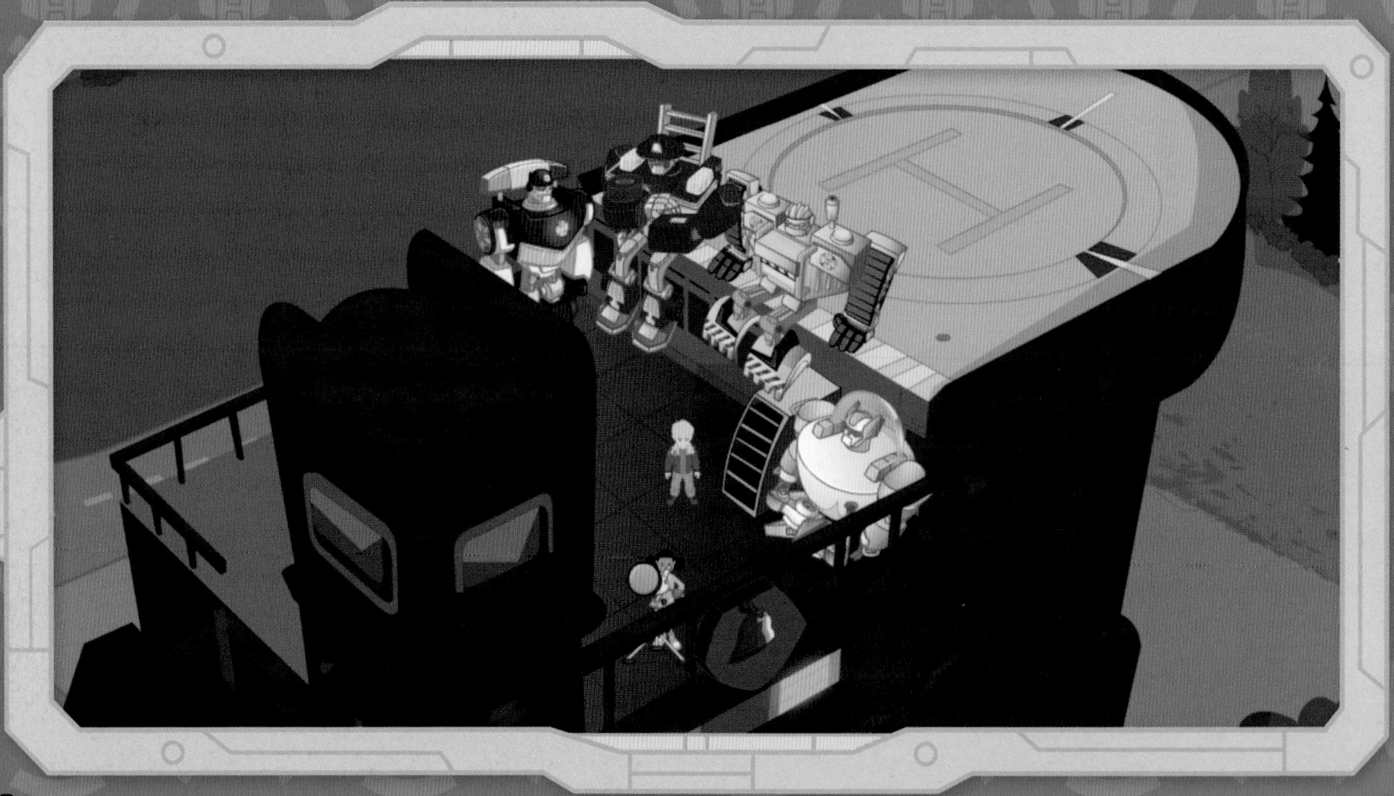

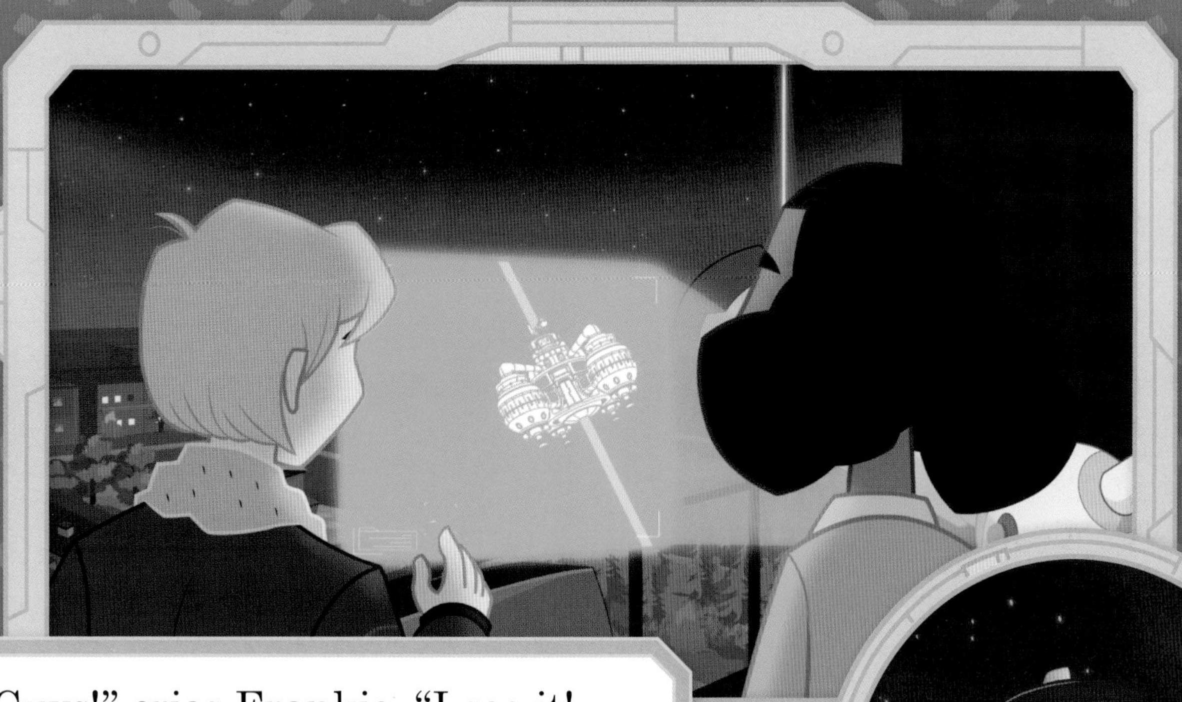

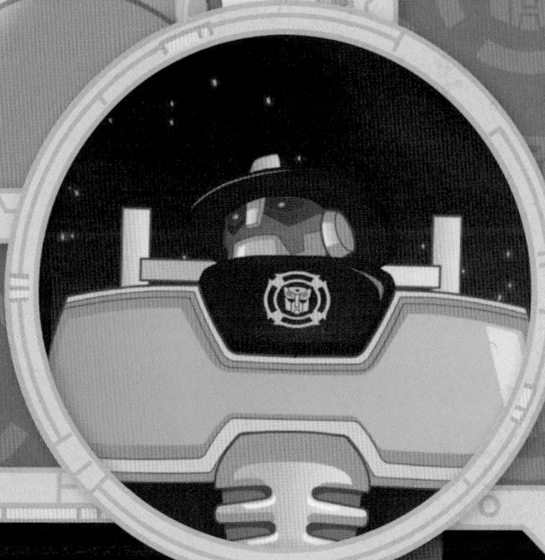

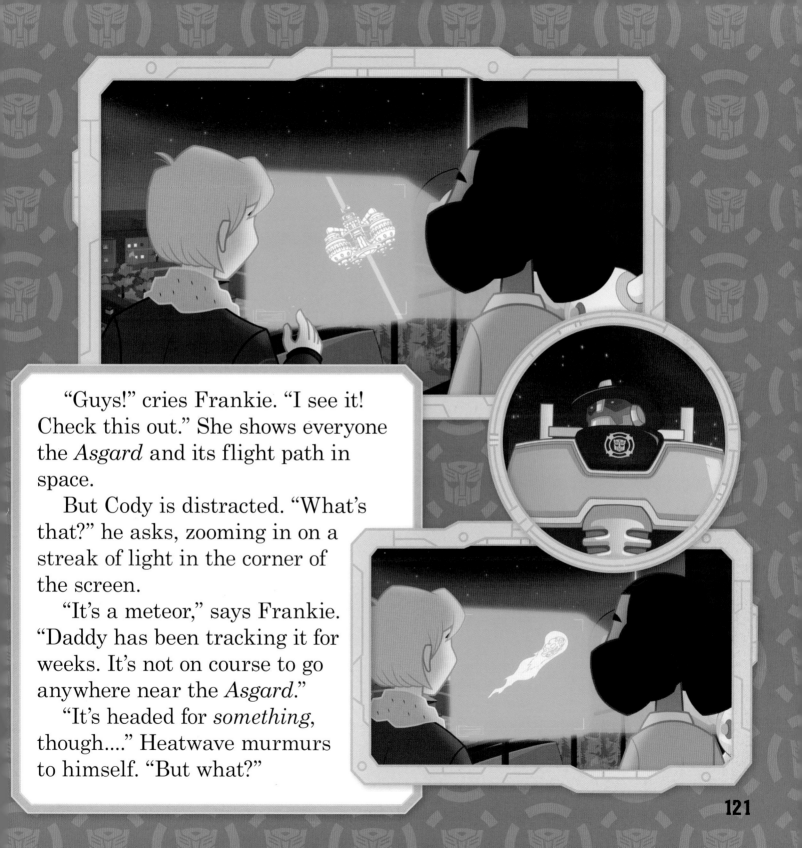

“Guys!” cries Frankie. “I see it! Check this out.” She shows everyone the *Asgard* and its flight path in space.

But Cody is distracted. “What’s that?” he asks, zooming in on a streak of light in the corner of the screen.

“It’s a meteor,” says Frankie. “Daddy has been tracking it for weeks. It’s not on course to go anywhere near the *Asgard*.”

“It’s headed for *something*, though....” Heatwave murmurs to himself. “But what?”

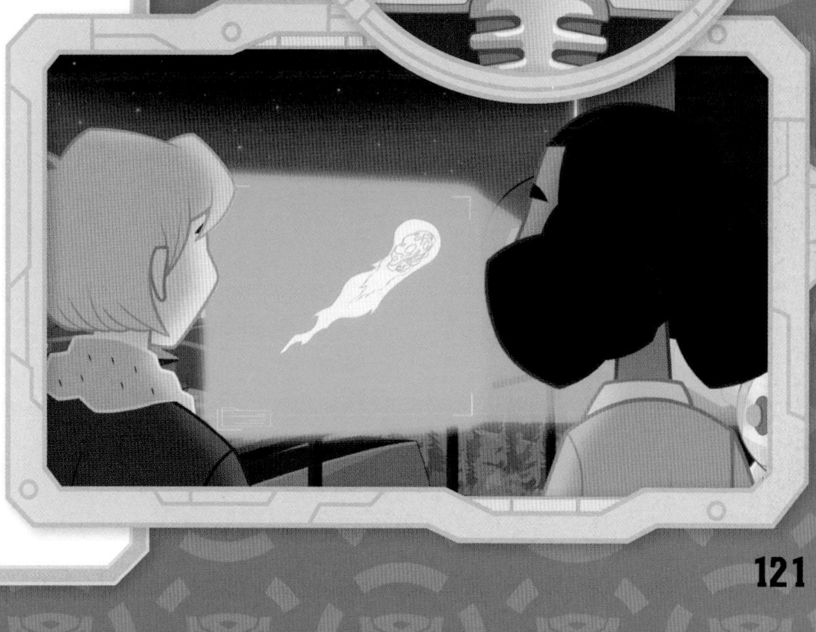

On board the *Asgard*, Graham and Doc Greene go through their checklist. Doc Greene calls out the names of the *Asgard*'s four pods as Graham looks at each of them on his computer screen.

"Everything is stable!" exclaims Doc Greene. "That means we did it! Phase one is complete."

But before Graham can even breathe a sigh of relief, the *Asgard*'s alarm begins to blare.

"What's happening?" asks Graham.

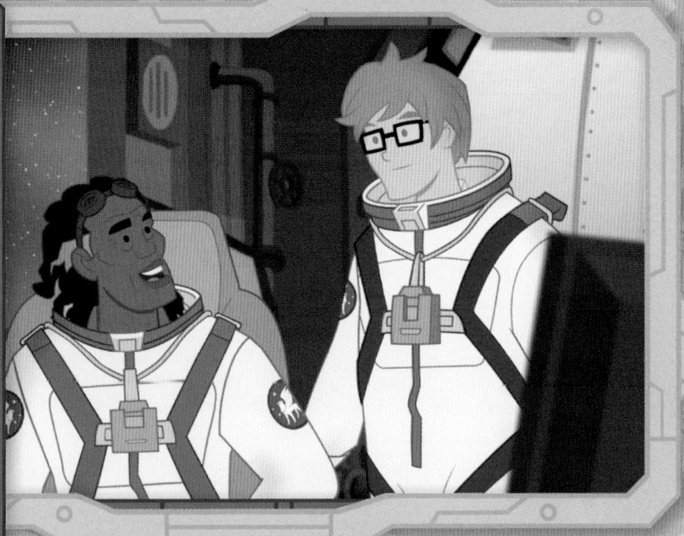

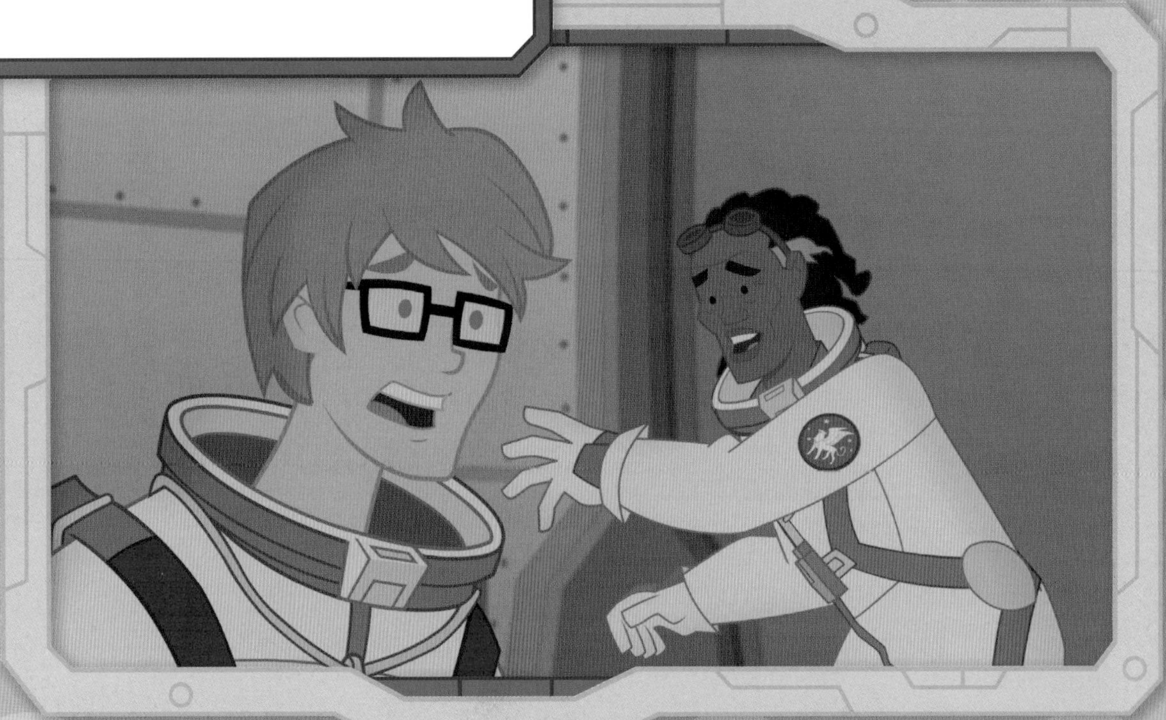

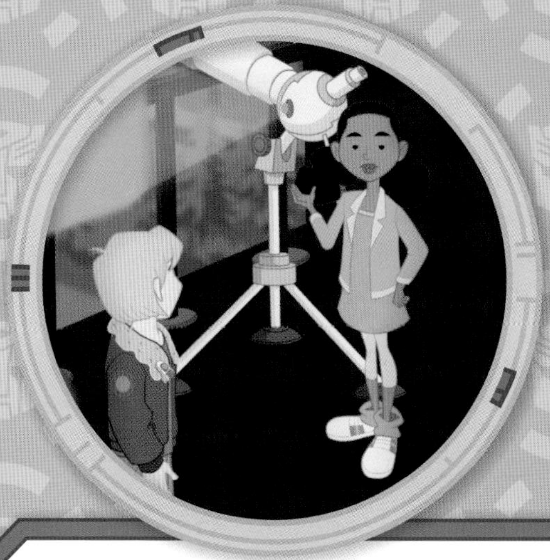

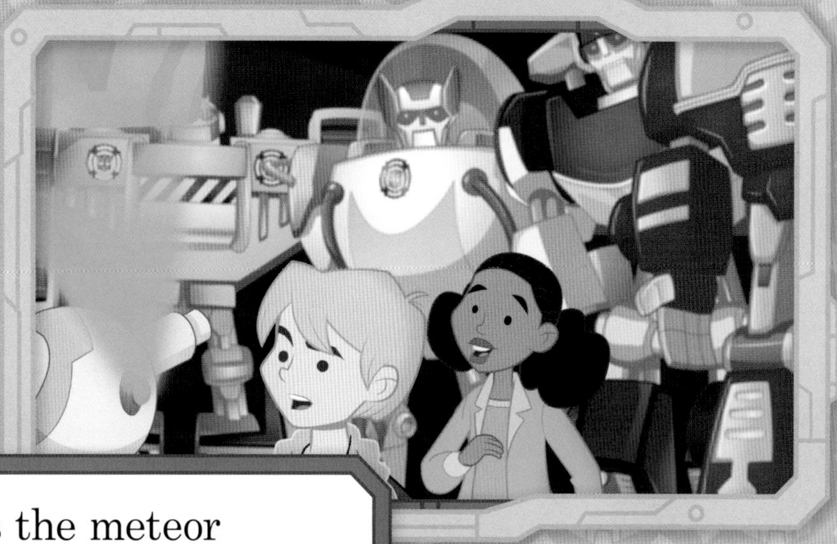

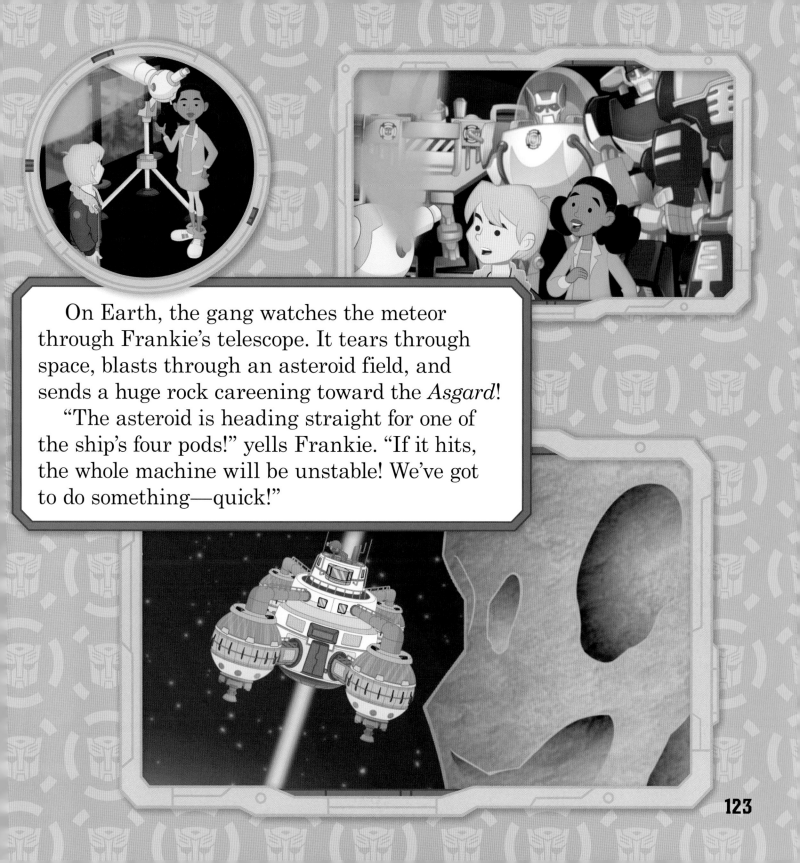

On Earth, the gang watches the meteor through Frankie's telescope. It tears through space, blasts through an asteroid field, and sends a huge rock careening toward the *Asgard*!

"The asteroid is heading straight for one of the ship's four pods!" yells Frankie. "If it hits, the whole machine will be unstable! We've got to do something—quick!"

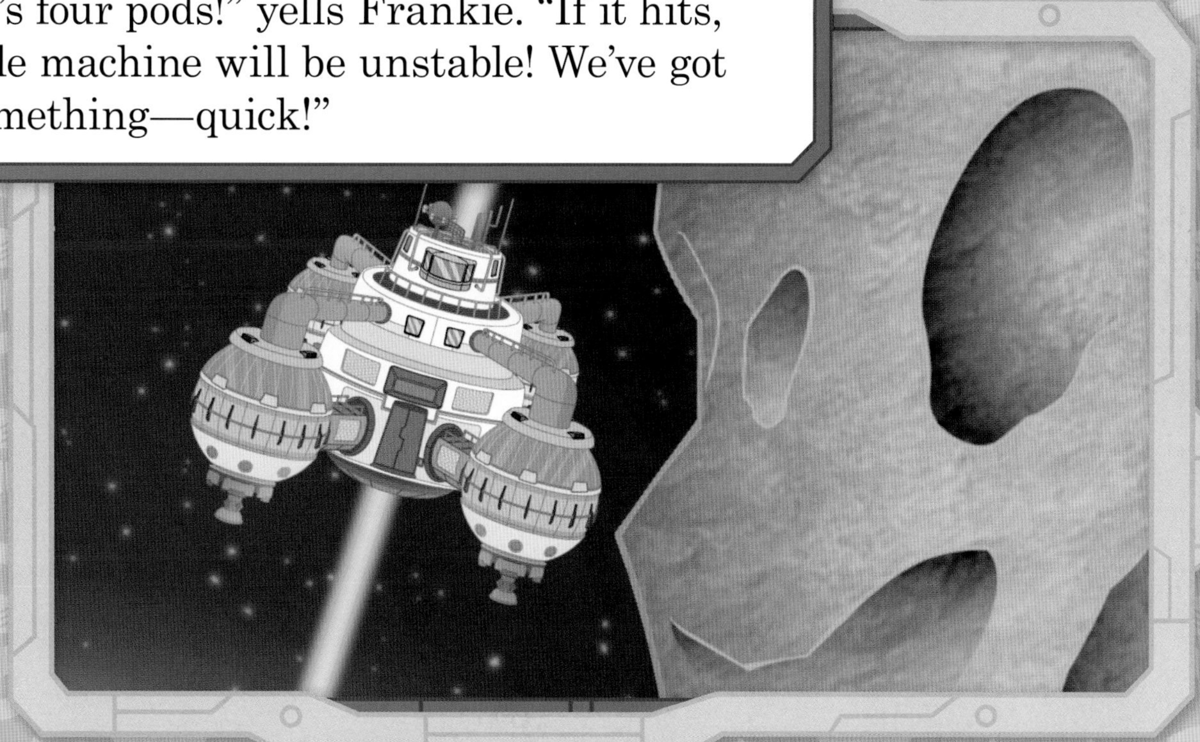

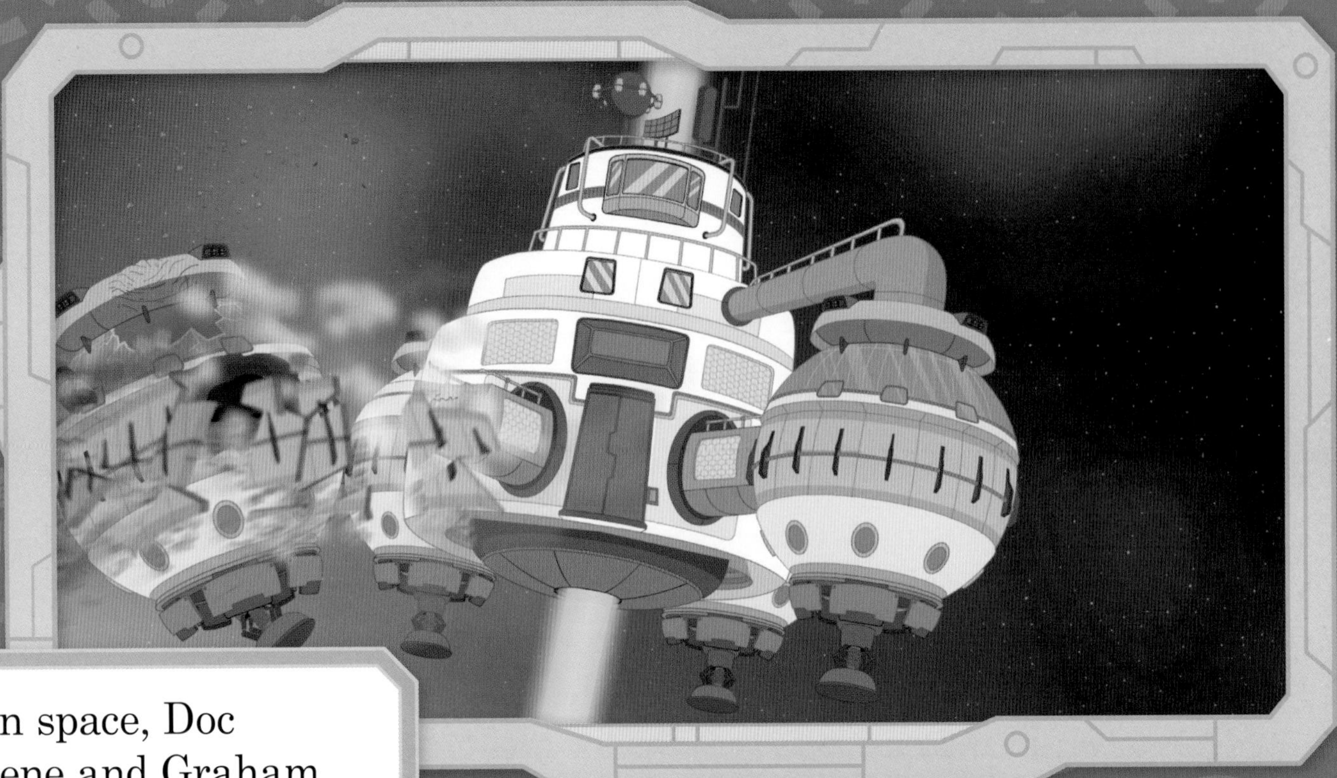

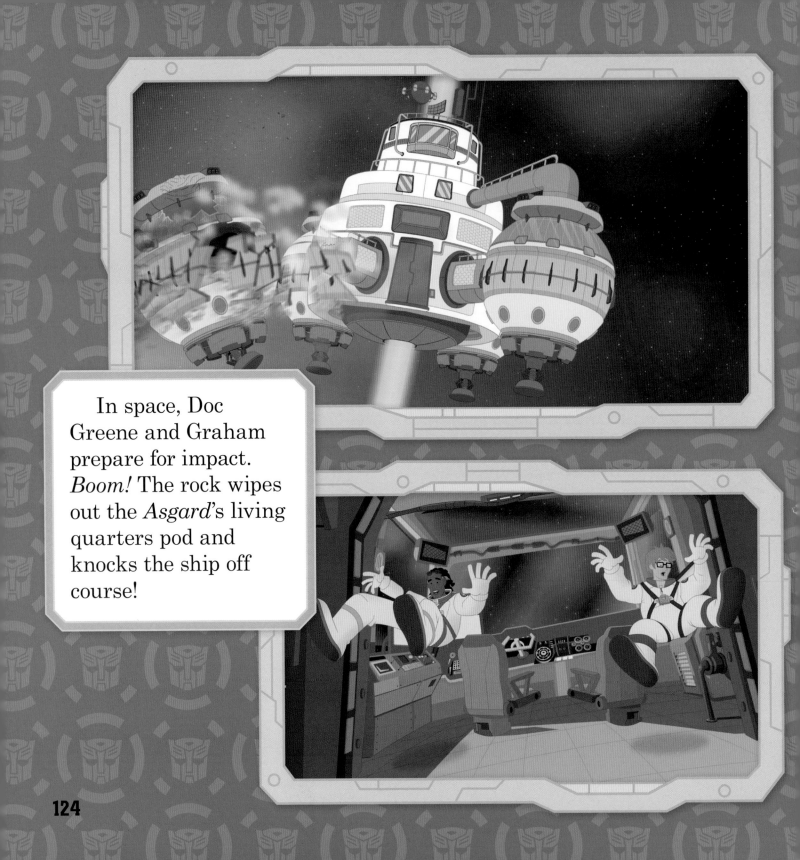

In space, Doc Greene and Graham prepare for impact. *Boom!* The rock wipes out the *Asgard*'s living quarters pod and knocks the ship off course!

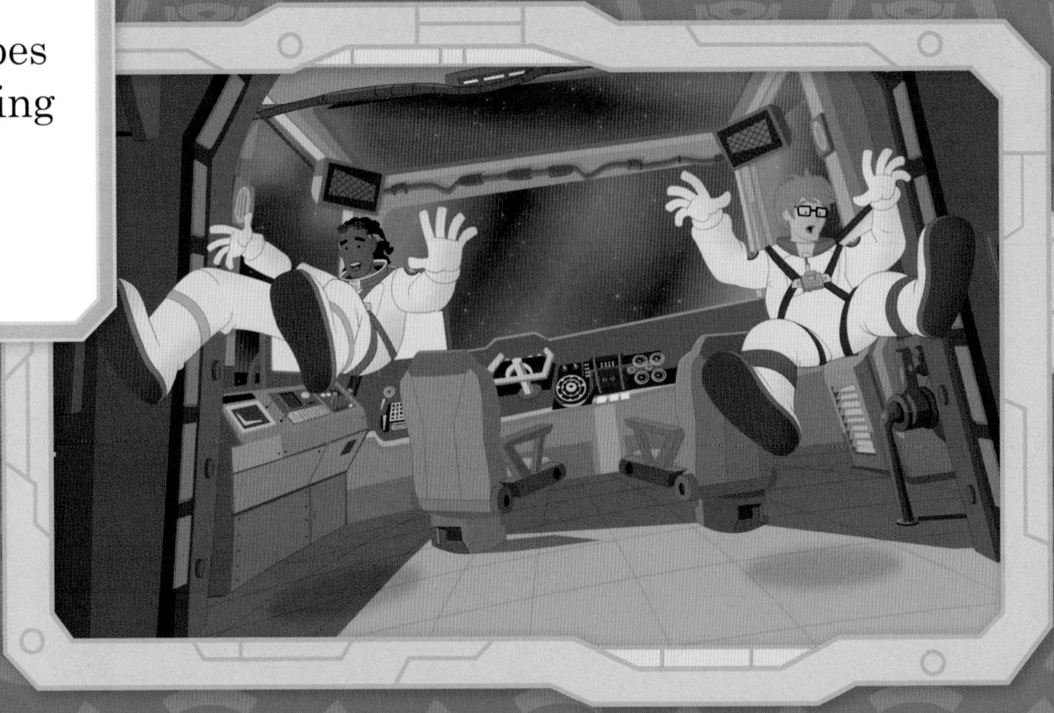

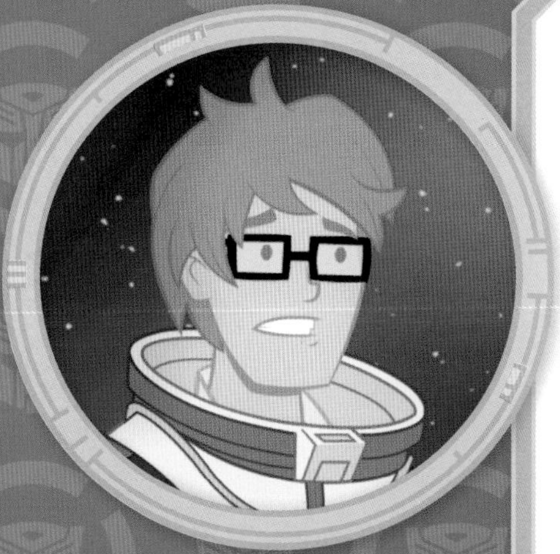

No one is hurt, but now the *Asgard* is floating through darkness with no way to get back on course. The radio is down. Graham and Doc Greene can't get in touch with anyone on Earth.

"What do we do now?" Graham whispers nervously.

"We wait for a rescue," says Doc Greene.

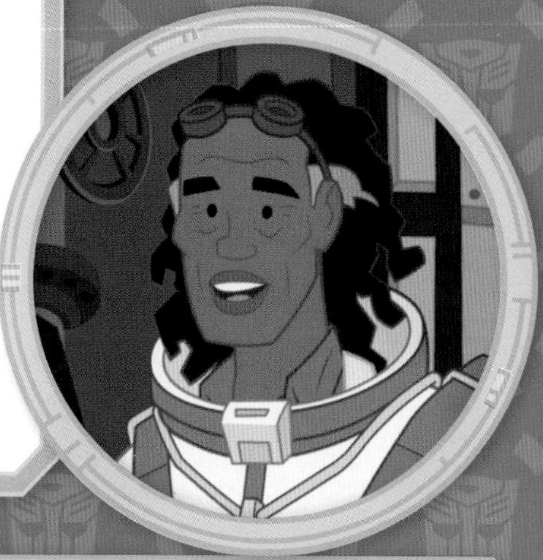

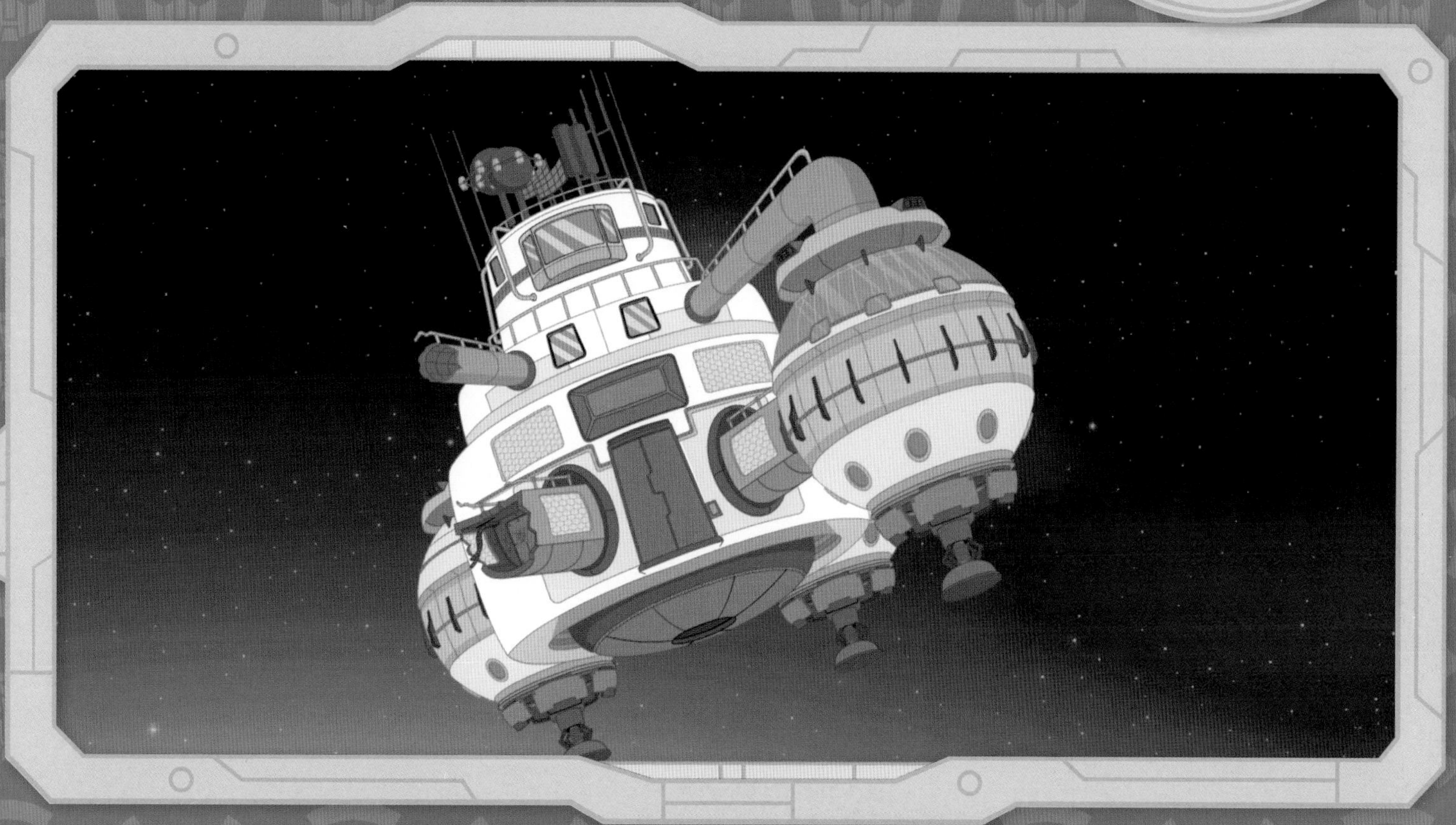

There is no time to lose. The Rescue Bots know what they must do.

"Rescue Bots, get ready," says Chase. "Looks like we're about to go on a space rescue!"

Cody and Frankie get Chief Burns. Together, the humans and the Rescue Bots head to a secret hangar, where the ship the Bots came to Earth in is hidden.

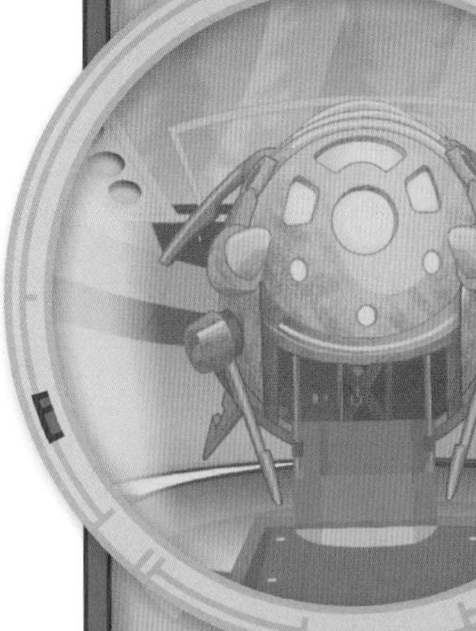

"The *Sigma*," Boulder marvels. "Think we remember how to fly her?"

"We're about to find out," says Heatwave. "Boulder, Chase, you're copilots. Everyone, strap in. It's time to rocket to the rescue!"

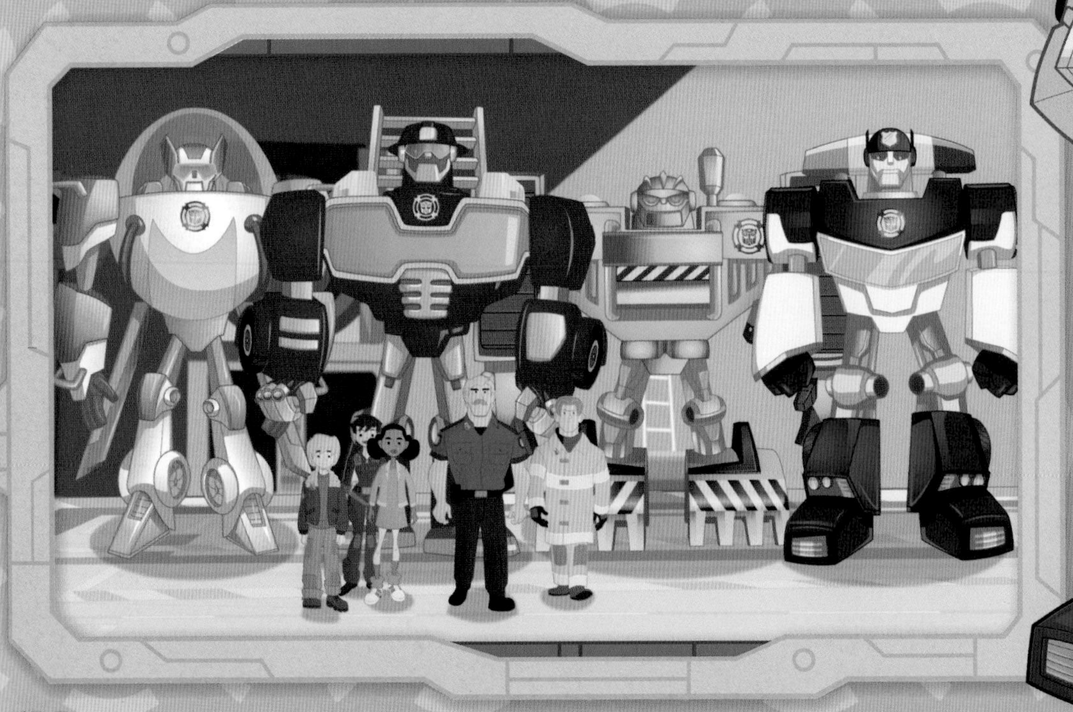

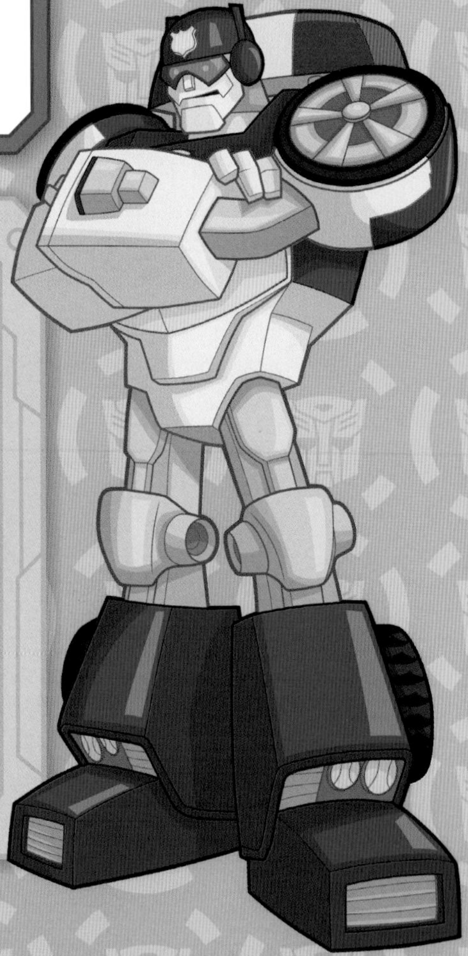

The *Sigma*'s engines roar. The ship lurches forward. With a blast, the spacecraft takes off into the dark night sky.

"Wow, Cody," says Frankie. "Don't you wish we were going, too?"

No one answers.

"Cody?" Frankie looks around. "Where is he?"

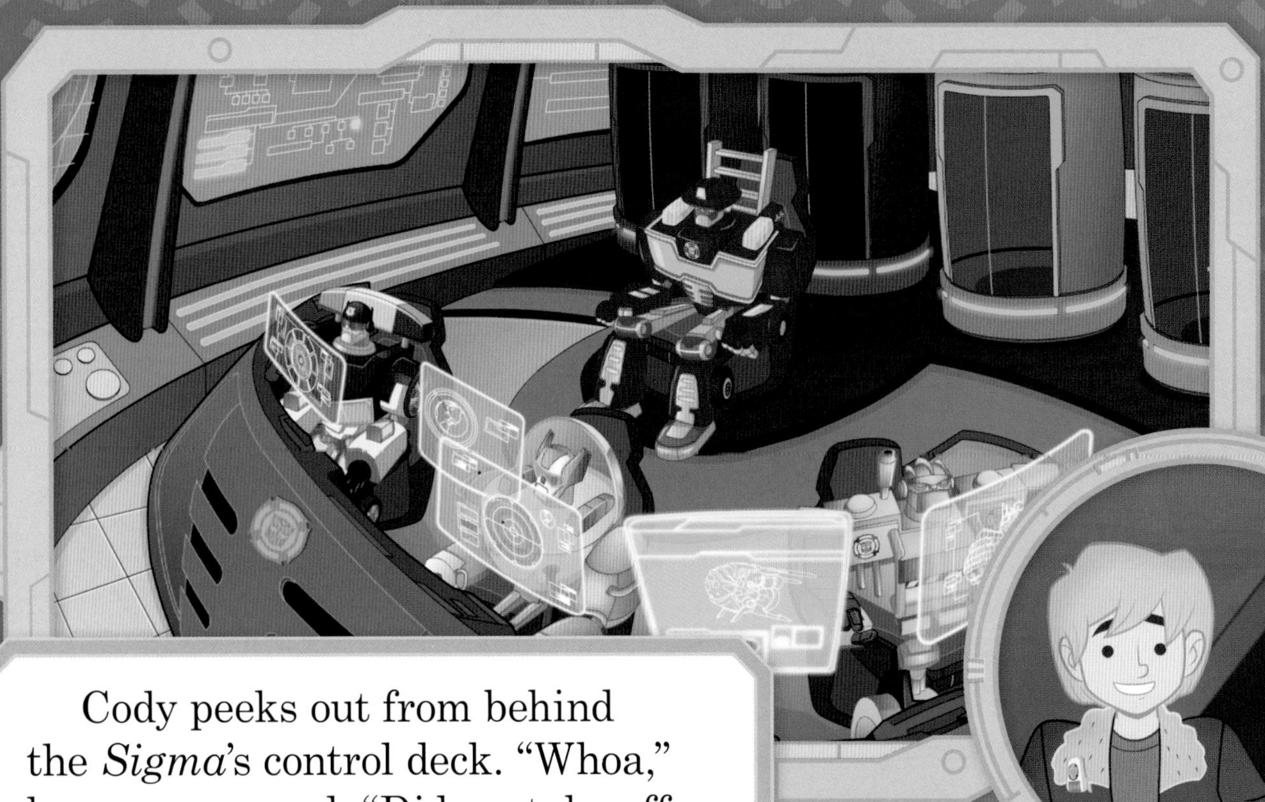

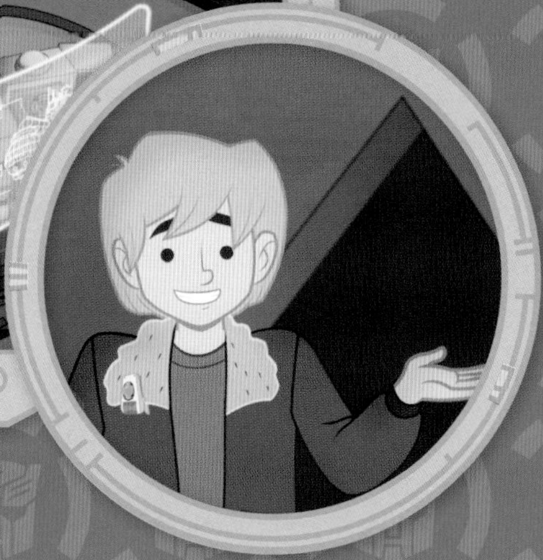

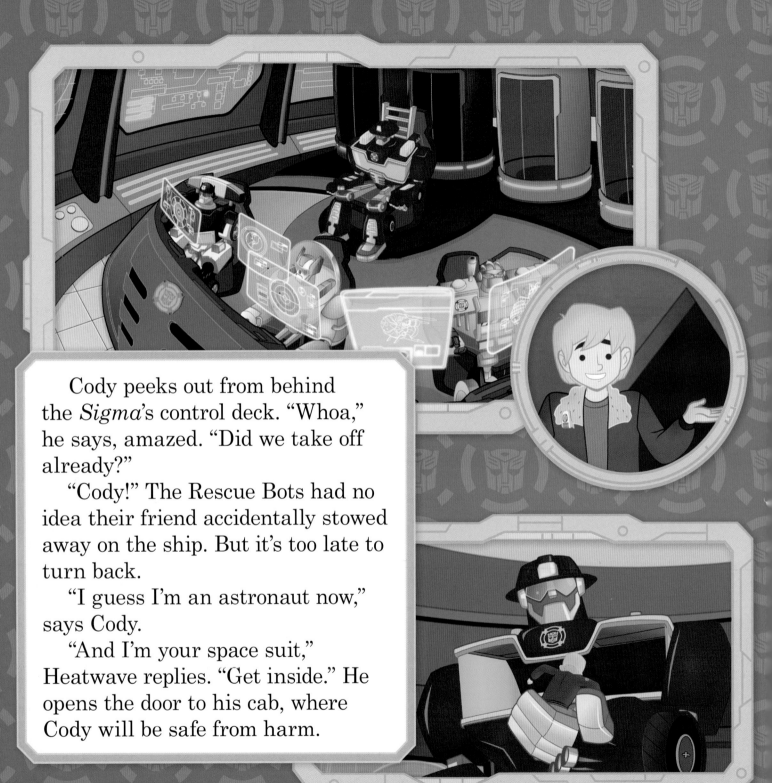

Cody peeks out from behind the *Sigma*'s control deck. "Whoa," he says, amazed. "Did we take off already?"

"Cody!" The Rescue Bots had no idea their friend accidentally stowed away on the ship. But it's too late to turn back.

"I guess I'm an astronaut now," says Cody.

"And I'm your space suit," Heatwave replies. "Get inside." He opens the door to his cab, where Cody will be safe from harm.

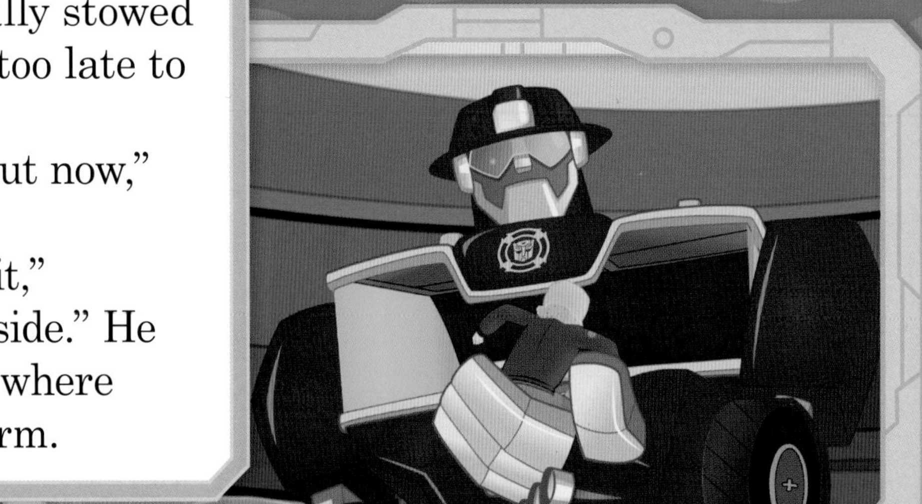

The *Sigma* climbs higher into space. Soon enough, the *Asgard* is just within reach.

"Boulder, move us closer," Heatwave commands. "I'll go get Doc and Graham."

As he pushes down the *Sigma*'s entry ramp, Heatwave speaks to his friend. "Buckle up, Cody," he says. "Looks like you're going on a space walk."

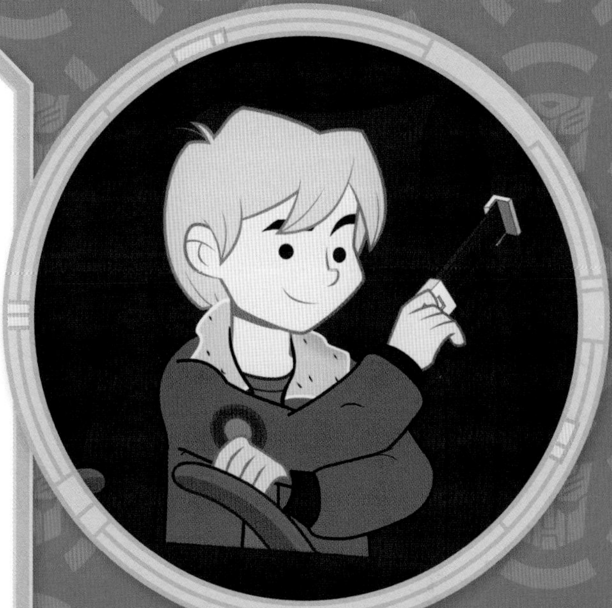

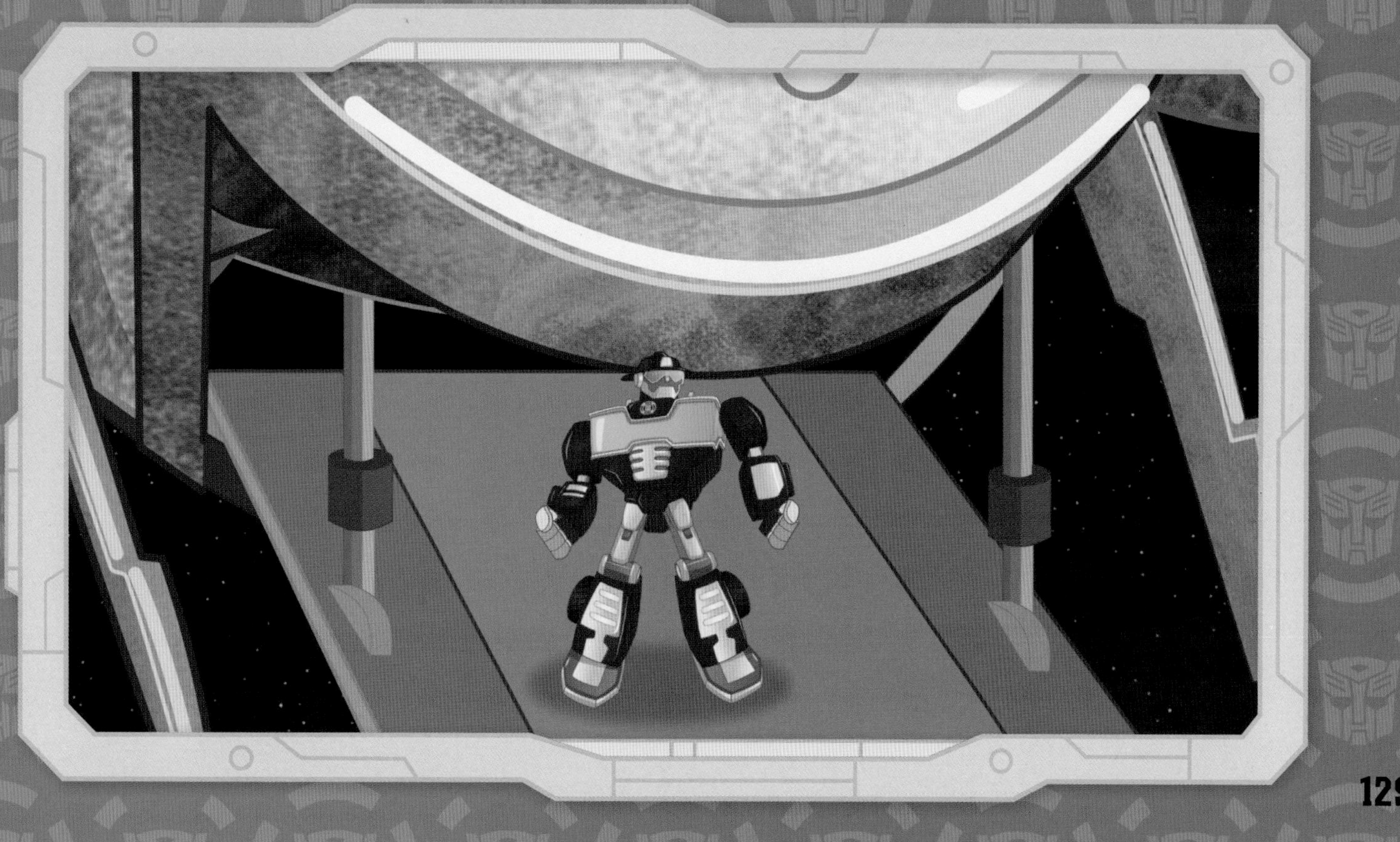

With a swift leap, Heatwave propels himself at just the right angle. His momentum carries him straight to the *Asgard*! As soon as he reaches the ship, Heatwave tears through each pod, searching for his friends. At last, he finds Graham and Doc Greene huddled in the greenhouse. "Get in!" he commands.

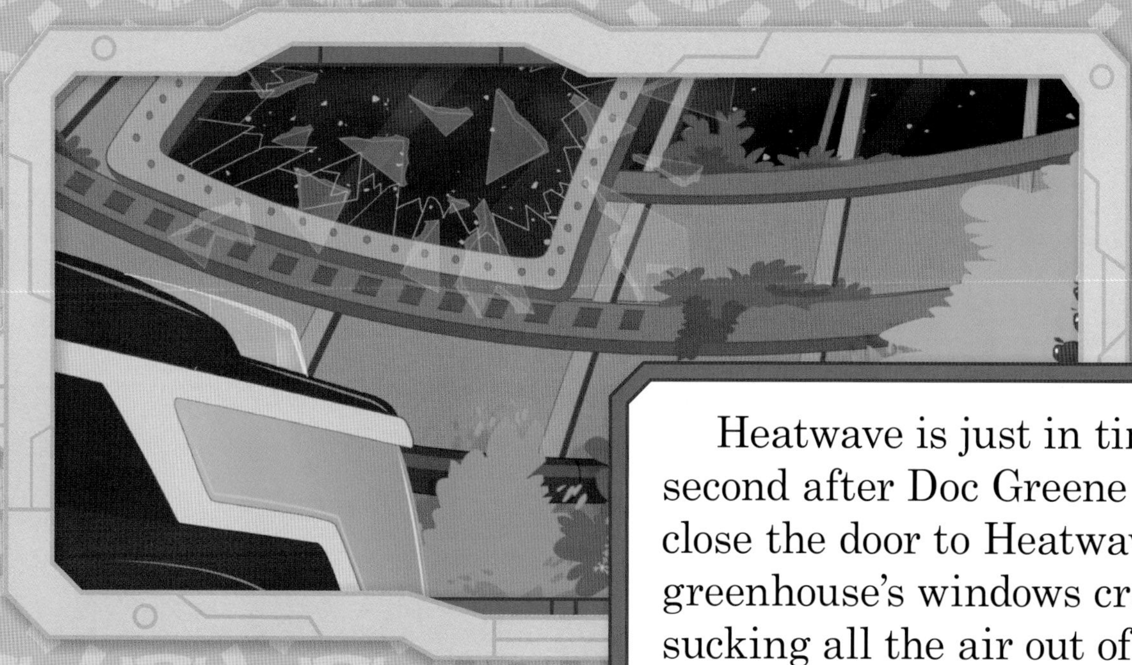

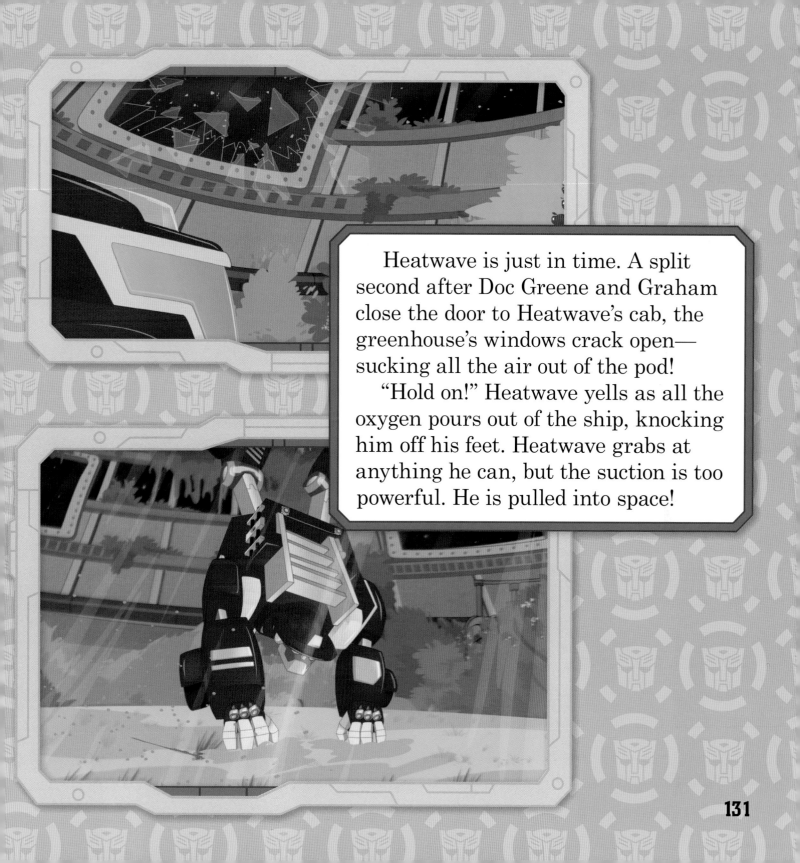

Heatwave is just in time. A split second after Doc Greene and Graham close the door to Heatwave's cab, the greenhouse's windows crack open—sucking all the air out of the pod!

"Hold on!" Heatwave yells as all the oxygen pours out of the ship, knocking him off his feet. Heatwave grabs at anything he can, but the suction is too powerful. He is pulled into space!

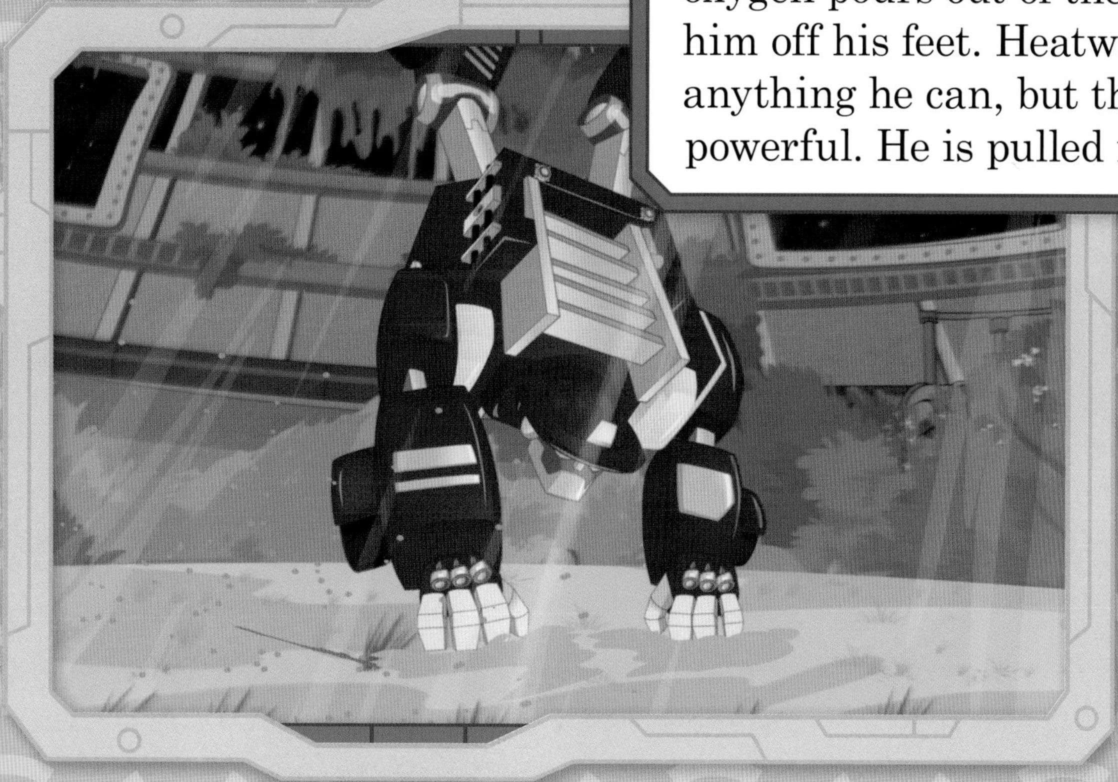

"We're adrift," Heatwave signals to his friends aboard the *Sigma*. "I don't have any propulsion."

"Now what do we do?" cries Blades in despair. "We did not train for this!"

"Keep calm, everyone," Heatwave says. "We'll think of something."

Just then, Cody has an idea. "Use your fire hoses," he says. "If you spray them, the force of the water will push us in the right direction!"

"Worth a shot," says Heatwave. "Here goes nothing." In a flash, Heatwave activates his water reserves. The burst of water sends the Rescue Bot flying!

"It's working!" Graham cries.

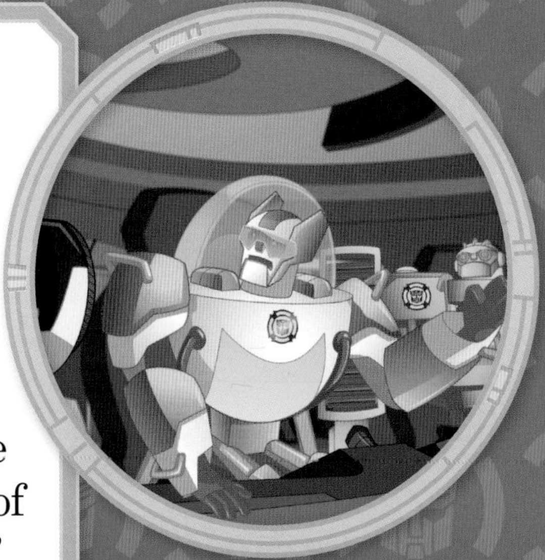

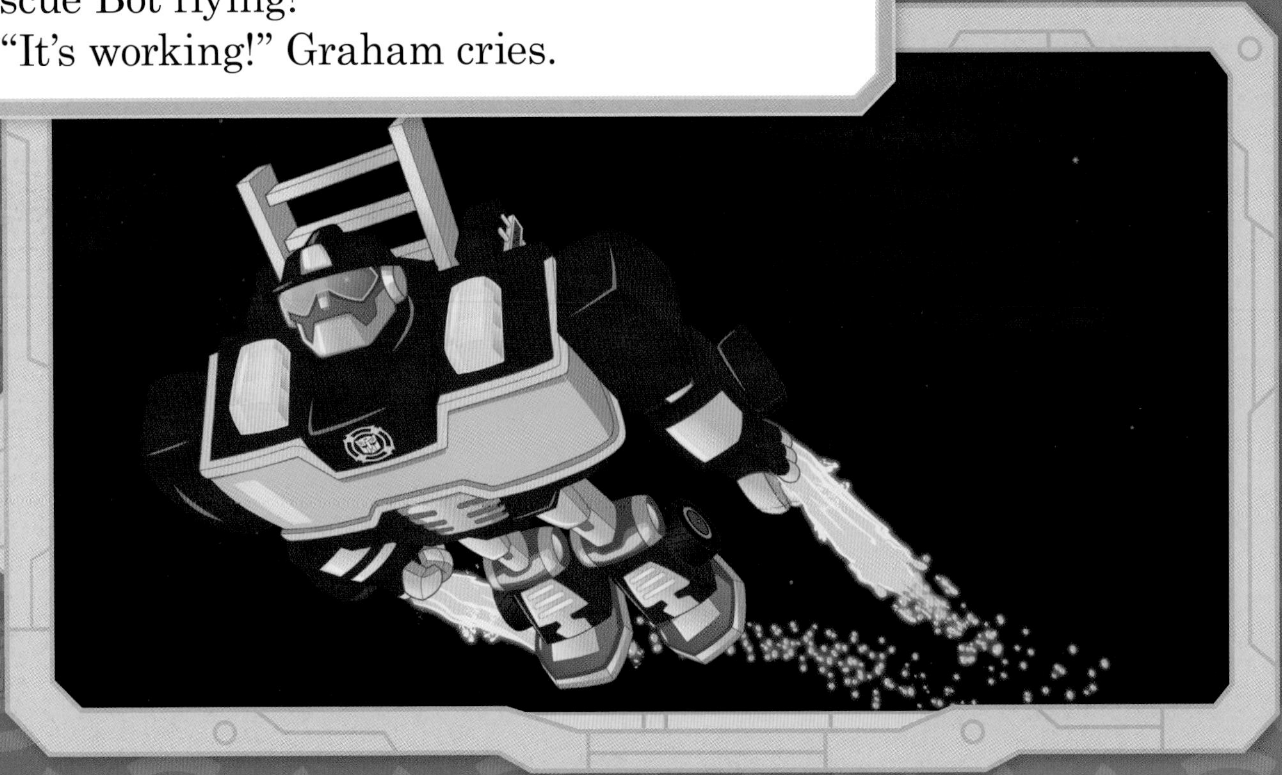

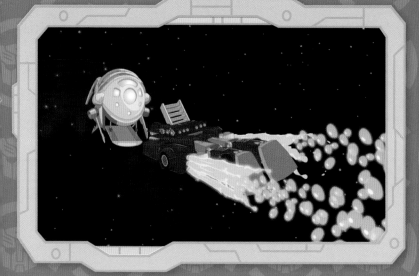

Once they're back aboard the *Sigma*, the Rescue Bots hitch the *Asgard* to their spaceship.

"Looks like we got everything we came for," says Boulder. "Next stop—Griffin Rock!"

The gang lands back on Earth in no time.

"Daddy!" Frankie rushes to Doc Greene's side.

"Welcome back, son," Chief Burns says to Graham.

"You had us worried," Dani tells him.

Everyone is so relieved to see the space travelers back home safe and sound. Even Kade gives Graham a hug!

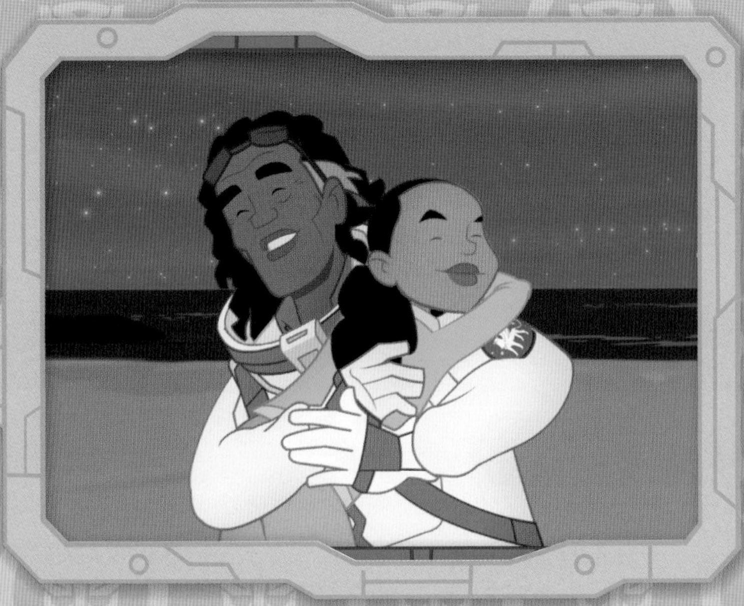

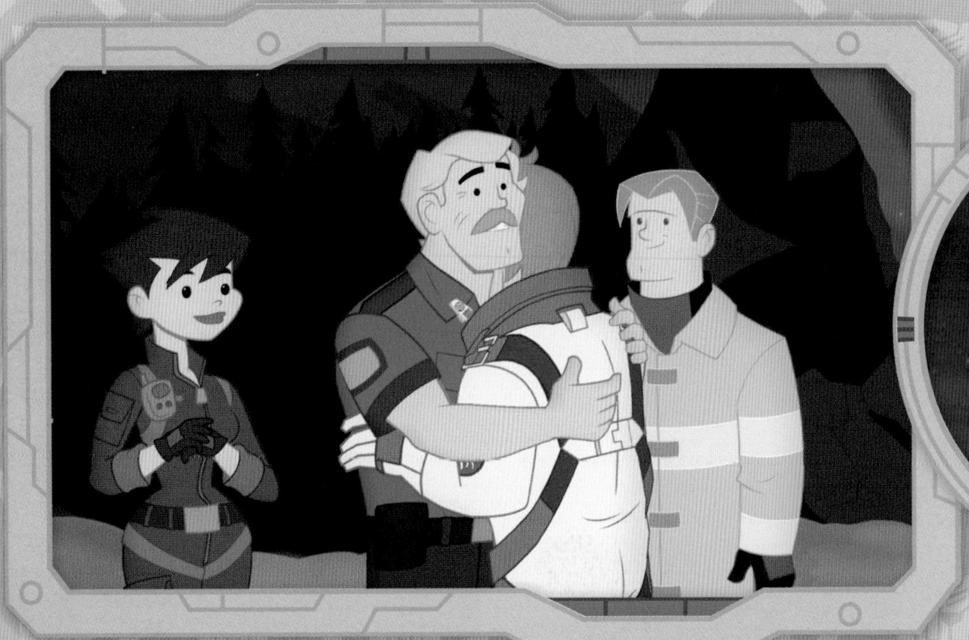

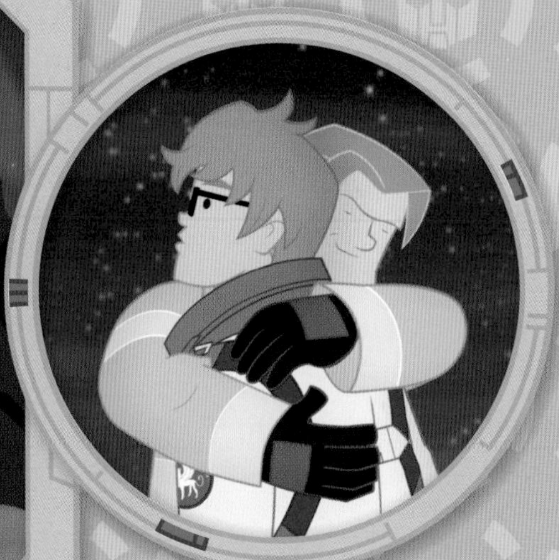

"Well, Rescue Bots," says Blades, "it looks like our space rescue was a success."

"Yes," says Boulder. "And it was kind of nice flying the *Sigma* again!"

"Perhaps we'll get the opportunity to use her again someday," Chase remarks.

"Maybe," Heatwave says. "But nothing beats rolling to the rescue on good old terra firma."

"What is that?" asks Boulder. "Earth?"

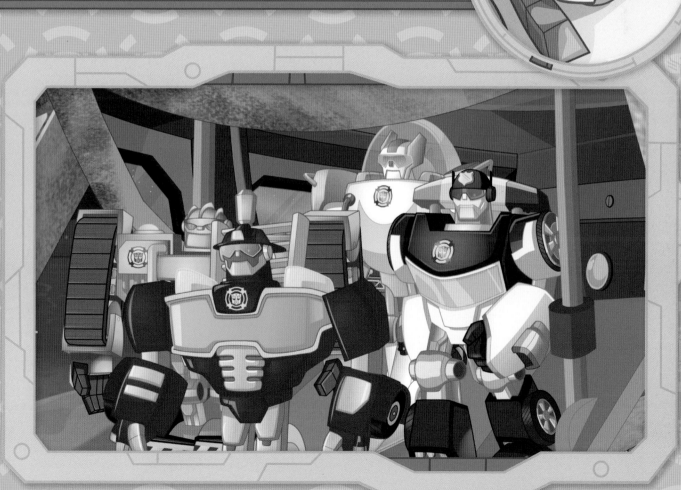

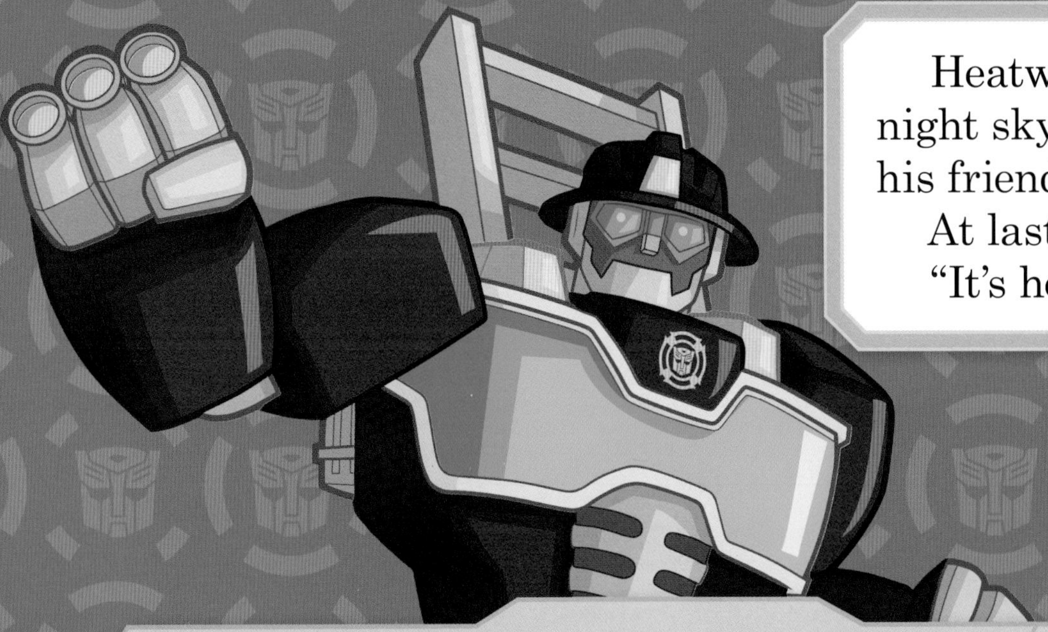

Heatwave looks at the night sky. He looks around at his friends on Griffin Rock.

At last, he speaks.

"It's home."

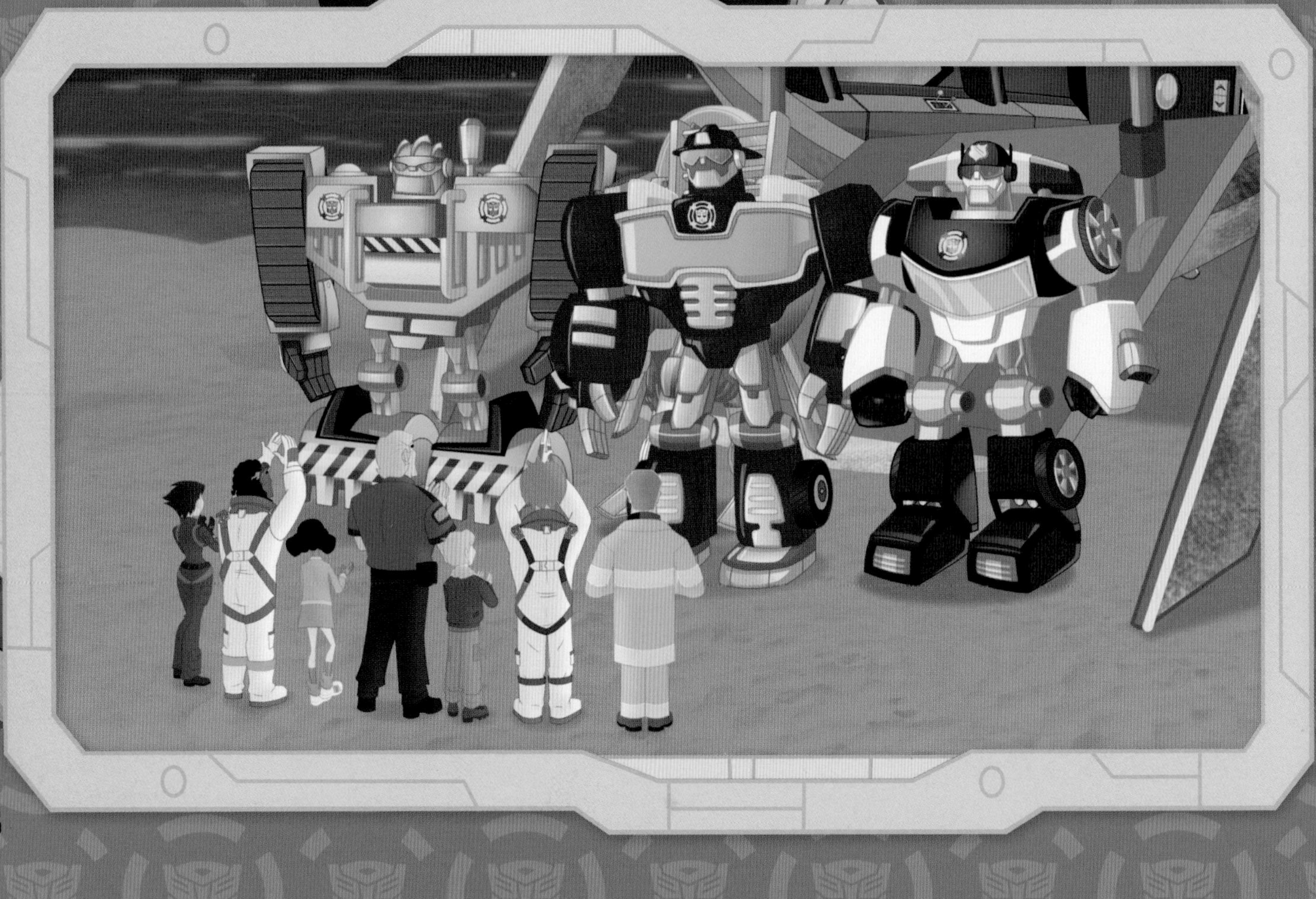

TRANSFORMERS RESCUE BOTS

Attack of the Movie Monsters!

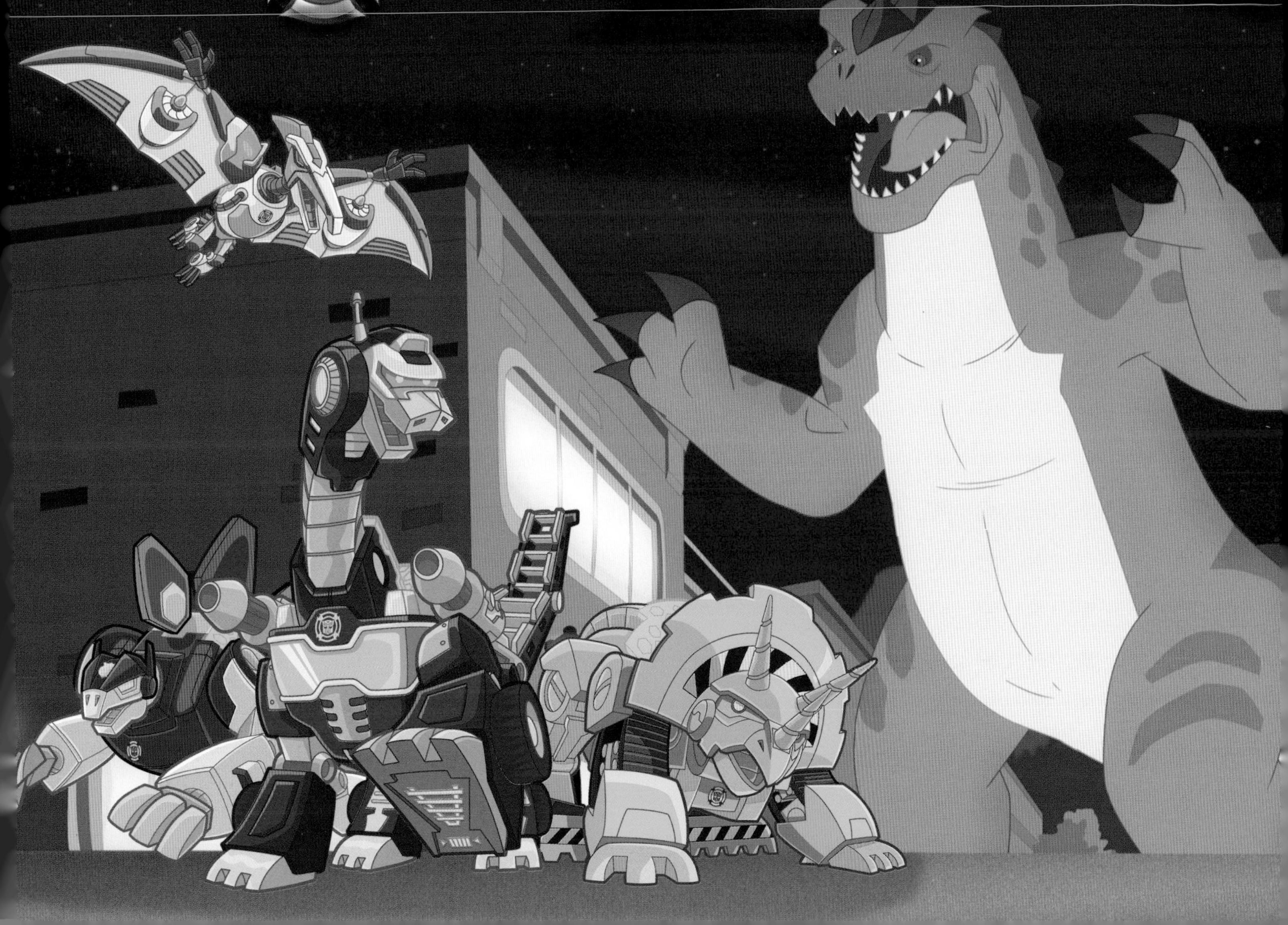

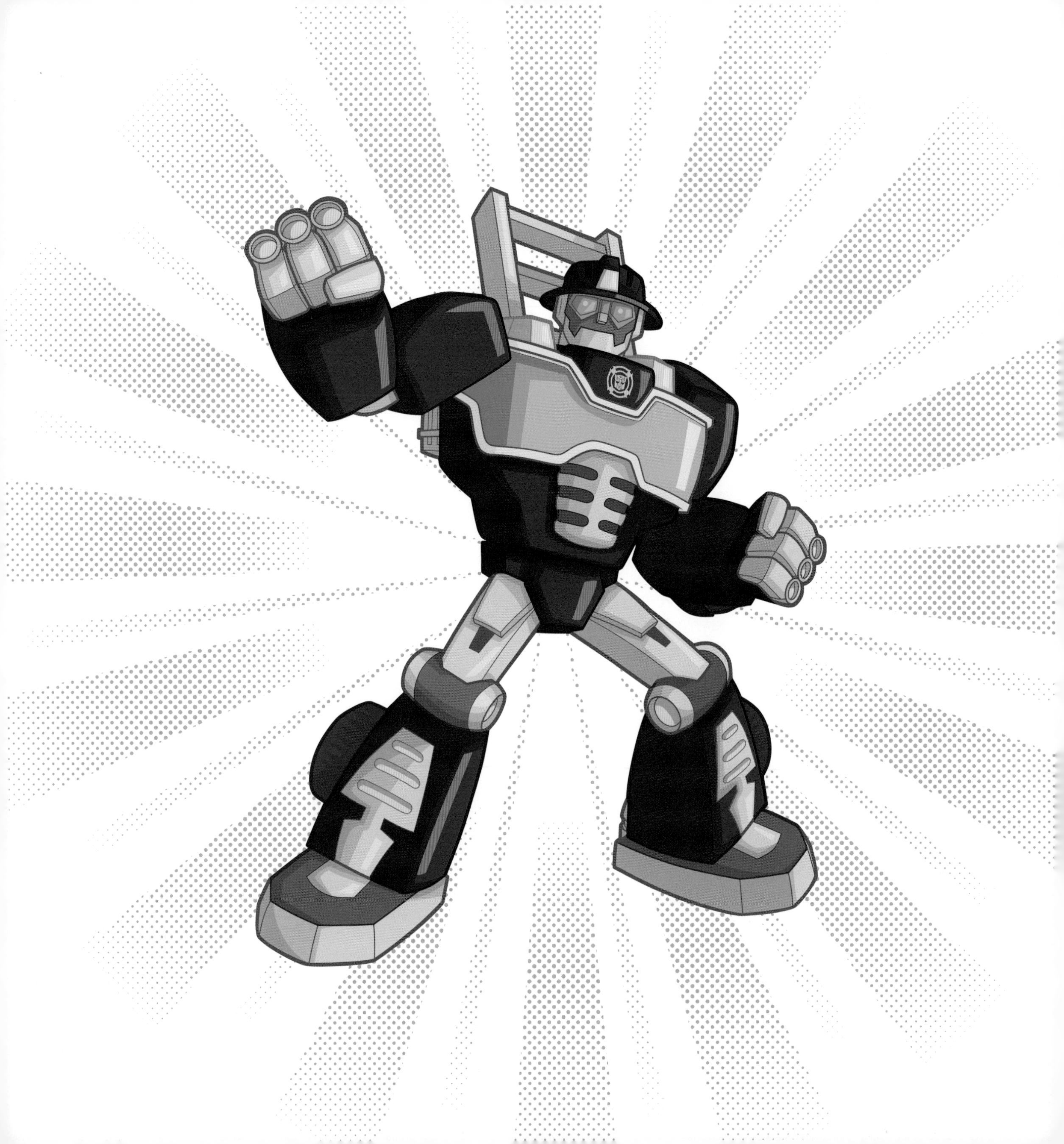

TRANSFORMERS RESCUE BOTS

Attack of the Movie Monsters!

Adapted by Brandon T. Snider
Based on the episode "The Attack of Humungado"
written by Shannon McKain and Jackson Grant

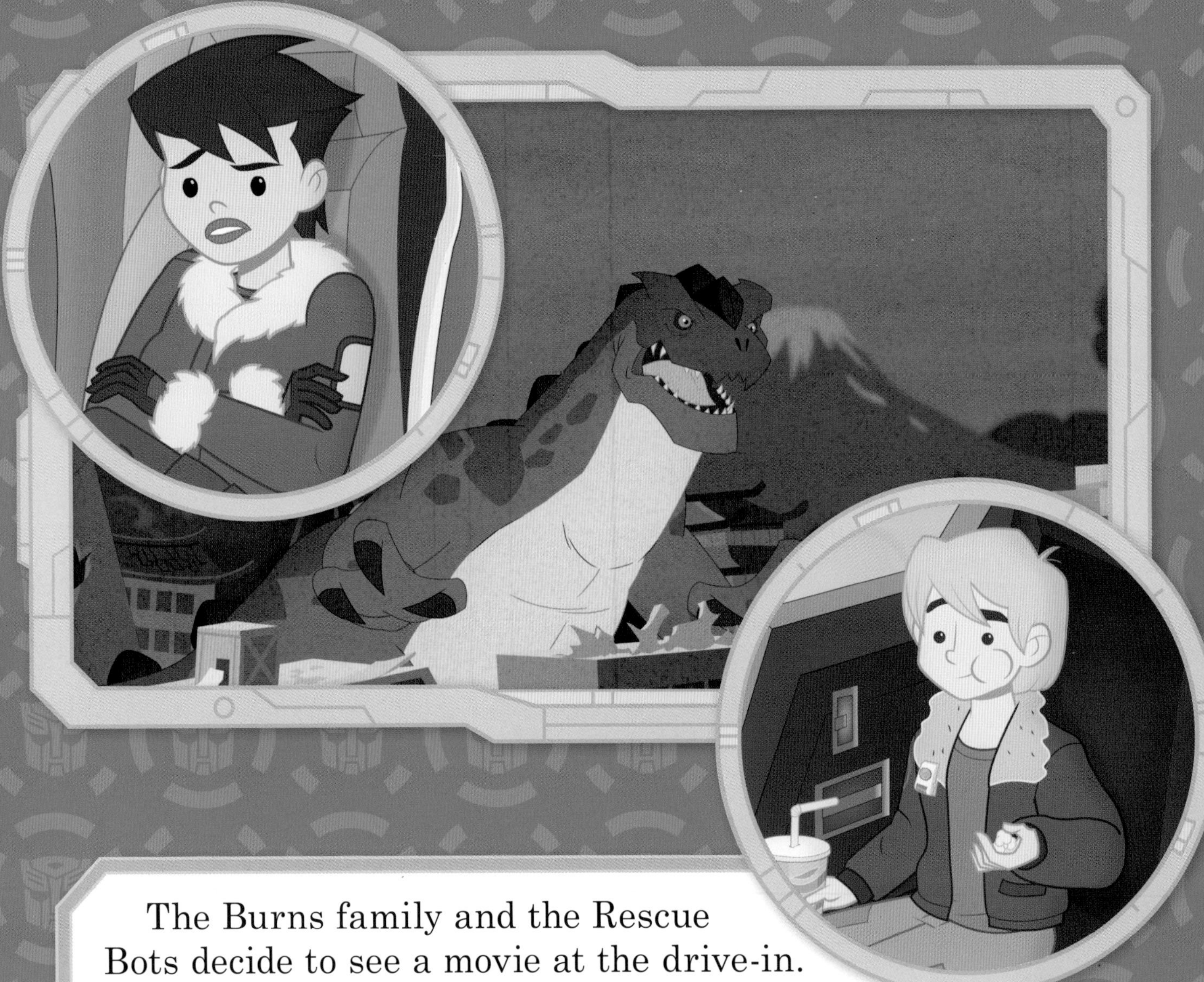

The Burns family and the Rescue Bots decide to see a movie at the drive-in.

"Why do we have to watch some silly monster movie?" grumbles Dani.

"*Attack of the Humungado* is not just *any* silly monster movie," says Kade. "It's a *kaiju* classic!"

"And there's nothing better than movie popcorn!" says Cody.

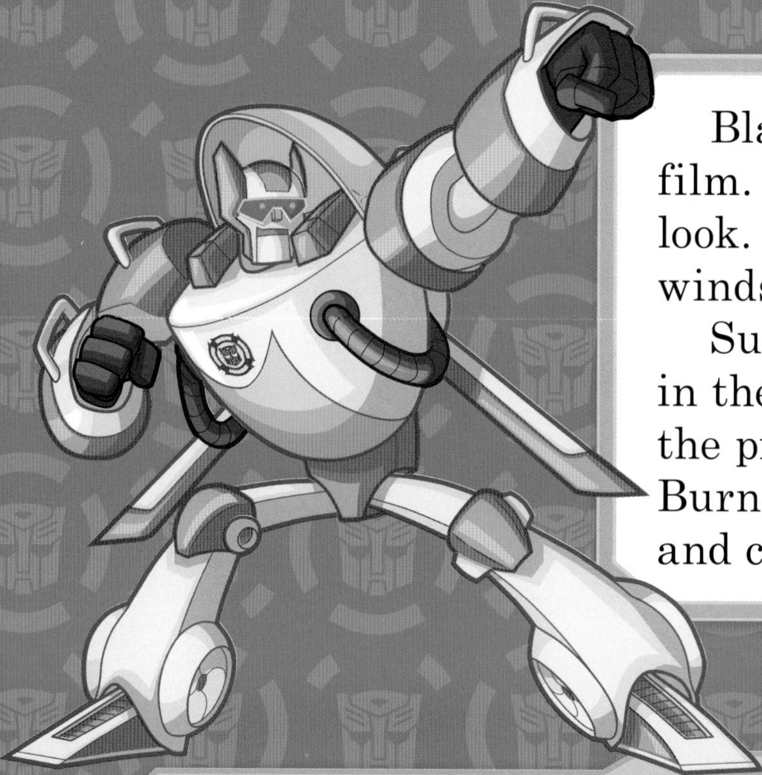

Blades is unimpressed by the old film. “Look at how fake those monsters look. I’ve cleaned scarier stuff off my windshield,” he says.

Suddenly, a terrible fire breaks out in the projection booth! Mr. Bunty, the projectionist, is in trouble. Chief Burns spots the flames from the hill and calls the Rescue Bots to action.

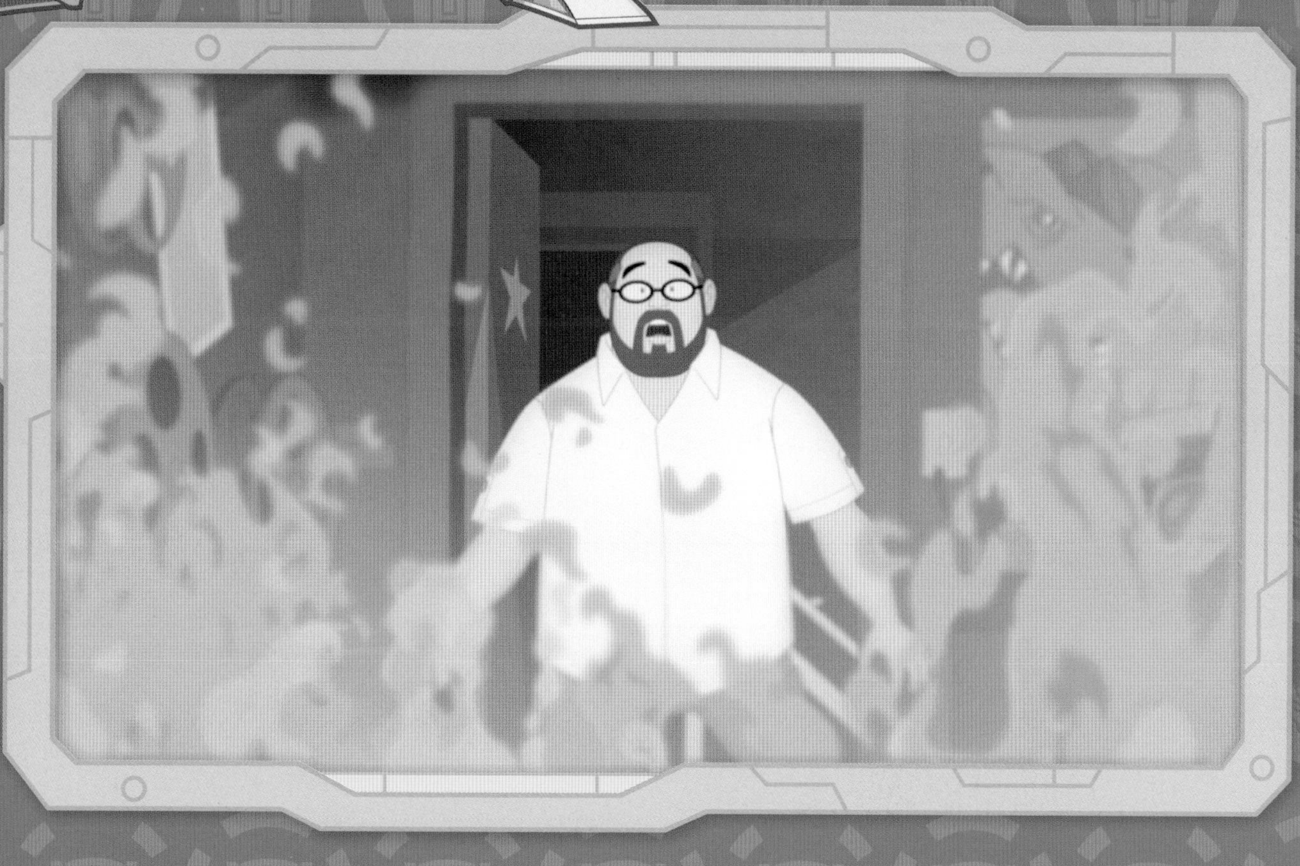

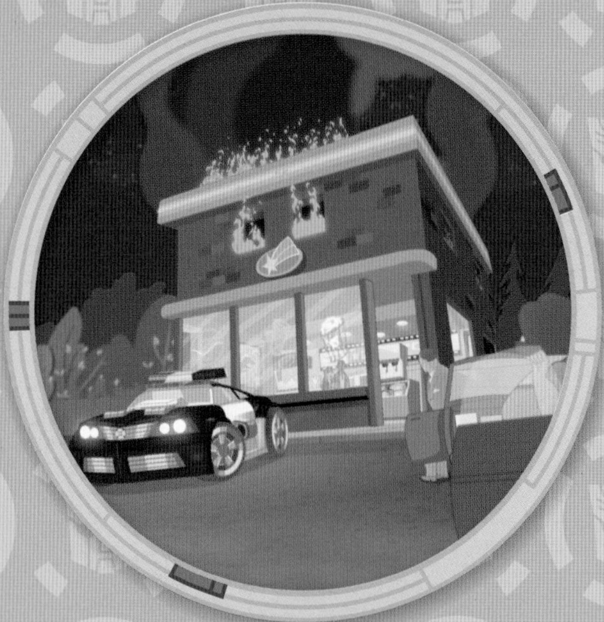

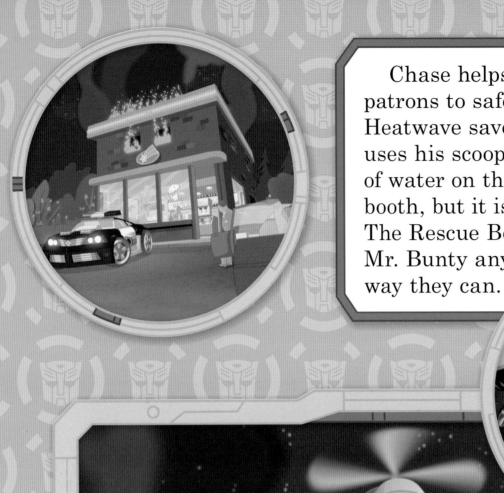

Chase helps guide the movie patrons to safety while Kade and Heatwave save Mr. Bunty. Blades uses his scoop claw to drop a load of water on the blazing projection booth, but it is burned to a crisp. The Rescue Bots promise to help Mr. Bunty any way they can.

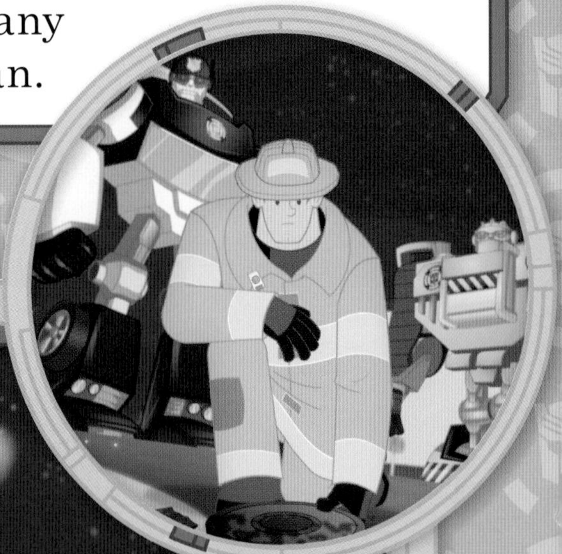

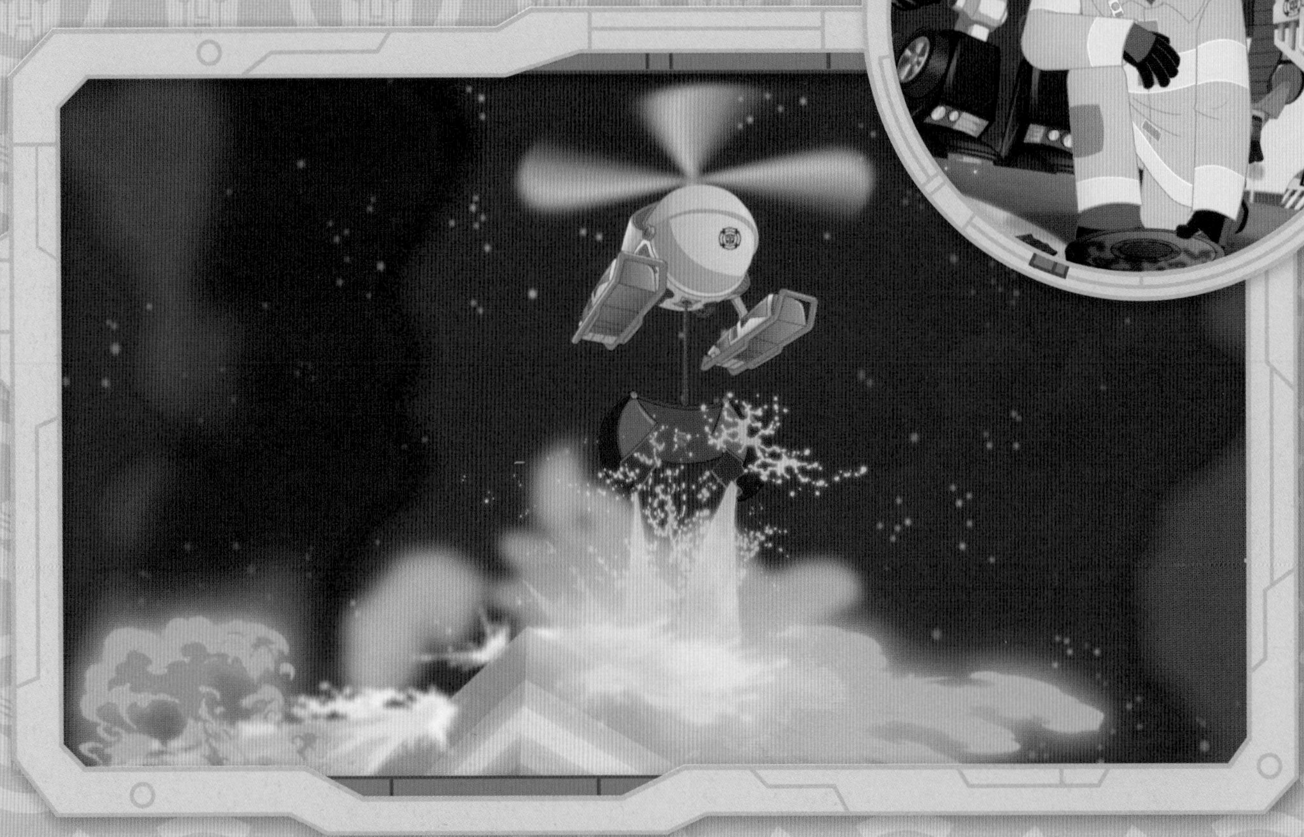

The following day, the Rescue Team helps rebuild the building. Heatwave, Chase, Boulder, and Blades put the finishing touches on the projection booth by fixing the roof in place. Mr. Bunty is grateful for the team's kindness.

"Thank you! It's never looked better. I wish I could say the same for my projector," Mr. Bunty says.

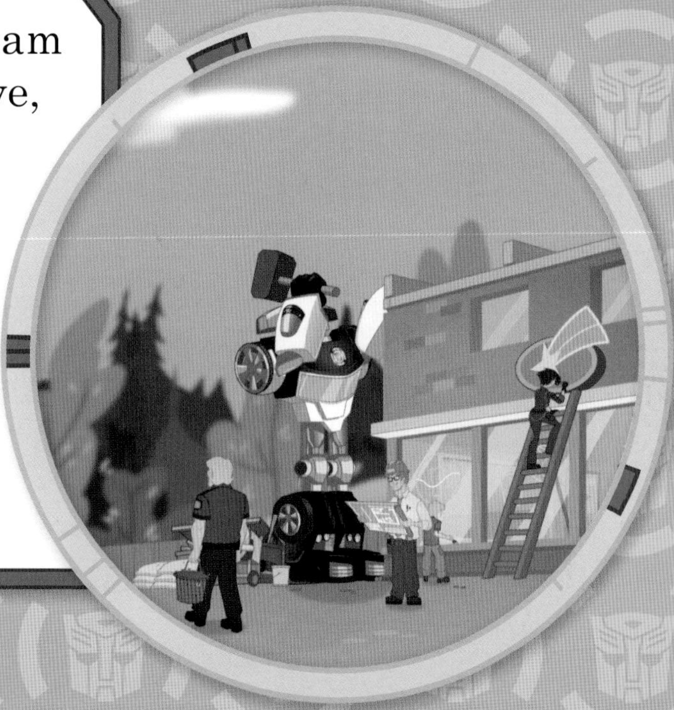

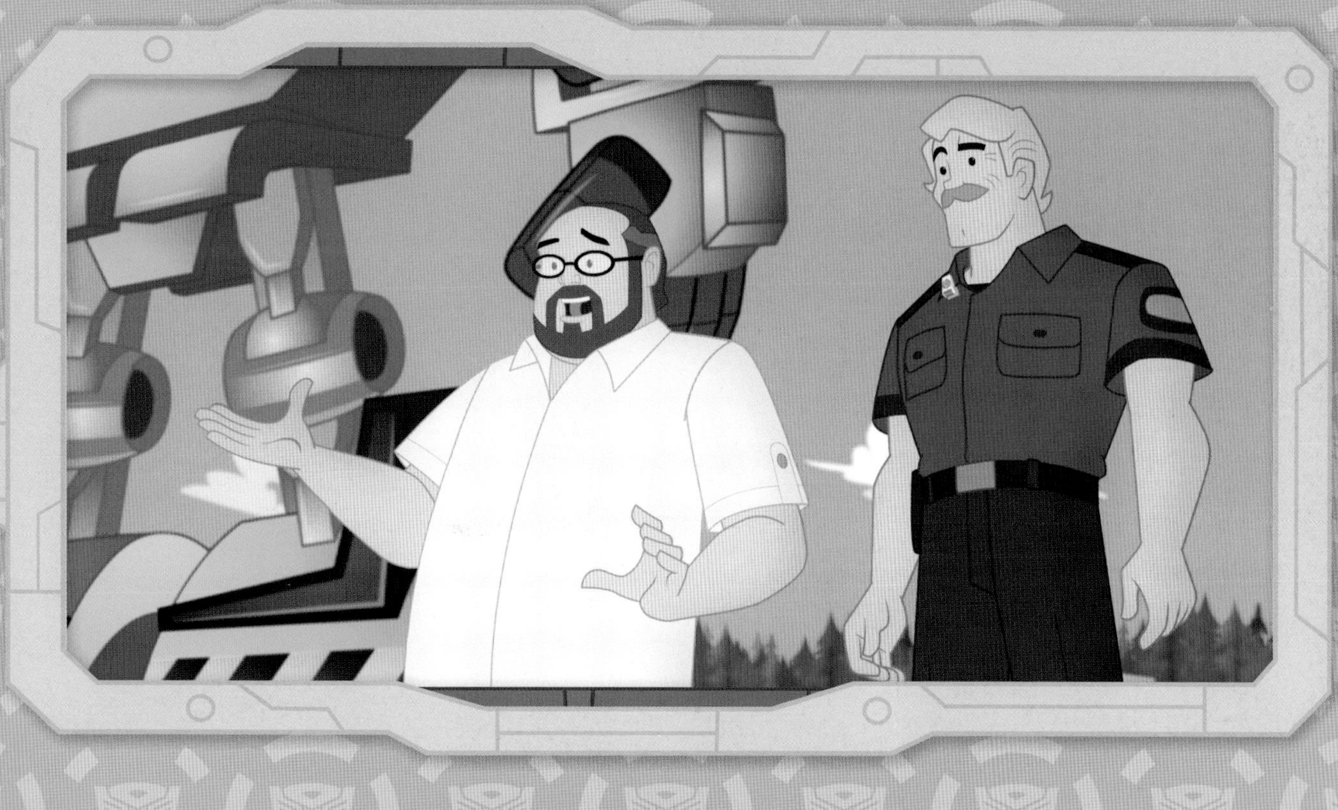

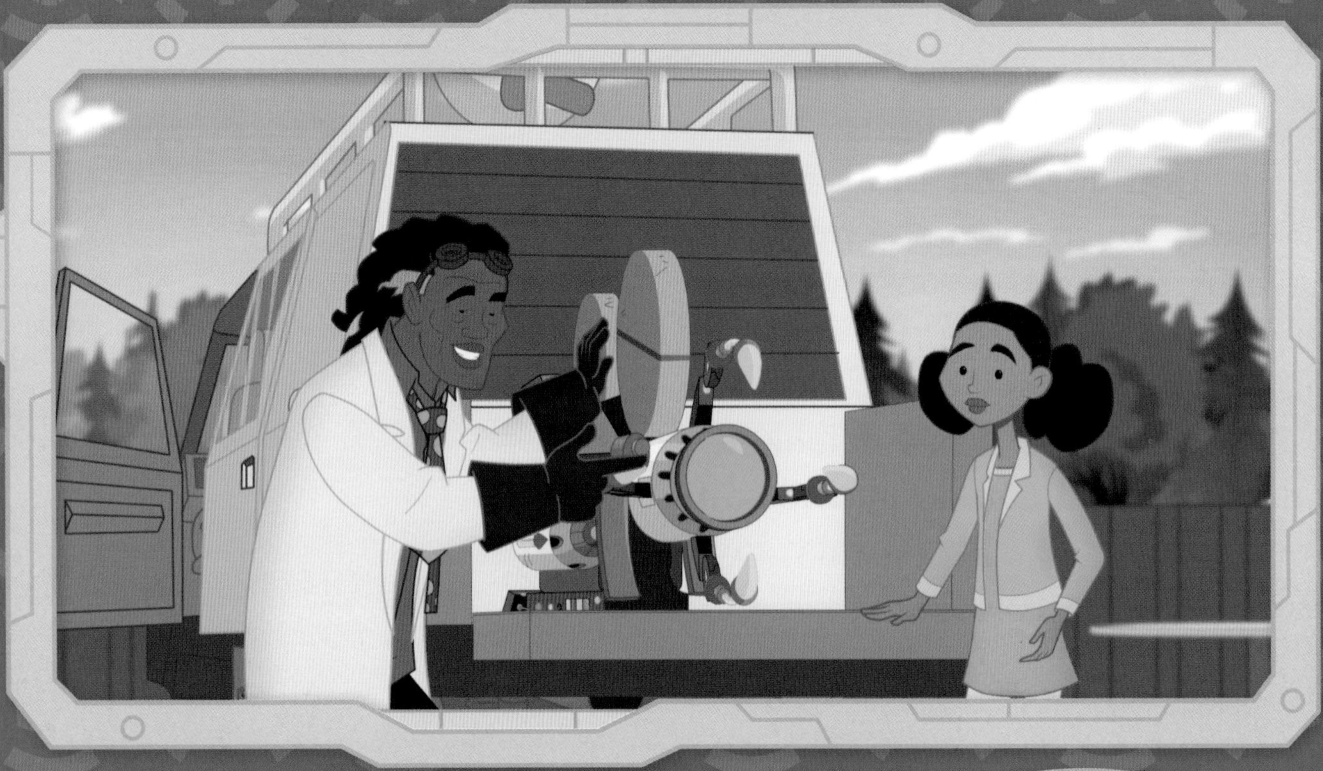

Luckily, Doc Greene has a brand-new device for Mr. Bunty. "This is a Holomorphic Projector," explains Doc Greene. "It turns a two-dimensional movie into a hologram!"

"So the monsters can stomp around in the audience?" asks Cody.

"Indeed. They'll look more lifelike than you could ever imagine," says Doc Greene.

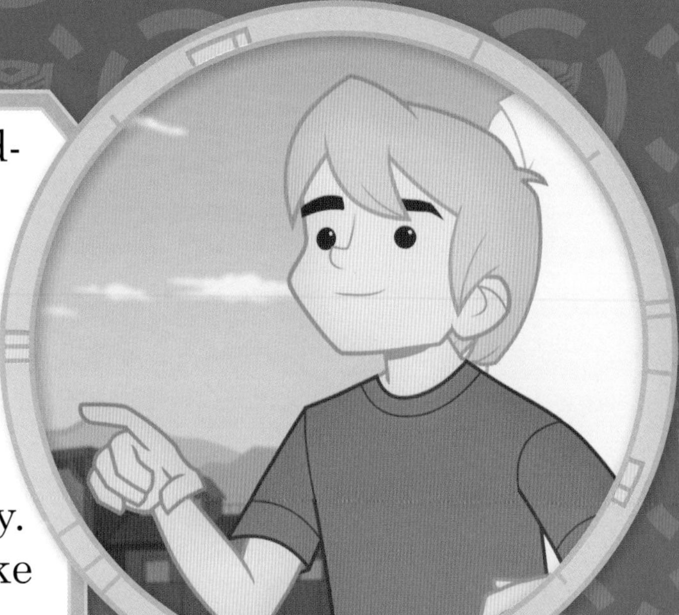

At the drive-in the next night, Kade and Mr. Bunty watch another *kaiju* movie, starring the monster Rayvenous. As Rayvenous appears on the screen, a power surge occurs, causing the projector to malfunction. Kade and Mr. Bunty don't notice that Rayvenous has actually come right out of the movie and into Griffin Rock!

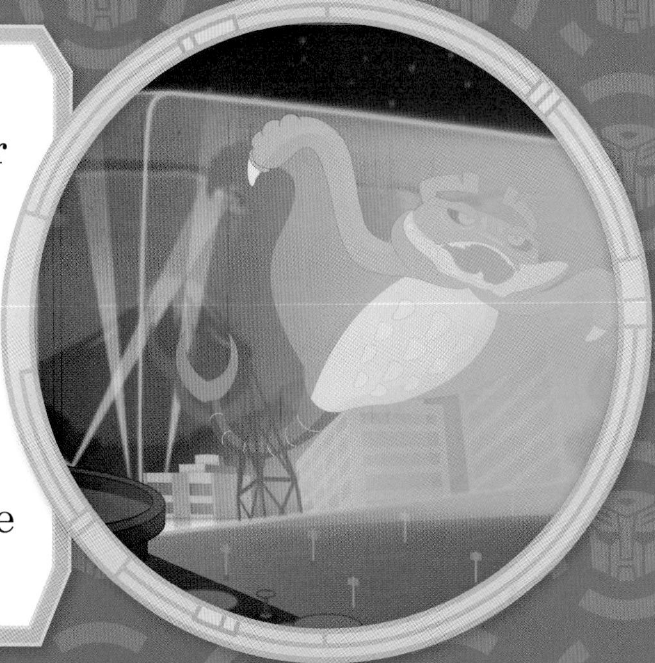

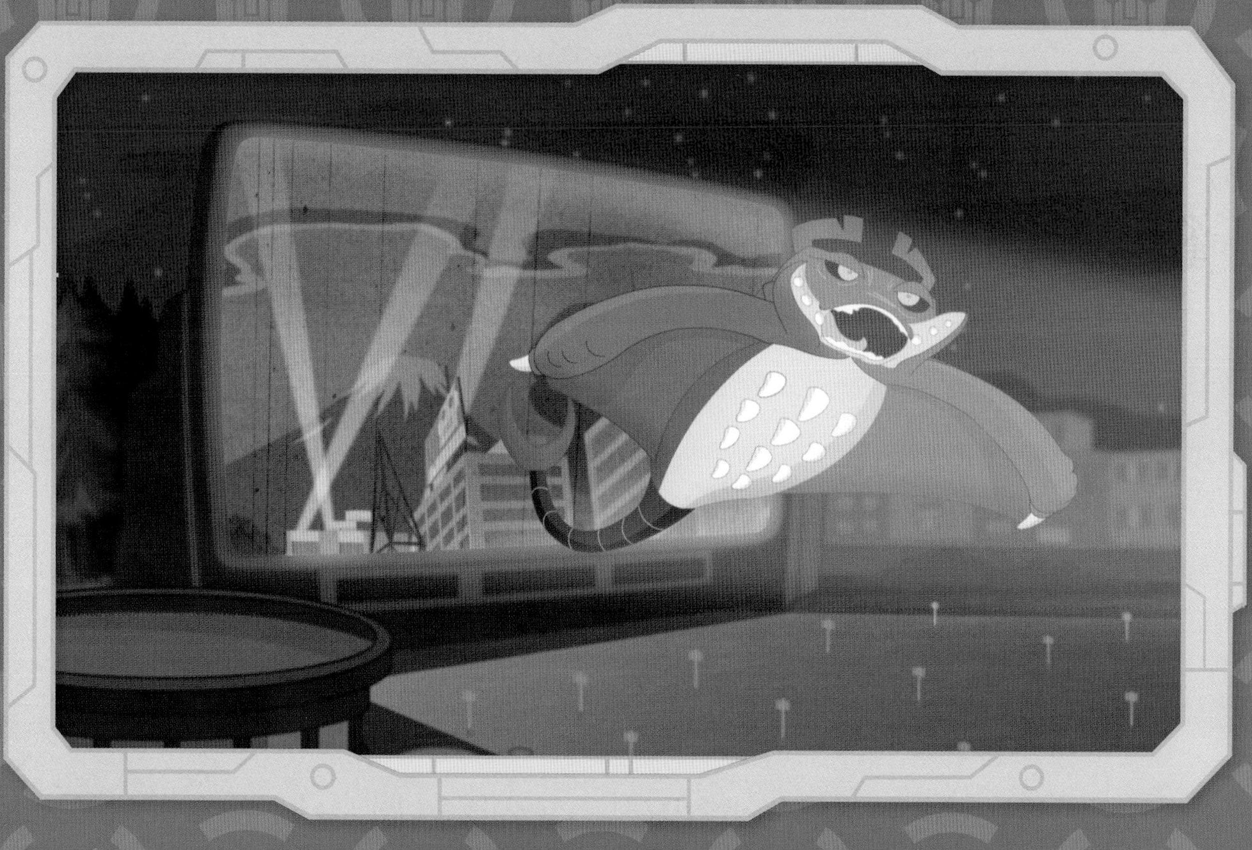

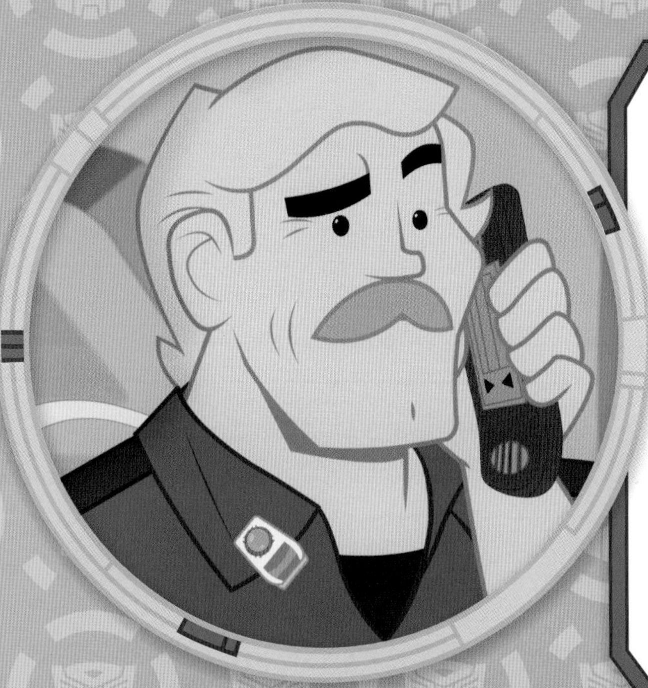

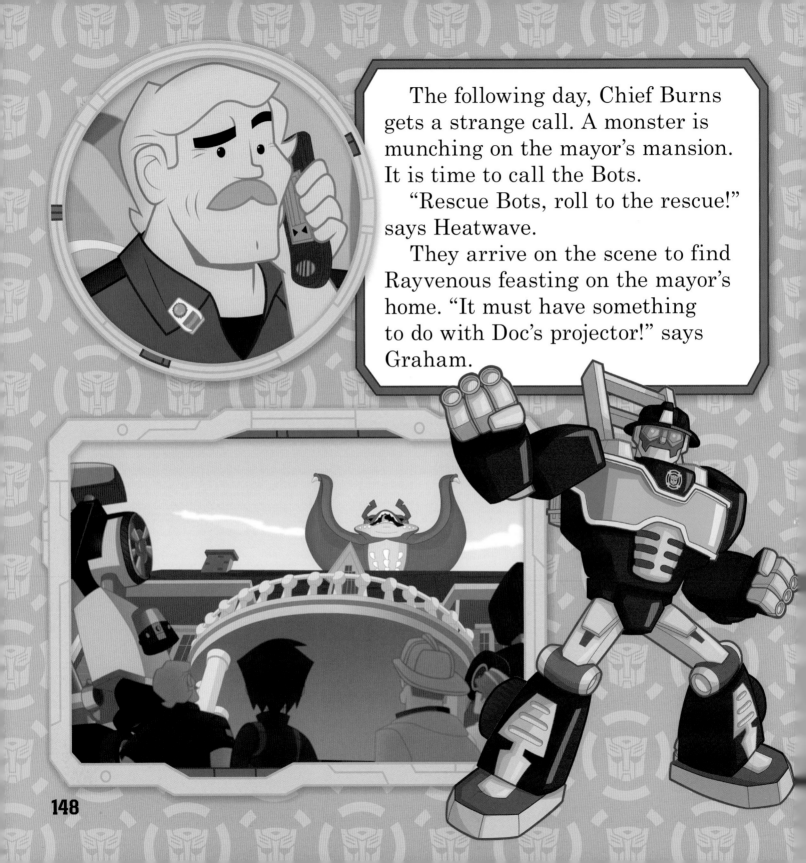

The following day, Chief Burns gets a strange call. A monster is munching on the mayor's mansion. It is time to call the Bots.

"Rescue Bots, roll to the rescue!" says Heatwave.

They arrive on the scene to find Rayvenous feasting on the mayor's home. "It must have something to do with Doc's projector!" says Graham.

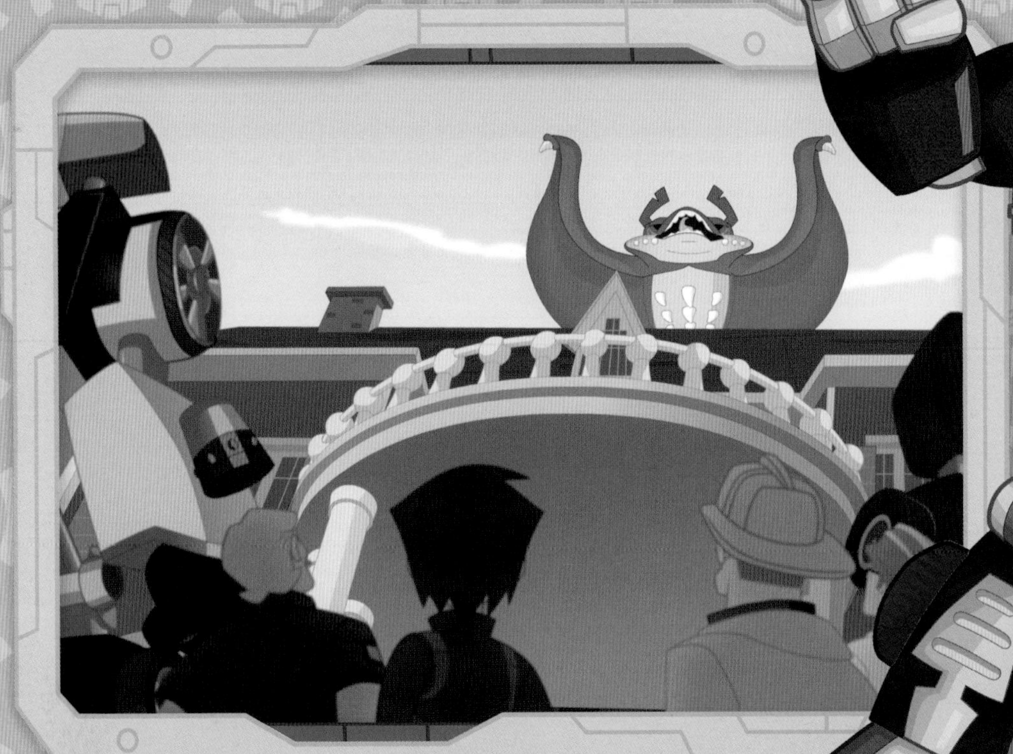

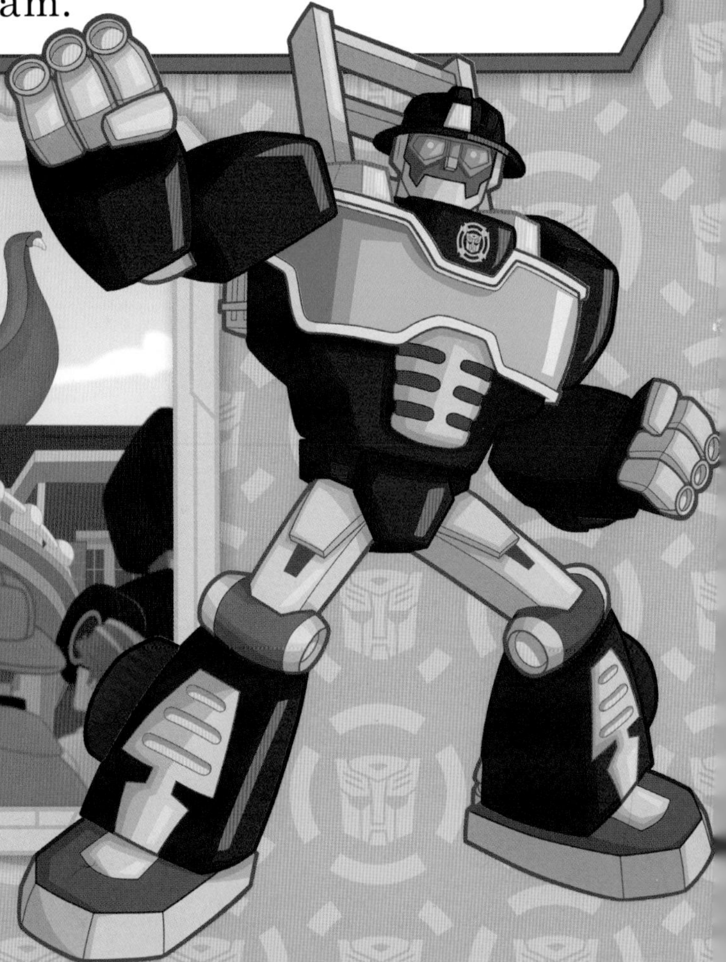

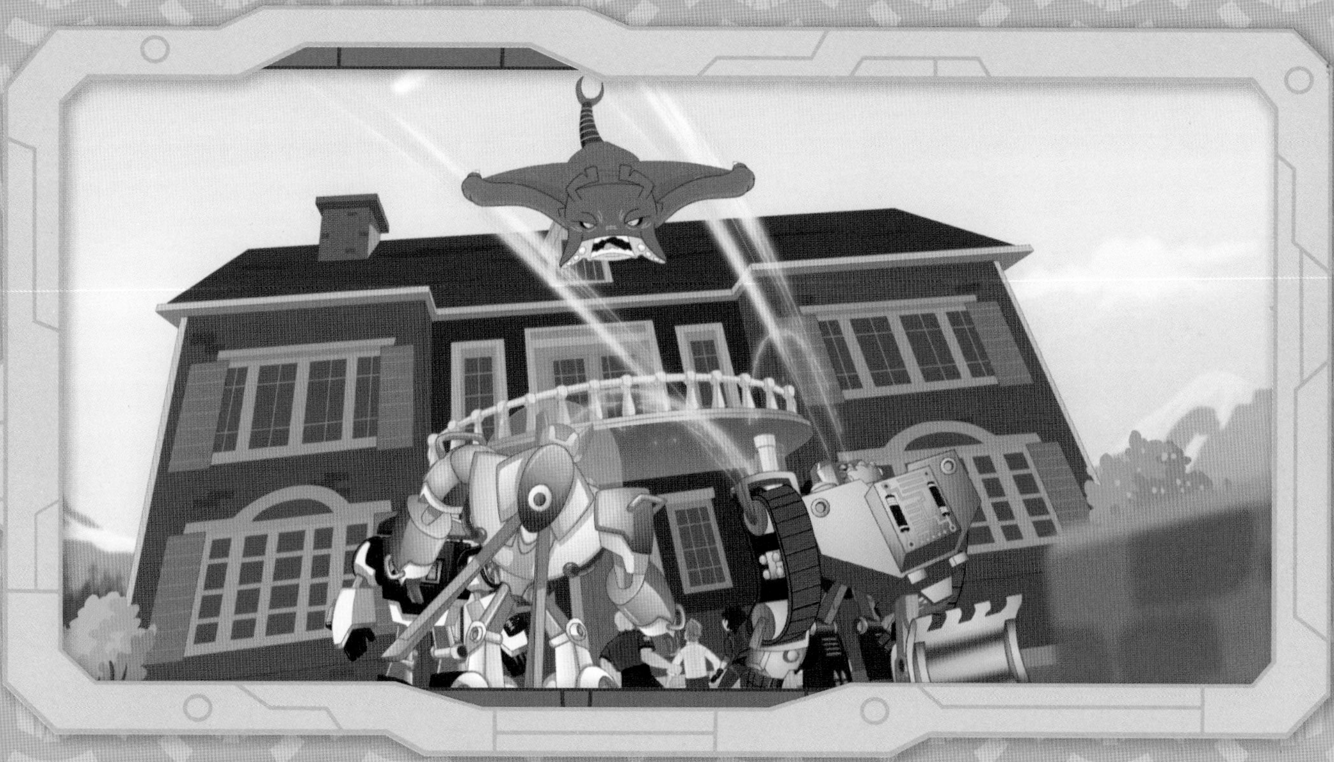

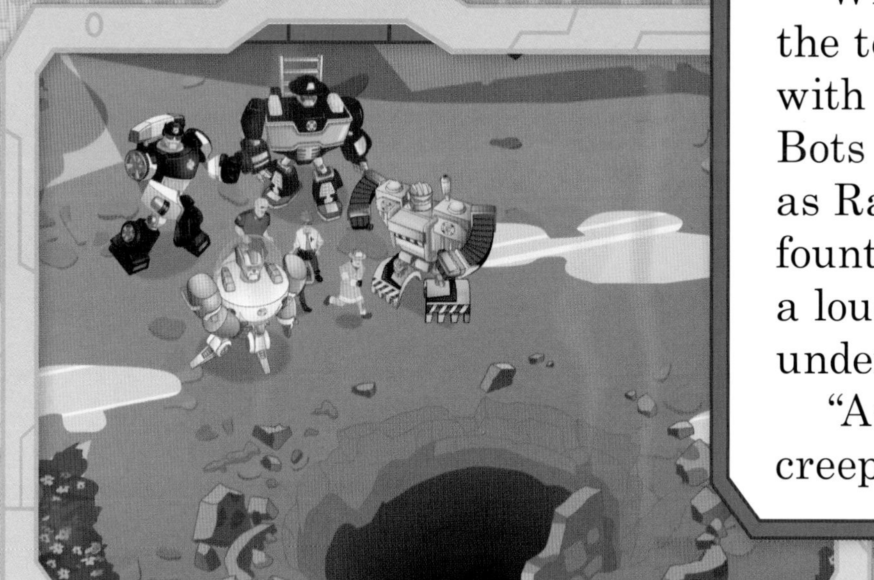

When Rayvenous dive-bombs the team, Heatwave blasts him with his water jets. The Rescue Bots shield their teammates as Rayvenous crashes into a fountain. The monster lets out a loud screech and flies into an underground tunnel to escape.

"As if it couldn't get any creepier," Blades says.

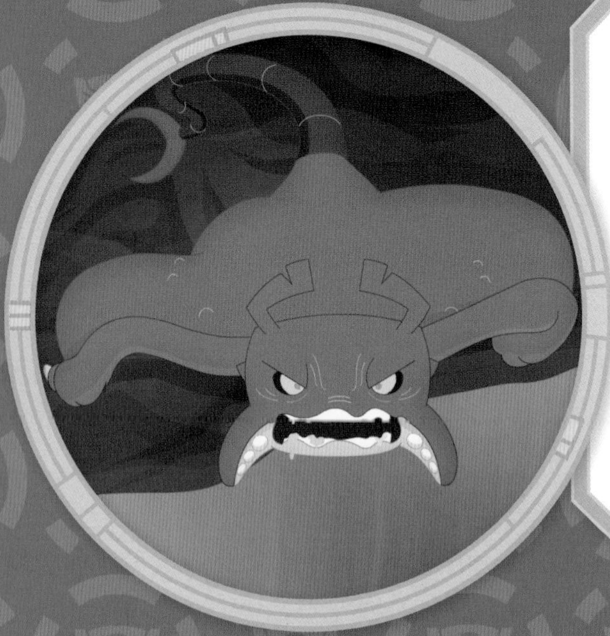

The Rescue Bots find Rayvenous snarling in a corner of the cavern. He attacks the Bots and starts chomping on Blades.

"Why me? There are others in the room, you know," says Blades.

Heatwave steps in to save Blades, and the Bots trap Rayvenous. They take him back to the drive-in for observation.

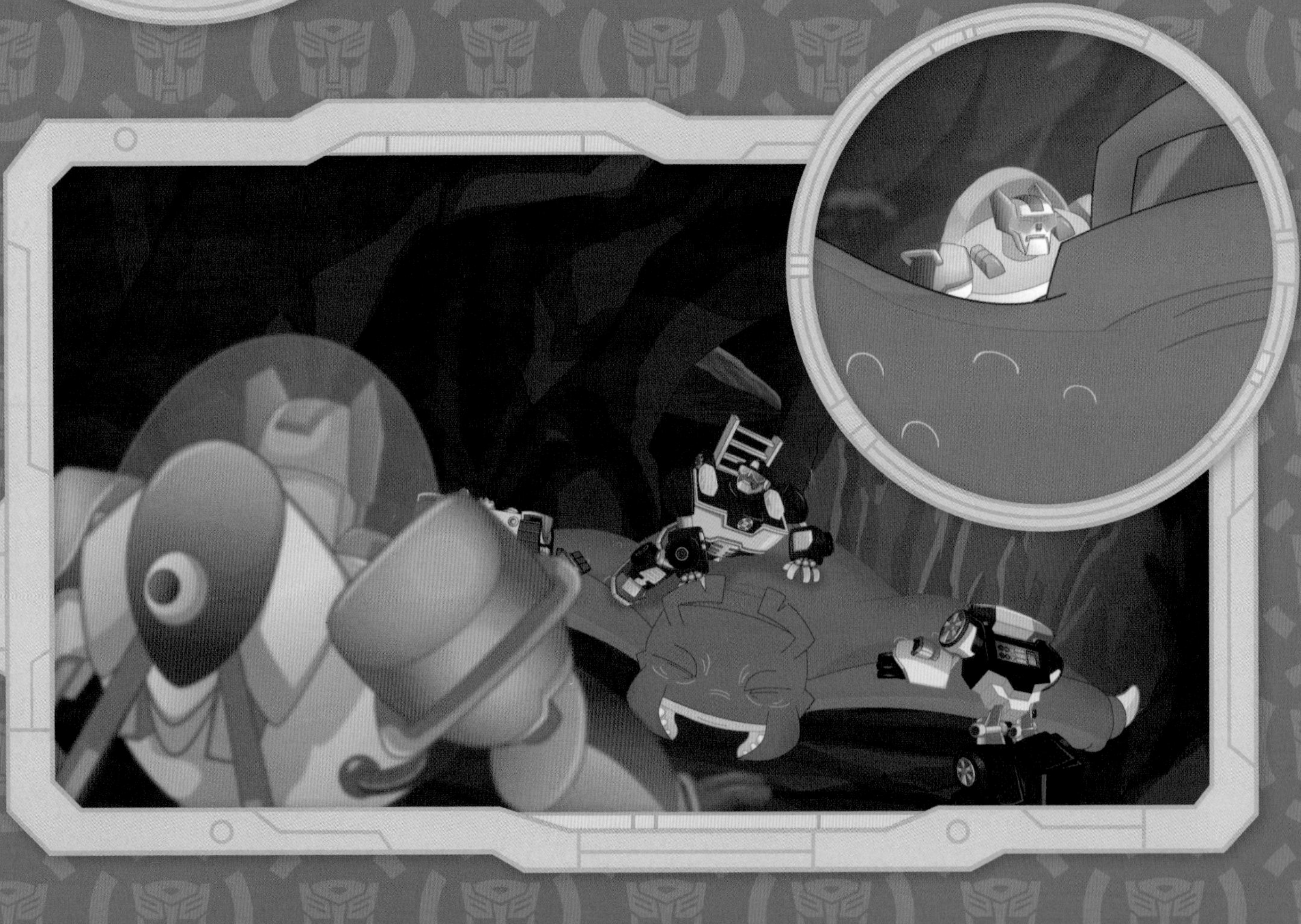

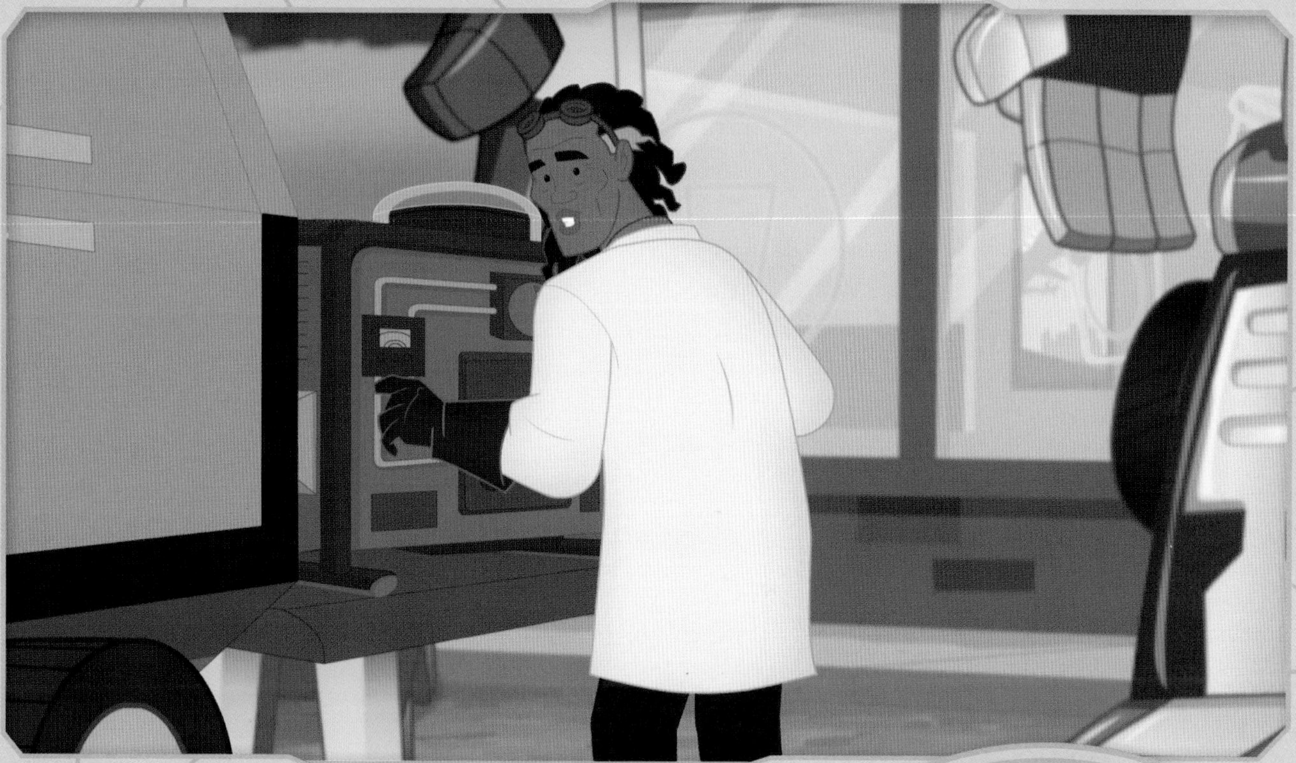

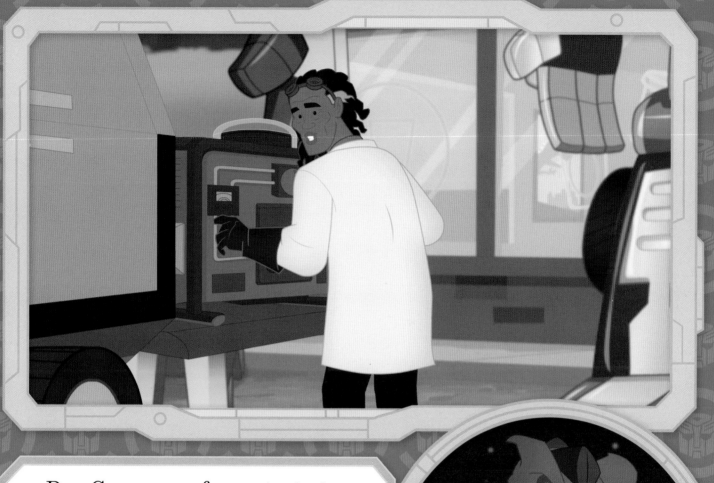

Doc Greene performs tests to determine what happened. He concludes that the power surge turned the hologram of Rayvenous into a solid creature with a taste for destruction. Doc re-creates the power surge, hoping to return Rayvenous to his previous state, but instead he brings forth a scary new menace: HUMUNGADO!

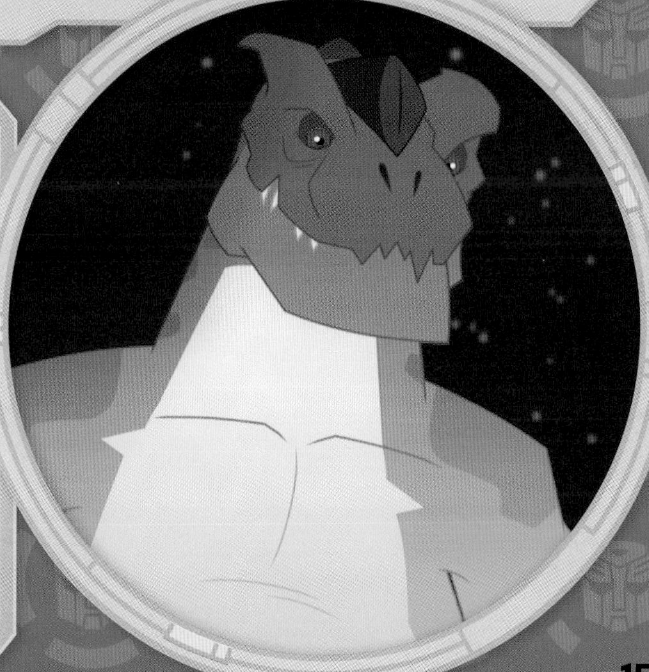

Humungado blasts his fire breath high into the sky and uses his massive tail to crush the Holomorphic Projector. Then he turns his attention to Rayvenous, who tries to zap him with ice. Heatwave and Chase grab Humungado's arms, and Boulder grabs his tail. The Rescue Bots aren't giving up without a fight.

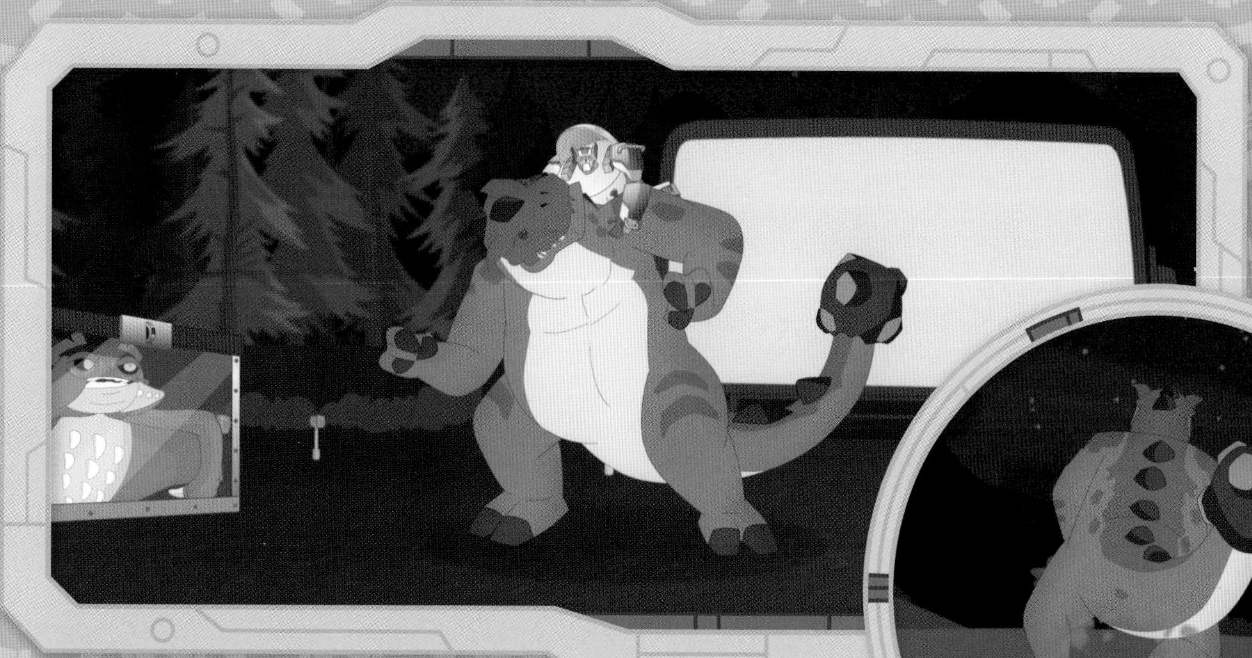

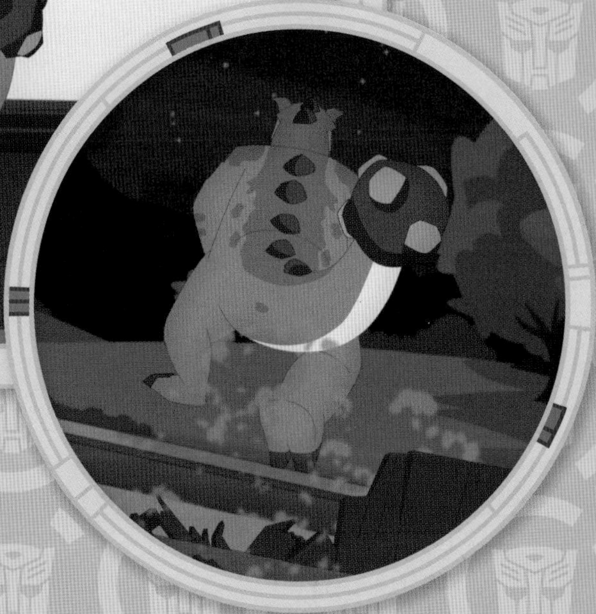

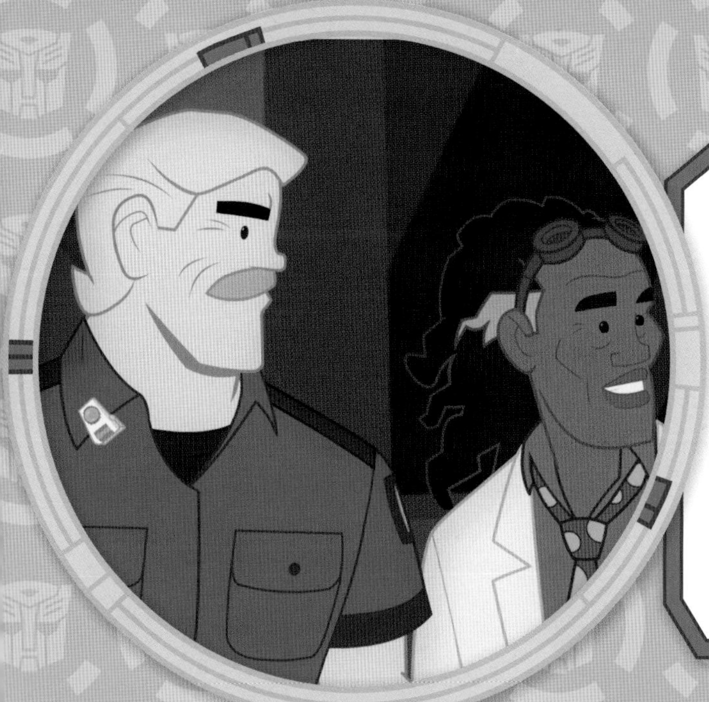

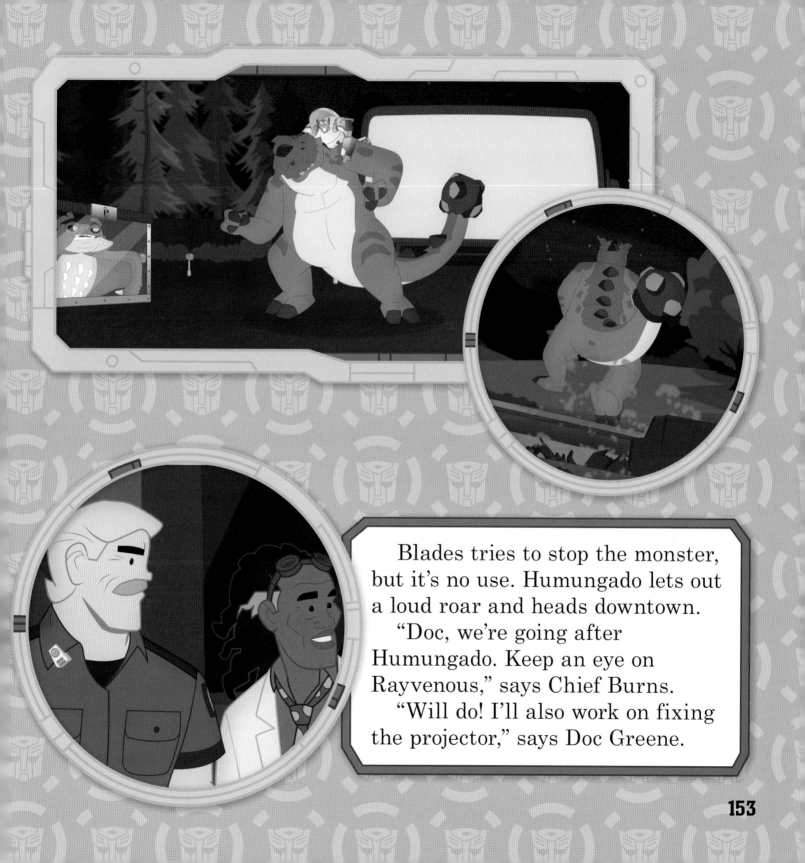

Blades tries to stop the monster, but it's no use. Humungado lets out a loud roar and heads downtown.

"Doc, we're going after Humungado. Keep an eye on Rayvenous," says Chief Burns.

"Will do! I'll also work on fixing the projector," says Doc Greene.

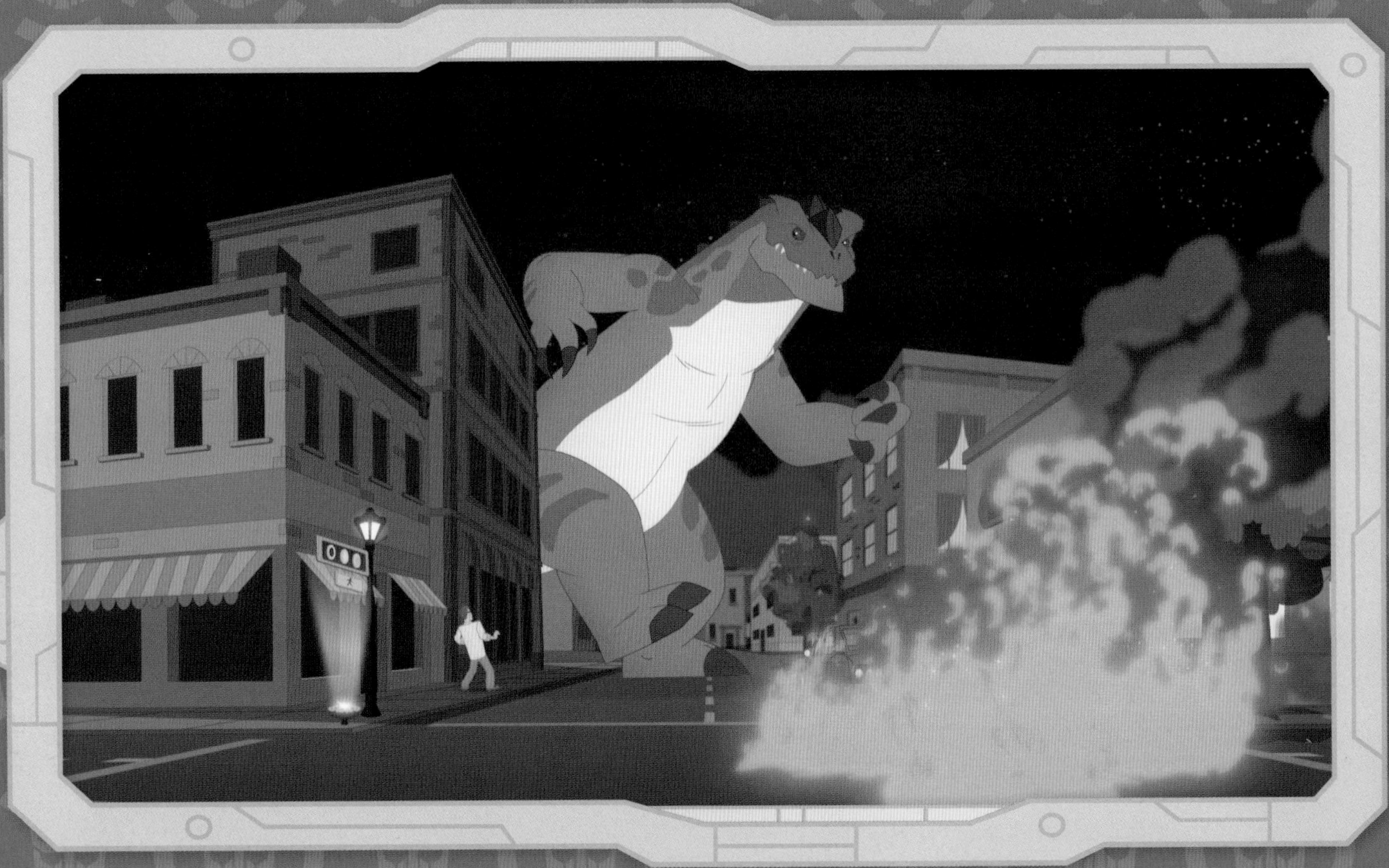

The chief and Chase watch as Humungado rampages through the city. Blades tries to distract Humungado, but it doesn't work. Nothing seems to be working. Is Humungado unstoppable?

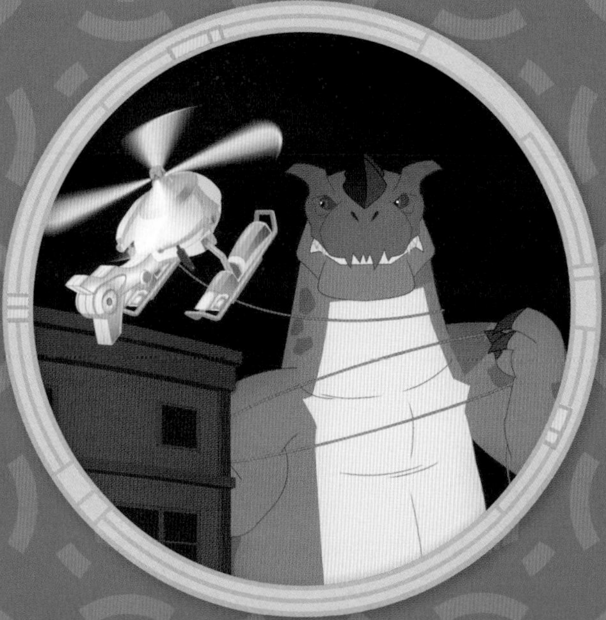

It is time for Kade, Heatwave, Graham, and Boulder to try their luck. They grab a gigantic steel beam, hoping to trip Humungado as he walks by.

"Hey, Humungado! Have a good *trip*. See you next *fall*," jokes Kade.

The monster snaps the steel beam like a toothpick.

"I guess he doesn't share your sense of humor," says Heatwave.

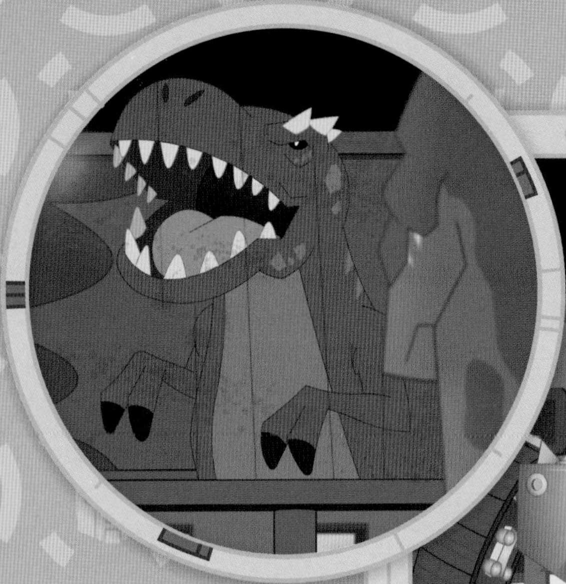

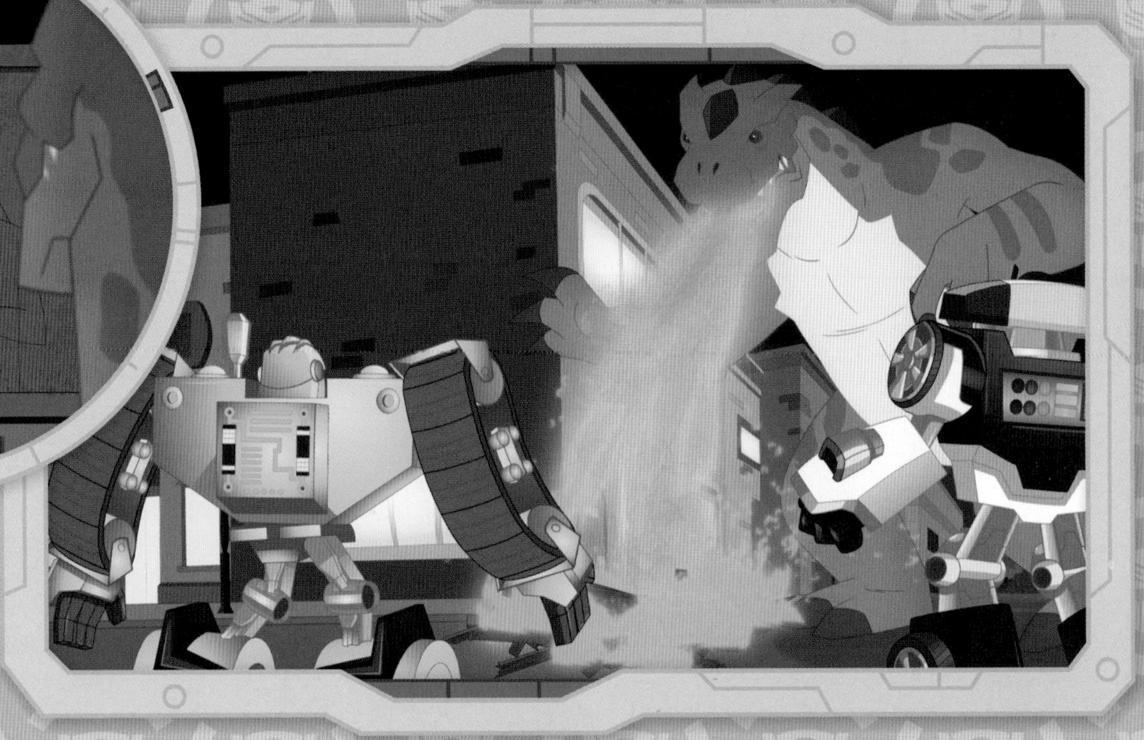

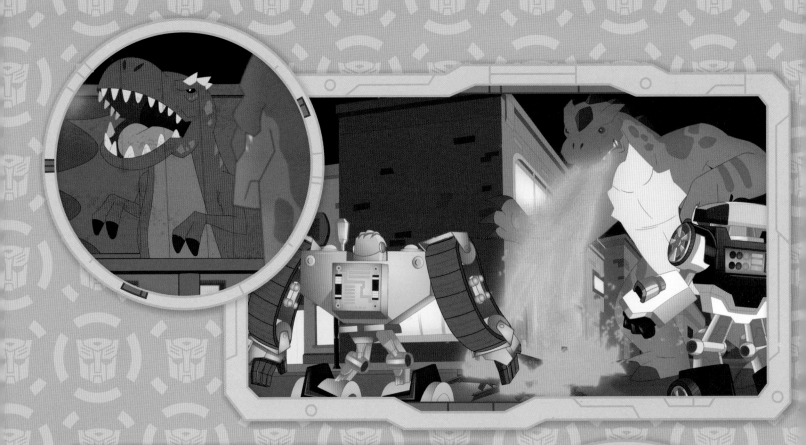

Humungado spots a billboard for the museum's dinosaur exhibit. It features a Tyrannosaurus rex. This makes Humungado *very* angry. He lets out another heart-stopping screech and angrily knocks over the billboard. Then he burns it to ash.

"Whoa! He must *really* hate dinosaurs," says Cody. "Or billboards."

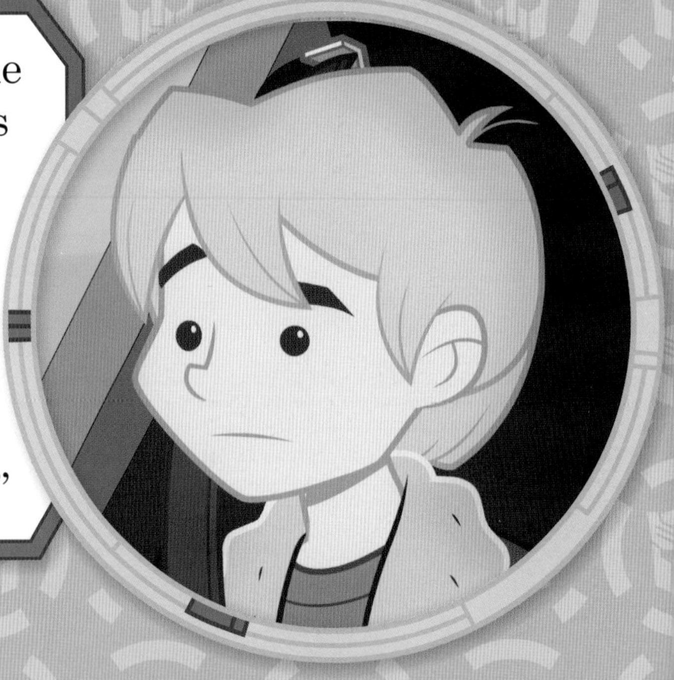

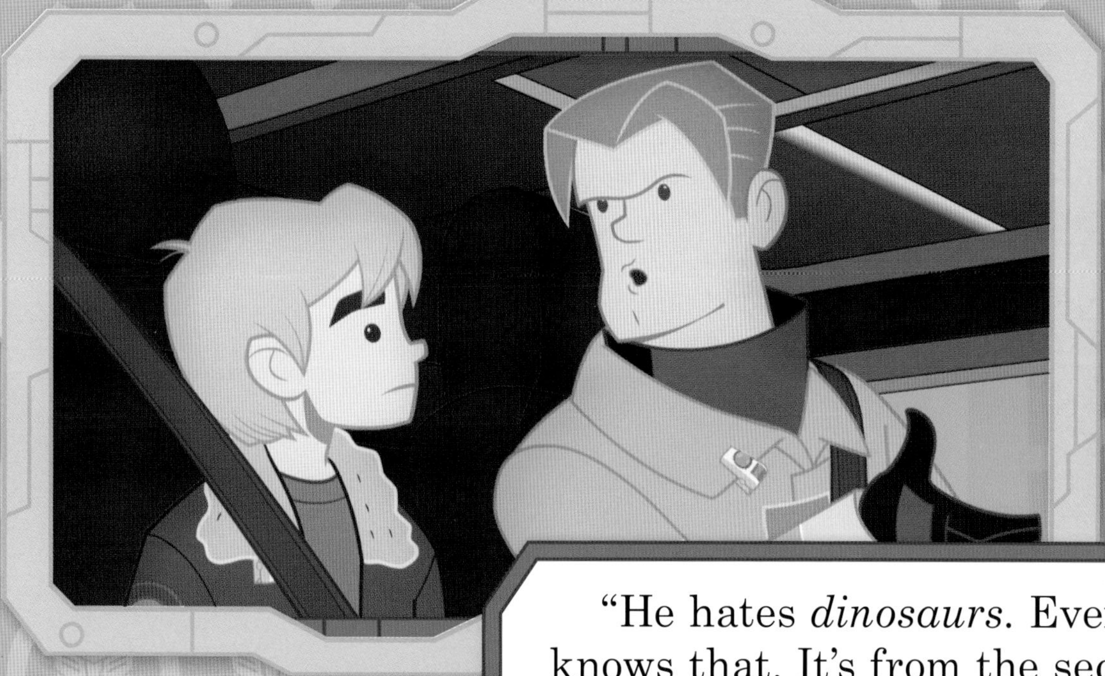

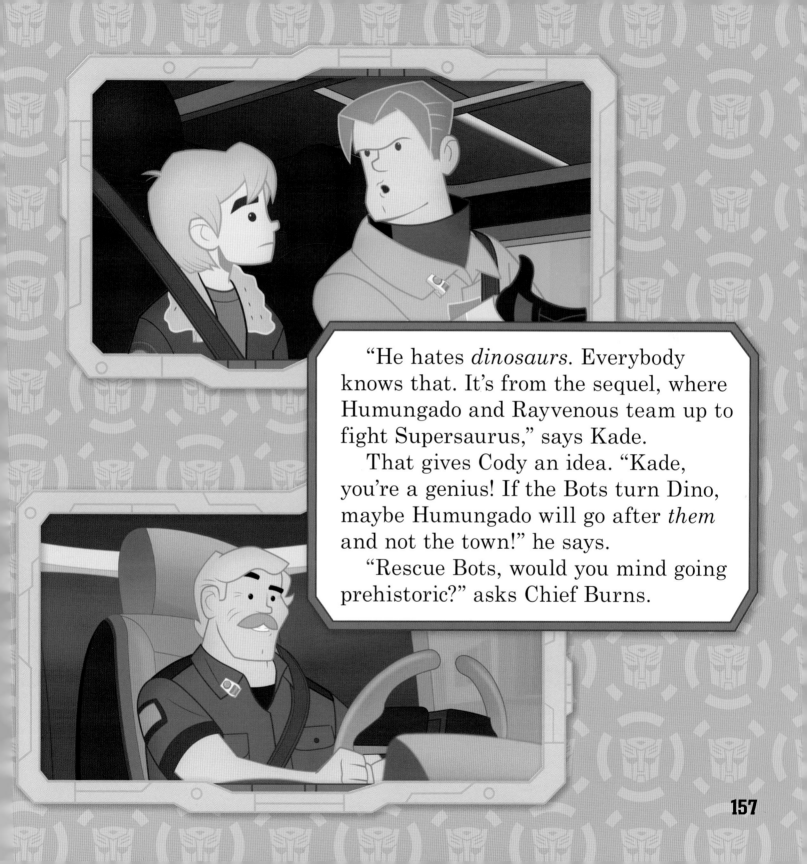

“He hates *dinosaurs*. Everybody knows that. It’s from the sequel, where Humungado and Rayvenous team up to fight Supersaurus,” says Kade.

That gives Cody an idea. “Kade, you’re a genius! If the Bots turn Dino, maybe Humungado will go after *them* and not the town!” he says.

“Rescue Bots, would you mind going prehistoric?” asks Chief Burns.

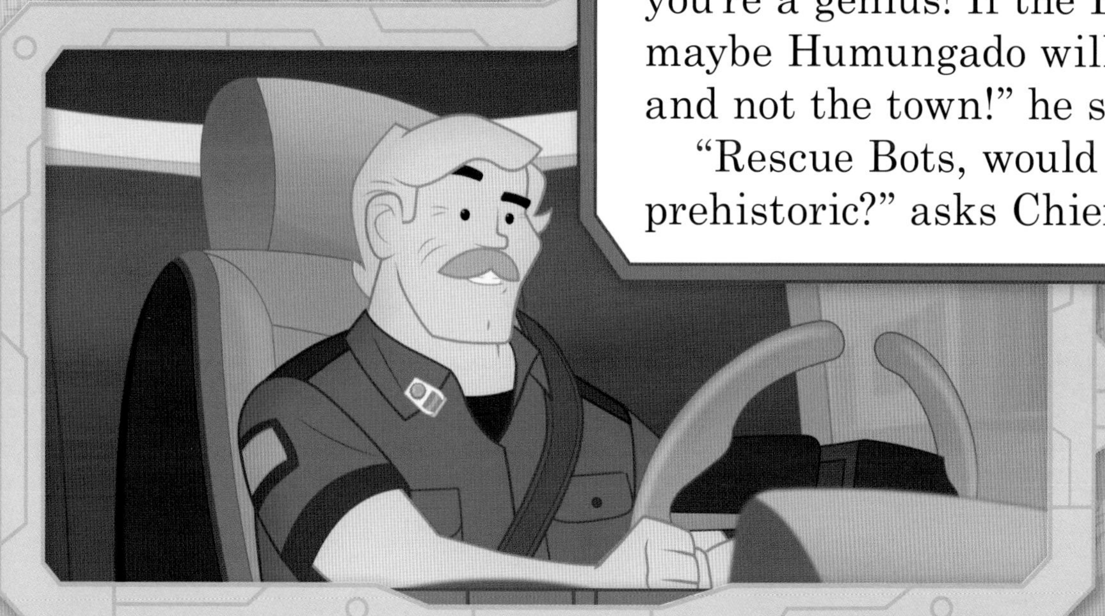

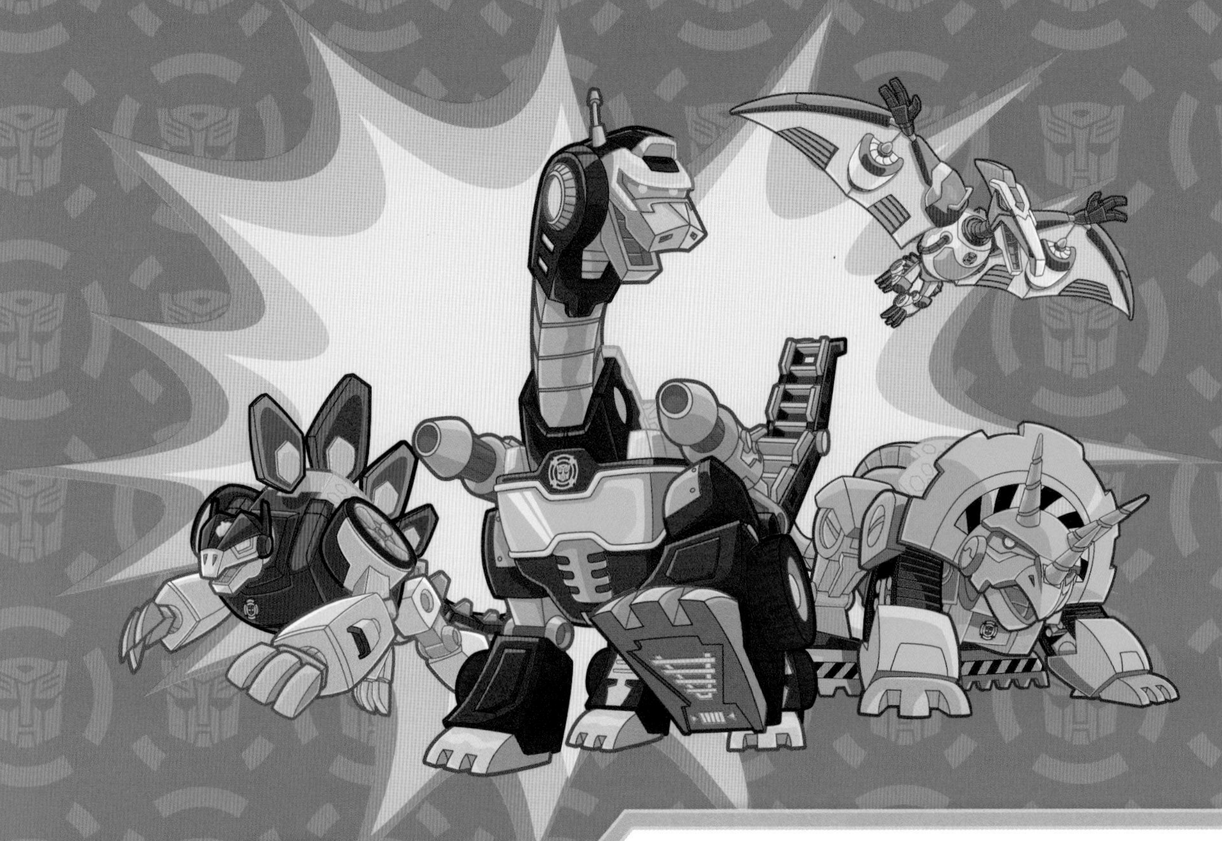

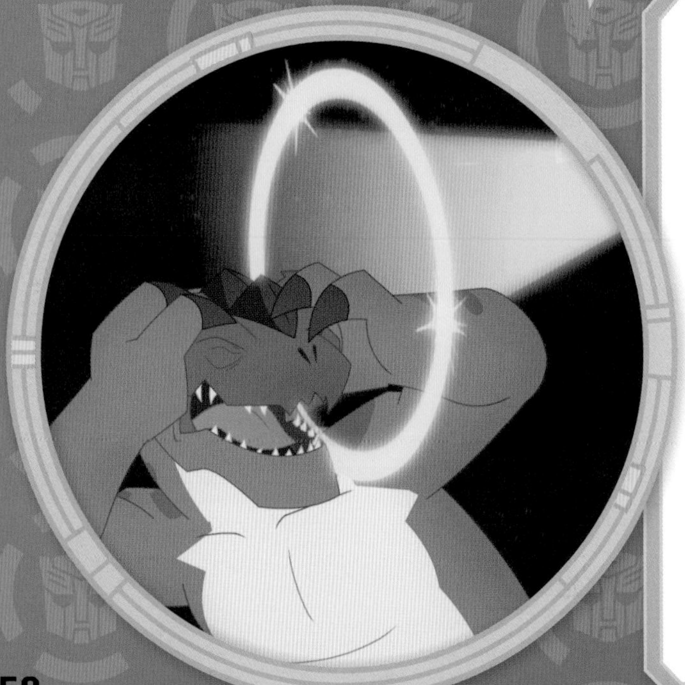

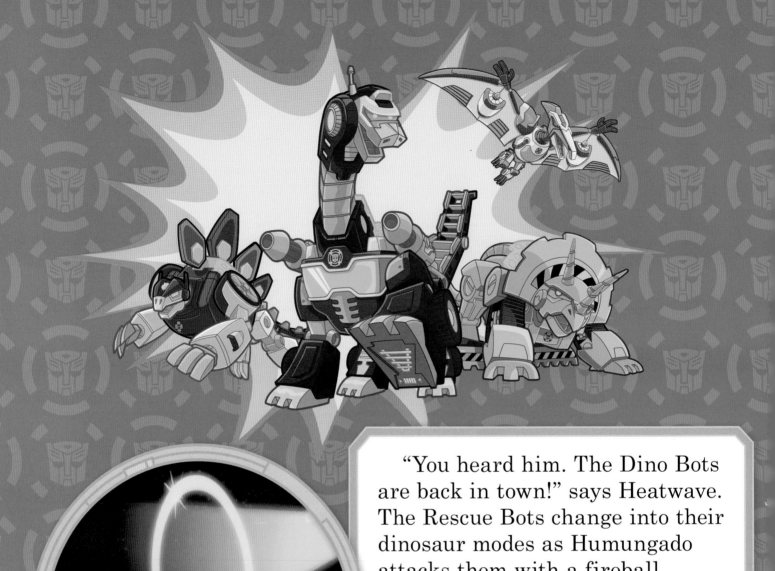

"You heard him. The Dino Bots are back in town!" says Heatwave. The Rescue Bots change into their dinosaur modes as Humungado attacks them with a fireball.

Heatwave neutralizes the fireball with a burst of water.

Boulder uses his seismic stomp to shake Humungado to his core.

Blades hits him with his sonic scream. Now Humungado is on the run.

Humungado comes upon a four-way intersection, but Chase is ready for him and blocks Humungado's path with his electrified tail. Humungado takes off toward the beach.

"It's working!" says Boulder. The rest of the Dino Bots follow Humungado to the ocean and corner him. The monster is now furious.

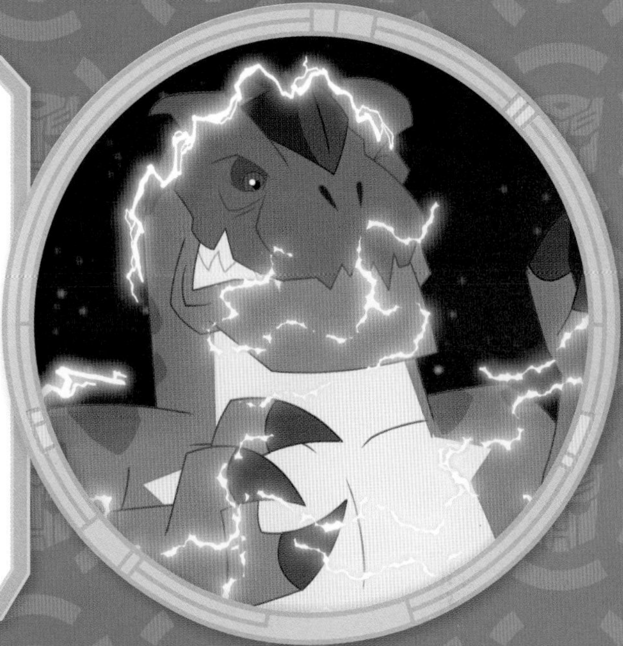

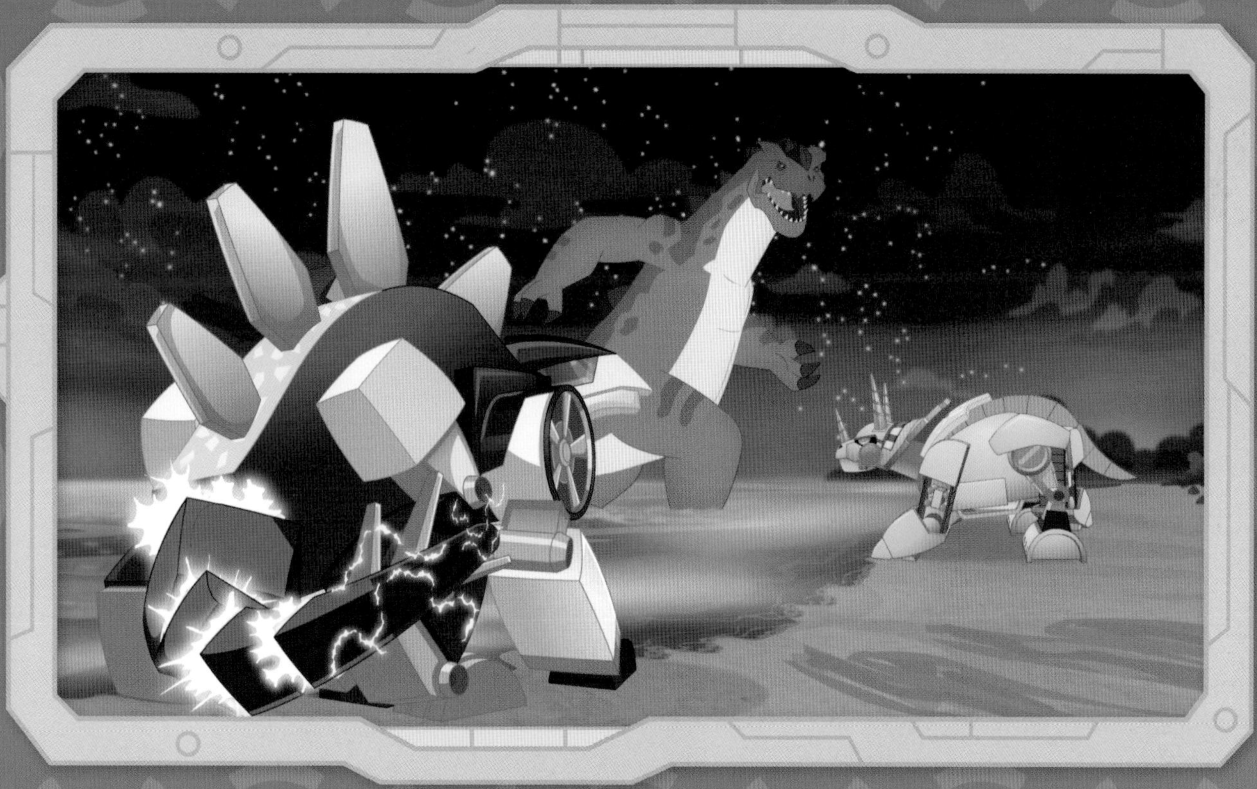

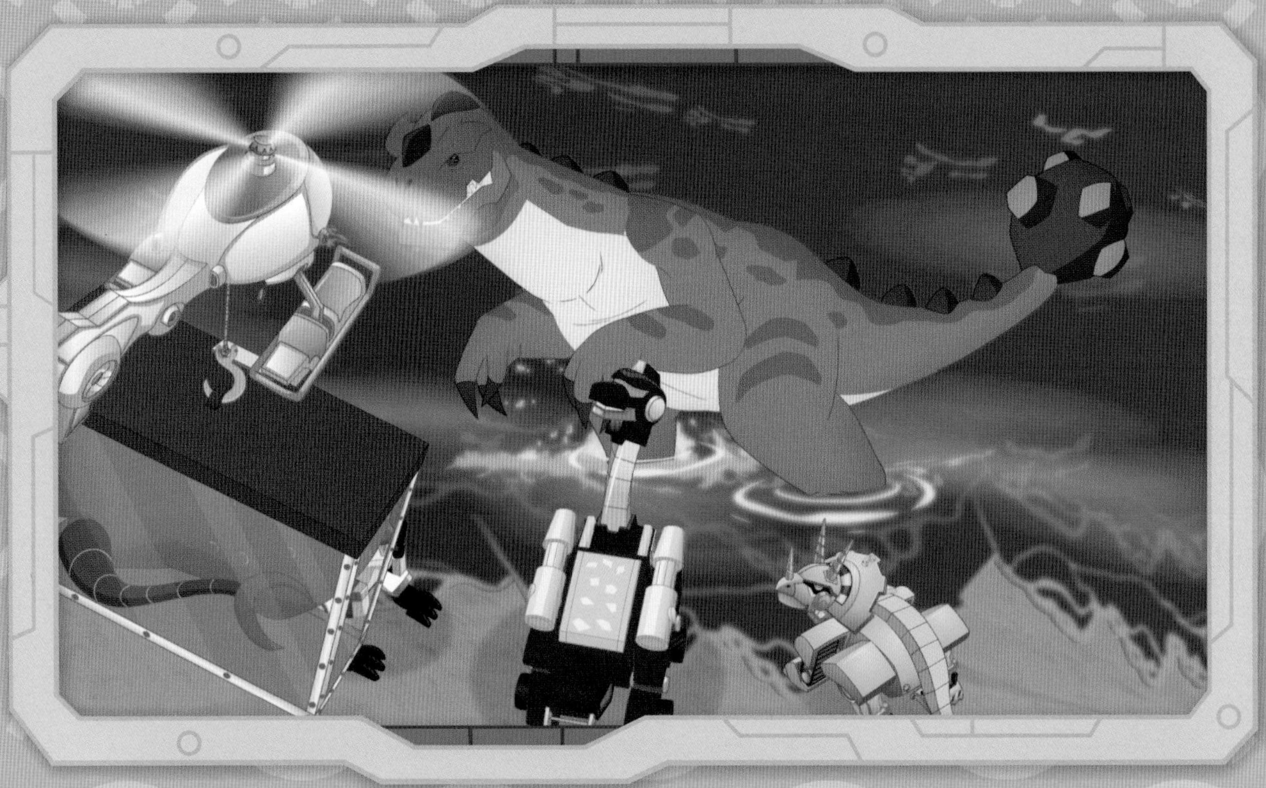

Blades uses the caged Rayvenous to lure Humungado back to the drive-in. Humungado is on the move again, letting out fiery belches along the way. A blast of fire hits Blades and sends him to the ground.

Now Rayvenous is free. Rayvenous and Humungado both hate dinosaurs and are going to join forces to destroy the Rescue Team!

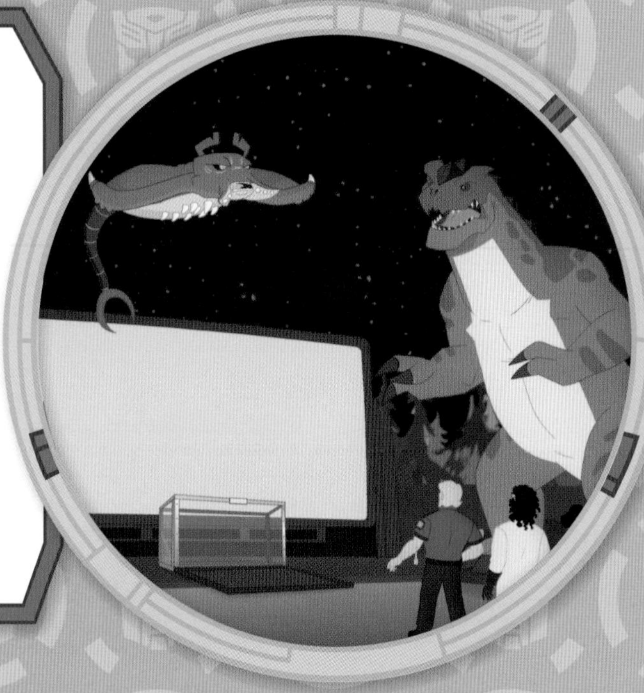

Doc Greene is ready to use his Holomorphic Projector to send the monsters back into their movie world.

"We only have one shot at this. We need both creatures inside the holographic field in order for this to work," says Doc.

The Rescue Bots struggle to contain Humungado and Rayvenous. The Bots charge at them with everything they have and force the two creatures into the holographic field.

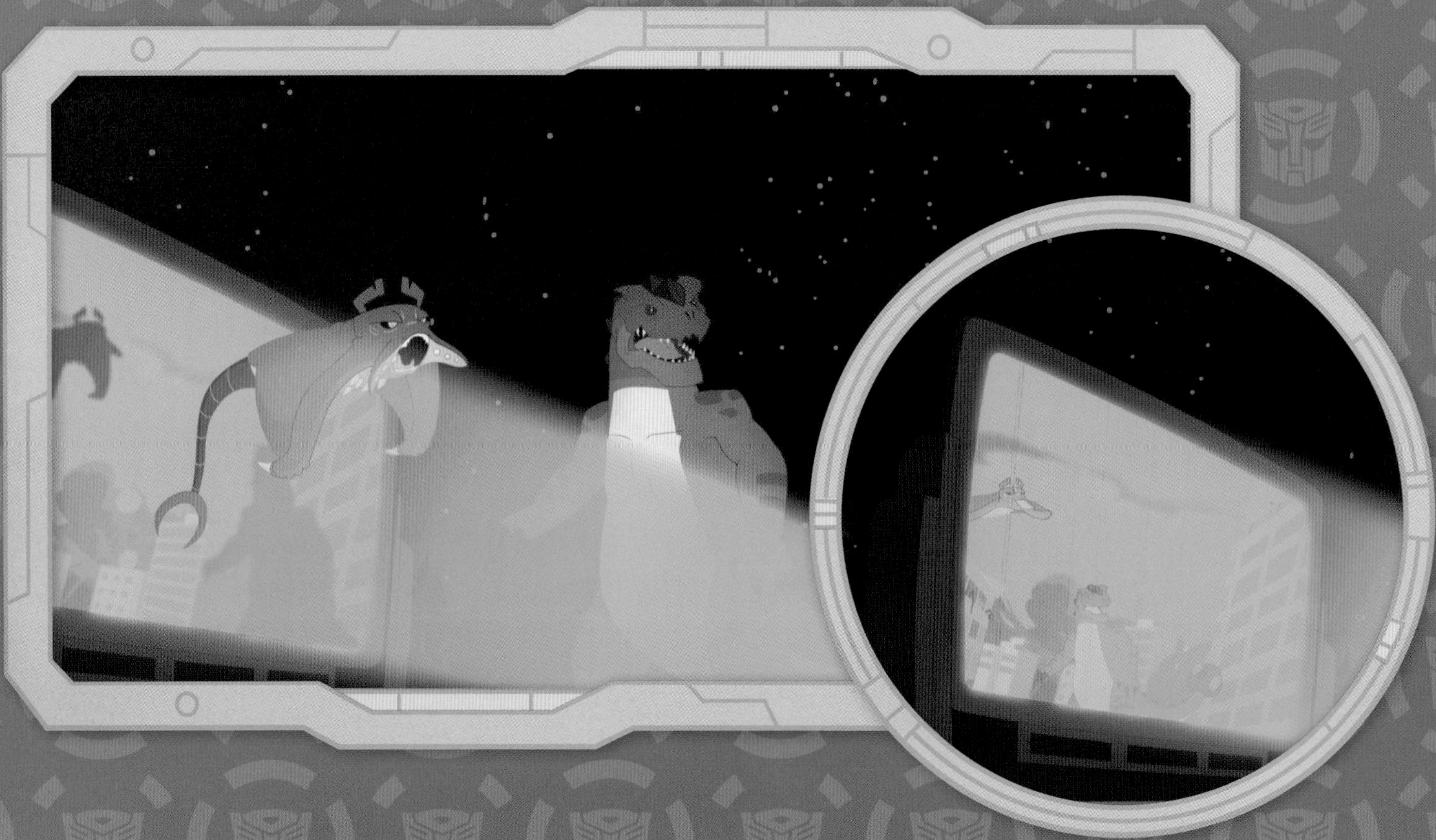

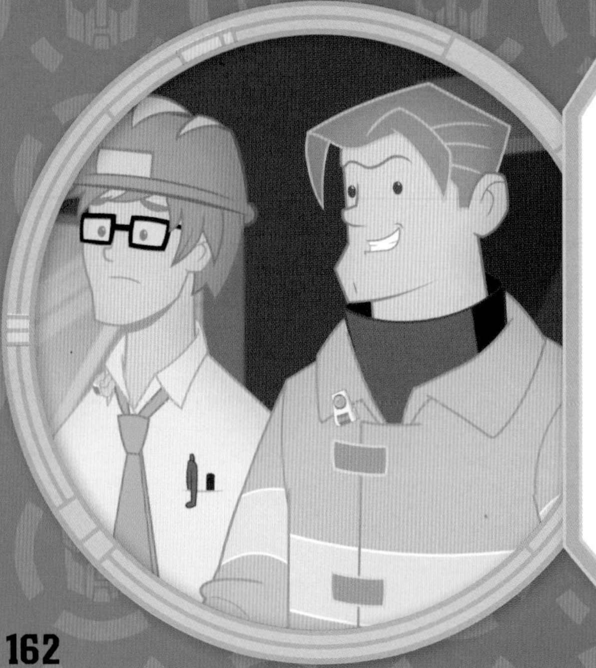

Doc Greene flips a switch that activates a power surge, which creates a huge blast of light. Then he turns on the lens of the projector. Humungado and Rayvenous are sucked back into the film. Griffin Rock is safe again, thanks to the Rescue Team.

"Now *that's* what the sequel should have looked like!" says Kade.

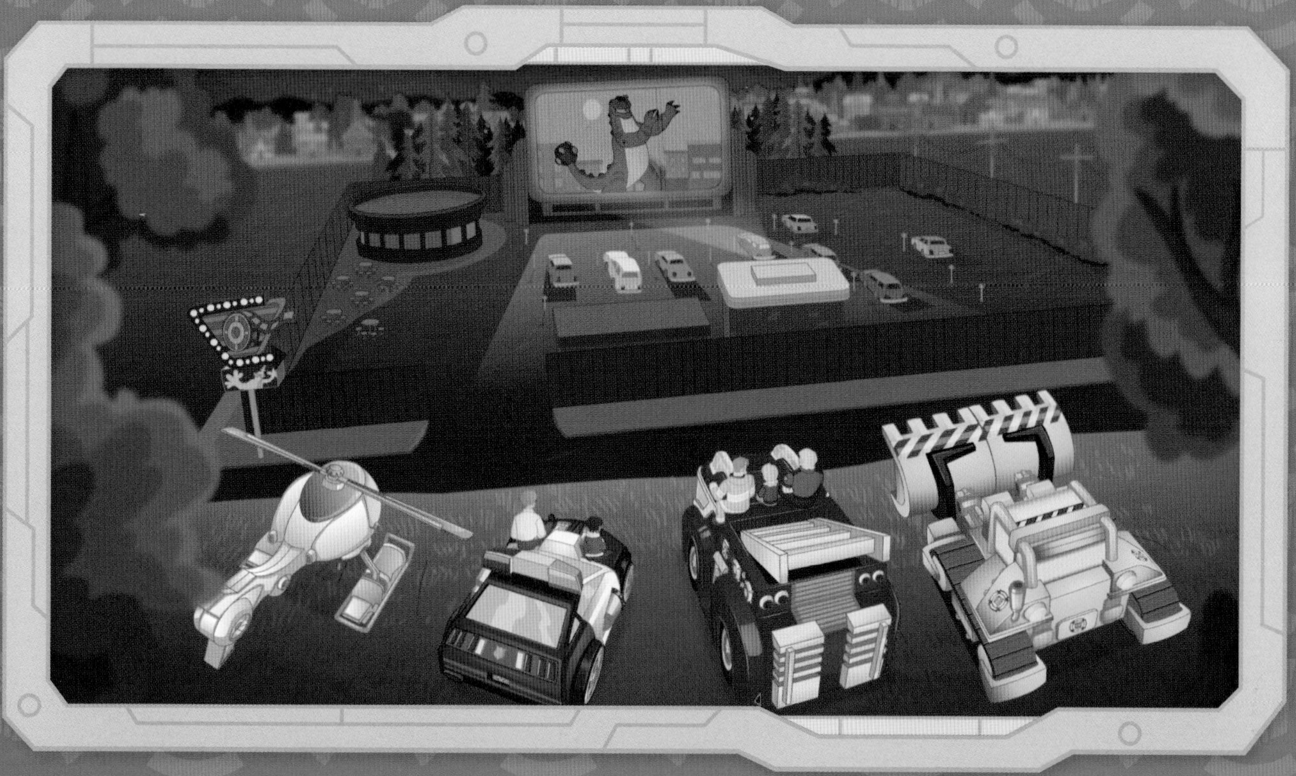

The next night, everyone settles down at the drive-in to finish watching *Attack of the Humungado* and all its sequels, upon Kade's request.

"Thanks, guys. It means a lot more with all of you here," says Kade.

Cody smiles. "That's what family does."

"Even if these movies are terrible," says Dani.

"Pass the popcorn?" askes Graham as Humungado roars safely on the screen.

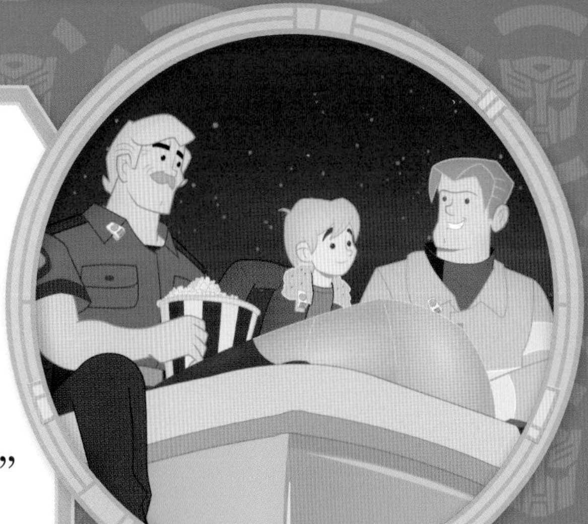

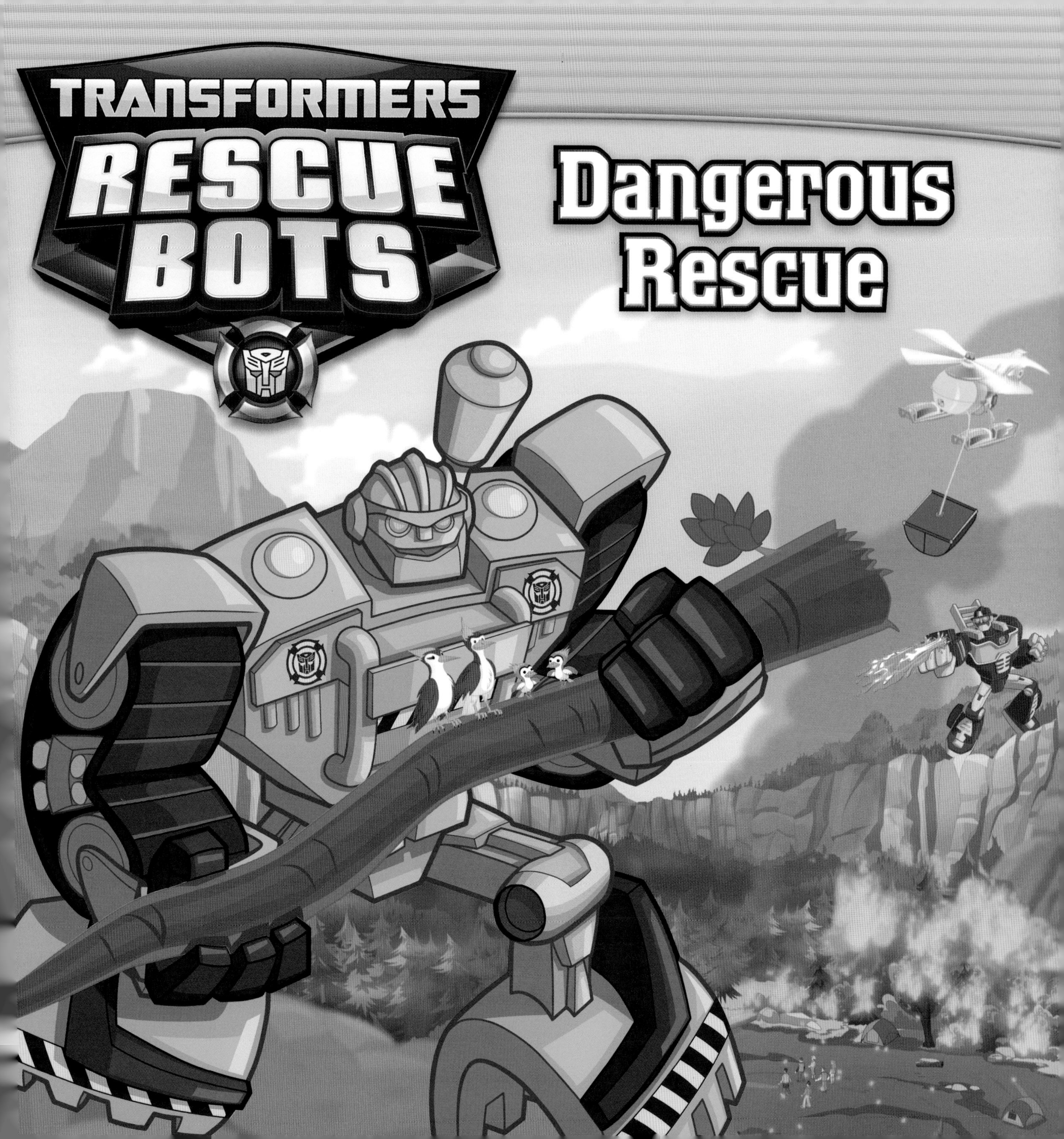
TRANSFORMERS
RESCUE BOTS
Dangerous Rescue

TRANSFORMERS RESCUE BOTS

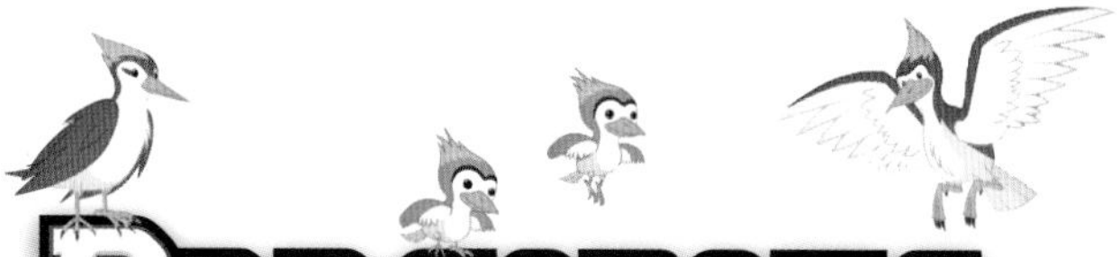

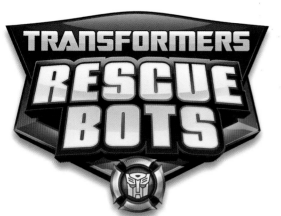

Dangerous Rescue

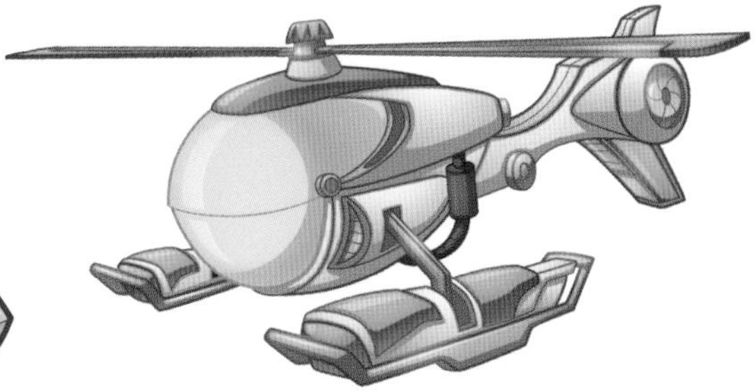

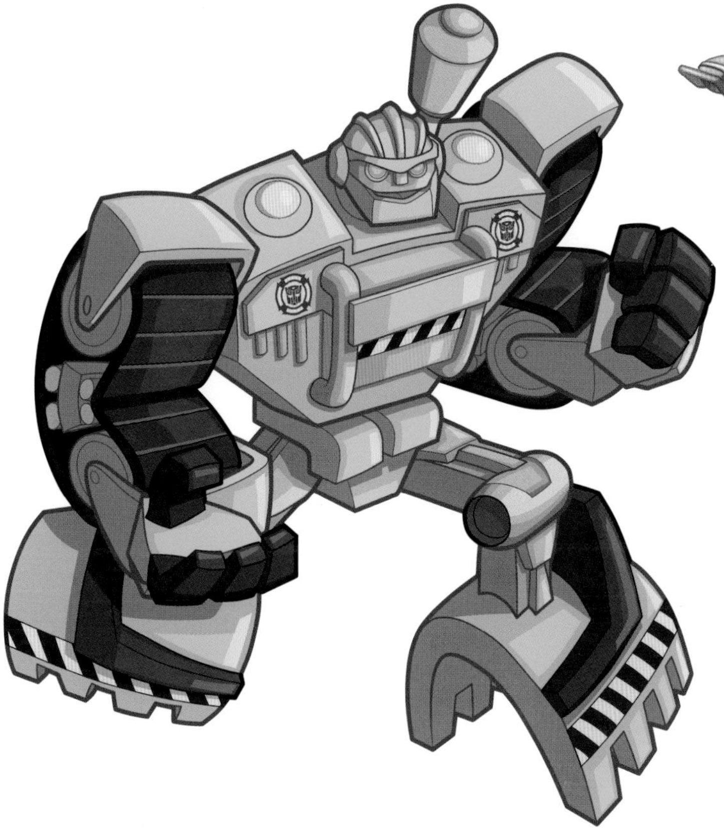

Adapted by Brandon T. Snider
Based on the episode "Endangered Species"
written by Andrew Robinson

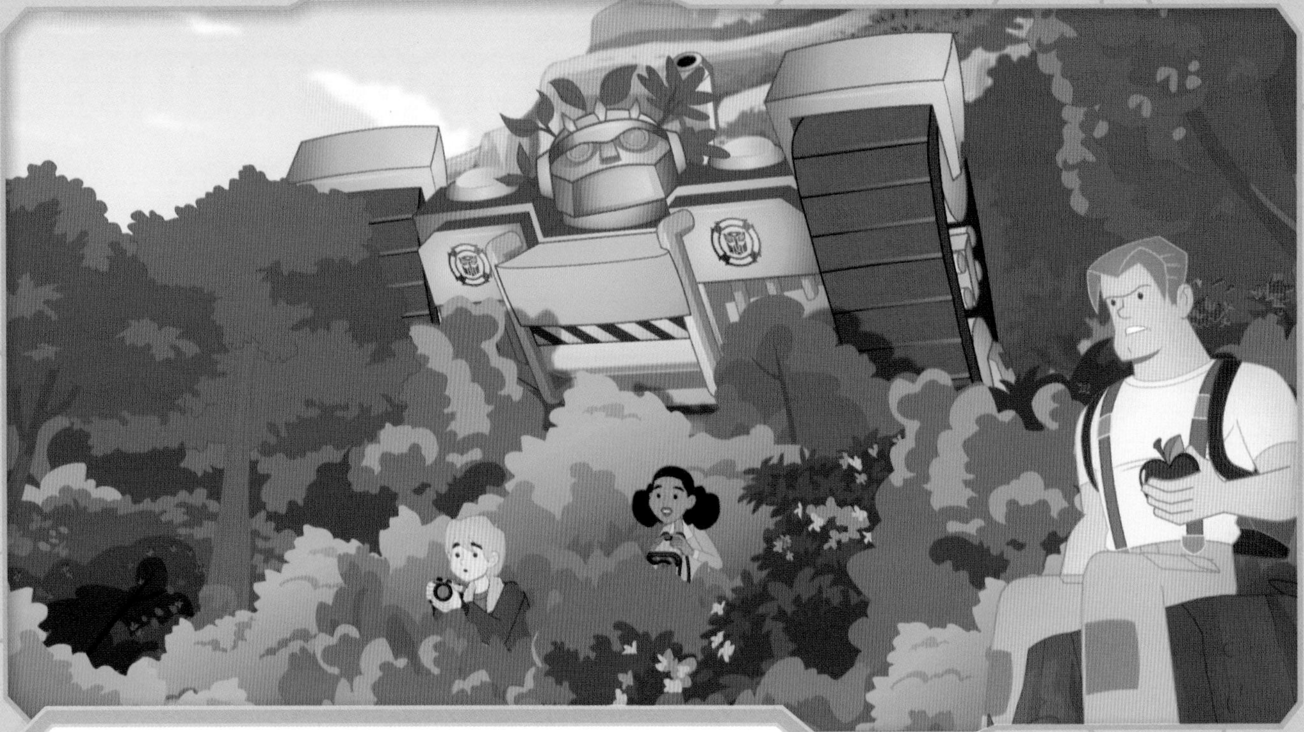

One beautiful spring day, Cody, Frankie, and Kade join their Rescue Bot friend Boulder for some bird-watching in the park.

Kade sighs. “Only Boulder could enjoy a pastime that even *humans* know is boring.”

“I find the variety and beauty of Earth birds to be inspiring. Cybertron doesn’t have anything like this,” explains Boulder. He checks his bird-watcher book.

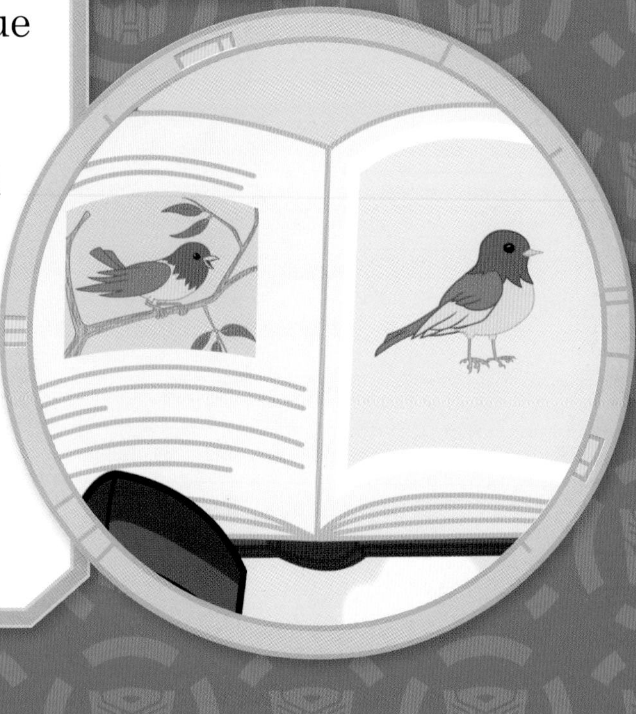

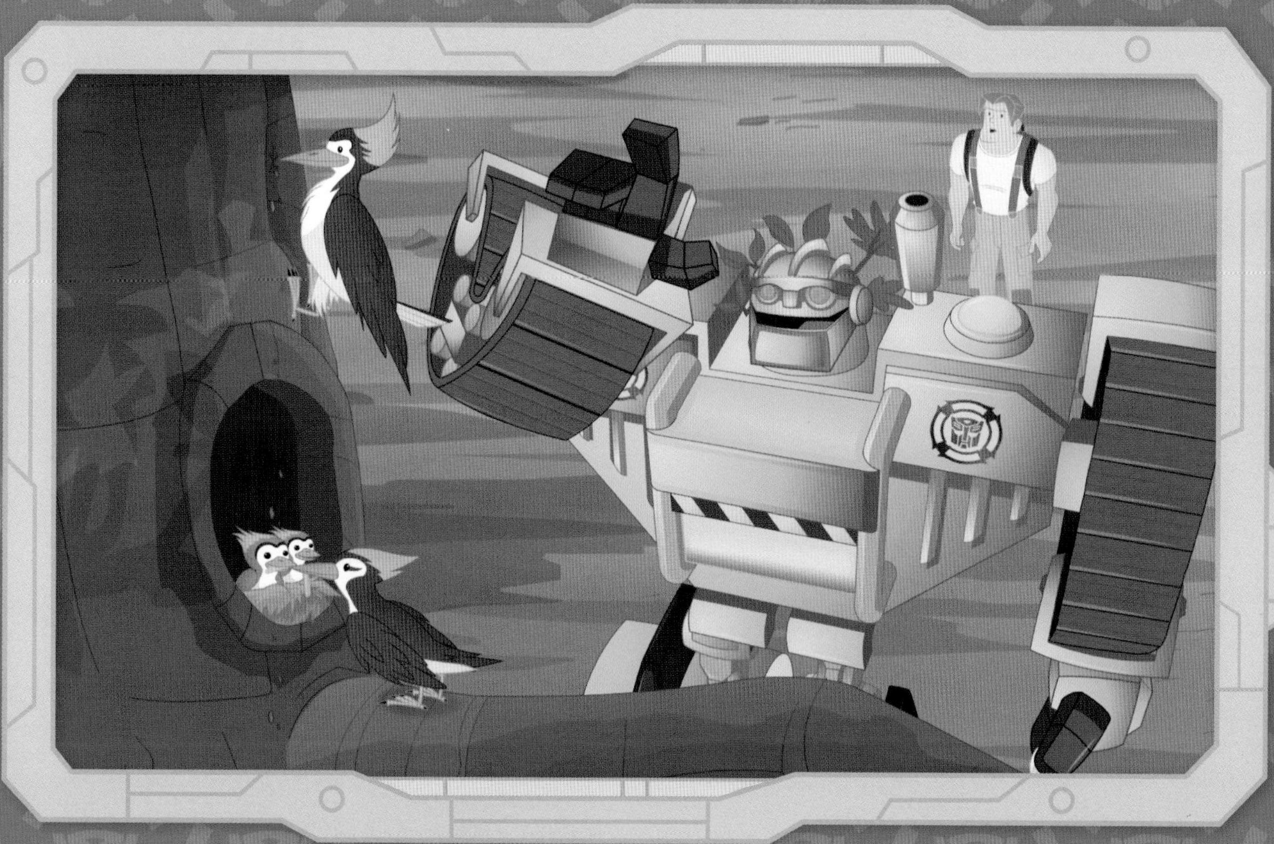

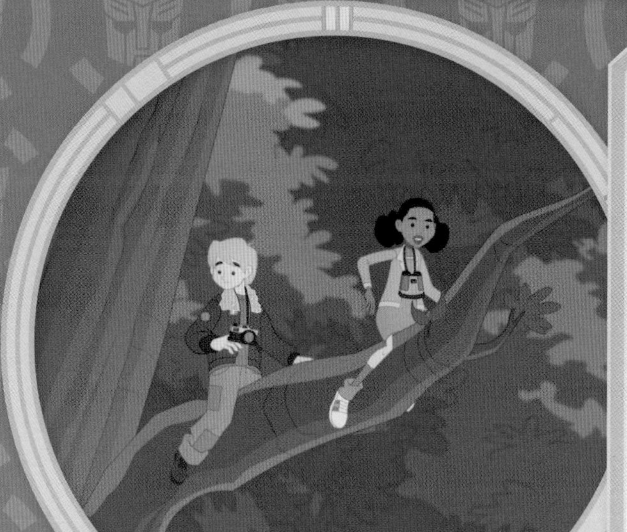

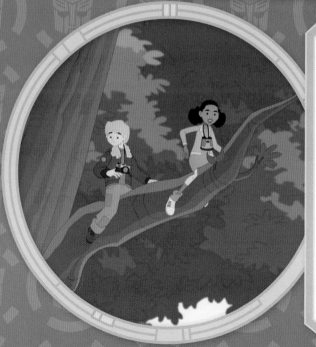

"That one is a woodpecker, and she has *babies*!" whispers Boulder. Cody and Frankie climb to a high branch so they can get a better look.

"Hey, kids! Climb down from there! It doesn't look safe," says Kade. Suddenly, the tree branch snaps, and Cody and Frankie start to tumble toward the baby birds.

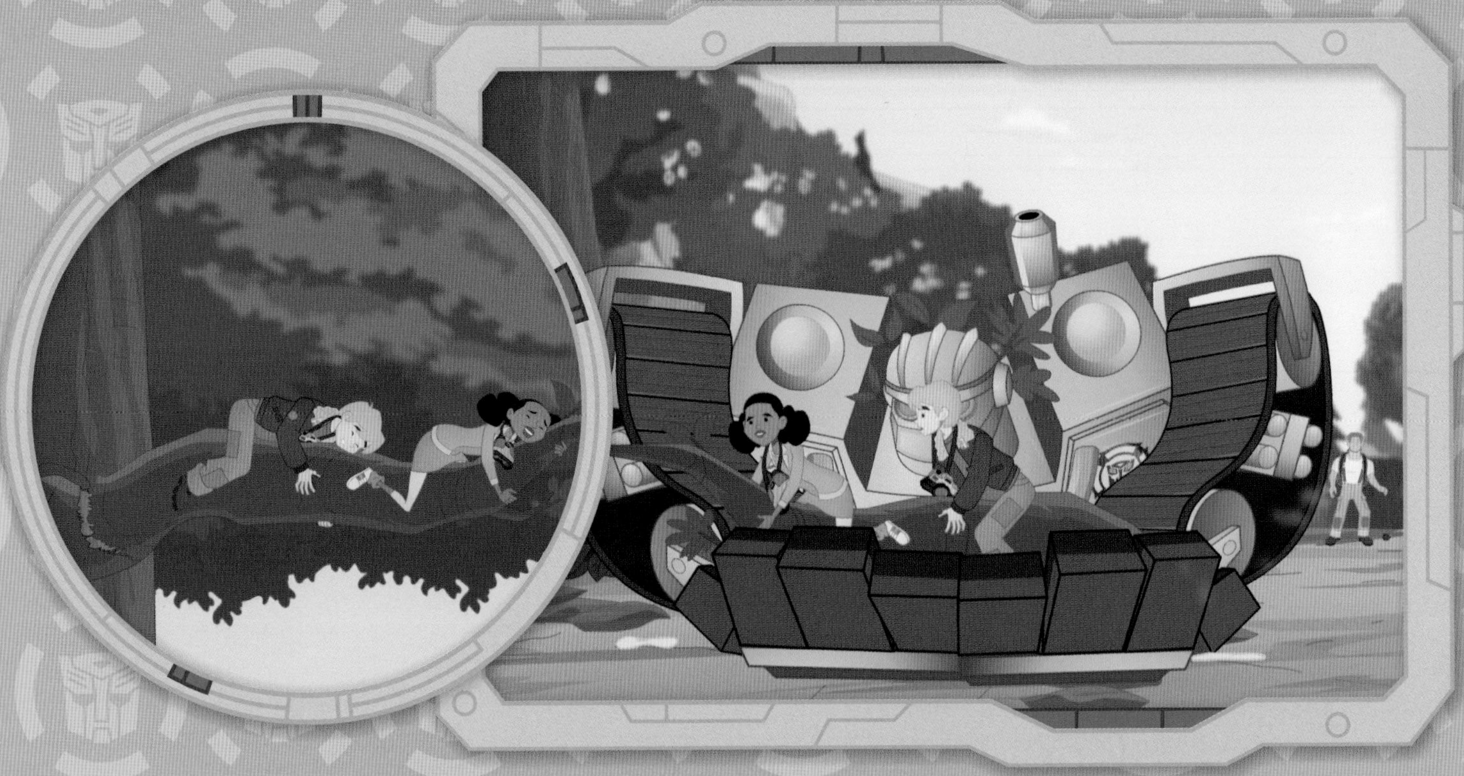

“Power up and energize!” says Boulder, springing into action. He catches the kids in one hand and uses his laser to slice away the tree branch with the other.

“Are the baby birds okay?” asks Frankie. The tiny creatures hop onto Boulder’s hand.

“They’re wonderful,” Boulder says, smiling. The mother bird hops onto Boulder’s head and gently pecks him. “Hey, that tickles!”

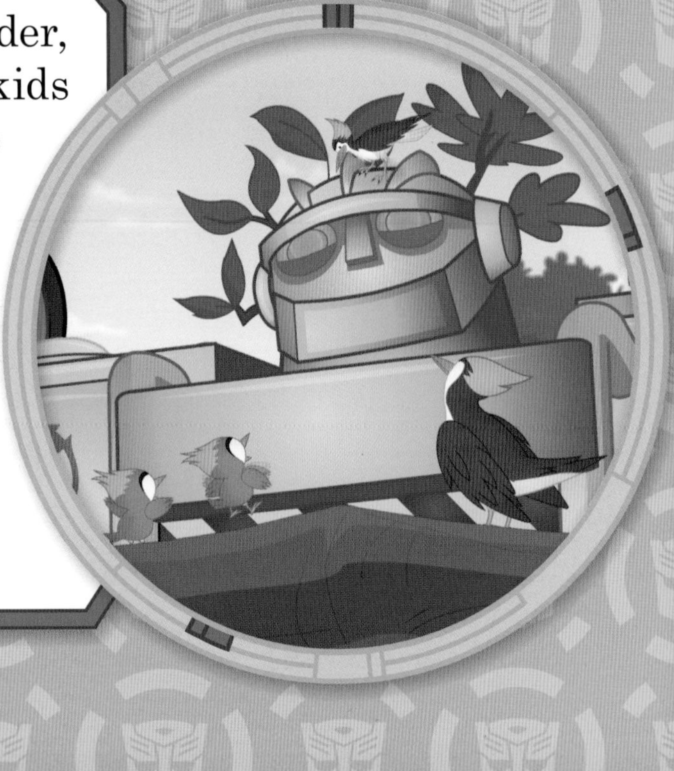

Back at the firehouse, Doc Greene explains the meaning behind Boulder's discovery. "That's the first golden-crested woodpecker anyone has seen in forty years. We mustn't tell anyone about this. These birds need to be protected as an endangered species. The worst possible thing would be a crowd of tourists trampling through their habitat."

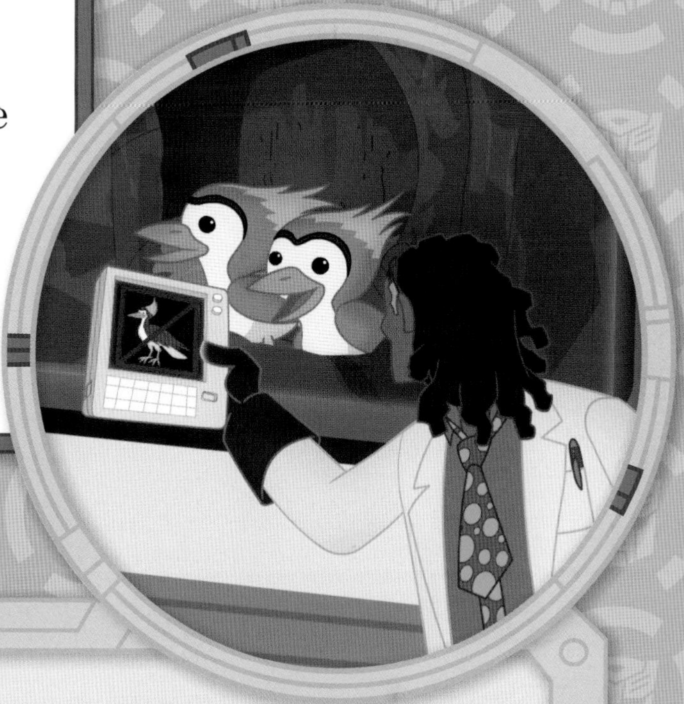

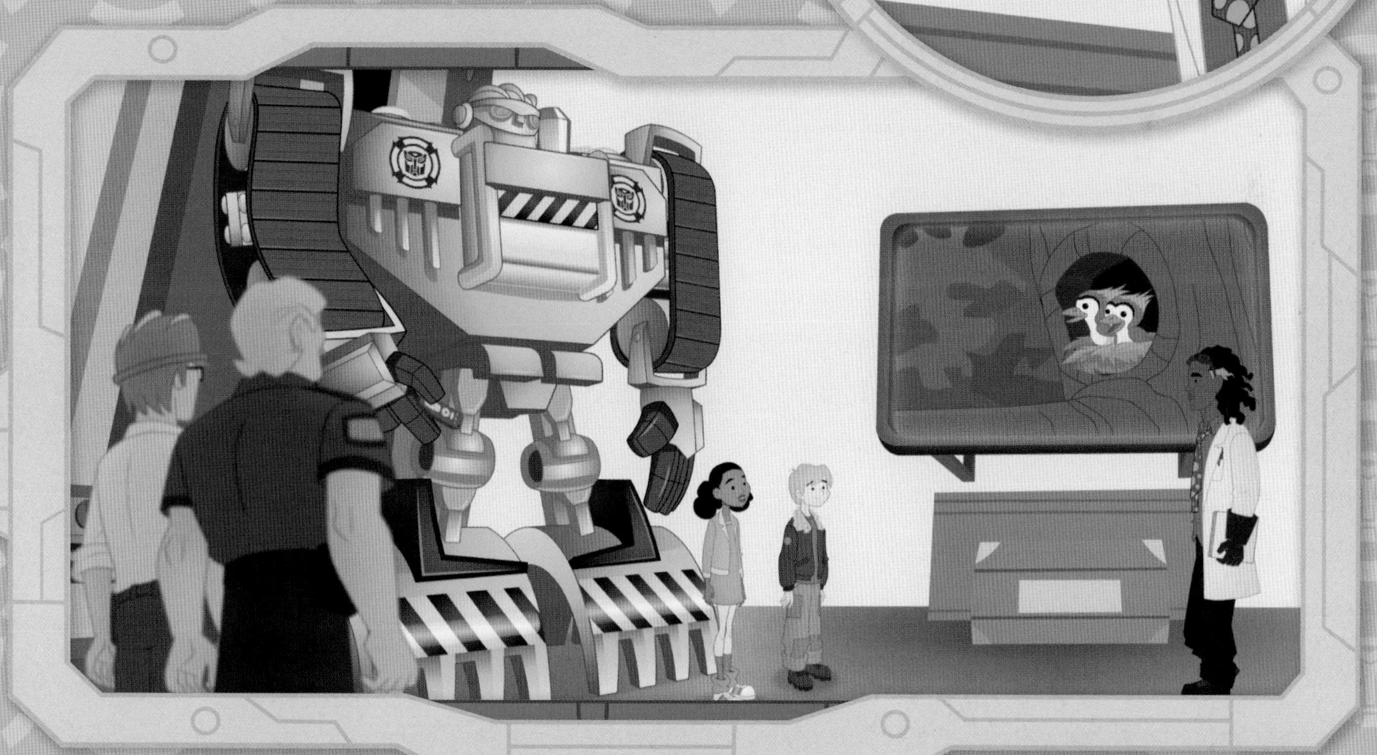

"What's an endangered species?" asks Boulder.

"An endangered species is an animal that's in danger of becoming extinct," answers Doc Greene. "If we can get those birds on the endangered species list, the government will step in to protect them."

Boulder loves protecting humans, but he thinks the birds should be kept safe, too.

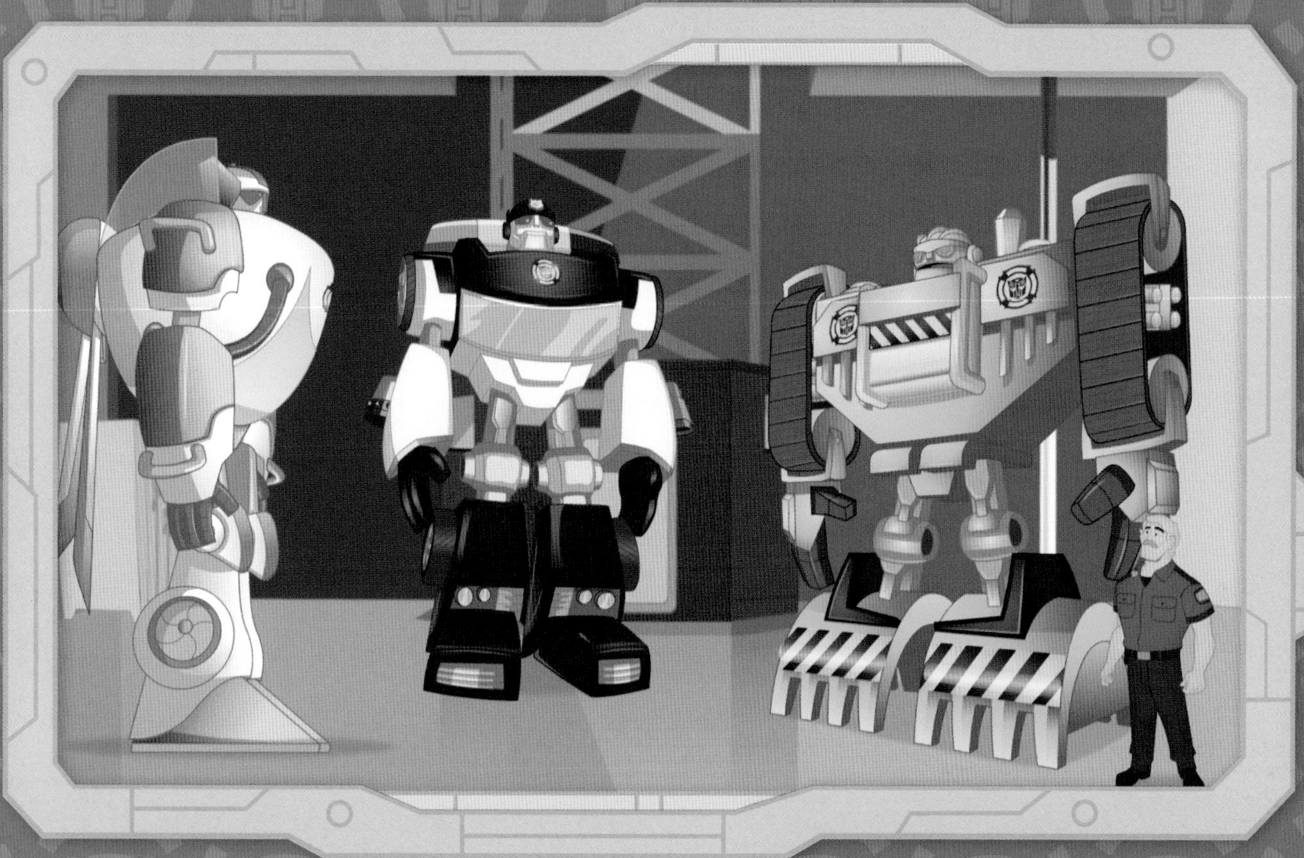

Boulder talks with Chief Burns about the birds' safety. "Our mission is to serve and protect humans. But what about those creatures who need protection *from* humans?" he asks. "Those baby birds need guarding until Doc Greene can get them on the list."

But Chief Burns has concerns about the Rescue Bots protecting the birds full-time.

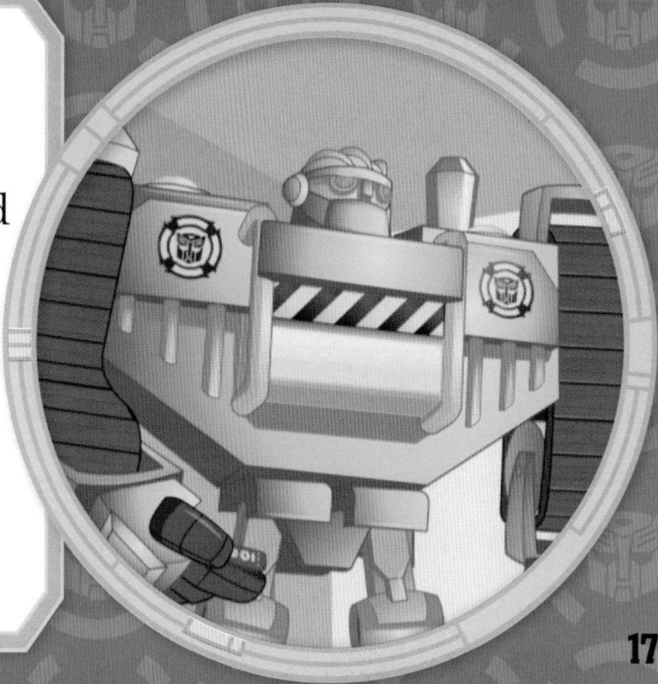

"I'll allow it on *one* condition: You can't neglect your *real* jobs," says the chief.

"Great!" exclaims Boulder, but not all the Rescue Bots want to be part of Boulder's mission.

"Our job is keeping people safe, not birds," grumbles Heatwave. "Count me out."

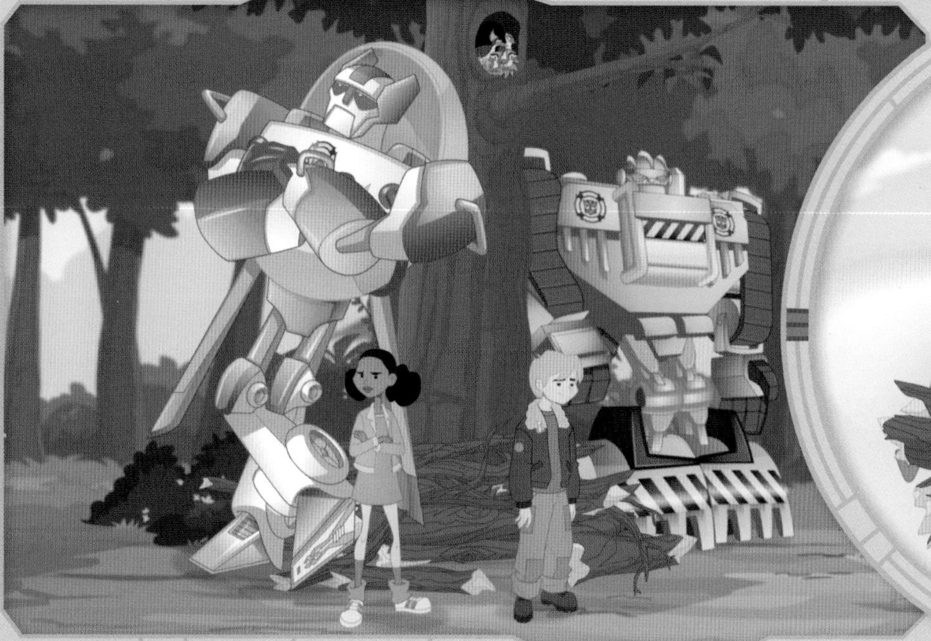

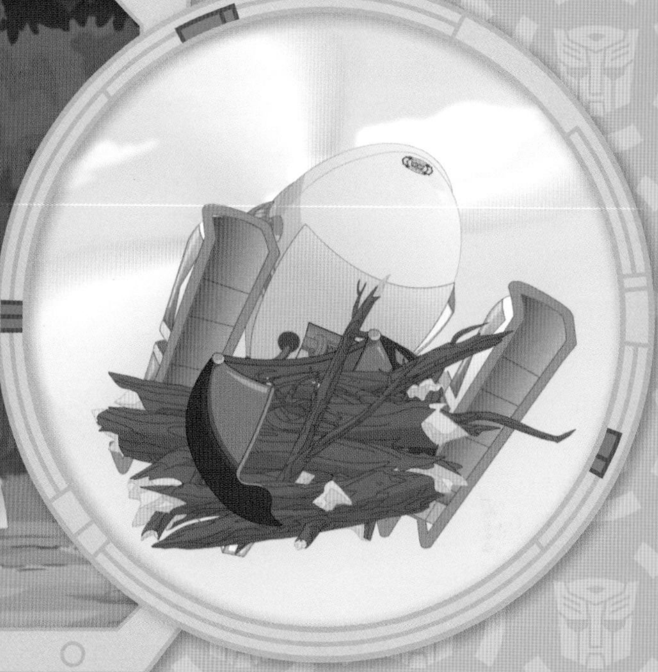

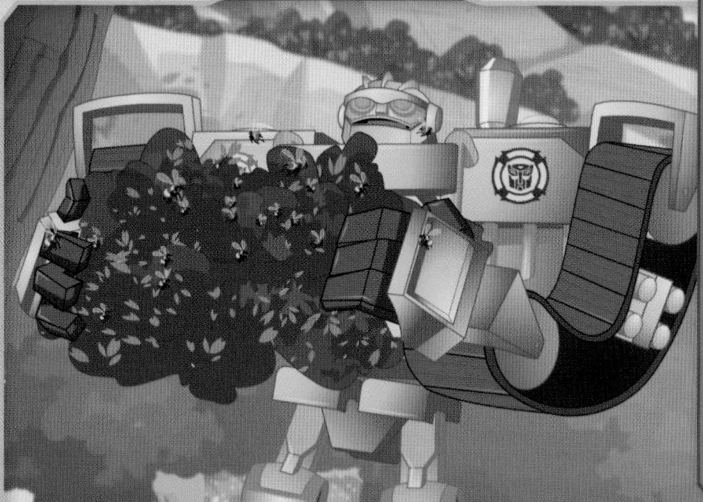

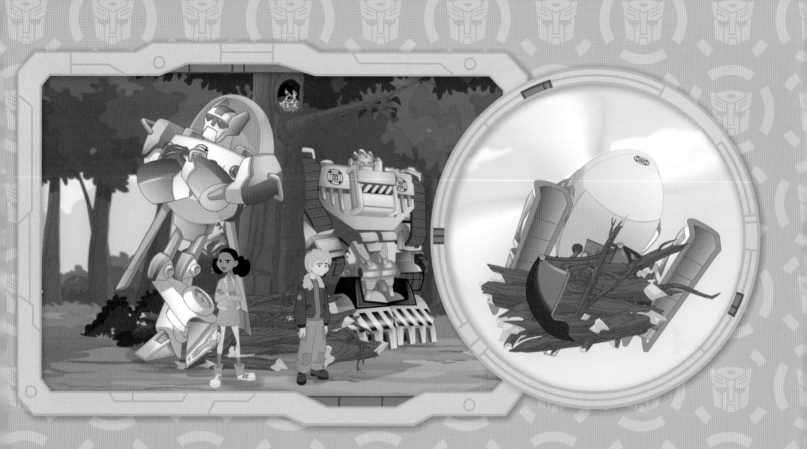

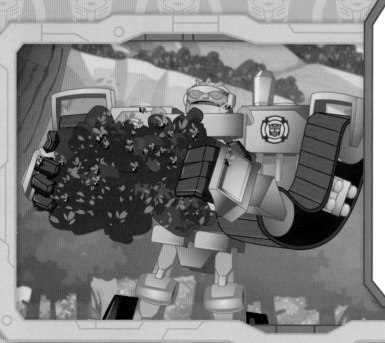

The next day, everyone else heads to Woodpecker's Grove to stand guard. Boulder suggests they clean up the area and plant some new flowers. He thinks the birds might like something pretty and fresh. The flowers attract a swarm of bees! Boulder has to plant the flowers a bit farther away.

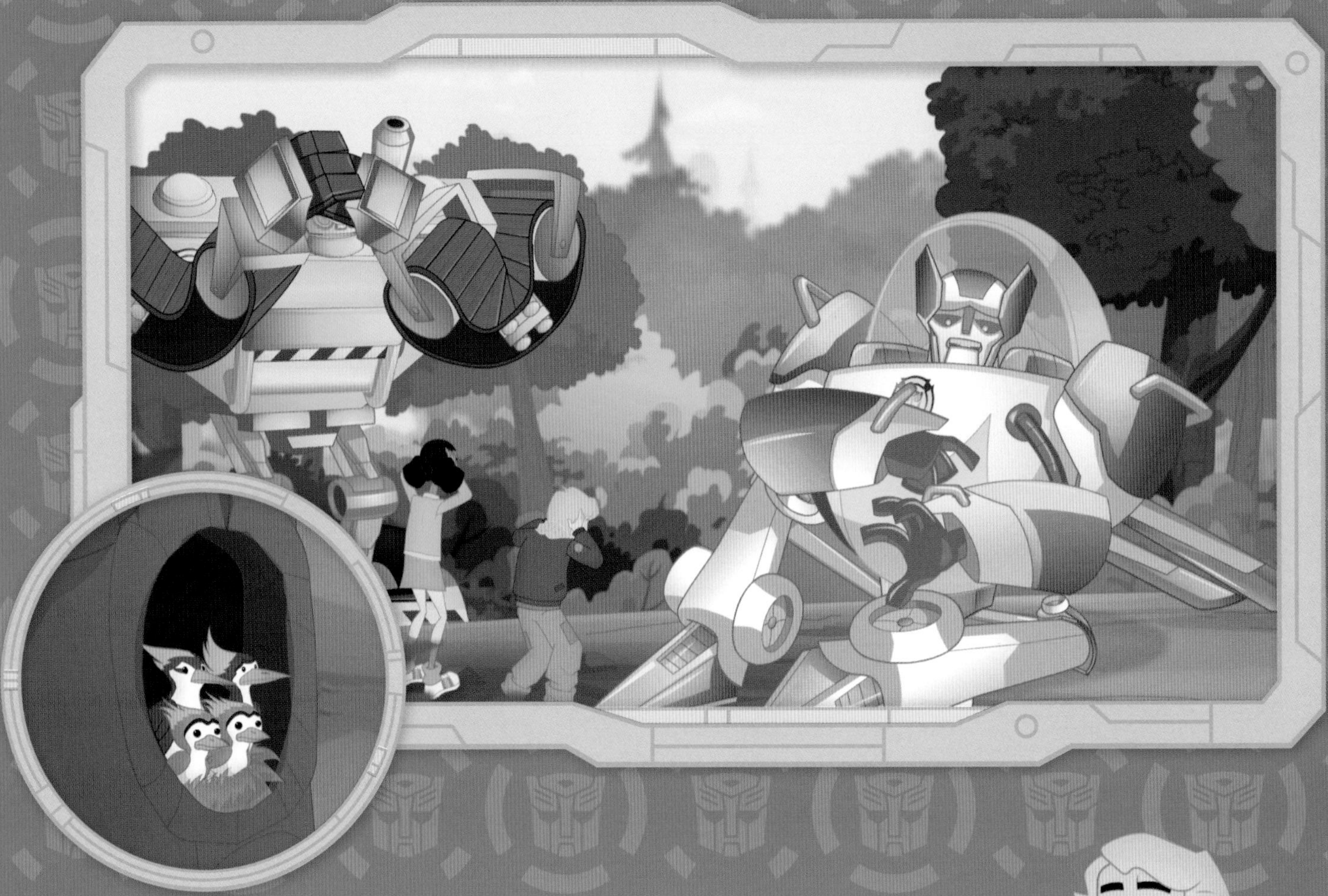

Boulder thinks some nice, soothing music would calm the birds down after all the activity. He and Blades play some music, but it's too loud. The birds are even more frightened. Blades fumbles with the controls until he is able to lower the volume. Chief Burns stops by to see how things are going. He is surprised.

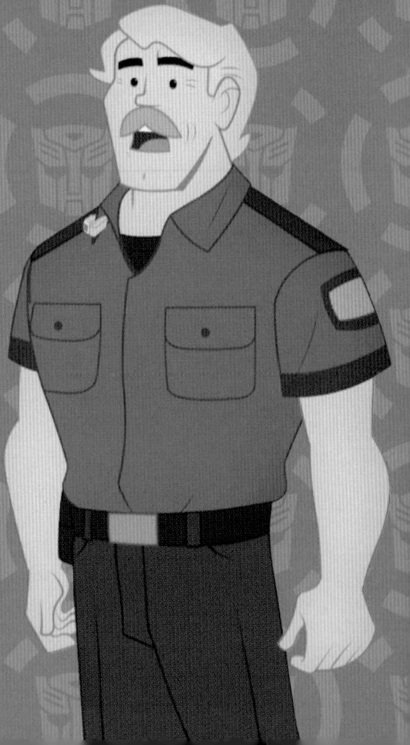

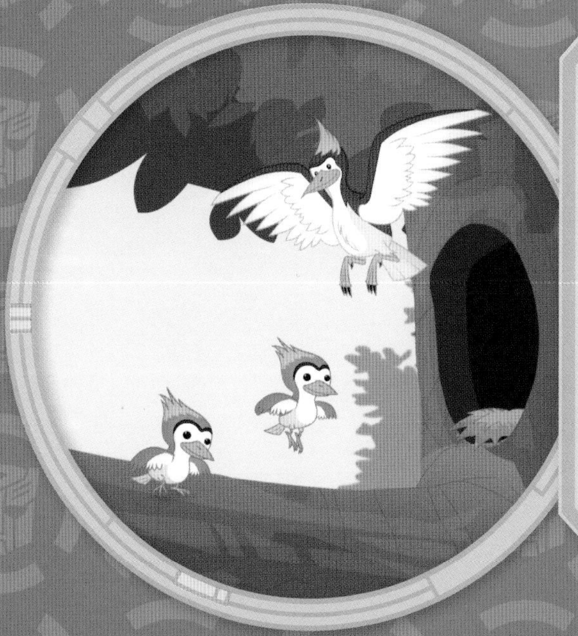

"I didn't realize your plan to protect the woodpeckers included scaring them," jokes Chief Burns.

Soon the babies come out of their hiding place. They look like they are ready to fly. Blades has some advice for the little birds. "Do what I did the first time. Just close your eyes and scream." Blades laughs.

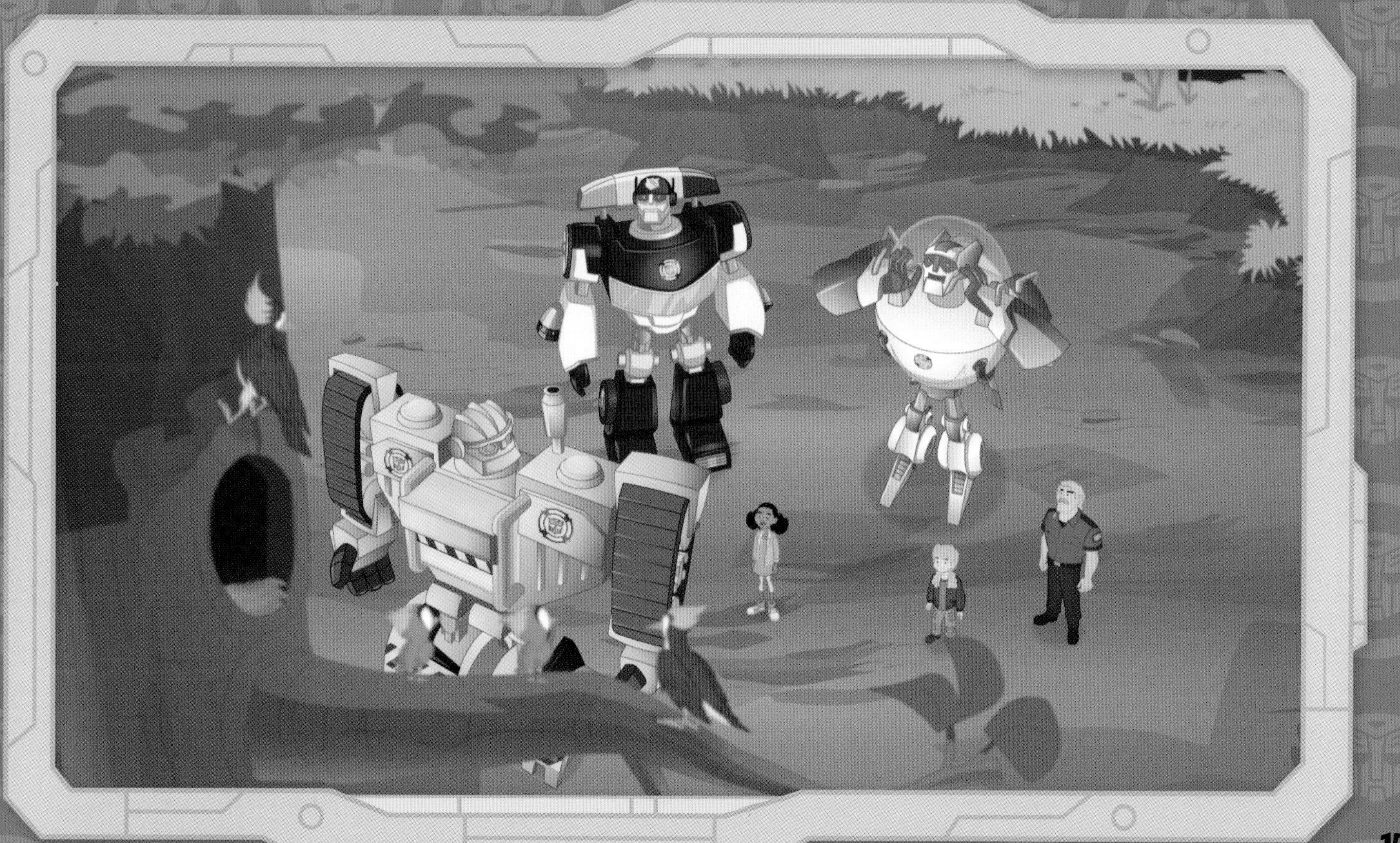

Back near Town Hall, Mayor Luskey's car falls into a ditch. Heatwave and Kade rush to the rescue by themselves!

"We're carrying this whole load while everyone else is babysitting. Those birds don't look so endangered to me," says Kade.

"Did you say *endangered*?" asks Mayor Luskey.

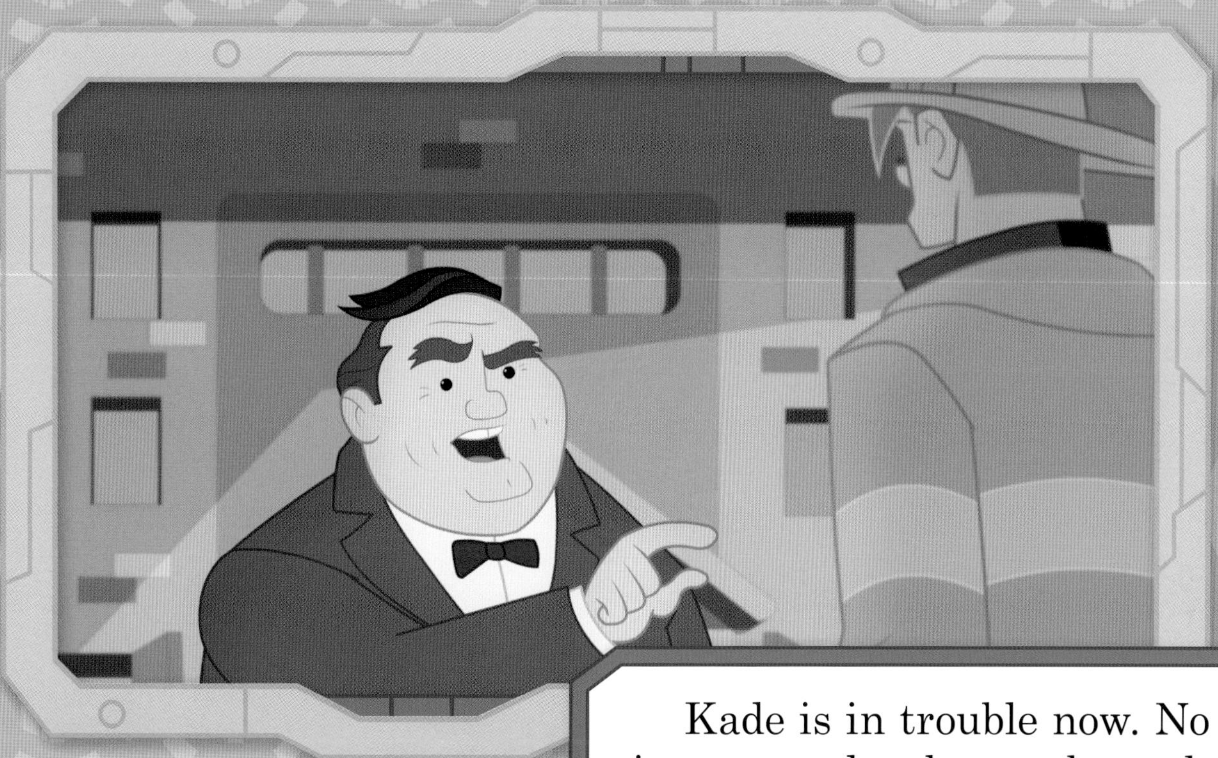

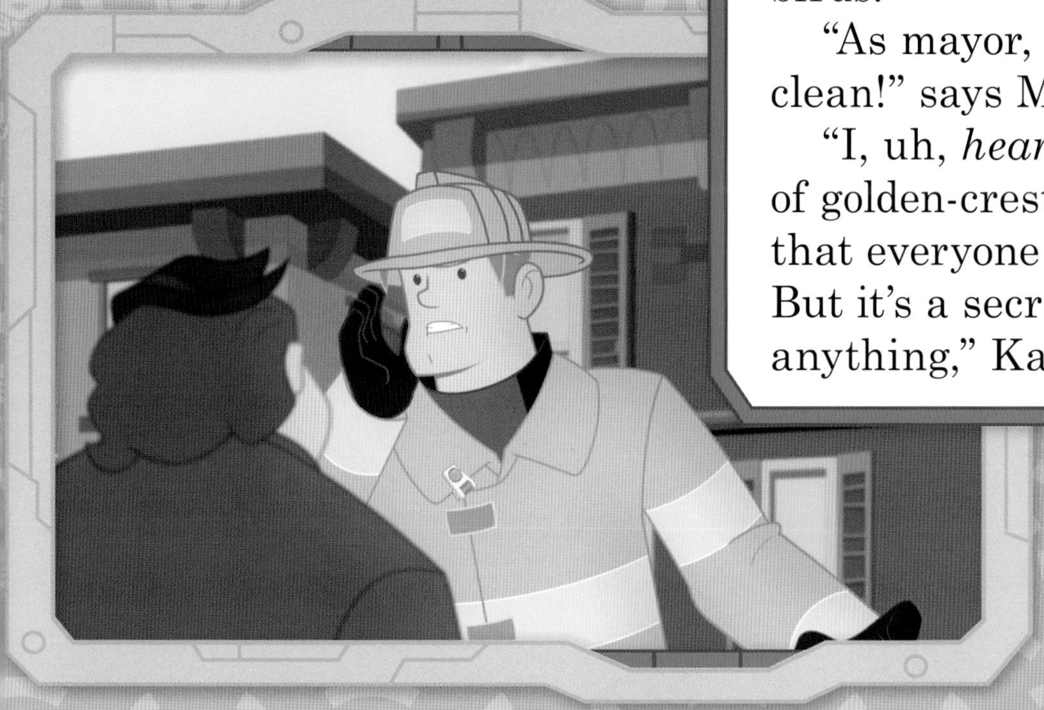

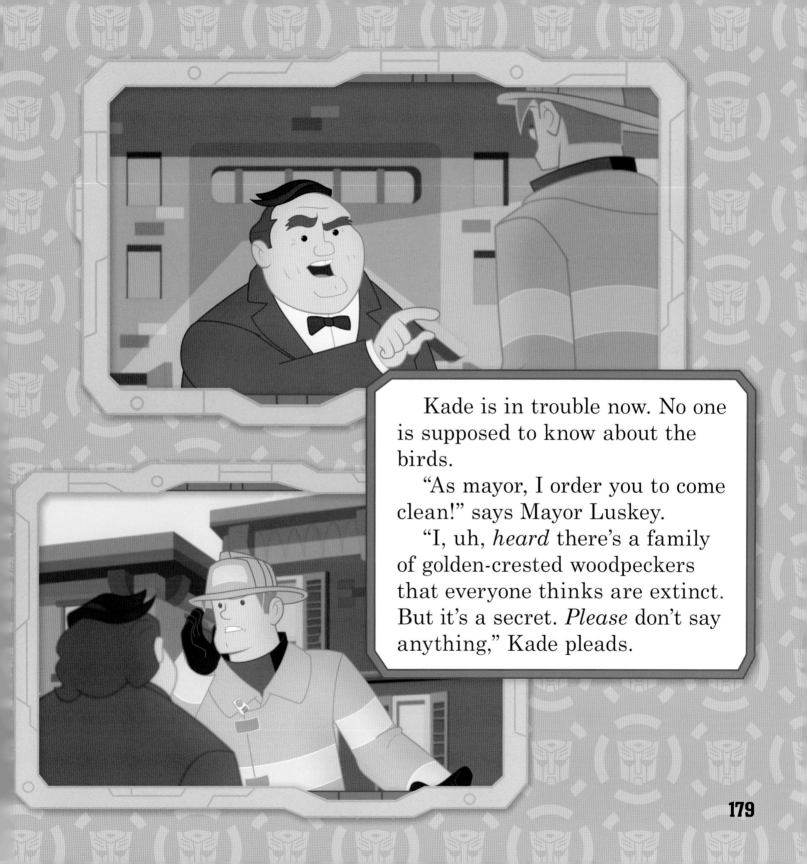

Kade is in trouble now. No one is supposed to know about the birds.

"As mayor, I order you to come clean!" says Mayor Luskey.

"I, uh, *heard* there's a family of golden-crested woodpeckers that everyone thinks are extinct. But it's a secret. *Please* don't say anything," Kade pleads.

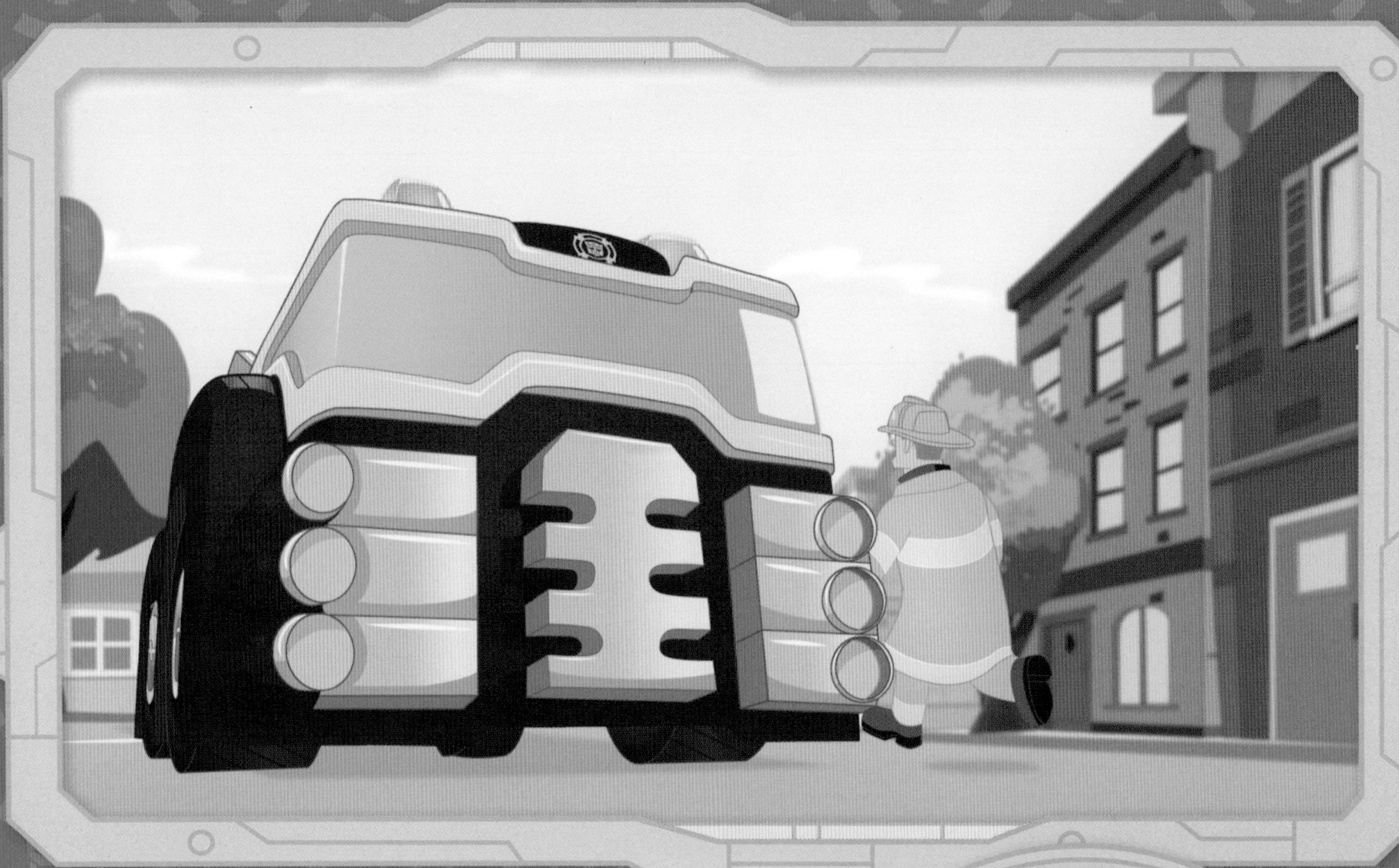

“Don’t worry, my boy. I know how to keep a secret,” says Mayor Luskey.

Heatwave changes into his vehicle mode. Kade hops in, and they drive away. Mayor Luskey smiles and waves as they depart.

Mayor Luskey makes a phone call. “Get out your floaties, because we’re about to be swimming in tourists.” He is up to something.

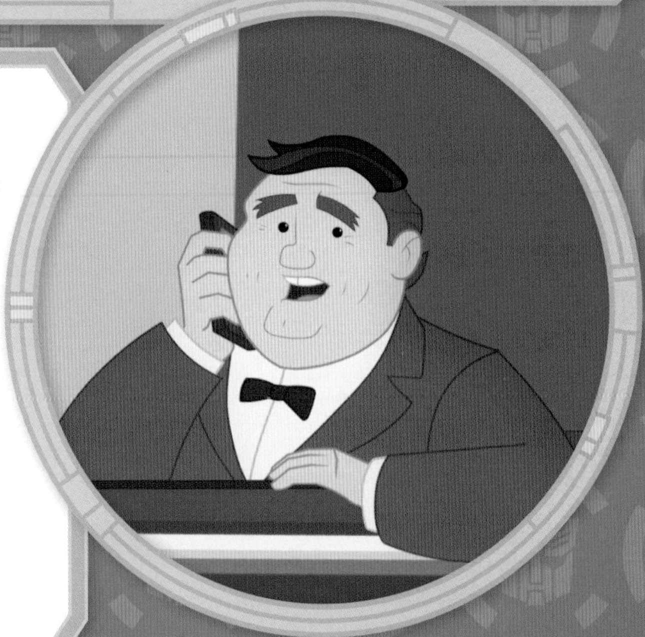

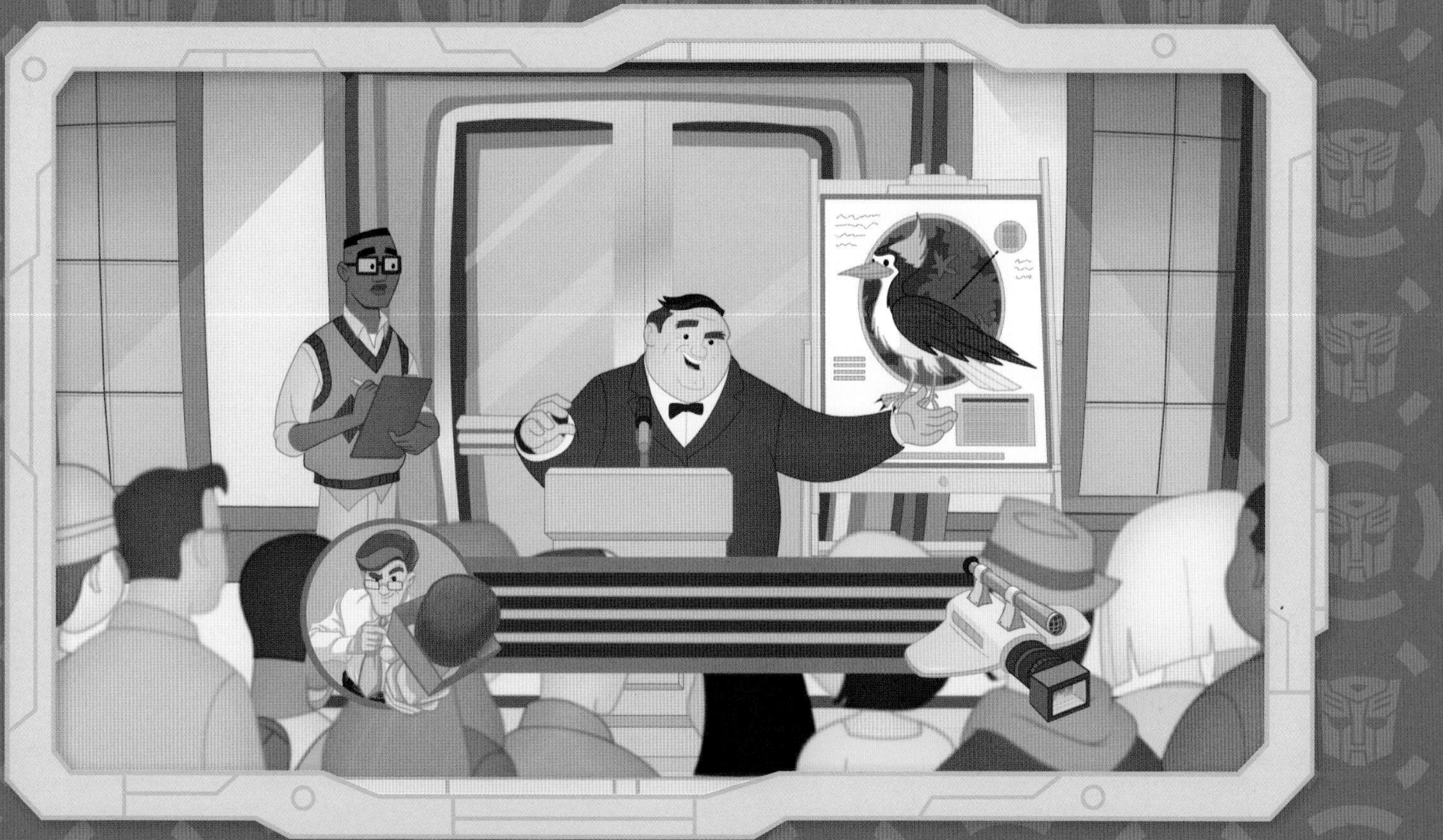

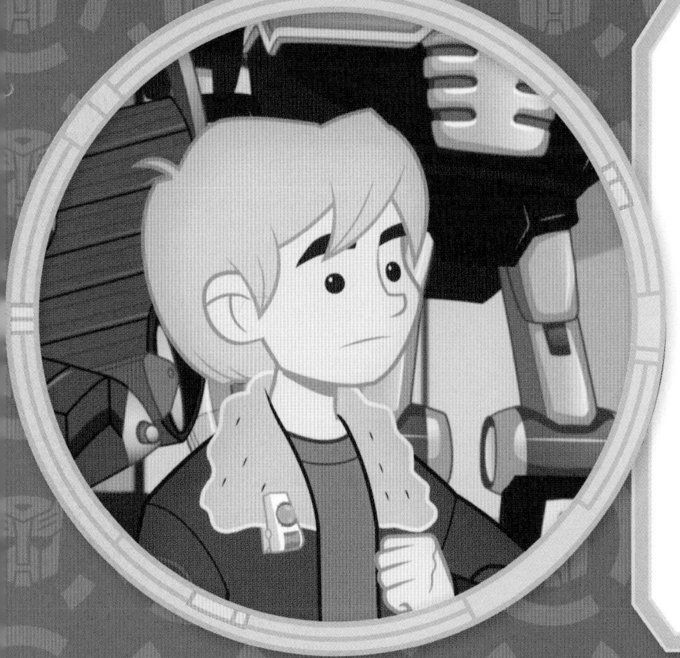

Later, the Rescue Bots and Cody watch as the mayor makes a big proclamation on the steps of Town Hall. "I'm thrilled to announce the rediscovery of the golden-crested woodpecker, right here in Griffin Rock!" says Mayor Luskey.

Cody can't believe what he is hearing. How did the mayor find out about the birds?

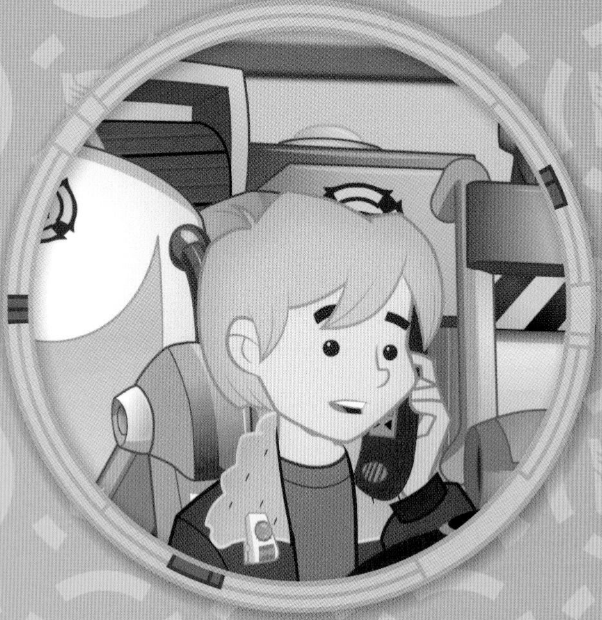

Cody gets a call later from reporter Huxley Prescott demanding to know who discovered the birds and where they are located. Boulder disguises his voice and handles the situation. He tells Huxley that the birds need to be left alone.

"That's the end of that," Boulder says, hanging up the phone. But he is wrong.

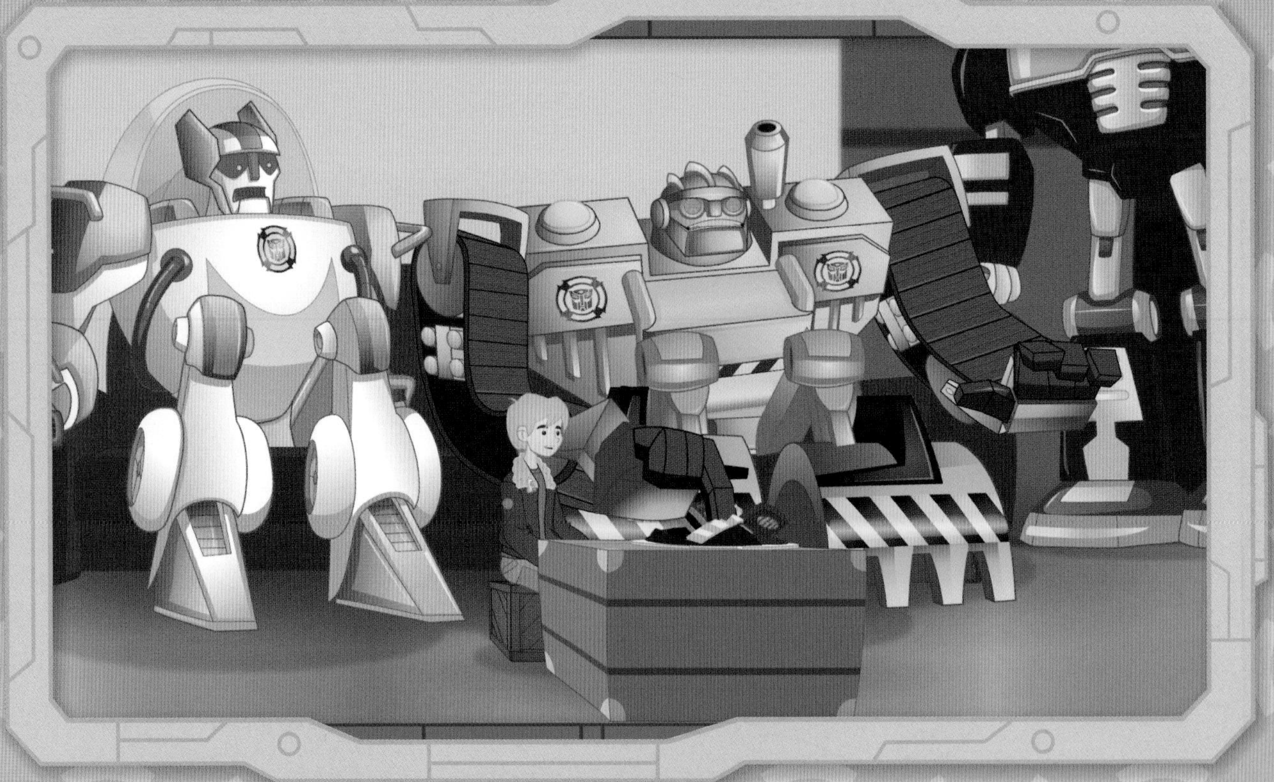

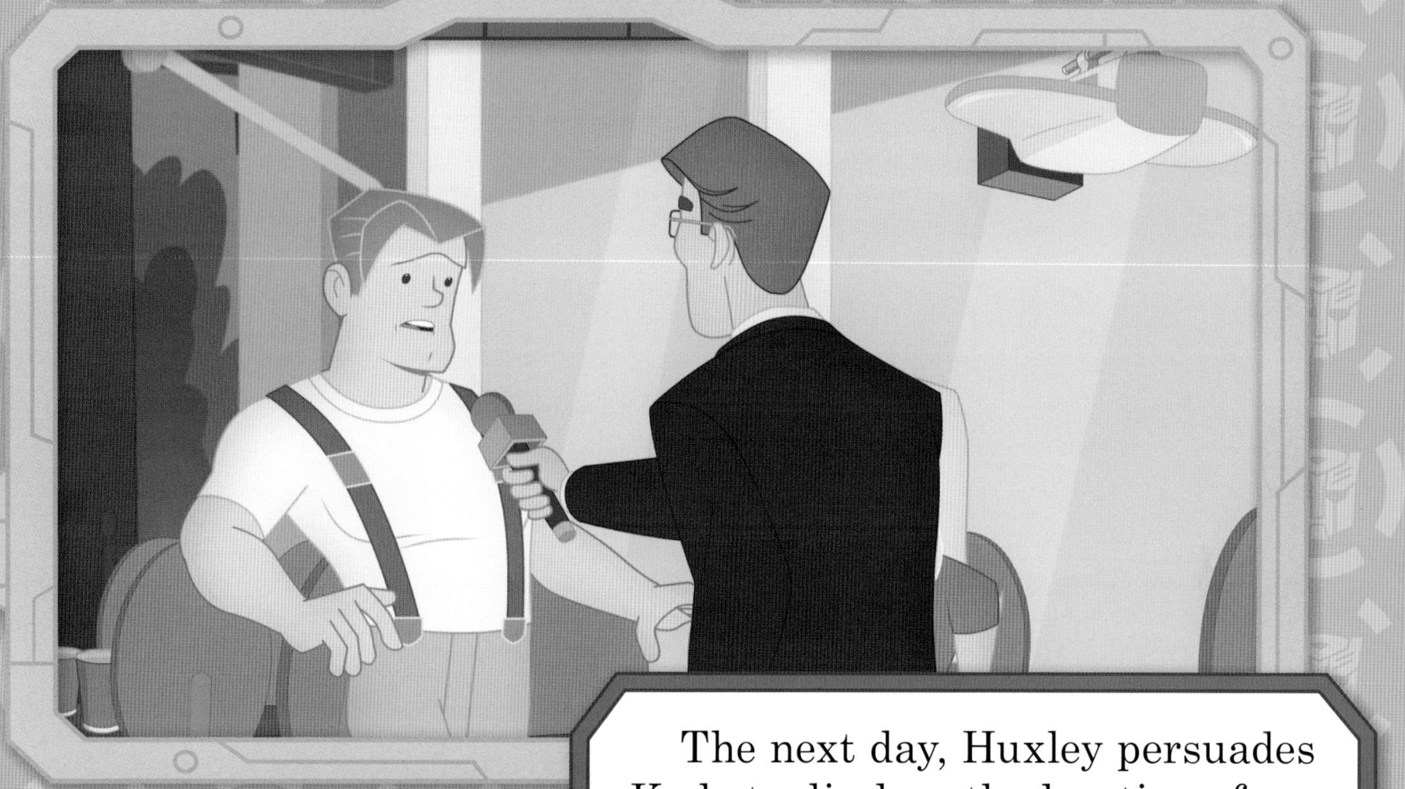

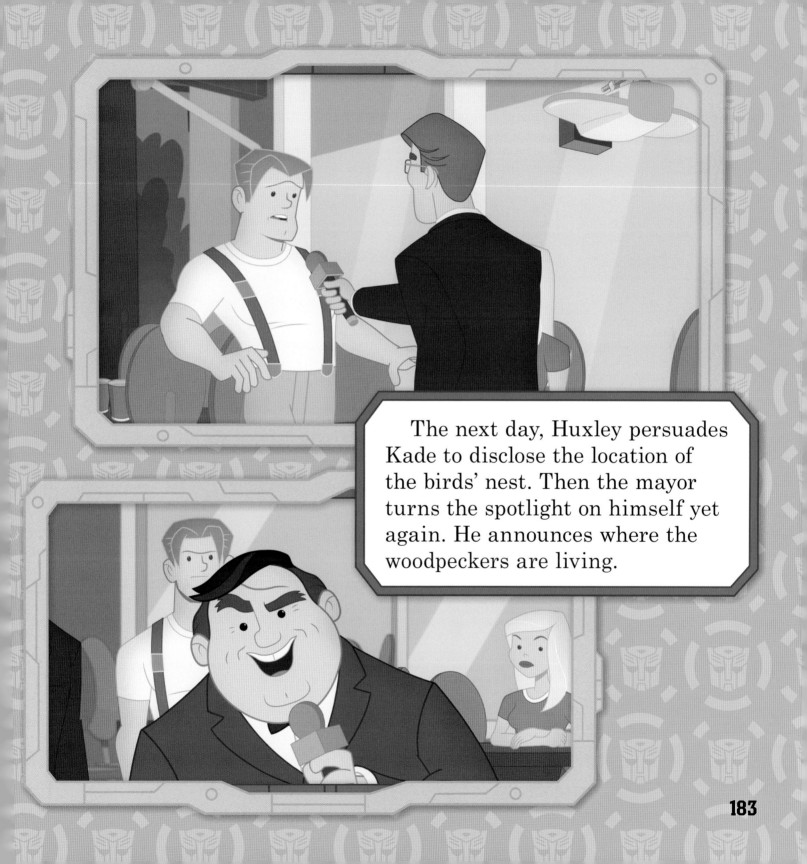

The next day, Huxley persuades Kade to disclose the location of the birds' nest. Then the mayor turns the spotlight on himself yet again. He announces where the woodpeckers are living.

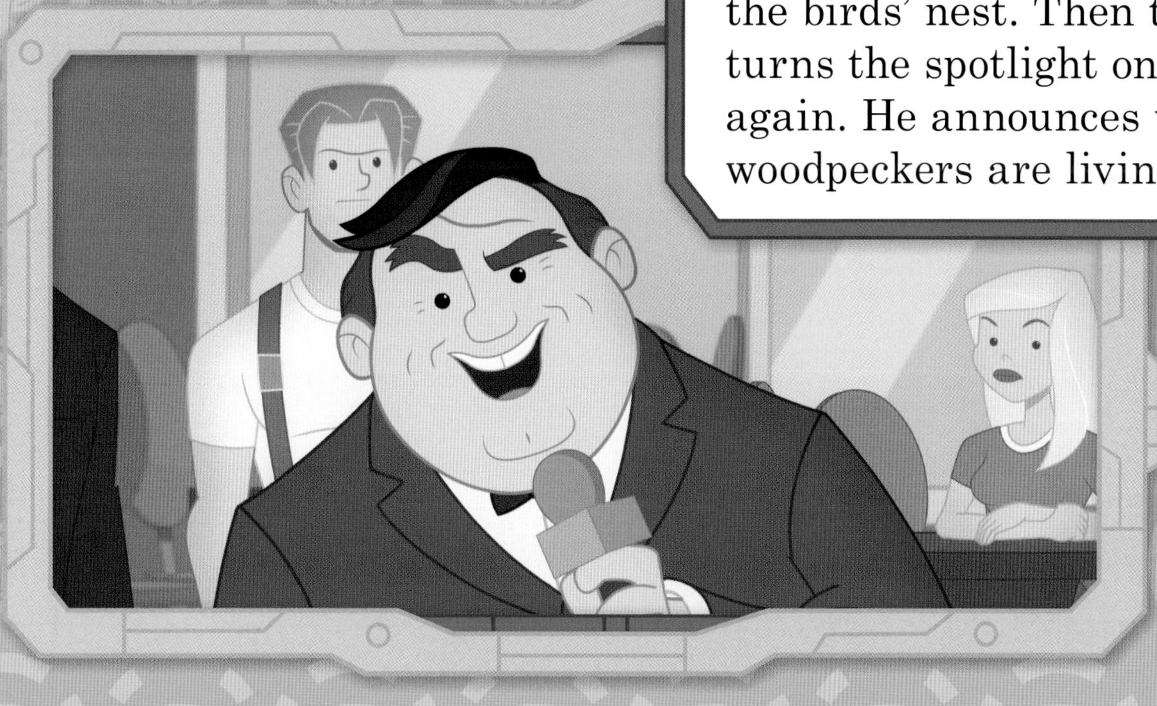

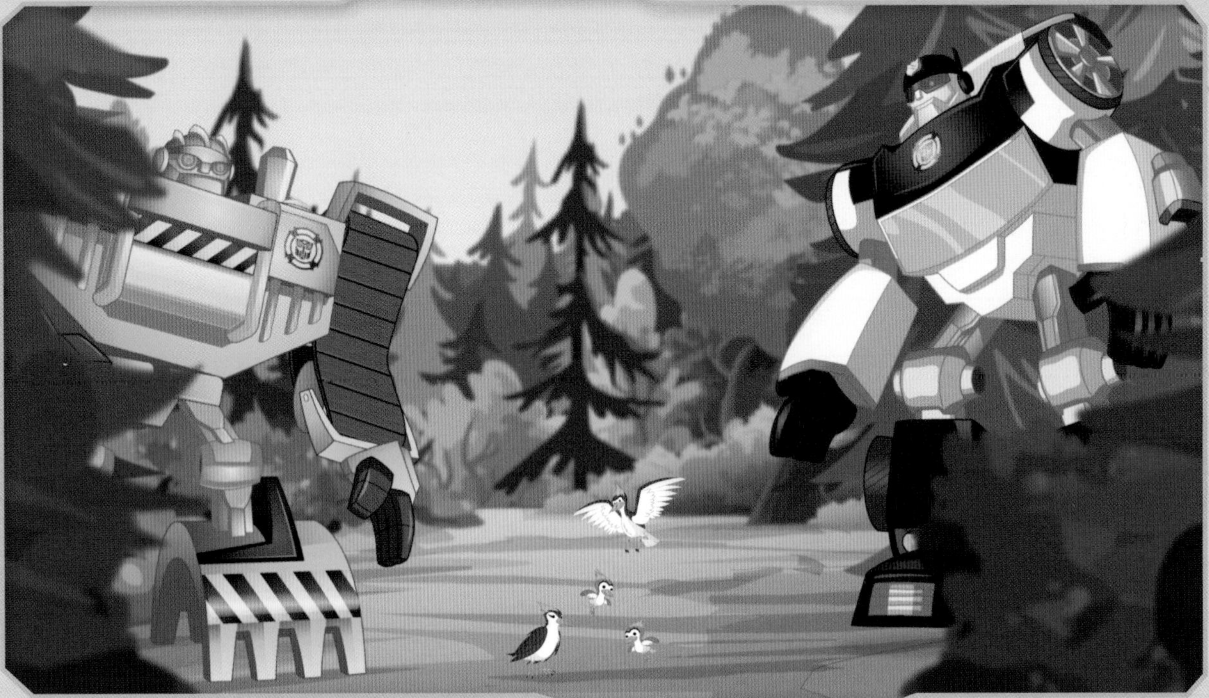

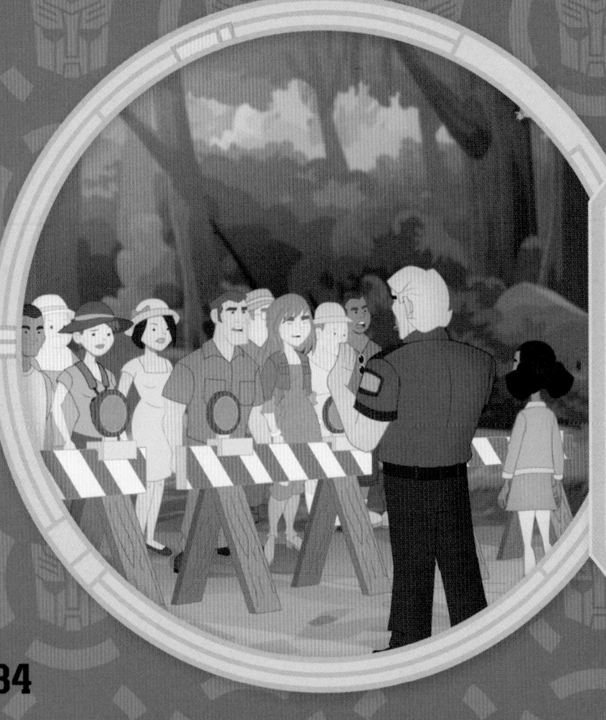

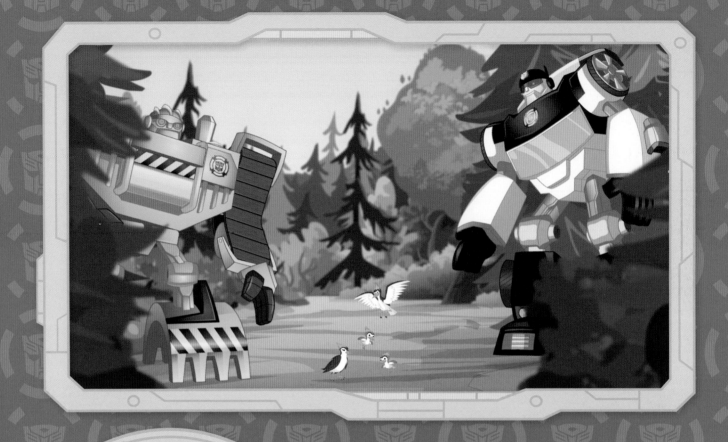

The Rescue Bots arrive to protect the birds from the tourists, bird-watchers, and campers who are showing up in droves. Chief Burns is worried that all the activity could mean danger—not just for the birds, but for the people as well.

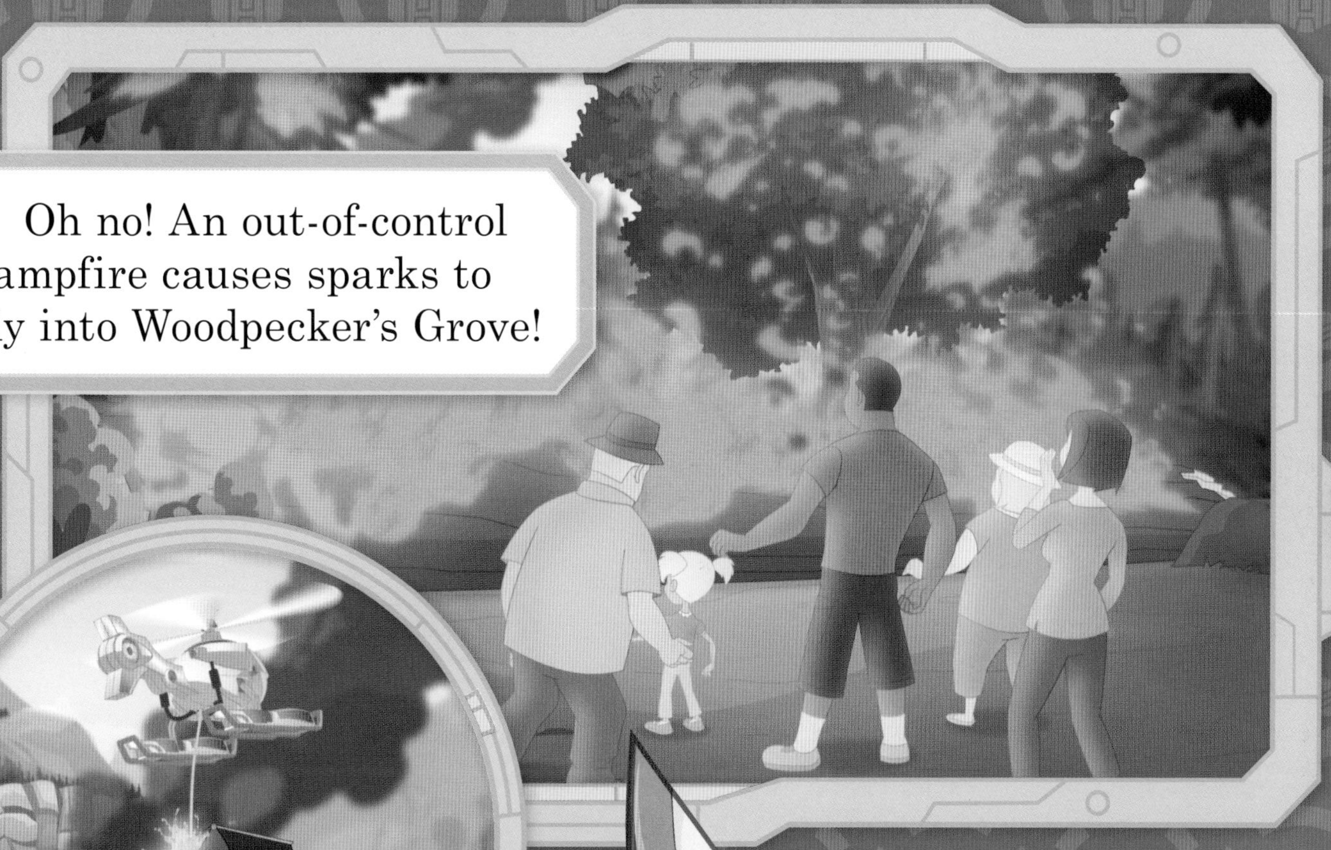

Oh no! An out-of-control campfire causes sparks to fly into Woodpecker's Grove!

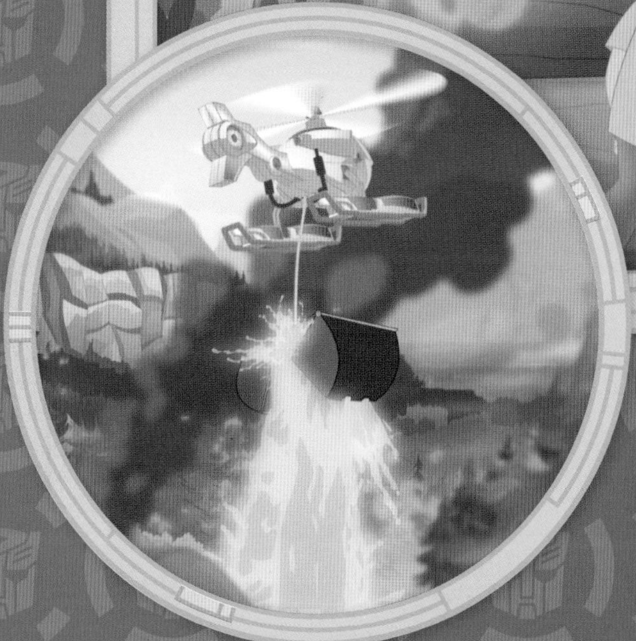

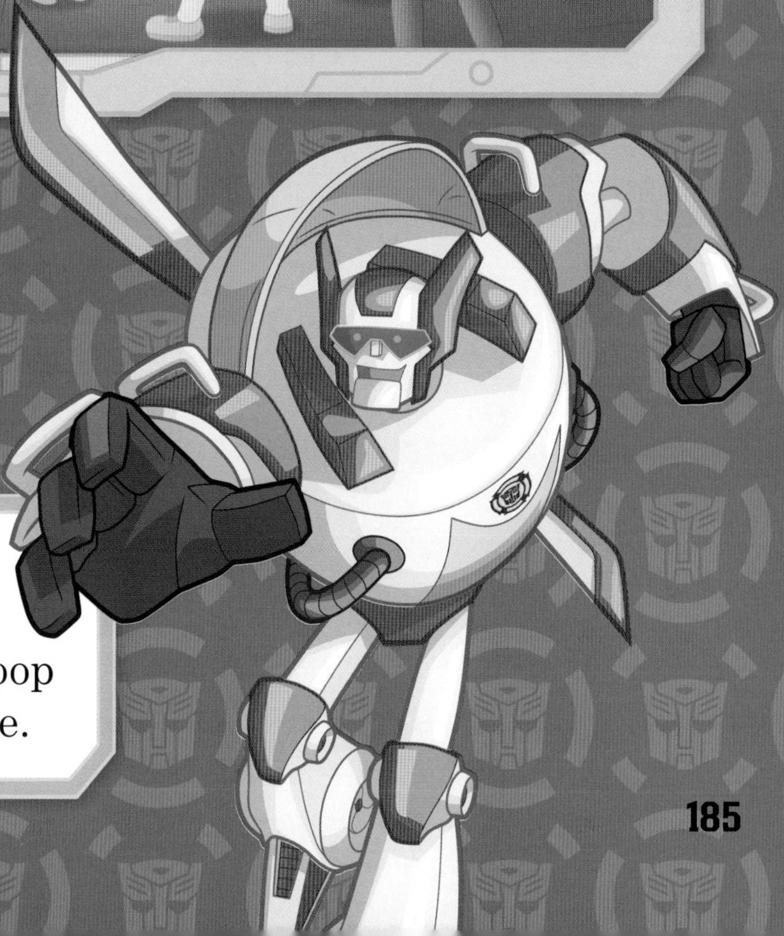

Quickly, the Rescue Bots roll into action and help the people get to safety. Blades uses his scoop claw to douse the fire from above.

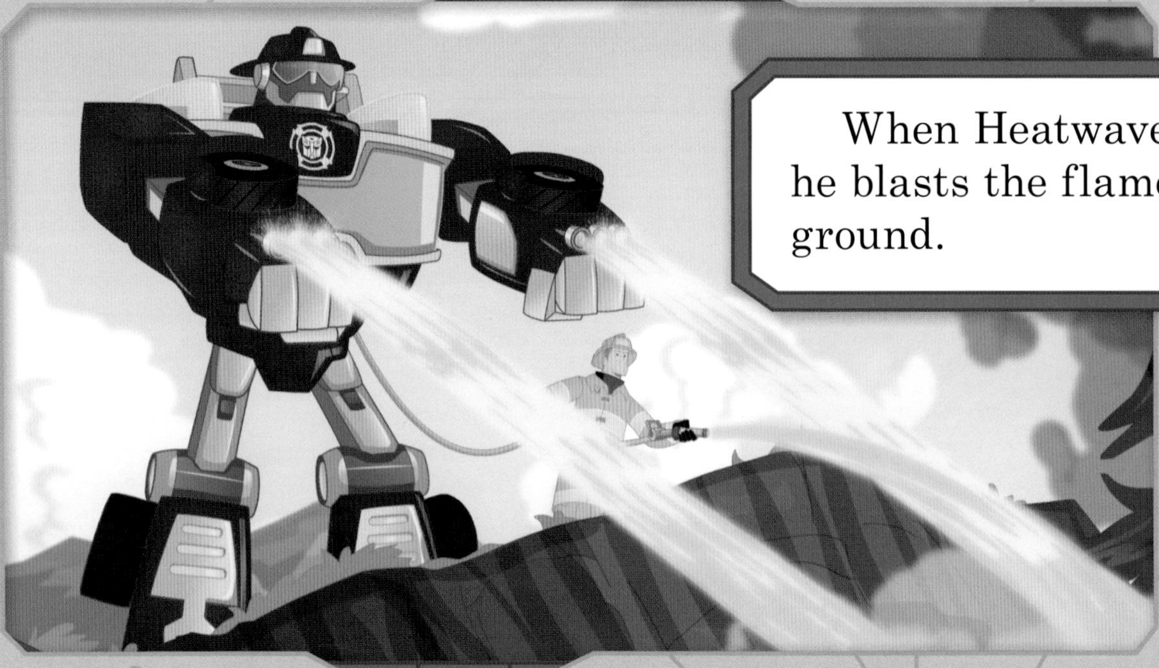

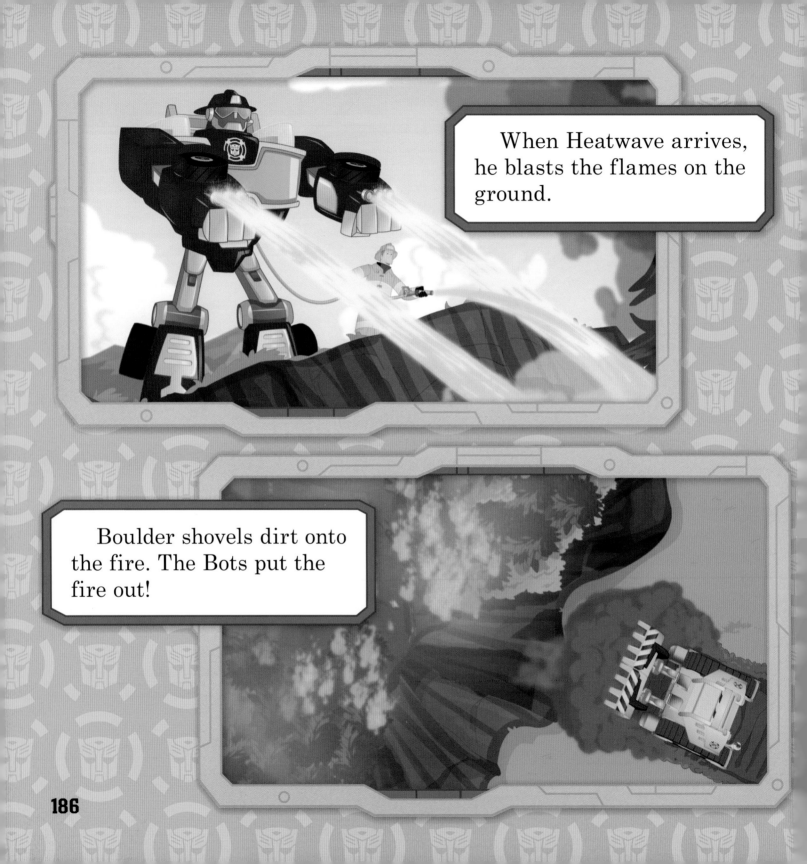

When Heatwave arrives, he blasts the flames on the ground.

Boulder shovels dirt onto the fire. The Bots put the fire out!

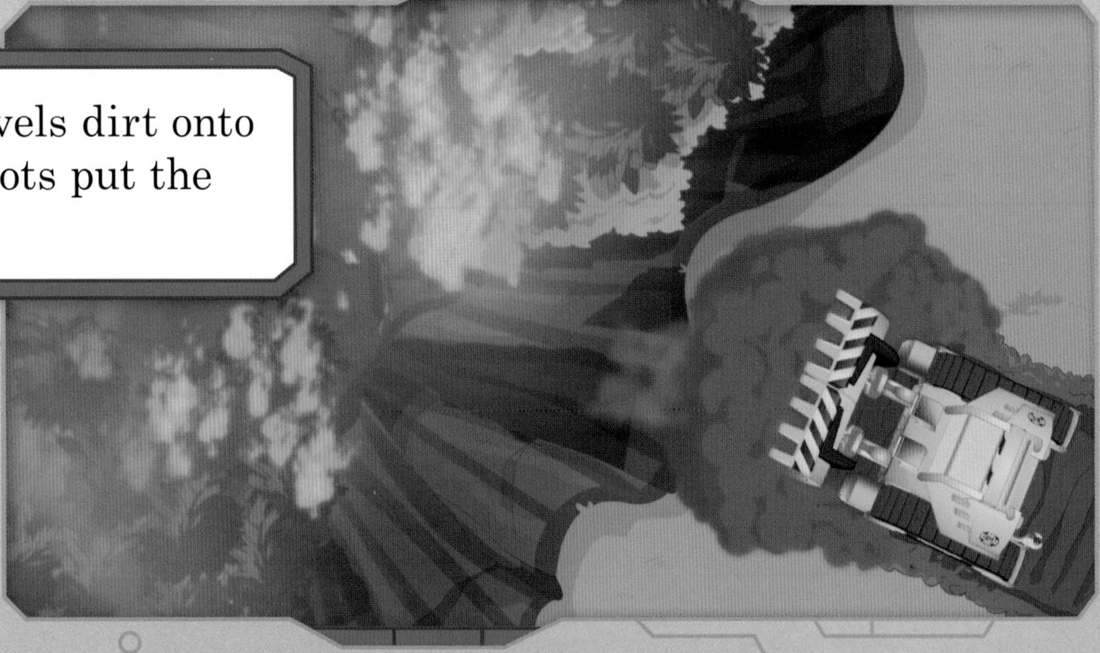

The townsfolk are saved! But the birds flew away during the commotion. Luckily, Doc Greene tagged them so he could track their location.

"I am sure the birds will return to their home in no time," says Doc Greene.

"Perhaps there's a way the birds can be safe and a way for people to still see them?" wonders Cody. That gives Doc Greene an idea.

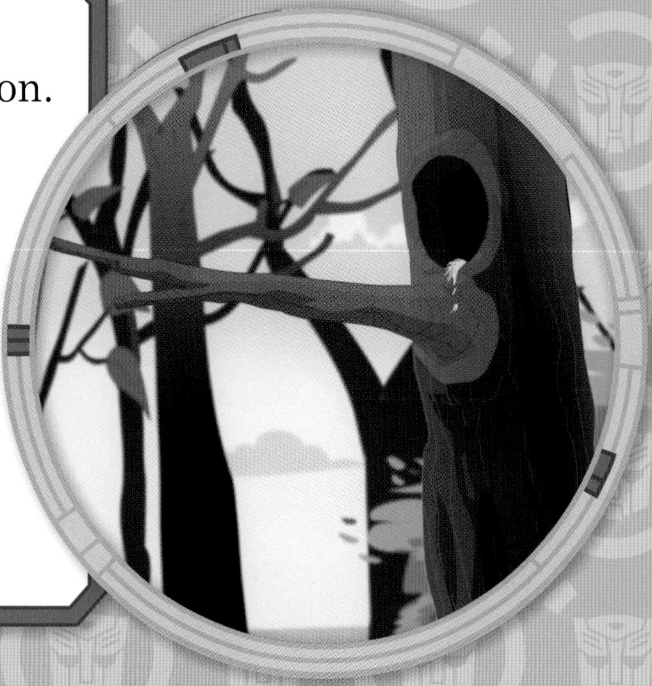

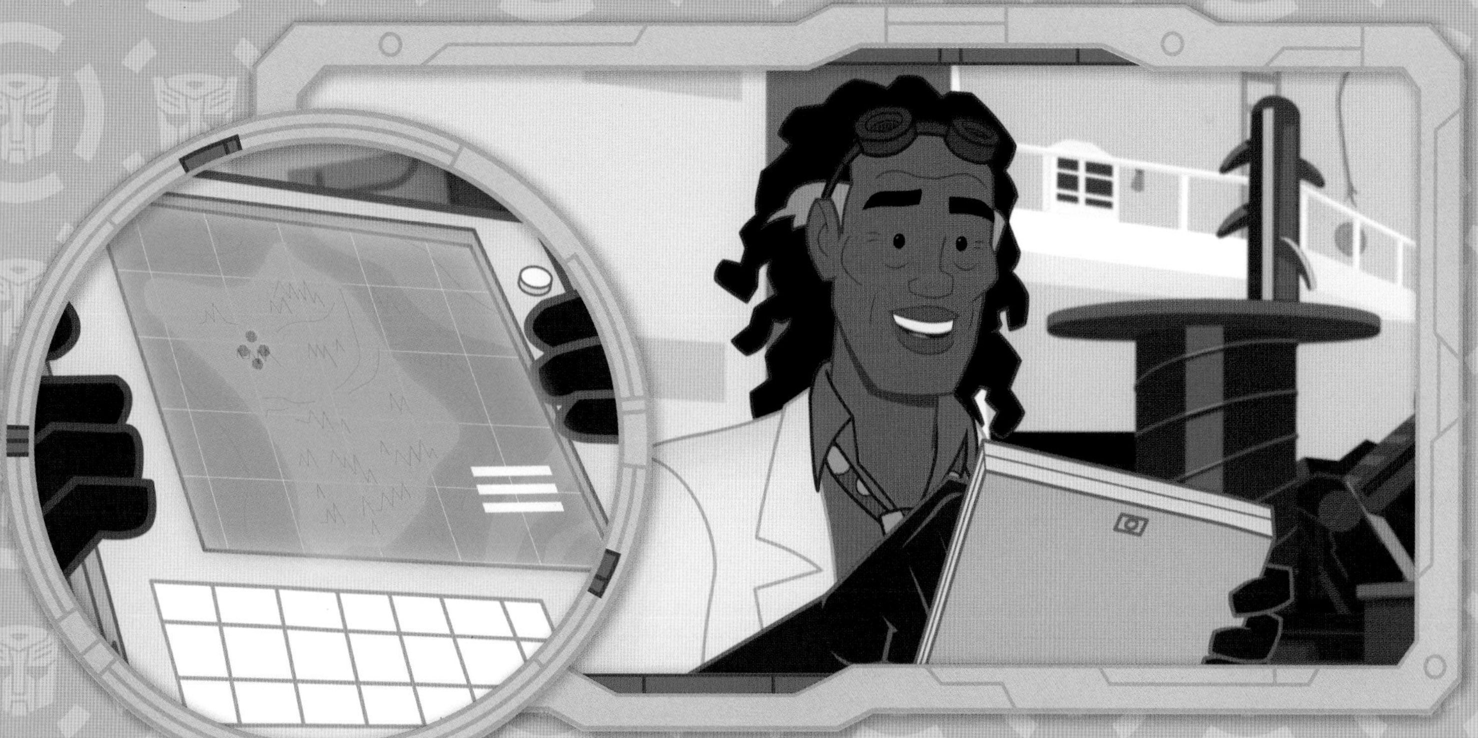

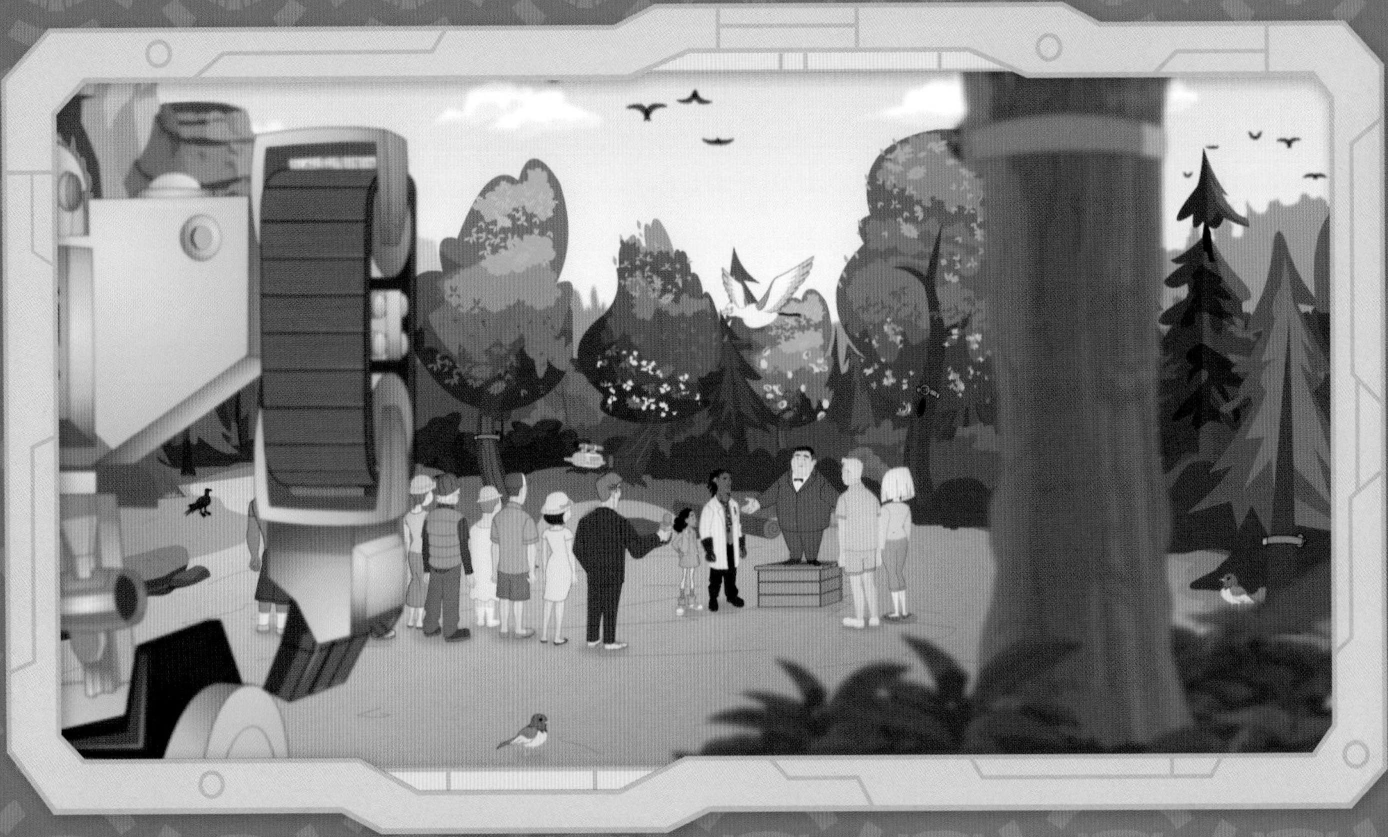

“After consulting with Doc Greene, I’m pleased to announce the opening of the Luskey Bird Sanctuary: a haven for endangered birds and the people who will pay to see them,” says Mayor Luskey. Thankfully, Doc Greene has some points to add.

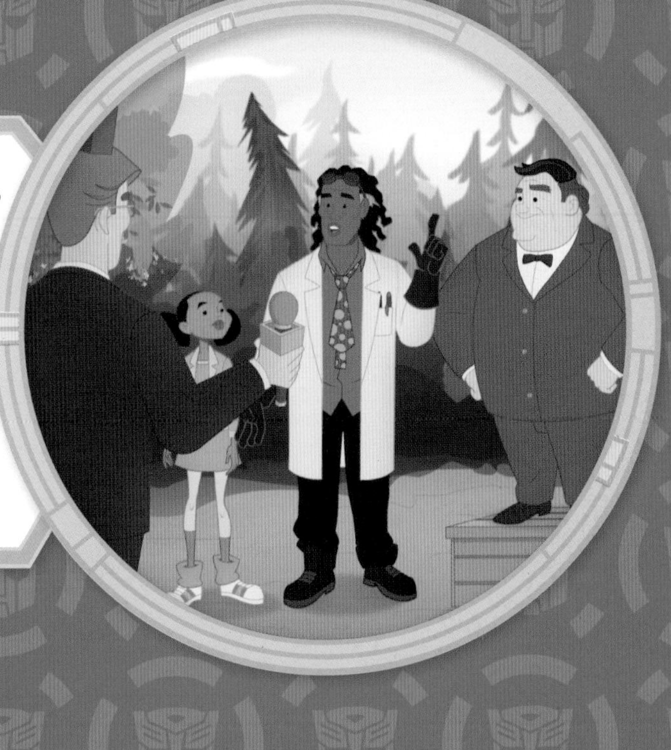

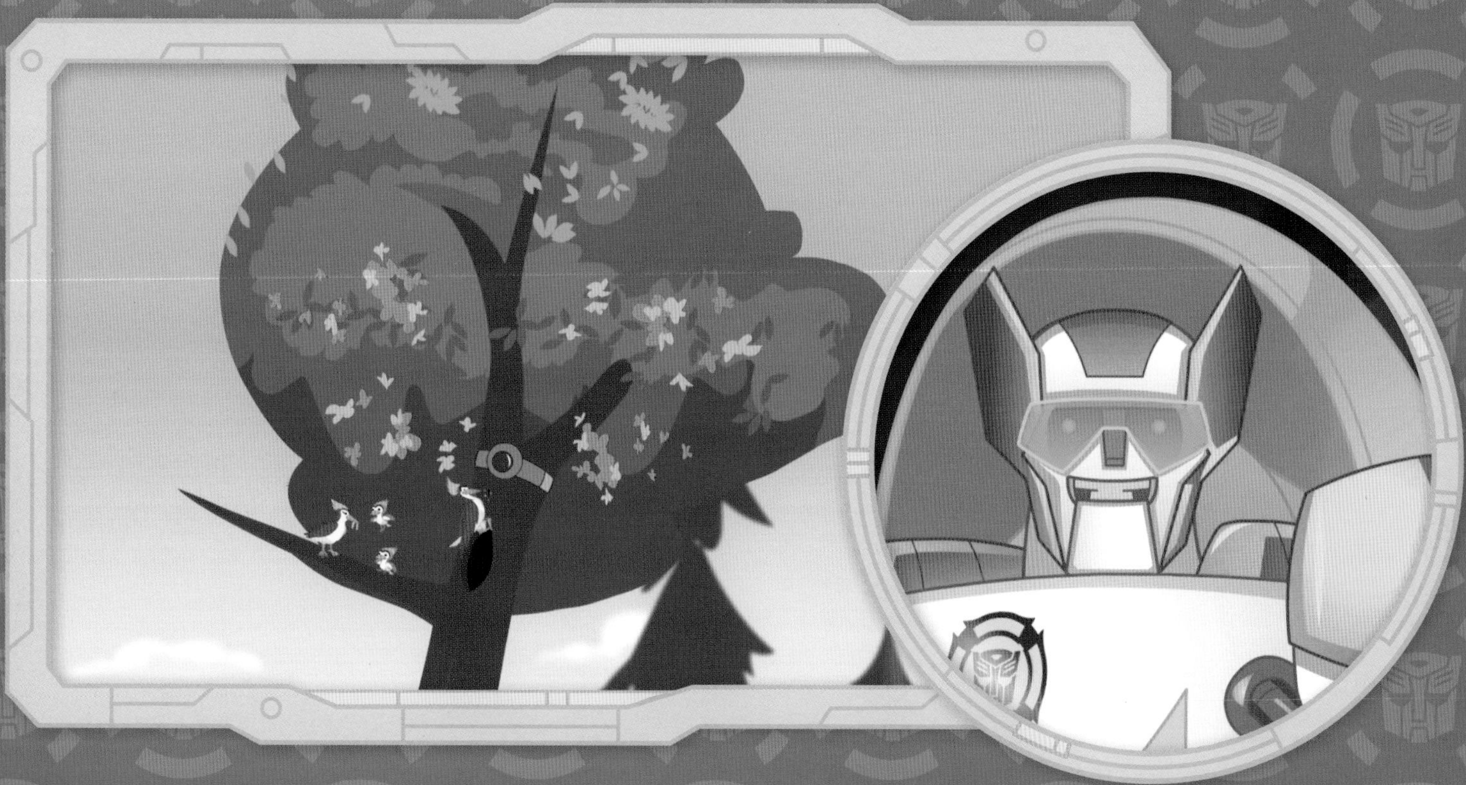

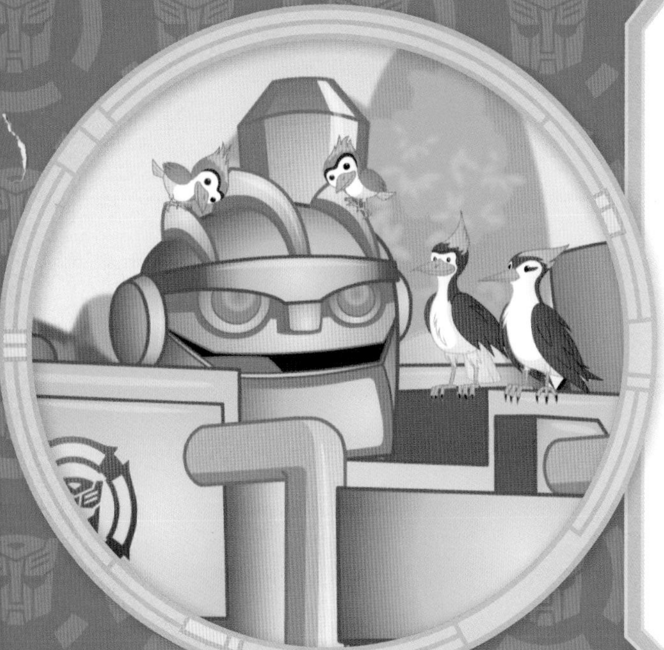

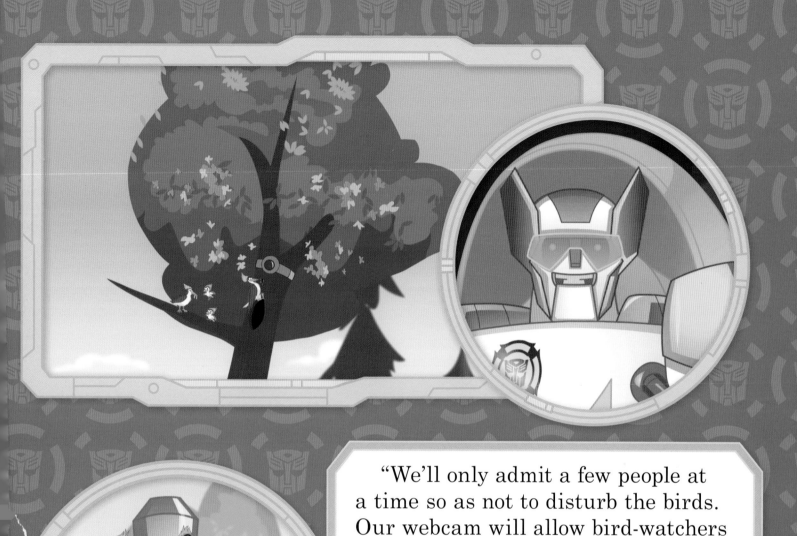

“We’ll only admit a few people at a time so as not to disturb the birds. Our webcam will allow bird-watchers all over the world to enjoy our golden-crested friends as they rebuild their population,” says Doc Greene.

A great compromise has been reached, and now everyone can enjoy the birds without troubling them.

“Yay us!” shouts Boulder as the baby woodpeckers take a seat on their hero’s head.

SERVE & PROTECT

A routine patrol with four Bots in stasis,
Years later awoke in the strangest of places.
Earth was their home now and in addition,
Optimus Prime gave them this mission:

"Learn from the humans, serve and protect,
Live in their world, earn their respect.
A family of heroes will be your allies,
To others remain robots in disguise."

Rescue Bots, roll to the rescue,
Humans in need, heroes indeed.
Rescue Bots, roll to the rescue, Rescue Bots.

With Cody to guide them and show them the way,
Rescue Bots will be saving the day.

Rescue Bots, roll to the rescue,
Rescue Bots.

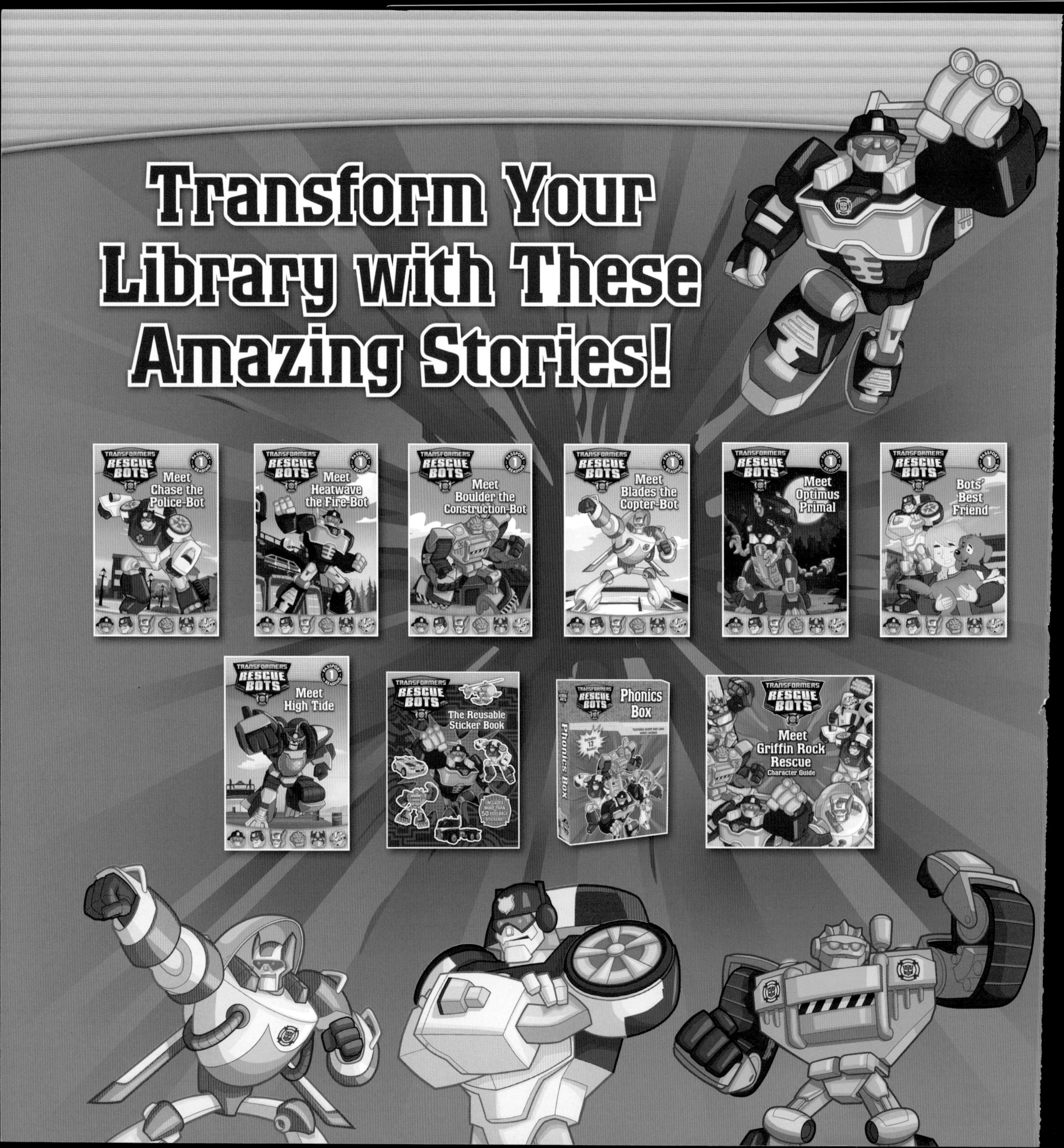

Transform Your Library with These Amazing Stories!
Meet Chase the Police-Bot
Meet Heatwave the Fire-Bot
Meet Boulder the Construction-Bot
Meet Blades the Copter-Bot
Meet Optimus Primal
Bots' Best Friend
Meet High Tide
The Reusable Sticker Book
Phonics Box
Meet Griffin Rock Rescue
Character Guide